IBENUS

THE VALDUCAN — BOOK 3

BY SETH SKORKOWSKY

MYSTIQUE PRESS

Bottle still his hand, Matt wriggled across the dead. The ancient bones crackled beneath him like dry rotted sticks. His padded knees and elbows sank into them with each movement. Chaya's boots pistoned inches from his face as she crawled, and he had to keep his head down to prevent one from taking him in the face.

Above the pops, rattling, and scrapes as they hurried, a baby's soft coo echoed from up ahead. Shit.

They scrambled faster. A giggle. Gabi's chubby face flashed in his mind, a sound that once brought joy now perverted.

"Visual!" Luiza called.

Children's screams erupted in the tunnel, echoing all around them. How many? Four? Five? Matt's pack slammed into the ceiling as he tried to hurry and his foot became buried in bones. They were almost halfway through now. They needed to get out before they were trapped. He glanced at the compass. The blood sphere had split.

"Two demons!" he called. The minions wouldn't show on the compass, only the mantismeres themselves. Six screamers per monster.

He winced at the sharp clack, clack of a suppressed pistol but they kept crawling.

One of the red beads slid away from the other, moving around. More shots came from ahead. Wisps of gun smoke danced in the beam of Matt's headlamp.

A giggle came from behind, sending a cold shiver down Matt's neck. He rolled and looked back down the passage past his own boots. A pale, doll-faced insect stood in the opening, its eyes liquid black.

Its mandibles opened and it cooed.

Shit!

Spidery legs reached around the edge and a second screamer crawled up into the trough.

"They're behind us!"

*For Curtis. We might fight like sisters,
but we'll always be family.*

CHAPTER 1

SIX MONTHS AGO

"When's this cocker goin' to get here?" James shifted in his seat with a grunt. "My ass is fallin' asleep."

Victoria watched through the rain-streaked window as a van rolled past, wet asphalt gleaming red in its wake. Something seemed off tonight, and not just the drizzle and emptiness or James' mood. She bent to look up at the nearest streetlamp.

"What is it?" James asked.

"Streetlights," she answered. "Not working."

"Kids." He grunted. "Smashin' 'em up for kicks or to hide whatever mischief they're up to."

"No mischief at the moment," Victoria said. "Makes it harder to whore if no johns can see you."

James snorted. "Probably better for business." He stretched his mouth into an ugly scowl, drawing a chuckle from Victoria.

"Maybe." She scanned further up the street, hemmed in between brick buildings, most of their windows dark or broken. Layers of graffiti encrusted the steel-shuttered shop fronts. Four lights were out. How many were out the night before? One? Funny how you don't notice some things until they're absent.

"Maybe the bugs got 'em," James offered, with a campfire story flair.

"You saw the latest video?"

"Of course." He scratched his stubbled head. "Internet's all abuzz about 'em. Some wanker's got a remote control toy and everyone's gone mental."

Victoria nodded, her eyes still on the apartment across the street. The video, captured by CCTV cameras, showed a lone pedestrian being attacked by a giant insect, like a tailless lobster. The victim screams mutedly on the silent footage, falls, then gets dragged away. Three videos in two weeks. No witnesses. No positive IDs on the apparent victims. All three *attacks* took place within two blocks of where they now sat. Maybe that was why no one was out. "I think it's a dog."

"Dog?"

"Yeah. Little terrier in a rubber suit."

He shrugged. "Could be a dog, I suppose. Last video showed two of 'em."

They sat silent for several minutes, the rain softly pattering the car roof, before James cleared his throat. "Detective Sergeant," he said, using her formal title, "Carpenter isn't coming back. If he were, we'd have seen him by now, and he's not going to come in this pissy weather. Trust me."

Victoria looked back out the window so he wouldn't see her clenched jaw. One girl was already dead and the other in hospital with a brain injury. Miles Carpenter was the only suspect they had. This was her first case since her promotion, and a failure. Three weeks and no new leads. Her queue was already filling with four new cases that DCI Brown listed as higher priority. She had to get this bastard. But James had a point. He always seemed to know these things, what he referred to as the "Manchester Way." He'd been a copper for eighteen years. Had he not been so open with his opinion he might have been promoted for something beyond just Detective Constable. However, his tendency to be right most of the time, and the fact that most of his younger superiors, including herself, had learned from him, meant he was still in the Criminal Investigation Department. James might rub the wrong way but there was no denying he knew the streets.

Victoria turned to him, meeting his broad face. "Another quarter hour." It was more of a request than an order. They had no solid lead and it was James' car. Hers was in the shop.

James nodded slow and enormously. "All right. I can do that."

Smiling, Victoria turned back toward the street. Carpenter had better show. Time was ticking down and hours of breathing James' farts needed some sort of payoff.

A dark van rolled slowly by. It appeared to be the same one that passed only minutes before. It stopped in the middle of the street and the side doors opened. A pair of black-clad figures in masks hopped out.

Victoria straightened in her seat. "What the hell?"

They appeared male but it was difficult to tell in the scant light. One was broad and tall, everything about him huge. The other slender. The thin man slid out of the vehicle and shut the door behind him in one fluid motion, as if practiced a thousand times. They each held something in their hands but carried them low against their sides.

"Who the hell are these bastards?" James asked.

The van drove away the moment the men were out. They hurried off and disappeared in an alley. Before the van turned at the next intersection, the taillights lit the objects in their hands, silhouetting them in a moment of crimson. The giant carried a club of some kind, its bulging end jagged. The other held a sword, its blade bowed forward in a D-shaped curve.

"Call it in," Victoria said, her voice rising. "Get Tactical here."

James fumbled the radio from the console. "This is DC Kettington.

Do you read?"

Victoria continued to watch the alley and street. "This is DC Kettington. Do you read?"

Silence.

"Piece of shit," James growled. "This is DC Kettington," he repeated, his voice clear and loud. "Do you read?" He twisted the volume control and a buzzing hum came through the speaker.

"What is that?" Victoria asked.

He clicked through channels but the hum continued. "Not working."

Victoria fished out her phone. The screen's light filled the car, momentarily blinding her. "No bars."

"Oh," James breathed, shaking his head. "Oh you bastards. They're jamming."

A spike of fear welled in Victoria's chest. "Mob?"

"Yeah."

Victoria's mouth went dry. Two men with primitive weapons, lights destroyed beforehand, mobile and radio frequencies jammed. Someone was about to die with no one to stop them. Not on my watch. "Come on."

"What?"

"We're the police," she said.

"You plan on using a pair of batons to stop men with swords?"

"Yes," she snapped. "If not, we can get a report on them. Nick them later."

James held her gaze, his lips tightening into a flat line. He pulled the keys from the ignition and leaned over her, jamming them into the glove box. "Open it up."

She dropped the little door open and a mass of crumpled papers nearly spilled into her lap.

"Pouch in the bottom," he said.

Victoria rifled through the chaos before finding a brown vinyl bag shoved into the back corner. It was heavier than she expected. Something metal bulged inside. Her eyes widened as she felt a handle, the cylinder. She pulled it open to see the black revolver. "What is this?"

"You know what that is," he said frankly. "Got it off a tosser I busted some years back. Numbers had been filed off. Held on to it."

"You shouldn't have this, James."

"Neither should the crooks but it don't stop them. Manchester Way."

Nervous tingles danced along her fingers she reached inside, gripping the gun by its plastic handle. "Is it loaded?"

"Of course."

Victoria swung open the cylinder, verifying the six loaded rounds. An icy confidence swept through her veins, cooling the nervous jitters. "You ever fired it?"

"Best if you didn't know."

She nodded. "Manchester Way." Her hand tightened on the grip and she pushed open the car door into the cold drizzle. "Come on."

They hurried across the street. The glow of the city lights reflected down from the clouds, casting everything in shades of gray. Victoria pressed herself against the wall beside the alleyway, the rough brick digging into her back. She took a breath, then peered around the corner.

Empty.

Scanning the shadows, Victoria followed the narrow canyon, James behind her. Their feet sloshed through the shallow puddles.

"There," James mouthed, motioning to an open doorway leading into the abandoned building.

Splinters of wood clung to the hinges. A dull silver padlock hung uselessly to the other side.

Victoria closed in, and peeked inside. Shards of smashed wood that had once been the door littered the hallway beyond. Wet footprints led into the darkness.

James glanced over her shoulder and looked at her. "What now?"

"Keep trying to call Tactical. We know they're inside."

He stepped back from the door and whispered into the radio. "This is Detective Constable Kettington requesting assistance. Do you read?"

Hiding behind the wall, Victoria continued to peer inside, hoping to see movement.

"Does anyone hear me?"

The shrill cries of babies echoed out from the blackness. Victoria's eyes widened in horror. How many were there? Four? Five? All screaming.

James turned from his radio, his thumb still on the button. "My God."

One of the baby voices abruptly cut off, followed by another. Then another.

Victoria's grip tightened on the gun. "James … we have to …"

"Yeah." James pocketed the radio and removed a stubby torch. He clicked the button, unleashing a brilliant white beam and shone it through the open door.

Victoria fished her keys from her pocket and removed a tiny LED light from the ring. She held it in the hand supporting the gun. It wasn't much, nothing compared to James' torch, but it was something.

A long hallway stretched nearly the length of the building before ending at an intersection. Empty bottles and crumpled papers littered the peeling linoleum tiles. Doors lined both sides. Most of them stood open. Others were missing entirely.

The last of the children's wails came from deep inside, high and terrified. It suddenly ceased and the building once again fell silent.

Victoria took the lead, only a step ahead of James, to her right. They scanned each room as they passed, their lights finding discarded mattresses and sleeping bags, but no occupants. It stank of piss, mildew, and stale cigarette smoke. Squatters had obviously lived here, but where were they?

Halfway to the split, the pungent, sweet stench of rotten meat assaulted Victoria's senses.

"Smells like dead cat," James grumbled, tucking his mouth in the crook of his elbow.

Victoria wished she could do the same but she needed both hands to steady the revolver. The stink worsened as they moved onward, but not because they were moving closer. It was growing stronger, as if someone had opened a broken and long-sealed refrigerator and now the reeking air was boiling out, desperate to escape. Tears welled in her eyes from the smell, but she pushed onward. She had to find those babies and the bastards who might have hurt them.

At the intersection, James shined his light up one branch, pausing momentarily on a discarded white sneaker that seemed completely out of place amongst the grime and filth.

Victoria motioned down the other hall, the direction of the smell. "This way."

James' light swung around and stopped on a black smoking shape a few steps away. It looked like some sort of insect or crab, split in half and its shell stripped away from the rubbery flesh. It sizzled and hissed. Victoria realized it wasn't black smoke rising from its surface but quickly dissipating vapor. Bile rose in her throat at that ungodly stench.

"What is that?" James asked from his elbow.

She shook her head, unwilling to open her mouth for fear of tasting it. Giving as wide a berth as the hallway allowed, Victoria stepped around the steaming black mess and continued on. They passed a dank stairwell, its walls emblazoned with orange and red spray-paint, and came to a wide lobby.

Four more fetid corpses littered this room, two crushed to a paste with awkwardly jutting spider legs. The stench was incredible. Dark steam curled through the beam of James' torch as he scanned the room, stopping on one of the ghastly black things splattered against the wall.

A loud thump sounded upstairs, like a ram hitting a door. James' light shot to the ceiling, finding nothing but cobwebs.

Another baby cry sounded. Distant. Terrified.

"Come on," Victoria said, barely moving her lips.

They crept up the stairs to the second floor. The baby's wails had ceased but it sounded like it had come from here. She shined her light up the stairwell, verifying it was empty, then stepped out into the hall. James followed behind, so close Victoria could hear his rapid breaths.

She started down the hallway when scratching sounded beyond a door to her right. The numbers had long since been pried off, but the missing space in the crackled paint read, "137."

They shared a look. Victoria stood back, holding the gun, arms stretched before her. James leaned in, threw open the door, and shone his light into the darkened room.

Nothing.

A baby's coo came from the corner.

Something shuffled across the trash-strewn floor. Victoria's light went to the movement, finding a pale, waxy shape the size of a bread loaf. James's brilliant light fell upon it, revealing a chitinous insect. The creature's face resembled a porcelain china doll, its oily black eyes completely filling the sockets. A pair of segmented pincers twitched outward from its bristle-lined hole of a mouth.

It looked up at them and a shrill infant's sob issued from that hideous maw.

What ... no ... no ... it's not real. Victoria stepped back, struggling to grasp the thing before her. *It's not real.*

A second cry issued from the room and a second baby-faced insect scuttled into the light's beam. It clacked its mandibles and sprang toward James.

"Gah!" He stumbled back, swinging the light away from the room as he batted the creature mid-air with his baton.

It hit the wall with a hard *thock* and fell to the floor, one of its legs broken.

The creature giggled and shuffled back onto its belly, the broken leg twitching awkwardly.

James screamed and kicked it. It hit the wall again, wailing its baby's cry. He stomped it over and over, crushing its plated armor, and squishing its guts out onto the filthy tiles.

More screams poured from inside. Victoria swung her light around to see the other insect charging toward James and a third one scurrying out from an open air vent.

She fired. The gun's booming report was louder than she would have thought possible. The round missed, kicking up shards of linoleum. Victoria pulled the trigger again, blasting the hideous thing nearly in half. Its legs and mandibles shuddered. Black ooze hissed out from the wound.

Her ears rang in a shrill hum.

The third creature was coming toward her, its mouth open in a scream Victoria could no longer hear. It crawled onto a broken sofa frame, readying to jump when she raised the gun and fired.

The creature fell back into the shadows, black ichor splattering onto the wall behind it.

Heart pounding, Victoria reached into the damnable room, grasped the door's handle and yanked it shut before any more of the monsters could appear. That awful rotted stench flooded the hall.

"What the hell? What the hell?" James blubbered, his voice

barely audible above the muted hum. Sweat streaked his white face. His wide eyes were locked onto the smashed bug in undeniable terror.

The creature's pale shell blackened and evaporated into misty vapor, leaving the gooey meat to sag and shrivel.

"What the hell?" James repeated, shaking his head.

"We need to go," Victoria said.

James only stared at the dead thing.

"DC Kettington!"

He looked at her. A smear of black ooze spattered his chin.

"We need to go," she repeated.

James blinked, then nodded. "Yeah. Need to go."

Victoria started toward the stairs when James froze, his eyes locked on the hallway behind her. She spun to see a man's shape silhouetted against the far window. James' light came up, revealing the smaller of the two black-clad intruders. He held his strange, curved sword before him.

"Stop right there!" she ordered, raising the gun. "Police."

The masked man cocked his head.

"Put the weapon down!"

The man straightened. "Move!" He charged, swinging his sword.

Victoria fired. But the man was instantly on the other side of the hall, still closing in.

He swung. She fired again, but the man was now a full meter from where he should have been.

James screamed and slammed into Victoria from behind. The gun fired harmlessly into the wall as she pitched forward. Her foot slipped on a discarded bottle. A white-hot shock of pain exploded from her rolling ankle and she fell onto the gritty floor.

The sound of ripping fabric and an awful clicking, and James' screams silenced.

Teeth clenched, Victoria twisted around to see an enormous man-sized insectile creature on top of James. Its cluster of scythe-like mandibles clacked madly against each other. Two of its four arms ended in long, serrated points. It raised one and slashed down into James' shoulder.

He screamed again and bashed his baton against the monster's head to no effect. The beast rammed its blade-like arm straight down into James's chest. He coughed blood but continued to bat his stick against his attacker.

Victoria screamed. She raised the still smoking gun and pulled the trigger.

Click.

Then the sword-wielding stranger was above her. The creature's head snapped towards him. Before it could move, the man slashed his blade into its back. Its chitinous shell split with a loud crack. The monster hissed and lashed one of its blade arms, slinging James' blood across the walls.

Dodging the wild swing, the stranger ripped the sword free. He vanished and was suddenly directly behind the monster, his weapon coming down into the back of its skull.

Cool blue flames burst from the monster's mouth.

"No!" Victoria cried as the burning monster collapsed on top of James. She reached for him and the stranger took a wary step away. Blue fire flickered along his golden brown sword.

"It won't burn him," he said. "But he does need an ambulance."

The strange fire spread over the creature's body but hadn't ignited James' clothes yet. He gasped weakly. The blood pooling beneath him was black in the spectral light.

One hand still on his sword, the stranger grabbed the dead monster by the shoulder and rolled it off James. The fire didn't seem to hurt him at all. The creature didn't appear to be burning either. There was no smoke. No heat.

Footsteps thundered up the hall. The second man, the big one, was racing toward them. He held a flanged medieval mace. "Are you all right?" he asked with the deepest voice Victoria had ever heard.

"Yeah," the swordsman said.

The big man looked down at Victoria. Instinct told her to look away. The men might kill her if they thought she could ID them. But the brief glimpse at his masked face revealed that he was black.

"Who are they?" he asked. That accent? French?

"Police." He tore open James' bloodied shirt and winced. "This one's banged up bad."

The big man growled rather than grunted his agreement. "We need to go."

"Yeah. Hey," he said to Victoria.

She looked at him.

"You hold this here," he said, motioning to the ball of torn shirt he pressed against James' chest. "In one minute, call 999."

James moaned.

"Who are you?" Victoria asked, reaching a tentative hand for the rag. Hot blood squelched between her fingers.

The swordsman rose. "Tell them whatever you wish but the truth. No one will believe you."

"Come on," the Frenchman urged. "Let's go."

"Who are you?" Victoria repeated. Tears of fear and rage welled in her eyes.

The big man was already headed down the stairs. The swordsman started after but looked back at her. "I'm sorry this happened to you both." Then he was gone.

CHAPTER 2

TWO WEEKS AGO

"What have we here?" Victoria leaned in toward her monitor, trying to make out the magnified, pixelated shape. She saw a scarecrow with a stag's head, but only because the description called it that. To her, it looked like a strange tree. Why did all sighting photographs have to be so damned dark? She sipped her lukewarm tea and copied the image, saving it to her "Monsters" file under the name, "Wendigo?"

The phone beside her erupted into Phantom of the Opera, giving her a start. Victoria eyed it, wishing it to disappear. Only one person had that ringtone.

The caller ID only verified what she knew. *Shit. Sunday already?*

Victoria straightened in her seat, cleared her throat, smiled fakely, and picked it up. "Hi, Mum."

"Victoria, how are you going?" Mother asked in an overly cheerful manner.

"Oh, I'm doing much better. Everything's ..." She scanned the filthy flat, every surface cluttered with food wrappers, dirty dishes, loosely arranged rainbows of Post-it Notes, tissues, dirty clothes, and unpaid bills. "... great."

"Wonderful. And ... therapy is going well?"

There it was, straight for the throat. No small talk, no skirting it, just the principal concern: *Are you still mad?*

"Well," Victoria said, forcing the smile to remain. Mother could always hear a frown. "We've made a lot of progress. Doctor Abbington believes the trauma of my attack and DC Kettington's death caused only a temporary hallucination. But he still wants to make sure my recovery is complete, you know."

"Good, good. That's wonderful dear. So ... CID will take you back soon?"

"Looks promising." She ran her fingers through her blonde, uncombed hair.

"Wonderful, dear. I'm so happy to hear that. It's been so terribly hard for you, I know. Soon it can just return to normal."

Normal, she thought with a bitter smile. "I can't wait. Listen, Mum, this is a bad time. I was just about to head out?"

"Oh. Plans?"

"Yes, I'm meeting a friend."

"A man friend?" Mother asked with that leading edge. Now that the first business was done she could begin her normal nagging. Mother seemed to believe that Victoria being single at twenty-five was the single greatest tragedy since Margaret Thatcher's resignation.

"That is none of your concern," Victoria said. If she was going to lie she figured she might as well go for it. "But, as a matter of fact, yes. And ... I'm running late."

"Best not to leave him waiting," Mother said, a delighted spark in her tone.

"I won't. I'll talk to you next week, Mum."

"And you can tell me all about him."

"I will. Love you."

"I love you too, dear."

Victoria clicked the phone off and released a tired sigh. Eventually she'd have to explain that CID had let her go. While they might have been able to look beyond her entering the building without calling it in, an action that resulted in James' death, her fantastic story of baby-faced monsters and giant insects had made it unsalvageable. By the time anyone had arrived, the dead bugs had become rats and a small dog that had been missing for the previous week. The burning monster had turned into an Oliver Grey, a truck driver who had also been missing for nearly a month. There was of course no trace of the knife that been used to kill DC Kettington or the blade used in the death of Mister Grey. Then there was the illegal firearm that, even though she had claimed was found at the scene, contained James' fingerprints on the brass casings. Once it was all put together, the conclusion was that Victoria's career was over.

Her mind again focused on the two men and whoever had been driving that van. Who were they? How did that one move the way he did, seeming to teleport? The strange sword was a bronze khopesh, an Egyptian weapon. She'd been able to figure out that much. Victoria had assumed the primitive weapons were for silence, but why those particular ones?

But that was only the very tip of the iceberg. What were those monsters? Oh, she'd told her therapist she believed it was a terror-induced fantasy, but she knew better. Why did they change after death? What was with that eerie fire that didn't burn?

Suspension, then unemployment, had provided ample time to search for the answers and, like most things these days, the internet knew all.

There were websites and uploaded videos. Some called them monsters, others said aliens, or the living power of Satan. Conspiracies upon conspiracies. Victoria would have written them off as nutters once, and some undoubtedly were. But now, finding herself lumped in with them, she could see sages among the madmen. All she had to do was sort the wheat from the chaff, as they used to say in CID. She read and watched every single one she could find. The comments below the videos insulted their creators, laughing about tin foil hats. But one in fifty was a kindred soul, someone who sheepishly confessed, "I, too, have seen something."

And while she did share this with her newfound contemporaries, Victoria possessed something they didn't: Cop Instinct.

She was a detective. Searching chaos for patterns was what she did, and she was bloody damned good at it. Those men were out there. The facts were out there. She only had to gather and sort them.

Victoria had files upon files, a bulletin board shingled in scrawled notes and printed photographs. She had grid-work of information laid out before her couch like tarot cards. She would find the truth.

The stories were always different. The weapons, the monsters, nothing was the same but yet it was.

One mobile-phone video showed a madman with a machete chasing a man through a New Orleans street. Then the would-be victim hurdled a three-meter fence and ran off with unbelievable speed. Another, a shaky video from Rio, captured a woman in nothing more than a thong, battling a huge flaming man on a hotel balcony. She cut his head off with a sword to a burst of pyrotechnic fire. Further research on this revealed that while considered a Carnival stunt at the time, police found a real body. It wasn't burned, but there were other burn marks at the scene. The suspect had used a fake ID and was presumably still at large. This led her to researching stories that involved archaic weapons.

Victoria found a security feed from the mid-90s that showed a woman holding a spear step directly through a brick wall as if it wasn't there. A body was later found inside the building she had entered. Stabbed to death. From Japan, there came a video of a man with a bladed staff outrunning a car. A long-range video from Australia showed a person launch a bolt of lightning out of what appeared to be an axe, and killing a man in fire. Like with Rio, and with her own personal experience, the recovered body was nude and wasn't burned.

One *insane* theorist brought up how many of the murder sites had lurid pasts. Not discounting anything any more, Victoria researched this and found it also true. There were patterns. So many patterns that it couldn't possibly be coincidence. Could it?

She researched each site before the videos and pictures had been made, also finding a distinct fingerprint. Old deaths, recent deaths, unexplained sightings and phenomena, and then nothing. Sometimes a body, usually naked. Sometimes an arson with a burned body inside. Then the killings stopped.

This only reminded her of her own debut in this secret play. The videos of giant ants, then the men appearing in their clandestine black van, a nude corpse, and then the ants were forever gone.

Yes, this was all related.

She could find these men. It didn't matter if they were Illuminati, agents of the Catholic Church, aliens, or the bloody Knights Templar, she would find them.

Victoria re-read a recent forum post. Someone had seen a monster. No one believed them. No one but Victoria and a few of her kindred new family.

She would go there. She would watch. James had taught her well. Victoria would have her answers, prove she wasn't mad. She'd do it the Manchester Way.

CHAPTER 3

PRESENT DAY

Gerhard sat on a hard bench, peering at his tablet and trying not to watch the uniformed school children. At least, he hoped to appear as if he weren't watching them. They talked and giggled, their bored eyes passing over the relics safely encased behind glass and lit with clean white lights. His fingers tightened as the children reached the half-circle weapon display, its blades thrusting outward like a steel-spoked star.

Did they notice it? Could they see its beauty?

They shuffled past, none seeming to fathom the flawless magnificence before them.

Their teacher herded them onward, deeper into the museum, toward the Aboriginal Collection. Their footsteps and chatter faded off down passage, leaving him alone once more.

Gerhard released a shallow breath. No one had seen it. While he wanted to shout, "Look! How can you be blind to such perfection?" he enjoyed the knowledge that no one but him knew the secret.

Licking his lips, he rose and slowly approached the high window separating him from that perfection. There, second from the top, a polished keris, the graceful curve of its wooden grip beckoning to be held. Gold erupted at the wide base of its blade, trailing down along it like dragon scales, following its waving curves. Thirteen there were, undulating back and forth, back and forth, hypnotically. Gerhard's palms began to sweat as he studied the dark steel of the blade, the folds of different metals like wood grain.

Oh, there were more elaborate ones than this, true. Its neighbor with its ivory and jeweled handle and decadent blade. It only had nine waves, not the masterwork thirteen of his. *His*, as he now thought of it, was elegant in its function and simplicity. Sheathed it would be restrained, not gaudy, holding its gold and art within the plain scabbard like a beautiful secret only known when drawn.

Gerhard looked around, verifying that he was alone. He was positioned so the black domes of the security cameras could not observe as he lifted the tablet to his chest and snapped a picture of *his* keris. He had done this act many times in the three weeks since he first saw it. Nearly two hundred photos he had now, each one capturing a new facet, a new hidden beauty that it had revealed to him.

In those three weeks, Gerhard had devoured more knowledge of the Indonesian blades than he would have thought possible. He'd found many for sale online, hoping one might satisfy his need to hold it. Some were garbage. Many were works of art themselves, fetching thousands of euros. But none could match his. None could fill the void.

He so wanted to touch it, hold it in his hands, feel the weight of it. He wanted to press it against his cheek, feel the cool, smooth metal against his skin. He wanted to taste it, wanted to absorb it into his own body and become one with it.

Was he going insane?

Movement at the corner of his eye, a reflection. Gerhard had become skilled at noticing these things, fear of someone walking in on these private moments.

He sidestepped along the display and scanned the other relics, feigning admiration.

Two men entered the room. Gerhard glanced back, smiling. One of them was old with white hair and sunken cheeks. He walked with a cane but stood straight. He smiled back. The man beside him was tall with broad shoulders, high, sharp cheekbones, and close-cropped blond hair. He looked more like a bodyguard than any son or grandson of the old man.

"Indonesian keris blades," the old man said as he stepped up to the glass. The accent to his raspy voice sounded British. He turned to Gerhard, his sharp eyes friendly. "Beautiful, yes?"

"Yes," Gerhard answered.

"You must forgive me. My German is not so good. Do you speak French, English, Italian?"

Gerhard pursed his lips. He'd taken a course in English but wasn't very skilled. "French."

"Ah, good," the old man replied in smooth French. The British flavor was gone. He returned his gaze to the displayed weapons. "Which one is your favorite?"

"Excuse me?"

"The keris. I noticed you looking at them. Which is your favorite?"

Paranoia tingled along the back of Gerhard's neck. He gave an embarrassed smile, hoping the hairs weren't standing on end. "There are ... many beautiful ones."

"There are," he agreed. "Do you know which one is my favorite?"

Gerhard shook his head. How did he have a favorite? He just arrived. There hadn't been time to study them, see which one outshone the—

"That one. Second to the left." He gestured with his cane. "Wooden handle. Gilded blade."

"Mine as well," Gerhard gushed, a little too enthusiastically. "It's magnificent." He suddenly felt embarrassed by such excitement, but it felt so good to know someone else saw it.

"It is," the old man said, seeming unfazed by the sudden outburst. "Sixteenth Century from Java."

Gerhard blinked. "How do you know that? There's no card saying its age."

The old man smiled. "I own this display."

"Oh, I ... I see," Gerhard stammered, fighting to hide the complete shock. This, this was the man who owned such a beautiful thing. What would that be like? And here he was blubbering like a destitute child introduced to a rich boy's toys. This man was laughing at him.

The old man offered his hand. "Alexander Turgen."

Gerhard looked at it a moment before accepting it. "Gerhard Entz."

Alexander motioned to the blond man, warily watching from behind sawed-off glasses. "This is my associate Taras Orlovski."

Taras nodded and Gerhard realized it wasn't wariness like a bodyguard, but more like a brother meeting his beloved sister's fiancé for the first time. "Good to meet you." His accent was Russian.

Alexander motioned to keris. "Would you like to see it up close, Mister Entz?"

Gerhard blinked.

"I can arrange a private viewing." The old man winked. "I know people."

"Yes. Yes, I would love to." Excitement fluttered through his stomach. He felt dizzy with it. A private viewing! Would they let him touch it? Surely not. He shouldn't get his hopes that high, but a *private viewing*! "When, when could we do that?"

"You're here now."

A knot clenched in Gerhard's chest. "I ... my lunch is nearly over. I need to leave, but I can come back later today." His supervisor had already reprimanded him for tardiness from lunch this week. Further infractions would result in disciplinary measures.

Alexander nodded understandingly. "But you'd much rather now." It wasn't a question. Simple truth.

Gerhard slowly nodded. "I'll need to call my office. Let them know."

"Of course." The old man smiled. "Take your time. Taras and I shall arrange the viewing while you do."

Cabinets lined one wall of the windowless viewing room. The pristine coldness of the white and ash gray aroused memories of a hospital, the so many visits while his mother wasted away, becoming frailer and frailer each time. Gerhard ran his fingers along the rubbery edge of the laminate table, trying not to shift in his chair. The urge to stand, to pace, to burn off the anxious energy was overwhelming. Soon, he assured himself. *Soon we will be together.*

Taras leaned against a side counter, his gaze following the lines where the ceiling joined the wall. He met Gerhard's eyes and smiled. "Are you originally from Stuttgart?"

"Yes."

"What do you do?"

"Accounting. My office is about a kilometer from the museum."

Taras nodded.

"And yourself?" Gerhard asked. He didn't really care for small talk at the moment but conversation might help pass the time.

The Russian seemed to think about this. "Crisis Management."

Gerhard nodded, but had no idea what that could mean. Aid relief after a natural disaster, he guessed. Maybe something military. He carried himself like a soldier. What would a rich collector like Alexander be doing with a soldier?

He drew a breath to ask, but then the door opened.

"Here we are," Alexander said, stepping inside. A suited man in white gloves followed, carrying the sheathed keris is upturned palms, like a nurse with an infant.

Gerhard straightened in his seat, eyes fixed on the carved and polished scabbard, seeing them joined for the first time. His heart thumped so fiercely he was sure the beats were visible beneath his shirt.

The museum man removed several white cotton gloves from one of the cabinets and set them on the table. Still holding the keris he nodded toward them, his demeanor telling that he had no intention of releasing the artifact until precautions had been taken.

A pang of disappointment prodded Gerhard's stomach that he wouldn't be allowed to actually touch the keris, but if the oils or salt of his skin were to damage it, he'd never forgive himself. Swallowing, he picked the gloves up and pulled them on, the sweat of his palms making it difficult.

The museum man's lips tightened into a satisfied smile. He

offered the weapon across the table like some holy vestment presented before the Pope.

Hands trembling, Gerhard reached out and accepted it. A faint shudder trembled through him as he wrapped his fingers around the scabbard.

"Thank you," Alexander said to the museum man. His voice seemed a thousand kilometers away. "I'll call once we are done."

Gerhard caressed one hand toward the handle, slow, savoring the way the light reflected off the polished wood. In the distance, he heard the door close as the suited man left. His fingers found the rounded grip. They tightened around it, fitting perfectly as if centuries ago some prophetic craftsman had fashioned it specifically for his hand. Gerhard closed his eyes for a moment, relishing the feel of it. Then carefully drew the blade, seeing the gold, that hidden secret emerge, one wave at a time, thirteen there were. Thirteen waves.

Tears welled in Gerhard's eyes. It was the most beautiful thing he'd ever seen. A warmth blossomed in his chest, spreading out through his veins. Euphoria. Was this love? He'd felt this before, his mother, lovers, friends, and family, but this was different, more intense, a combination of those and so much more. Yes, this was love.

Gerhard set the scabbard down onto the table and touched the blade, imagining its history, the men who carried, the men … no … monsters who died along it. Normally such fancies as monsters might cause him to laugh but that is what Gerhard imagined, and it made him smile.

"Beautiful, isn't it?"

Gerhard blinked, now embarrassed to be caught in such an intimate moment. He'd forgotten the men were even with him. "He is."

"He?" Alexander asked, seemingly amused.

"Yes … it feels like a he." Gerhard smiled shyly. "I'm sure you find that funny."

The old man shook his head. "Not at all. He has a name." A teasing glint shone in Alexander's eye. "Would you like to know it?"

"Really? Yes. Very much so."

"Umatri."

"Umatri," he repeated, the word sounding like something he'd heard in a dream. Umatri. Of course it was. Somehow he'd always known that, like a deaf man finally hearing his own name for the first time. "Thank you."

"It's my pleasure, Mister Entz. It's fortunate to have met you and let you see Umatri like this. I'm sure his new owner feels the same."

Gerhard's fingers flinched at the words, tightening around the handle. "New owner?" he asked, trying to hide his shock.

Alexander nodded. "Yes. My reason for coming to Stuttgart was to pick it up."

Gerhard's mind reeled, unable to fathom it. He'd finally touched him, learned his name. Now they were coming to take him away like thieves. "I … I see." He licked his lips. "Mister Turgen …"

"Please, call me Alex."

He nodded absently, his head swimming in a torrent of grief, panic, and anger. "Alex, is … can you tell me who purchased it?"

Alex's lips tightened and he shook his head. "I'm sorry, I'm not yet able to say who the new protector is."

"Is it a museum? Please tell me that."

"No, it is a private party."

A weight pressed against Gerhard's lungs, cold and inert. He struggled to breathe. "Would they sell it?" His savings was healthy, six months' salary, but probably not enough. Definitely not enough. How could you put a price on such a treasure? But someone had. Alexander had! A hot coal of anger ignited in his guts. How could he put a price on Umatri?

"I can inquire." Alex touched his fingertips to the table. "But … it will be expensive."

Gerhard's gaze returned to Umatri. "Let me worry about that."

CHAPTER 4

Allan slowed and peered out the side window as the van crested the narrow bridge. Stone and wood embankments lined the River Somme as it stretched out, curving away behind enormous willows, their feathery branches brushing the water's surface. The only boats were the small flat-bottoms tied and stowed for the night, their hulls lightly bobbing against the banks' sheer walls. In the distance, the faint glow of Amiens' light shone through the trees. "Not much longer," he said, continuing on. "You ready for this, Chaya?"

"Definitely."

He eyed her through the rearview. "You sound pretty sure. You want me and Luc to take this one off? Let you handle it by yourself?"

The young knight grinned. She shared a look with Samantha, the Australian redhead on the bench beside her. "Why not?"

Luc snorted from the passenger seat, the big man's head nearly brushing the ceiling. He scratched his sharp-chiseled jaw with the back of his fingers as if considering the offer. "I'd be willing to let her," he rumbled in his deep bass voice, his first words in over half an hour. The knight's humor was so dry that Allan couldn't always tell when he was kidding, which only seemed to encourage him more. "But Master Sonu would have our heads if we did."

Chaya shrugged. "Maybe next time, then."

"Don't get too eager," Allan said. "These things are deadly."

"I know," she said. "This isn't my first hunt."

"True," Allan said. "But it's your first one since Master Sonu … cut the cord, we'll say. You know he'll be watching the videos after so we better be by the numbers."

Chaya nodded. At twenty-six, the lean Israeli wasn't the Valducan's youngest knight, a title Allan owned by a full year, but she was the newest. "Then, how's this for an idea?" she said. "You and Luc go in with me, but if I get it without help we get a dog."

Sam perked up. "I'm in favor of this."

Luc growled a harrumph. "Dog? Dogs are noisy. So needy."

"Yeah," Allan agreed. "Besides, you know how Orlovski would pop his top if we brought a dog home."

"That's just big dogs," Sam offered. "If we got a little one, like a corgi, maybe he'd get over his issues. Serves him right for missing this. Out of commission for a year and first job that comes along he's off in Germany with a nice hotel."

"We all have our responsibilities." Allan turned the van onto a narrow road. The lights swung past white reward posters, emblazoned with images of animals, adorning nearly every post like paper scales. "I'm sure he'd rather be here than recruiting."

"Little dogs are worse," Luc said. "They have no idea they're little. Just mean. Yip, yip, yip."

Sam rolled her eyes.

"Why not a cat?" Luc asked.

"A cat?" Allan turned his eyes from the road to stare at him.

The big man shrugged. "I like cats."

"No," Allan said.

"Cats are little bastards," Chaya said. "Ungrateful things."

"A cat can hunt," Luc said. "Dog can't rid the mansion of mice."

"I'm good with a cat," Sam said.

Chaya shook her head. "No. You're not getting a cat on my big debut."

"I didn't get a cat on my first hunt," Luc said. "So I deserve it more."

"Why not both," Sam offered.

"No one's getting a cat!" Allan blurted.

Sam leaned forward, between Allan and Luc. "What about a ferret?"

"Seriously?" Allan snapped. "Can we focus on the job?"

Luc chuckled, then roared in laughter. Chaya and Sam joined in, laughing at Allan's expense.

Allan sighed and shook his head. "Just get it out. We're almost there." He'd gotten used to Sam's dumb humor before a hunt, but having Chaya to play off of made it exponentially worse. Although, and he'd never admit it, her jokes did alleviate the pre-hunt anxiety. Luc joining in on them was the biggest surprise. Normally the Frenchman had served as Team Leader, but now that the Valducans had begun replenishing their ranks, he and Allan had been swapping that duty. Soon they would have their own teams to manage, and Allan tried not to dwell on the fact that this might very well be their last assignment together. It felt like the band was breaking up.

They crossed a pair of narrow canals leading to the river. High hedges lined either side of the road. Allan flipped off the headlights before turning onto an earthen drive. By the pale glow of a half-moon above, he guided the van to a shaded spot between a tree and the hedge.

He killed the engine and turned the police scanner up. "Let's go to work, people."

The dome lights didn't come on as the vehicle's doors opened. Allan stepped out into tall grass and made his way to the back where Chaya had already begun pulling out their gear. The air was sticky. It smelled like a swamp, that combination of vibrant plant life undercut with wet rot. Frogs and insects chirped and hummed from every direction, mingling into a single, rolling wall of noise.

Allan flexed his hands, fighting off the pre-game jitters. Chaya handed him a ballistic vest and he strapped it on. He pulled out a sturdy web belt, weighted by several pouches and a long scabbard, and clicked it on. He then attached his throat mic and earpiece before keying up the radio near his hip.

"Testing. Testing."

"I got you," Luc's voice rumbled through the ear bud.

"Okay," Allan said. "Sam, you got me?"

"Gimme a second, boss," she said from inside the vehicle, wrestling with something in her lap. "All right, you hear me?" came through the radio.

"Loud and clear." As the others continued to check their radios, Allan wriggled his fingers and opened the flat case from the back. A golden bronze khopesh rested inside, glinting in the faint light. Carefully, almost reverently, Allan tore the Velcro straps apart and pulled Ibenus free. As always, the jitters vanished the moment he felt her smooth ebony grip. *Miss me, Love?*

Allan slipped Ibenus into her scabbard, designed to accept the bowed blade. Leaves shuddered in the trees as a sudden breeze swept through, washing the humidity away and cooling his sweat-beaded forehead.

"Check your ammo," he said, drawing a silenced Walther pistol from its holster and verifying it was loaded. The bullets themselves wouldn't harm the tengu but the cherry wood tips could. Even then, they'd only hurt the demon's host body. But better than nothing, providing Allan could even hit it. He'd never been a good shot.

"You really need to upgrade that sidearm," Chaya said, never passing a chance to bring up the old argument.

"I like it just fine."

"Have you even tried the pistol I selected?"

"Not my style. We can discuss it later."

"Promise?"

"Promise." Holstering the gun, he plucked a pair of black latex gloves from a bag Luc had set in the van door and pulled them on.

"Here." Sam thrust out a small plastic box, dangling from a bead chain necklace.

Allan nodded a thanks, accepting it. He put it on and wedged the GPS unit under the snug vest so that it wouldn't bounce. "All right, we ready?" he asked, sliding a thin balaclava over his face.

"Ready," Luc said, pulling on his own tracker. His black iron mace, Velnepo, hung from his side, its flanged head protruding up through a ring at his belt.

Chaya pulled her curly hair back as she slipped on her mask. She set her hand on her scimitar's crescent moon pommel. "Ready."

Allan still wasn't used to Khirzoor on the girl's belt. The holy sword had belonged to Ben ... before he'd died, forcing the weapon to choose a new protector.

"All right," Allan said. "Luc, you take the north side. Set eyes on a good vantage of the front. Chaya and I will move around behind. It'll make a break for the water the instant it feels threatened, so stay quiet."

"No problem for me," Chaya said with a smirk.

Allan turned back to the van. "Sam."

The young woman looked dutifully up from her station of monitors. The slender microphone curved down from her headset to the flat line of her mouth. All trace of Sam's usual joviality was gone. It was all business now.

"You know what to do." She gave a nod.

Allan pursed his lips. *Am I forgetting anything?* He fought the urge to look at Luc, maybe see the answer in his eyes. *No. That's everything.* He closed the van door. The dim light of Sam's screens glowed faintly through the tinted glass. He drew Ibenus. "Let's do it."

Keeping to the shadows, the knights hurried through the open field, Luc moving to the right while Allan and Chaya took the other side. Allan kept close to Chaya, sharing the bubble of silence emanating from her unsheathed scimitar. While he could hear the leaves crunching beneath their feet, no sound of it would carry beyond two meters of her blade.

Tengu were among the least aggressive demons, usually satisfying their appetite with fish, small animals, maybe splurging on a family pet. Opportunistic killers, they struck humans fast and without warning, usually drowning them. But most often they blended in society, holed up in their dens. Hermit hoarders living below humanity's radar. No telling how long this one had lived here but someone had seen it.

Not long ago, tabloid newspapers would have carried the story, then cheap mail-order magazines brimming with questionable bigfoot and Nessie photographs. Now, with streaming videos and worldwide chat rooms, all populated with self-proclaimed cryptozoologists, finding these elusive species was easy. But in many ways it was even more dangerous. People were becoming bolder. Would-be hunters, desperate for fame or vindication of their beliefs, were actively seeking these monsters, potentially making themselves prey, or inadvertently spotting the real hunters. Once, masks were only needed for urban environments. Now, in a world of inexpensive micro hi-res cameras, they were becoming standard procedure. That morning, on a scouting run, Chaya had found and disabled a game camera.

They crossed a narrow concrete footbridge over one of the small canals that separated each property into private islands and crouched at the gate on the opposite side. Allan peered through the wrought iron bars at a small house. A yellow light shone above the front door, but the rest of the home was dark. A line of small trees ran along one side of the property against the canal, coming to an abrupt end where it met the river. The gate handle was on the opposite side, its access blocked by a wire mesh stretched across the bars. Lifting Ibenus, he stepped back, then swung at the air as he stepped forward. An instant sensation of weightlessness accompanied a *whoosh* in his ears, and Allan's descending foot came down on grass and not the worn concrete.

He turned to see Chaya still at the gate, now four feet behind him. Allan moved back and opened the now accessible latch, and pulled it open. The grating *squeak* of the hinges sent shivers down his back, but thanks to Khirzoor's bubble, only he and Chaya could hear it.

"That's a cool trick," she said.

Allan nodded. "It is rather nice."

"What is?" Sam asked through the radio.

"Nothing." Allan replied. "Sorry about the chatter. We're in the yard."

He motioned his head for Chaya to follow and, maintaining a crouch, followed the tree line toward the rear of the property. Across the river stood a single-floor house. Shrubs and trees revealed only a partial view of the yard. Tengu liked their privacy. Pale light glowed through its open windows but Allan saw no one inside.

"Camera one is up," Luc's voice whispered through the radio.

"Got it," Sam replied.

Allan stopped about twenty feet from the riverbank and approached a metal bird feeder, standing about five feet high. He peeled the Velcro flap from a pouch at his belt and removed a tubular camera. Kneeling, he unfolded a trio of rubberized legs from its underside and wrapped them around the post before extending an antenna out the back. He clicked it on. "Camera Two is up." Allan peered along the top, aiming it at the right rear of the home.

"Little higher," Sam said. "Perfect."

Allan motioned across the yard and Chaya hurried to the other corner of the property. She crept to a flat rock and set her own camera atop it, its legs forming a tripod. "Three is on."

"I see it," Sam replied. "No movement inside."

"All right." Allan tightened his grip on Ibenus. "Let's shake the nest. Luc, give the front door a little knock, please."

"Moving in," Luc whispered through the radio. "Three. Two. One." A terrible crash sounded on the opposite side of the house.

There was a clatter, then a piercing shriek. The rear door of the house flew open as a brown feathered creature, like a bird-headed man, burst outside. Clawed feet extended from beneath its red silk pants. The tengu sprinted toward the river, cutting in Chaya's direction. She sprung from her crouch, scimitar raised to meet it.

"Get it!" Allan leaped up and ran toward her. He swung Ibenus and blinked forward a full meter before his foot hit the ground. He stepped, swung, and teleported again.

The tengu splayed its claws. Its shriek cut off as Chaya closed in, the silence bubble enveloping it. She swiped, but the beast hopped backwards, and then rushed in. She hacked downward, but the monster lifted an arm, taking the blow to its forearm. It slammed into her, sending them both sprawling.

"Chaya!" Allan cried. He was almost on them.

The demon scrambled atop her and raised its uninjured arm, talons out.

Allan launched himself toward it and swiped Ibenus, closing the distance. He hacked the khopesh, taking off the clawed hand before he hit the ground.

The demon's scream cut off as Allan fell outside of Khirzoor's radius. He spun just as Chaya rammed the holy scimitar up under the tengu's ribs and out its back. Brilliant green fire spewed from its wounds, then erupted from its mouth and eyes. Chaya rolled it to the side and wrenched the blade free.

"You all right?" Allan asked.

Panting, she turned toward him. Demon fire flickered along her bloodied blade. "Yeah."

Luc ran out from the house, mace in his hand. He slowed as he saw them above the corpse.

Allan nodded to the demon, the ghostly flames spreading over it. "Good work."

Chaya averted her eyes, the only part of her visible through the mask. "I shouldn't have let it get me like that." She shook her head. "I'm sorry."

"Sorry?" Allan grinned. "No one's hurt. Demon's down. That's a success."

"She got it?" Luc asked.

"Damn right she did," Sam answered over the radio. "Caught it all on camera."

"*We* got it," Chaya said. "Allan had to save me."

Allan set a hand on her shoulder. "Should have seen my first kill. Just about shit myself. Don't worry about it. You were great." He looked around. The yard and willows were all lit green in the firelight. The windows across the river were still vacant, but for how long? "Come on. Let's get this thing inside before anyone sees."

Sheathing his weapon, Allan grabbed hold of its arms, one of them ending in a bloodied stump, and lifted as Luc took its feet. The emerald fire flickered between Allan's gloved fingers and up his forearms. Chaya fetched the burning claw from under a leafy bush and hurried off to the house, holding it before her like a lamp.

Luc gave a little shudder as they carried the corpse toward the back door, swinging between them like a sack of melons.

"What?" Allan asked.

"I hate the way it feels."

"What?" The blood and feathers made it slippery, and Allan had to fight to keep hold.

"The fire." Luc shook his head. "Like ants moving up my skin."

"It's your imagination. It doesn't feel like anything."

"No it isn't," the big man grumbled. "Maybe I'm just more sensitive than you."

Chaya ran back toward them, a blanket in her arms. "Here." She draped the blanket over the corpse, shading the weird light from the neighbors' view. The green firelight glowed on the ground beneath it, like some street racer.

"Thanks," Allan said, still fighting his grip. He stepped backwards up onto the tiny porch and through the open door. "Keep your ear to the scanner, Sam."

"Roger. Find me something pretty."

They swung the corpse onto a plush sofa. Burning feathers clung to Allan's bloodied gloves. He wiped them across the cushions, smearing the fire across the cream fabric.

"All right." Allan fought the growing urge to pull the mask off his face as he scanned the baubles and trinkets blanketing every surface of the lavishly cluttered home. Shards of the smashed front door littered the entryway. "Time for fundraising. Three minutes."

Chaya moved toward a hallway as Allan bent before a cabinet loaded with silverware. The meticulously organized stacks were composed of at least four different pattern designs.

"I found this." Chaya carried in a brown leather suitcase, likely top of the line fifty years ago, at least. It clinked as she set it down.

Allan flicked the brass locks and opened it. Dozens of men's belts, each rolled into a tight coil, filled the case. Some appeared old and worn, others old but never used. He noticed a tarnished swastika on one of the buckles, and again wondered exactly how long this tengu had been living in Amiens. "It's perfect." Allan dumped the belts out onto the floor.

"I'll check the bedroom," she said, hurrying off.

Allan opened the cabinet doors and began shoveling the silverware into the case. Master Turgen could tell him if any of the sets were valuable, but if not, the silver alone was reason enough to take them. "Look here." Luc offered down a porcelain jar like he was offering Allan a cookie.

"Hello." Allan reached in picking a handful of rings. He accepted the jar and fit in into the suitcase. Luc handed him another, this one filled with necklaces. In ninety seconds a single tengu had far surpassed the total funds collected from demon nests in two years.

Luc moved to the kitchen and came back carrying a bottle of cooking oil. He unscrewed the cap and slung it out over the blanketed demon, the sofa, and poured the rest onto the rug.

After loading several more trinkets, Allan snapped the suitcase closed. "We ready?"

"Coming," Chaya's voice came from the hall and radio. She hurried in, a bulging orange backpack over one shoulder.

Luc removed a black rectangular device resembling a plastic hip flask from a belt pouch and fidgeted with it. After a few seconds he nodded. "Ready."

"All right." Allan reached for the pack. "Luc and I will carry these to the van and grab camera one. You pick up two and three and we'll meet you there."

"Me?" she said, a frown to her voice as she unshouldered the bag.

Allan grinned. "Price of your big debut."

Her dark eyes cocked but she remained quiet.

Allan checked his watch and gestured to Luc.

The big hunter twisted a knob atop the small bomb and dropped it onto the couch.

"Let's go." Allan was already moving. "Sam, we're on our way."

The two men hurried out the broken front door and across the yard. They stopped long enough for Luc to remove a camera from the wrought iron fence before they passed through a gate and over the canal.

Allan couldn't help but smile. If this was his last hunt beside Luc, it couldn't have been a better one. They neared the shadowy place where they'd parked the van and Allan's smile vanished.

The door was open.

Allan yanked Ibenus from her sheath. The suitcase clattered from Luc's grip as he reached for Velnepo. Allan didn't know if he saw it, too, or was just responding to him.

"Stop right there!" a woman's voice shouted.

Sam stumbled from behind the vehicle, arms behind her back. A lean woman clutched her forcibly by the shoulder and jerked her to a stop.

"Drop your weapons!" the stranger ordered. Her accent was British.

Allan took a step but the woman lifted a sawed-off shotgun. "*Drop* the sword. *Now!*"

Allan lowered Ibenus but held his grip. "Sam, are you okay?"

"Yeah."

Allan licked his lips. "I don't know who you are, but you're making a mistake. Let's just calm—"

"You don't know who I am?" She pushed Sam into the moonlight. The woman was young, mid-twenties. Intense eyes stared out from beneath short blonde hair. "I remember you. Now drop your weapons."

"Manchester," Allan said. "You were the policewoman."

"Good. Now I know I can't hit you. Tried before." She jammed the gun behind Samantha's head. "But I can hit *her*. And you have five seconds."

"Officer, I don't—"

"Four."

"You're making a mistake!" he knew he could get there, get the gun, but not before—

"Three seconds."

"Don't do it," Sam said through clenched teeth.

"Luc?" Allan asked.

"Two!"

"Do it." Luc dropped his mace.

Allan noticed Chaya moving up the other side of the yard behind the police woman. He opened his hand and set Ibenus on the grass. "There. Now remove the gun from her head."

The blonde's grip relaxed on the trigger but the ferocity still burned in her gaze. "Take off your masks. Slowly."

Palms out, and trying not to watch Chaya crossing the yard, Allan peeled the mask from his sweat-slicked face.

The woman just looked at them as if she hadn't known what to expect.

Allan broke the silence first. "What is it you want, officer?"

"I ... I want to know. I want to know what's going on."

"All right," Allan said with a purposeful nod. "We can do that. But first you'll want to put your gun down. Then we'll talk."

Her eyes narrowed, the cold determination still burned, but she lowered the shotgun from Sam's head. "Tell me who you are."

Chaya was running now, her feet silent on the fallen leaves.

"All right," Allan said.

Chaya was closing, her scimitar raised.

"Don't hurt her!" Allan yelled.

The officer's brow rose at the outburst. "Wha—?" and then Chaya's silence bubble enveloped her. That instant, she could hear Chaya's closing steps. She wheeled, bringing the gun up, but the Israeli was on her like a puma.

Chaya knocked the shotgun to the side. Orange flashed at its tip, followed by the sudden *thop* as the buckshot broke free of the bubble and blasted into a tree.

Allan dropped, grabbed Ibenus' handle, and swung as he sprang toward them. He blinked forward, and swung again before his foot even landed.

The two women grappled each other's weapons, knees and elbows swinging. Chaya yelped as the policewoman smashed her forehead into Chaya's eye. Hands cuffed behind her back, Sam spun and kicked the policewoman to the ground as Allan closed the distance.

Chaya screamed, raising Khirzoor.

"Stop!" Allan thrust his blade between Chaya and the fallen officer. He looked down at the woman.

Fierce intensity blazed in her eyes, not the fear he remembered that night in Manchester.

"Search her."

"I'm sorry," Sam said. "My radio went out and she was just there with a gun on me."

"It's all right," Allan assured, his gaze still on the woman as Luc patted her down.

"What are we going to do with her?" Chaya growled.

"We'll see," Allan said.

Luc quickly found a yellow radio jammer, about the size of a walkie-talkie. "Here we are." He removed a small billfold attached to a key ring from her back pocket. He unlocked Sam's cuffs, then handed it to Allan.

Allan squinted at the ID, trying to read it in the moonlight. "So … Victoria Martin, what brings you to France?"

Victoria eyed the sword points aimed at her, then met Allan's gaze. "I came for answers. I want to know what's going on."

"About Manchester?"

"About everything. The monster. Your weapons. You."

"You had a partner," Allan said, scanning the darkness.

Her lips tightened. "He's dead."

Allan nodded. "I'm sorry about that."

"How did you find us?" Luc asked.

Victoria gave a little snort and looked at him. "I'm a detective … At least, I was a detective."

"Then tell us how?" Luc asked.

"I found a report online from a person that said they saw a monster swimming in the river. That brought me here."

"And you found it and waited for us to show up?" Allan asked.

She shook her head. "Instead of looking for it, I watched for you to come looking for it. Then I followed you."

Clever, Allan thought. "For answers?"

She nodded.

"We're running out of time," Chaya said.

She tracked us down. She knows about the weapons. What else does she know?

"What's the plan?" Luc asked.

"You know what I want to do," Sam growled through clenched teeth.

"We don't work like that." Allan closed the billfold. "Where's your car, detective?"

"Why?"

"Because there's about to be a house fire in about seven minutes and you don't want your car to be found nearby. Now where is it?"

"Up the road. Hundred meters."

"All right. You want answers." He nodded to the van. "Get in."

"Hell with that," Sam snorted. "Not after she pressed a gun to my head."

"It was a misunderstanding." Allan held out the keys and wallet to her. "You take her car. Follow us."

"But—"

"No buts," Allan scolded. "Do it. Call it in. Tell them everything." He mouthed, *Get Uwe on it.*

Luc leaned toward him. "Are you sure about this?"

"Yeah." Allan turned back to Victoria. "Let's go."

CHAPTER 5

Within the darkened bedroom of his fourth-floor apartment, Gerhard slept beneath green cotton sheets and dreamed. He walked through the middle of lonely streets, canyoned between stone buildings, rising impossibly high toward an overcast sky that was neither night or day. Movement flickered beyond those blackened windows, but no matter how quickly he turned to see who might be watching them, they were empty. The air was still, silent, except for his own footsteps and a distant howling of wind through far away avenues.

He clutched Umatri in his hand, his only companion is this deserted world, and the only one he'd ever crave. The smooth wood seemed to move beneath his grip like a flexing muscle. The movement continued up along the wavy blade. It flowed with serpentine grace, undulating back and forth, back and forth.

Mesmerized, he held the weapon before him, eyes transfixed on the slithering blade. The rippling movement suddenly ceased. The edges bristled into serrated thorns. Umatri stretched and bent to the side like a sapling in a strong wind.

Following its curve, Gerhard turned to see a bat-headed thing leering out from an open door. It shrieked, revealing crystalline fangs, like broken glass, and the monster charged.

Gerhard wheeled to face it. The beast raced toward him, claws extended before it. He ducked the hungry claws and thrust the keris up, missing his mark, but the blade bent midair and plunged into the beast's chest. The bat-headed creature howled. Light swelled beneath its dark fur and it came apart, dissipating into a luminous cloud of vapor.

Umatri's blade moved again like a dowsing rod. Gerhard turned to see another monster charging on all fours. It looked more dog than human. Behind it, a skeletal thing crawled out from an open sewer grate.

The dog-thing leaped and Gerhard sprung to the side, lashing the keris toward it. The blade shifted like liquid metal into a L-shape and speared the monster straight through the ribs. Before he could withdraw the weapon from the still airborne corpse, the monster exploded into more glowing mist.

Snarls and howls sounded through the now growing fog, but Gerhard was not afraid. He had Umatri and, together, they would conquer all. The skeletal creature loped toward him. A greasy black ball of worms or eels writhed within its yellowed ribcage, slithering between the bones. With a scream of exalted fury, Gerhard lunged. He thrust—

Gerhard awoke to darkness. His sheets were soaked in sweat. Panting, he rolled over to check the bedside clock, the damp sheets clinging with the movement.

1:57.

He let out a long sigh, hoping to still his pounding heart. The dream lingered in the back of his mind like the afterglow of a bolt of lightning imprinted on the watching eye. Gerhard rolled from bed and padded naked across the cool laminate floor. He crossed to the window and opened the shade.

Directly opposite the street, stone and brick façades of luxurious houses stared back at him with haughty indifference. Gerhard confessed some mild amusement that his own apartment building was what they had to see, nothing like their manicured shrubs and twisting cast iron railings. Above their roofs he could just make out the treetops of the park beyond, a park those wealthy enough to afford such luxuries could gaze out upon. Did those within their walls appreciate such a view? Not so long ago he had coveted such wealth, such decadent possessions: a house, a luxurious automobile, inlaid redwood floors buried beneath oriental rugs. Did they appreciate them?

Would Umatri's anonymous owner appreciate him? Or would they merely hang him on a wall, another bauble coveted away from those who could appreciate it?

Gerhard closed his eyes and pressed his forehead against the glass. Had Alex relayed his message to the buyer? If so, why hadn't he called?

Probably not enough time yet, he answered to himself, but it didn't satisfy the nagging question. The dreams before, when Gerhard hadn't yet touched the keris or known its name, were only that, dreams. In the two nights since, they had evolved into something else, so vivid, so real that he could still feel Umatri in his hand as together they slew monsters. He opened his eyes. Below, a single car cruised the empty street, riding the line between the envied and the envious.

Gerhard looked to the phone on the table, its green LED pulsing as it charged. Alexander Turgen's crisp white card rested beside it, its face stark, marred by nothing more than name and phone number in raised sans-serif type.

Maybe I missed a call, he hoped, picking the phone up. The screen only verified what he already knew. Without giving himself time to think, he called the old man's number.

Fear seized his chest as it rang. What was he doing? It was two in the morning. He wanted to hang up, but Caller ID would have already betrayed him. *He won't answer. I'll just leave a message.*

The ringing stopped.

"Hello?" a husky voice asked.

"Uh ... Mister Turgen, I'm sorry ... but—"

"Gerhard," he said with an audible smile. "Please, call me Alex."

"I ... I didn't mean to disturb you, Alex. I apologize. My phone ..."

"It's quite all right, my friend. I was expecting your call. How may I help you?"

"Well." Gerhard licked his lips. "I was wondering if you've spoken with the buyer yet, about Umatri."

"I have spoken with the new owner, yes." There was a mischief to the old man's voice.

"Yes?"

"And Umatri is yours."

"But … I … how much?"

"No money," Alex said. "It's yours. The weapon has chosen you and you may have it."

"What?" he asked, unable to unwilling to believe the old man. This was a joke? Some cruel payback for a late-night call?

"It's yours, Gerhard. But you must do one thing."

"And that is?" Excited tingles danced across his skin. Surely this was a joke. But he couldn't help himself.

"You must come pick it up. Leave in the morning for Brussels. Tell no one where you are going. You must stay one week. After that, Umatri is yours and you may do whatever you wish."

"A week? Mister Turgen, I can't—"

"For Umatri," he interrupted. "You can."

Gerhard's supervisor wouldn't let him have a week off. It wasn't possible. He'd lose his job. He'd lose everything. *Everything but Umatri.* He'd already planned to spend his savings on it. How was this different? "All right," he said, finally. "One week."

"Excellent. I'll pick you up at the station when you arrive."

CHAPTER 6

Victoria sat silent on the bench seat, staring out the window as they followed empty streets lined with sleeping houses. The giant black man was driving. She'd recognized his voice and that iron mace from Manchester. The other one had called him Luc. A slip. His face looked familiar, but she couldn't place it. Maybe from one of the internet videos, but she knew that wasn't it. The short-haired Englishman with the Egyptian sword had admitted he was the one who had tried to save James after leading them into that godforsaken building. Victoria had assumed that the redhead, Sam—a second slip—had been the last of their team; likely the van's driver in Manchester. If only she'd been prepared for the fourth member, the dark-haired woman now seated behind her with an unsheathed sword. Victoria had assumed there were three and, as her old IPLDP instructor had drilled into their heads, to "assume makes an ass of you and me."

They'd handcuffed her wrists in front and not behind her back, thank God. With some luck, she might be able to grab the door handle, maybe a weapon if there was an opening. They also hadn't killed her. But what of the elderly man living in the house they'd gone into? Was he dead? She'd seen him the day before when she trailed them. He looked odd with his enormous nose, but he wasn't a monster. Why would they murder an innocent recluse and keep her alive after threatening them? "Where are you taking me?"

"Quiet," the woman behind her growled. "You're lucky to be alive right now, so shut up."

"We're taking you somewhere to talk," the Englishman said, not looking up from his phone screen. "You wanted to talk, so that's what we're going to do."

"Then why am I handcuffed?"

The man turned around. He'd have looked handsome with his dark hair and sharp chin if he didn't appear so angry. "Because you pressed a shotgun against my friend's head, and I'm not going to risk you doing that to anyone else."

Victoria ground her teeth and looked back out the window, dark images of water boards and bright interrogation lights playing through her imagination. She knew why they were keeping her alive. And once they discovered what she knew and how she'd found them, she was dead. Well, they'd never get it from her. Victoria wondered who was on the other end of that phone.

Five minutes later, the Englishman nodded ahead. "There. That's good."

Luc pulled the van up to a concrete biking trail alongside the river. A lone picnic table sat beside it, looking out over the water.

The Englishman stepped out of the vehicle and opened the sliding door. He'd left his gun belt and khopesh in the front seat. "All right." He held up the handcuff key. "Let's talk, Detective Martin."

Victoria eyed the key. James had taught her this trick. The false promise of freedom for information or to merely wear down the prisoner's resolve. She could play this. A faint grin pulled at her lips as she extended her cuffed wrists.

He unlocked them and dropped them in his pocket.

"Thank you," she said, hiding her surprise.

He led her to the table and sat down. A symphony of frogs and insects droned along the riverbank. "Please," he said, gesturing to the other side.

She took the seat and the brunette with the scimitar sat down beside the man, her sword still in her hand.

"Don't worry about the sword," he said, catching Victoria's gaze.

The woman gave a wicked little grin. Her left eye had swollen a little since she'd peeled off her mask. A little memento from their fight. "It keeps you from screaming."

"No," the man said, a scolding edge to his voice. "It prevents anyone from hearing you scream. But you're not going to do that, and we're not going to hurt you." He gave a cold look to the young woman. "Are we?"

The sound of rolling tires drew Victoria's attention. The girl, Sam, parked Victoria's car behind the van. The blue LED of a phone's headset glowed from her ear and she was speaking. How many people were they talking to?

The bench creaked as Luc sat down beside Victoria, but he kept his distance.

"You said you wanted answers," the Englishman said. "Ask."

Victoria swallowed, her mind stumbling as the ten thousand questions all raced to the front. But the most important, the simplest, pushed itself out first. "Who are you?"

"We're demon hunters," he said plainly.

"Demons," she repeated, eying his tactical attire. "You don't look like priests."

"Not that kind of demon. We kill monsters … physical manifestations of demonic possession."

"Monsters? Like that thing that attacked me?"

He nodded.

"And that's what was in that house tonight?"

Sam approached and handed Luc a computer tablet without even looking at Victoria. She walked back to the car as he scrolled through the screen.

"Yes," the Englishman said, ignoring them. "That was a tengu. It's a … different breed."

"I don't understand. How is a monster a demon?"

"It's …" He sighed and ran his finders through his dark hair. "There are thousands of monsters in folklore from all over the world. Most of those are just superstition, but some of them are real. They're demonic spirits, that when they possess a host, human or animal, they transform them into a monster. *That's* what we kill."

Victoria nodded, remembering the witness reports and

fuzzy photographs, the insane ramblings of internet nutters now making sense. "Why the weapons?"

He shared a moment's look with the brunette, as if debating how much to reveal. "Demons can only die from a holy weapon. Guns and other weapons can't hurt them."

"And just to get this straight," she said. "We're discussing monsters like werewolves and vampires, ghouls, goblins."

"Correct." He gave a little smile. "Except for goblins. Those aren't real."

Luc grunted a chuckle.

"So tell me, if a holy weapon is the only thing that can kill them, why haven't they just taken over?" she asked, channeling the most common naysayer mantra from the websites. "Infected everyone?"

"It's not like that," he said. "It's not some disease that passes around." He rubbed his fingers, as if trying to articulate the thought. "Let's say a demon bites you … well, it doesn't have to be a bite necessarily. Some use sex, or some other type of domination. In that act they mark your soul, and that means they can take you over. But that's all it means. A werewolf bites a hundred people, there's not a hundred werewolves, there's only a hundred potential werewolves, but there's still only one."

Victoria chewed her lip. It made sense. About as much as everything else did. Then she saw the hole in the logic. "All right," she said carefully. "You say normal weapons don't hurt them?"

"Correct."

"They killed those baby-faced things just fine. How was that possible?"

Luc offered the tablet to the Englishman, showing him something. The Englishman nodded. "Those weren't demons. Those were … minions."

Victoria raised a brow.

"Some demons can imbue their power into other creatures. Sometimes as a familiar, which is essentially human, but under the demon's control. Others times they can do it to a corpse. Those screamers you saw in Manchester were made from dead vermin. Those you can kill with mortal weapons."

Screamers, she thought, the memory of the doll-faced bugs sending shivers along her neck. *Fitting name.* "So that's why you carry guns?"

He nodded. "Partially. But certain elements can also harm a demon's body. Shoot a werewolf with a silver bullet and you can kill its host. The spirit moves to another, unharmed, so we try not to do that unless we have to. Which brings up a point." He leaned closer. "How exactly did you come to know there was a demon in Amiens? It's not like it even matched the description of the one that attacked you."

Victoria tongued her cheek, her gaze passing over the graffiti-etched table. "I started by looking for those but didn't find anything more than what I already knew. But it led me to a lot of cryptid websites and forums. Mostly rumors and questionable photographs of Loch Ness and Black Shuck."

"Any particular sites?"

She brushed at a mosquito buzzing in her ear. "Not especially. Mostly useless, except that they turned me on towards monsters in general. So then I thought about the weapons. At first I assumed that they were for silence, but then I thought, 'Why those weapons?' A khopesh isn't exactly a normal choice. Why not a fire axe or crop knife. So I started searching for unsolved killings or monster sightings related to primitive weapons." She met his eyes. "That got results."

"Websites about us?"

"No." She shrugged, hiding the lie. "Nothing so organized. But I found some rumors, other weapons, more bad photographs. But that led me to broaden my search. More than once a sighting was followed by an unrelated murder or fire and then no more sightings. So I decided to keep the search up for new sightings, try to figure out which ones might be real and not just some prank or cry for attention, and go check it out."

"You lost your job after the attack?"

"Yes."

"Because you told them about what you saw?"

Victoria chewed her lip, biting back the anger. "A good man died."

"I'm very sorry that happened." He drew a breath, about to

say more, but turned as Sam approached.

She pulled the headset from her ear and offered it to him. She mouthed something. Durgen? Turgen?

He quickly accepted it and hooked it onto his own ear. "Yes?" He held up a finger to Victoria, and stepped away, speaking low and his back to her.

There was no need to question who they were discussing. *What*, was a different matter. She turned, looking up at Luc. "I have another question."

He nodded.

"Why the secrecy? You know these things are real. You know they're killing people. Why are you hiding it?"

His jaw tightened, the muscles rippling. He appeared as though he wasn't going to answer, but finally he spoke. "How do you propose we tell people?"

"Well, you start by telling them."

"Oh." The corners of his mouth tightened into that little smile you give a child that excitedly tells you something obvious. The black void of a missing tooth at the corner ruined the line of white. "And they'll believe us? Tell me how. Demons change back to human when they die, leaving no trace. No blood. No DNA. Nothing someone can hold up and show as real. Footprints? Photographs?" He shook his head. "Those can be faked."

"But they are real," she said, hearing the weakness in the statement as she said it.

"Prove it. That's what they'll say." He opened his broad hand. "Look at alien conspiracies. You were a police officer. Would you believe those without proof?" He shook his head. "But let's pretend. We'll say that people do believe. What will they do when you tell them that there are monsters living among us? That there's no way to prove who is human and who isn't? What would happen if police said that there was a psychopath living in a community, someone who would eat them and their children?"

Victoria turned from his gaze and looked out across the black water, its ripples crested with moonlight. "They'd panic."

"Panic?" He gave a humorless chuckle. "They'd go insane.

Begin searching for any telltale signs. Then the accusations. Old hatreds would surface. Now they're not just the wrong race or religion or just different, but not even human. No guilt to be had by getting rid of them. Don't think that won't happen. Hatred thrives on justification. "Now let's tell them that the only way to kill these monsters is with a holy weapon. What then?"

She didn't answer. The buzzing mosquito returned.

"Holy weapons would become celebrities," he said. "Everyone would know them and their owners. Reporters would follow them. Do you think we could just show up in a city without anyone knowing? Everyone would know and then the demon would simply jump to a new body and escape.

"But that's just the beginning. If holy weapons are the only true way to rid ourselves of demons, then holy weapons become national security. Nations will fight for them. A new arms race. Everyone will want one, and they'll want to have the most. There are more countries than holy weapons and people will come for them. So now you have Russia, China, the United States all sitting on their stockpiles and other countries will have to beg for their protection. Now the politicians can say, 'No, you didn't sign this trade agreement, or we don't like your policies, so now your people can get eaten and die without help.'" He held her gaze. "Don't tell me it can't happen."

Victoria shook her head. Over Luc's shoulder she saw the Englishman click off the phone. He walked back and slid into his seat as Luc started speaking.

"Good," Luc said. "But why stop there? Now your country has a stockpile and can kill the monsters. Now the monsters can become your weapons. You can *control* them."

She snorted. "No. I don't see that."

"Really?"

"No. Not if they knew that much about them. That's too big of an assumption."

Luc shrugged. "History says otherwise. You ask me why we don't tell the world the truth? The reason is because humanity can't afford it."

"That's right," the curly-haired brunette said from beside her.

"But keeping innocent people ignorant of the threat leaves them victims," Victoria said. "How many lives might be saved if people only knew what was out there?"

"Now there's one less." The Englishman set his hands on the table, one atop the other. "You wanted answers. There they are. That's all we can give you."

"Wait." She straightened. "That's it? That's all you're going to tell me?"

He nodded and checked his watch. "We need to leave."

"But I have more questions."

"I'm sure you do." He licked his lips. "So, you can go back home with the answers you have and do whatever you like with them." He leaned closer, his brown eyes peering into hers. "Or … you can come with us and I'll teach you to be a hunter."

"What?" the curly-haired girl and Victoria blurted in unison.

Luc stared at him, brows creased in some dire, unspoken question. "You've lost your job. And no police force is willing to hire you. You've dropped off social media. Your bank accounts are nearly depleted. There might be something in private security, but—"

"Stop." Victoria clenched her teeth at the feeling of being violated. They'd gone through her accounts, her life, and the wreck they'd become. "Are you … offering me a job?"

"I am, yeah. You've experienced something terrible and nothing is going to change things back to how they were before. You've seen what's going on so I'm offering you a chance to look further, to do something about it." He shook his head with a little smile. "You tracked us down. There's a lot we can learn from you and there's a lot I can teach you."

Victoria studied his face. He seemed sincere.

"Of course if you don't wish to, that's all right. We can—"

"No," she blurted. "I'm interested."

"Good."

"Just one thing, though. I don't know your name."

He smiled and offered his hand. "Allan Havlock, protector of Ibenus. And I'm happy to accept you as my student."

CHAPTER 7

Gerhard watched out the rain-streaked window as the train glided alongside the platform into Brussels-South station. Running a hand along his bristled cheek, he regretted that he hadn't shaved before leaving. In the excitement and rush to pack after speaking with Alex, he'd forgotten about it. Only after boarding did he realize that he'd also forgotten his phone charger. No matter. Both were easy to correct. Though the untidiness irked him, if Alex could forgive a 2 a.m. call, then surely he could forgive a little stubble.

Passengers erupted from their seats as the train stopped, instantly flooding the aisle. Gerhard remained seated, waiting for them to pass as he scanned the platform for Alex or his Russian assistant, or bodyguard, or whatever he was. The five-hour ride from Stuttgart had afforded him ample time to ponder Alex's intentions. What exactly was Gerhard to do for Umatri? What services was he expected to provide over the next few days? Surely the old man required some compensation for such an artifact. Whatever it was, Gerhard would complete his payment and in a week's time return home, the keris his. He'd told his supervisor he had a family emergency, naming an aunt he hadn't spoken with in the three years since his mother's death, and he hadn't been sacked. His job secure, his savings again safe, Gerhard looked forward to when this strange adventure would be but memory. With a hopeful smile, he slid from his seat and made his way to the exit.

The noise of shuffling bodies and a thousand conversations in Belgium-accented French and German accosted him as he stepped off the train. Rain pelted the metal ceiling above. Gerhard looked around, and spotted Taras, dressed in a tight, gray T-shirt tucked into jeans, headed toward him, a paper coffee cup clutched in one hand. Bright tattoos of monsters sleeved one arm down to the forearm. Their snarling faces and bloodstained fangs stirred a shiver, reminding Gerhard of his dreams.

"Good to see you," the Russian said, offering a thick hand.

Gerhard shook it, returning the man's firm grip. "Good morning. Is Alex here?"

Taras motioned his head toward the entrance. "His leg is acting up today. Come on, I'll take you to him."

Gerhard had to hurry to keep pace as they strode through the crowd to where Alex was pushing himself off a bench near the glass doors into the station. Unlike Taras' casual dress, the old man wore a light-colored suit with shiny Italian shoes of chocolate brown.

"Ah, Mister Entz." Alex offered a hand which Gerhard accepted. "So happy you could make it. I trust you had a good trip?"

"Yes. Thank you for having me."

"Have you eaten?"

Gerhard shook his head, his stomach tightening at the reminder.

"We have food at the house, but if you prefer we can stop on the way."

"I can wait." Gerhard hoped no one heard the accompanying growl of his stomach.

The old man smiled. "Excellent. I'm sure you're eager to see Umatri."

They led him through the building and down into a parking garage to a silver Mercedes. Gerhard ran his fingers along the smooth leather seats as Taras drove them up the ramp and out into the streets. A glass skyscraper towered before them, overlooking the entirety of Brussels. Gerhard peered up at the glass-and-steel monolith standing against tarnished pewter sky.

"Have you been to Belgium before?" Alex asked from the front.

"Once. But I was very young."

"Hopefully you'll have a chance to see some of it while you are here."

"What is it I will be doing here?"

"Ah," Alex smiled. "I'm certain that question is foremost in your thoughts. I'll explain everything once we're at the manor and you have Umatri."

Manor? Gerhard again wondered what sort of man this was who gave away valuable antiques and rode in luxurious cars driven by a bodyguard. "What is it you do?"

"That is part of what I wish to discuss," Alex said. "I am on the board for an organization. A very old one. Among my duties, I locate lost relics and find homes for them."

"What organization?" he asked, thinking of Crelan, BNP Paribas Fortis, or any of the other Belgium banks. He'd told them he was in accounting. Perhaps this was a job offer.

"We are called the Order of Valducan. It's an international group like no other." He raised a hand. "Do not worry, my friend. All will be explained once we arrive."

They rode for another forty-five minutes before turning into a narrow drive. A high wall encircled the property, broken only by solid gate crowned with black iron spikes. It swung open as they neared and they continued on.

Through the trees, across the plain, manicured lawn, stood a giant building of red brick. The drive turned, emerging from the trees and Gerhard's eyes widened. The mansion rose three floors with a high slate roof. Wrought iron cages of decoratively curving bars encased each window. "This is your home?"

"It is the Valducans' house," Alex said, "but it is my home, yes."

They parked beneath a wide carport alongside several other vehicles, only one of which was as nice as Alex's sedan. The rest were rather plain cars and vans, though they all had dark-tinted windows.

Taras opened the Mercedes' trunk and offered Gerhard his suitcase. He then opened a nylon bag and removed a large kukri knife with a black-and-gold handle adorned with tiny jewels. Gerhard paused as the man unfastened his belt and looped it through the leather scabbard.

"That is Amballwa," Alex said. "Taras is her protector, same as you are with Umatri."

"Protector?" Gerhard asked.

The old man smiled. "Umatri has called to you, Gerhard. He has chosen you and only you to protect him. Come. Let us go inside and reunite you two, and then I will explain."

They led him up stone steps to an arched metal door, painted like dark-stained wood and artfully studded in pyramidal points of brass, silver, and bronze. Taras punched a keypad lock and unseen bolts thudded somewhere within. Gerhard noticed the rectangular cameras mounted on the manor's corners, above the door, and along the carport, each painted to match their surroundings. This wasn't a house at all. It was a fortress. Again, the nagging fear that maybe he shouldn't have come tugged at the back of his mind.

Taras pushed the door open and stepped inside.

Hesitating, Gerhard opened his mouth, unsure what to say, but Alex placed a hand on his shoulder and gently led him through.

An enormous floor-to-ceiling mirror greeted him as Gerhard stepped inside. The fragrance of flowers and rosemary from a bulging bouquet atop a foyer table threatened to make his eyes water. A swirling pattern of green and white marble decorated the floor, the design mostly hidden beneath the bright pinks and blues of a Turkish rug. He followed Alex, passing a suit of armor elaborately etched in strange geometric designs, every centimeter engraved, and then past a large room.

A young woman with curly dark hair sat in a wingback chair, a curved, gold-hilted sword across her lap. She turned her head as they walked by, giving Alex a smile. One of her eyes was nestled within a purple bruise. A brown-haired man with a heart-shaped face sat across from her. A sword handle protruded from his waist. To his left, a blonde with an upturned button nose looked up from a laptop screen and watched the newcomers with open curiosity.

Alex gave but a moment's glance, nodded to the man, and continued on. "The Holy Order of Valducan," he said, his cane tapping on hall's wooden floor, "originated between the first and second Crusades. Consisting of eight knights, each armed with a sacred weapon, they swore an oath to eliminate the greatest threat facing mankind: demons."

Metal inlaid symbols glinted from the square mahogany floor tiles, their shapes reminiscent of the armor they had passed. Some of the glyphs adorned the middles, others the edges or corners, each one unique. Looking up, Gerhard scanned the portraits lining the walls, men and women of different eras and races, all holding a weapon before them. Was this some religious group?

"In 1148 they were excommunicated from the Church for refusing to destroy Khirzoor, a Muslim scimitar." Alex opened a door, its silver knob decorated with polished stones. "Since then, the Valducans have lived in secrecy, sworn to protect the sacred weapons of the hidden war."

Gerhard followed him into a long dining room. More portraits and antiques decorated the oriental red walls. A dark, polished table ran nearly the length of the room. Another bouquet crowned its center, filling the room with a strange aroma. Before it, laid out on a folded velvet cloth, rested Umatri, his gilded blade hidden within his polished scabbard.

Gerhard's mouth suddenly felt dry. He stepped closer, his hands trembling as he crossed a thick rug and reached for the keris. His fingers found the smooth wood and clutched it. He closed his eyes, pulling it close to his chest. The relief of their reunion washed through him in a euphoric wave. For an instant he imagined he felt the grip ripple beneath his touch as it had in the dreams, as if muscles moved beneath wooden skin. It was his. Or … was he Umatri's? It didn't matter. They were together and he'd never let him out of his care again.

"Would you care for a drink?" Alex asked after nearly a minute of silence.

Gerhard blinked.

The old man was pouring an amber drink from a crystal decanter. He turned, offering a stemmed glass.

"No," Gerhard said, finding his voice. "No thank you."

Alex nodded and stoppered the bottle. "The bond is such a beautiful thing." He pulled a chair out beside Gerhard and eased himself down. "If I could live a thousand years it would never grow old to see."

"The bond?"

"The bond with a holy weapon." Alex gestured to an empty seat. "Please."

Glancing back, Gerhard realized Taras had left the room, if he'd even entered it. Gerhard hadn't noticed.

"Taras is preparing food for us. It will give us some time to talk."

Gerhard pulled the chair out and sat, still gripping Umatri as if the old man might somehow try to wrestle it from him. "What do you mean, bond with a holy weapon?"

"Do you mean to tell me that you don't feel it?" Alex asked. "That feeling that your life has been somehow incomplete without Umatri? Perhaps you've even questioned your sanity because of an obsessive need to be with it, an un-living object has won your love, a love it could never return."

A spike of anger shot up Gerhard's spine. He stiffened. How dare this man think Umatri couldn't—

"Ah." Alex raised a finger, a triumphant smile across his face. "So you *do* know. Umatri does love you because despite all reason, you know him to be alive. Don't you?"

Gerhard pursed his lips, eyes averting from the old man's knowing stare.

"You felt its call at the museum. You returned day after day just to be near it. In your dreams you felt him, felt him calling, begging you to return. Then finally you touched him, felt him and that love. And then your dreams changed."

"How did you know that?" Gerhard lifted his gaze to meet Alex's matter-of-fact smile.

The old man sipped his drink. "Because within that blade lives an angel, Gerhard. And out of everyone alive he has seen your soul and has chosen *you* to be his protector, his champion to aid him on his quest. I know this because every Valducan knight has bonded to a living weapon, and Umatri has bonded with *you*."

"His quest?"

"To destroy demons."

A sharp laugh escaped Gerhard's lips. "You're serious?"

"I am." He swirled his drink, gazing at it like chemist studying a solution, then met his eyes. "Holy weapons have existed for thousands of years, magical weapons that slew monsters. Those myths are based on *real people* and *real weapons*. If you know Umatri to be alive, capable of returning your love, is it so impossible to believe that there are other things out there, beings that only Umatri could kill?"

Gerhard gave a nervous chuckle. He'd never believed in a god but didn't wish to offend or debate the old man. Alex's obvious response would simply be that Gerhard had just more or less admitted that he believed ... no, *knew*, Umatri to be alive. He decided on a different route, instead. "If Umatri wished for a warrior, then why me?"

"There is a military base in Stuttgart." Alex swirled the drink again, then sipped it. "That was part of why I selected that museum. Do you have any idea how many soldiers and their families walked past Umatri's display?"

Gerhard shook his head.

"Your mother passed away some years ago. Were you close?"

"Yes."

"As much as her loss grieved you, did you not feel that maybe it should have upset you more, as if you were somehow broken because you were able to move past it so quickly?"

Gerhard's fingers tightened again on Umatri, that remembered guilt pressing the back of his brain. He'd never told anyone that and, now hearing it from the old man's lips, a renewed anger barbed and twisted within him, anger at himself for not mourning her as deeply as he should have, anger at this man for reminding him of that failure.

Alex set the snifter down onto the table. "I know more than that about you. You lack most prejudices. You've always been in fine physical condition, especially hand-eye coordination. You've never once considered suicide, and you've never had, nor will you ever, suffer from post-traumatic stress."

"How could you know that?" Gerhard asked.

"Because a holy weapon has bonded with you. Being a great warrior is more than training. It requires a very specific type of person. Out of everyone who saw him, Umatri selected you. So say whatever you wish about what faults or shortcomings you might believe you have, but Umatri has seen your soul, Gerhard, and has judged you the worthiest."

A knock sounded from the door. Gerhard turned as Taras peeked inside.

"Ah," Alex said. "Come in."

Taras pushed open the door and carried in a pitcher with some glasses. A tall, auburn-haired woman followed with two plates of sandwiches. Gerhard's stomach tightened and rumbled at seeing the food.

"Sam," Alex said to the young woman, "I want you to meet Gerhard Entz, Umatri's new protector. Gerhard, this is Samantha Coxall."

She set the food down and offered her hand. Her large, bright eyes deceptively gave her the appearance of a teenager. "It's a pleasure to meet you," she said in German, a bare hint of some strange accent to it.

"And you," Gerhard said, accepting it.

"I look forward to working with you," she said. "I've never seen Umatri in action."

Gerhard smiled, unsure how to respond.

"Sam is Taras' squire, or student, if you prefer," Alex said. "She's also a language enthusiast. Fluent in four and always working on more."

"Five," she corrected with a little smile. "My Swedish just needs a little tuning."

"Don't brag," Taras said, filling the glasses. "Not until you can beat Master Sonu."

Her full lips curled into a pout.

Taras turned to the two men. "Is there anything else we can get for you?"

"This is fine," Alex said. "Thank you."

Sam gave Gerhard a final smile, then followed Taras out, closing the door behind her.

Not ready to let Umatri go, Gerhard laid the keris across

his lap and picked up the sandwich. He ate in silence, thankful for the interruption. Alex's conviction troubled him. This whole affair was so strange, so unbelievable. Demons. Modern knights living in a mansion. Angels inhabiting weapons. Yes, Umatri was special, that he was sure, but the rest ... This was a cult.

The old man nibbled at his food as he watched Gerhard. "I know this is all a bit overwhelming for you."

Gerhard nodded. He sipped his water. "It is ... a lot to process."

"I understand. That is why I requested a week for you to consider our offer."

"And what is that?"

"To join us, of course. There is safety in numbers and your particular skills would be very useful in our other businesses."

"Other businesses?"

"All of *this*," Alex gestured around them, "requires money. The Order has several businesses, real estate, and a rapidly-growing energy endeavor that finances us, but we have been without a proper accountant for some time."

"So this *is* a job offer?"

"Of course it is." Alex leaned closer. "Your life has changed now, Gerhard. Now that you have bonded with Umatri it will never be the same. I'm offering you safe haven, training, and the ability to work as a team. Independent hunters have lived long and prosperous lives, but those are rare. Police and media are a bigger threat than ever, and they become more sophisticated every day. If we are to win this war, we must align ourselves."

Gerhard shook his head, his fingers finding Umatri for comfort. "I'm ... I'm not joining any war. I don't know what this is about but I don't have any intention to *kill devils*, or whatever it is you mean. I came for Umatri. Nothing more."

Drawing a contemplative breath, Alex leaned back. "I see." He reached for his cane and pushed himself up. "Come with me, please. Let us take you to your room so you can make yourself more comfortable. But first, there's someone that I would like you to meet."

CHAPTER 8

Allan tipped his coffee cup, waiting for the last drop to roll out. The excitement from the night had waned since they got home. The exhaustion was coming, looming imminent on the horizon now. No amount of caffeine could hold it back. He just needed a little bit longer.

"It's just so weird." Victoria shook her head and tapped the keyboard. Rain pattered the carport outside, growing louder.

"What is?" Allan rubbed his eyes and peered down to the frozen image of Chaya standing above the dead tengu, captured in the night vision's green monochrome. He saw himself there, partially out of frame, looking like some kind of ninja with his mask and black attire. She pursed her lips, eyes as intent on the crumpled beast as they'd been when she first watched the video three viewings ago. "It was just living there like anyone else. No one even knew."

"Someone knew. Or at least someone finally saw it for what it was."

Her hazel eyes met his. "How long had it lived there?"

Allan ran his fingers along his rough cheek. He needed a shower and shave, then clean sheets, darkness, and the sound of the rain. "At least seventy years, I'd guess, with some of the things we found." He looked up at Chaya sitting in the chair opposite them, its burgundy leather seeming to match the mottled purple of her black eye. "You went deeper inside. Any guess how long it has been there?"

She tapped a finger on the sheathed scimitar across her lap. Sitting with a sword was always problematic. "At least seventy," she said, finally. "No relics from the first World War, so sometime between that and the Second."

"And no one noticed the same person living there all that time?" Victoria asked.

Allan caught a whiff of his own soured sweat and wondered how bad he must smell to Victoria. Then again, they probably all reeked. "Mimickers are pretty good about rotating bodies every few years."

"Mimickers?" Victoria scrunched her brow. "Ones that mimic people?"

"That's right," he said with an impressed nod. "Aside from their big noses, tengu look completely normal when they wish. But they're nesters. Won't abandon a place unless they have to. So they just mark a new victim, have them purchase the property, then eat the old body once it's finished. Nice and neat."

Victoria's mouth tightened as if about to say more, but turned toward the open doorway as footsteps approached from the hall.

Allan straightened as Master Turgen stepped into the room. The lean-faced German recruit followed closely behind him, Umatri clutched in his hands.

"I want to introduce you to Gerhard Entz, Umatri's newest protector." Turgen gestured as Chaya rose from her seat. "This is Chaya Dahan, protector of Khirzoor."

She offered a hand. "Pleasure to meet you."

Turgen motioned in Allan's direction as he stood. "This is Allan Havlock, protector of Ibenus."

"Good to meet you," Allan said, shaking Gerhard's soft hand.

"And you," the German said with a slight bow.

"And this," Turgen said, stepping closer, "must be Victoria Martin, Allan's new student." He extended his slender hand. "I am Alexander Turgen. Welcome to our home."

"Thank you," she said.

"I sincerely apologize that I was not here on your arrival. I assume Allan has offered you some refreshment?"

"He has."

He smiled in that warm grandfatherly way of his, but Allan noticed the fine, wary edge hiding in the old man's eyes. "Very good." Turgen stepped aside, allowing Gerhard access. "This is Gerhard, another guest, only just introduced to our fold." He waited until they had shaken hands before offering Gerhard a chair. "Allan, I was wondering if you could share the story of how you first became a hunter."

"Of course." Allan ran a hand along Ibenus' smooth grip until Turgen had lowered himself into one of the leather wingbacks, then he drew the khopesh from her sheath. If the old man was asking for this story now, it meant that the new recruit wasn't sold on joining the Order, yet. He sat down cradling Ibenus across his lap. "My great-great-grandfather, Gordon Havlock, was a treasure hunter. Fancied himself an Egyptologist, but ..." He shook his head. "Bit of a scoundrel, really.

"While on expedition in Thebes he discovered a small temple. Couple mummies, gold, artifacts. There, at the edges of their torchlight, resting on a pedestal before a statue of a hawk-headed god, was Ibenus." Allan patted the bronze blade. "So his team divided the treasure up, carried it all back to England, and made a fortune selling it to collectors and museums. He held on to some choice pieces for himself, Ibenus among them.

"When I was a kid, we used to visit my father's uncle every summer. He kept Ibenus in private museum and, as long as I could remember, I was fascinated with her. Whenever we'd arrive, the first thing I'd do was go and look at her." He shook his head, grinning. "They used to pretty much drag me away when it was time to leave."

Gerhard gave an understanding nod, but discomfort still seemed to linger in the tight corners of his lips, like a boy caught stealing cookies.

"Then when I was twelve, I fiddled the lock on Ibenus' case open. That feeling ..." Allan's fingers gripped the sword, "getting to touch her for the first time." He released a low breath, the memory tingling through his veins. "It was love." Allan glanced to Victoria, watching him intently, a question forming on her lips. A strange pang of guilt prodded his stomach but he couldn't say why. Why should he feel guilt?

"My uncle caught me, of course," Allan continued. "I was swinging her around, pretending I was some warrior. It's a wonder I didn't break anything. Got in a lot of trouble for that one. I thought he'd send me home for sure, but ..." He shook his head. "That was the last time I was allowed in there, though. Then when I was finishing secondary school, my uncle passed away. The estate was divided up and he willed me Ibenus as well as tuition to University of Liverpool. That was about the time the dreams began."

Gerhard cocked his head. "Dreams?"

"Yeah. I'd always had dreams about Ibenus as long as I could remember. Nothing too specific. Usually she was the goal, something I was searching for. They became more common after I first touched her. But now I was holding her in them. Fighting on some ancient battlefield or exploring a dungeon. See, I wasn't ready for her yet. I was too young. But then, once she was mine, they became nightly and full of monsters."

Gerhard leaned closer, eyes intent. "Tell me about them."

"The most common one, I was in a desert, dressed as Lawrence of Arabia or something. There was this wall of sand swirling around me, like I was in the eye of a storm. The wind was howling and monsters were coming out of the wall, or bursting up from the dunes, attacking me, coming for her. And no matter how many I killed, two more emerged, all of them different. Every one."

"I was on a city street," Gerhard said. "There was a glowing fog and the monsters were coming out of the windows and sewers."

Allan smiled. "Wake up sweating?"

The German nodded.

Allan raised a finger. "That's the call. Ibenus was telling me I was ready. I just didn't know for what. Then, when I was twenty, I heard about some farmers in Greasby, claimed a giant black dog was killing their sheep. Called it the Beast of Wirral. After a couple of months, a girl was found dead, torn apart by some animals. Tabloids pegged it on the Beast but no one actually believed in it."

"But you did," Victoria said, her voice a whisper.

"Yeah." He swallowed. "I didn't know why it struck me so hard, but I started obsessing about it. I'd head down there nightly, Ibenus tucked into a battered DJ case. I'd filled it with foam, cutout this shape of her in it so she could fit, like some television hit man." He chuckled. "Two weeks I did that, creeping around farms at night, crawling through fences. What started as this sort of game had completely taken over." Allan met Gerhard's eyes, his smile falling into cold sincerity. "Then one night I found it."

If the German was moved by the dramatic flair, he didn't show it. "What was it?"

"Hellhound," Allan answered. "Imagine a shaggy black dog, but huge, big enough to ride. At first I couldn't tell what it was. Just this shape in the shadows. Then I saw these two red eyes glowing like coals. It was that moment I realized it wasn't some fanciful game I was playing. It was real, and it was charging at me, teeth bared. It leapt at me. I stumbled backwards and brought up Ibenus, like I could somehow block it, then, *whoosh*, I'm a full meter away from where I fell, and was standing."

Gerhard's brows furrowed. "I don't ... understand."

"Ibenus grants me the gift to teleport a short distance when I swing her. Just a meter, meter and a half, but it's enough."

"Teleport?" Gerhard looked over at Turgen, skepticism filming the German's eyes.

The corners of Turgen's lips tightened into a smile.

"You didn't tell him?" Allan asked.

"It hadn't come up yet." He lifted a hand toward Allan, giving permission to share.

"The bond with a holy weapon is a bond to an angel," Allan said. "As that bond strengthens, we are gifted access to that angel's unique powers. Umatri's gift ..." Allan started, searching for the best words, "she moves, like a serpent."

"He," Turgen corrected.

"Apologies," Allan said, cursing his forgetfulness. "They used to call him the Steel Adder. Because he moves," Allan undulated his hand back and forth, "like a snake."

Gerhard sat back, his mouth a flat line, eyes fixed on Allan's slithering hand. He swallowed and gazed down at the keris in his lap.

That got through, Allan thought.

"In my dream," Gerhard said, "he moved like that."

Allan grinned. "At least he's warned you. Ibenus gave me no warning. Just *poof*. The hellhound snarled and wheeled toward me. I swing again. *Poof*. Suddenly I'm on the opposite side of it and Ibenus buries into its flank. Then it howls this unbelievable wail, echoing out across the moors. My muscles just turn to jelly at that noise and I stagger back, miracle I kept hold of the sword. Beast turns, about to lunge again. I swing, *poof*, I close the distance and bury the blade," Allan brought the side of his hand up in a karate chop motion into his forehead, "right into its skull." He lowered his hand, returning it to Ibenus. "In your dreams, did the monsters burn when you killed them?"

Gerhard shook his head. "They ... evaporated into mist."

"Then let me tell you the next thing I wasn't ready for. Bright blue fire spewed out from the monster's wounds and enveloped it. Beautiful, really, but bloody terrifying when you aren't expecting it. But demon fire isn't like normal fire. It's not actually burning, but its soul is. Looks like a hologram or a bad special effect, you know. Superimposed."

The German gave a puzzled grimace, as if unfamiliar with the term, but he didn't speak.

"About that time the leather grip tape I'd wrapped around Ibenus' handle swelled and split open as the original wood grip, long decayed, grew back good as new. Weird. So there I am, standing by this blue fire, covered in sweat, then I see that the monster is changing, transforming into a woman dead at my feet."

Allan sighed, the image of her cloven face tightening his chest. For some reason hers was the only one that still got to him. "I panicked." He glanced at Victoria. Sympathy lurked beneath her fascinated intensity. He licked his lips. "Thought I might have gone mad. Maybe just murdered some random naked woman, thinking she's a monster, but that fire is still burning. I briefly considered burying her, hiding the body, but ... I just got the hell out of there. Swore I'd never do anything like that ever again. Went home and tried to pretend it'd never happened."

He shook his head, eyeing the empty coffee cup. "But you see, Ibenus had me. She chose me because she knew me, knew I wouldn't resist. My eyes had been opened to this world I never knew about. Started noticing things, little things I'd not given any thought to before. Couple of my mates visited a massage parlor in Chinatown. Said they had a great time, if you catch my meaning. One of them, my friend Rob, he's going on and on about this one girl. Said it was amazing but he's also real sickly after that. Said it was stomach bug or the like, but couldn't wait to go back and see this girl again. Once I'd have just chalked it up as another bloke that fell for a prostitute, but I can't stop this uneasy feeling about it. Week later he's feeling his old self, goes and pays her another visit. Comes back, he's pale, tired, and still raving about her. Then that feeling come back, worse now. All I can think is succubus."

Allan sighed. "So just a month after I swore I'd never do anything crazy again, I go to Chinatown with Ibenus, bent on killing the succubus that's feeding on my friend. Luckily for me, the Order had gotten to her first. But they'd waited around, having heard of the body found in Greasby killed with a sword about the same time the beast sightings stopped. They found me and took me in. And here I am."

"Thank you, Allan." Turgen shifted in his seat and squeezed his knee. "Gerhard, I imagine you would like to freshen up, and be alone with Umatri. We have time to discuss this later. Chaya, would you mind showing Mister Entz to his room, please?"

"Of course."

"It was good to meet you," Gerhard said, rising.

"And you." A sudden apprehensive weight settled in Allan's chest as Chaya led Gerhard out, his suitcase rolling behind, the wheels rattling on the inlaid hall tiles. The entire drive from France, he knew this was coming, and now it was here. It was time for Turgen's interview.

Turgen smiled at Victoria, disarming in its absolute warmth. "So, Miss Martin, tell me about yourself."

"What do you wish to know?" she asked.

"Parents. Tell me about your family."

She shrugged. "Not much to tell. My mother lives in Nottingham selling real-estate. My brother, Charlie, is in the Air Force, stationed in Cypress last I heard. We never connected much."

"No father?" Turgen asked.

"None to speak of." She shook her head. "Haven't heard from him since I was fifteen."

The old man kneaded the side of his knee and squeezed. His face gave no indication how bad it must be hurting him. "So, brother in the RAF and you became a police officer. A detective, I understand."

"Yes. Detective Sergeant."

"How was your performance?"

"Not very good."

Turgen's thick brows arched in a look of mild surprise. "No?"

"I was only recently promoted when I got sacked. It was said that my inability to handle the stress of the position was what led to my ... breakdown," she said with a bitterly amused edge.

"When you saw a monster?" he asked.

"When it killed my friend."

Turgen swallowed. "I'm very sorry to hear about that. I'd read Allan's report of that night. Tragic. We try to be sure that no witnesses are in the vicinity before revealing ourselves." His eyes flashed to Allan. "We failed you."

Allan's jaw tightened. The old man accepting the blame with him was worse than having it all on Allan was where it rightly deserved.

Victoria didn't say anything.

"And after that terrible event you managed to track us down," Turgen continued. "I must agree with Sir Allan that you are a more skilled detective than your superiors believed. I can only imagine that we will benefit from such talent. Both in helping us locate demons as well as better hiding our own tracks."

"Thank you," she said.

"You've had a long night and must be exhausted. We can continue this another time."

That's it? Allan thought, fighting to hide his surprise. He'd expected a grilling.

Turgen touched the silver grip of his cane leaning against his chair. "I can assure that you'll be asked a thousand questions by everyone wanting to meet the new girl, but we have plenty of time for that. Despite this morning's excitement, two recruits at the same time is almost unheard of." He moved, as if to stand, but stopped. "One more thing I must ask."

Here it comes. Allan had known better than to think it was going to be this easy.

"Yes?" Victoria asked.

"Do you have any allergies or illnesses that we need to be aware of?"

"No."

"Any phobias?"

She shook her head.

"Very good." He pushed himself up and Allan rose as well. "I will see you at dinner this evening. Allan, once you've shown Miss Martin to her room please meet me in my office for debriefing."

"Of course," Allan said, the long-forgotten childhood dread of being summoned before the head teacher suddenly returning. Master Turgen never requested private audience immediately after a hunt. He turned to Victoria. "Shall we?"

Victoria stood and followed him out into the hall. "So these were all knights?" she asked, scanning the paintings. "Like you?"

"They were."

"Is there one of you up there?" He shook his head.

"Not yet."

"You know, I remember the Beast of Wirral." Thunder rolled outside, rattling the windows.

"You do?"

She nodded. "I hadn't heard of it until the second body was found, Iris ... something."

"Reeder," Allan said, turning into the staircase leading up

to the second floor. Like that bloodied face, framed in blue fire, he'd never forget the name of the first person he'd killed. The first he'd set free.

"That's it. So was that true?"

Allan stopped. Turned on the stairs. "What part?"

"All of it. Or was that only for Gerhard's benefit?"

"It was true. Every word."

Her tired, red-rimmed eyes studied him, searching. "That must have been terrifying."

"Everyone's first encounter is. It gets easier, just never easy."

"They say that about a lot of things."

"It's true, though." Allan continued up to the second floor. "Your next time you'll be trained, equipped, and so will those with you." He led her down a hall, lined with dark wood doors, their silver handles each encrusted with stones. "This is you," he said, opening one.

She followed him into a long bedroom the color of parchment, its sea gray curtains open. Through the rain-streaked windows, the trees danced in the wind. She touched her suitcase resting atop the bed. "Thank you for bringing this up."

"No problem at all," Allan said, choosing to ignore that Luc and Sam had carried it up in order to scour it. "Let me know of anything you need." He jammed a thumb to the right. "I'm next door. Washroom is down the hall to the left. Chaya and Sam sort of claimed it as the women's loo."

"Something tells me that they're not going to like me using it either," she said. "Didn't exactly start on the right foot."

Allan shrugged. "Not really. But they'll get used to you."

She cocked her brow. "You don't know women very well, do you?"

He chuckled. "My best friend Matt pointed a gun at my face when we first met. So did you."

"You sound like you need a better way of meeting people."

"Seems to work for me. We live a very unconventional life. Holding grudges doesn't serve any purpose. Not when we're risking our lives doing what we do. They'll get over it."

She smiled wanly, as if not wishing to argue the point. "Turgen doesn't trust me, either."

"Why do you say that?"

"I can tell."

Allan closed the door. "Master Turgen is just being cautious." He pulled the chair out from the desk and sat down, adjusting Ibenus so she slid beneath the chair's arm.

She took a seat on the bed, her knees nearly touching his.

"A few years back we took in a recruit, thinking she was a knight. She betrayed us. Several knights were killed, many holy weapons were destroyed, our records compromised. She even set fire to our home."

"What happened to her?"

"She offered herself to a demon goddess. Tiamat. We killed it, but we're still limping from what she did. Master Turgen took Anya's betrayal very personally. His own student and holy sword was destroyed by it."

"So why do you trust me, then?" she asked, looking straight into his eyes.

"Because," he said, meeting her gaze, "what you did was because of what you went through. It wasn't malice. You wanted answers. You tracked us down despite any fear of what you'd find. If I didn't take you in just you'd keep going. Your eyes are open and you're a warrior. I know what that's like. The least I could do is give you the tools."

Victoria studied him, searching his face, then she looked away. "Thank you."

"Now," he said, fighting the urge to put a hand on her knee, "rest up. Tomorrow I'll begin training you how to hunt and you get to teach me how to be a detective."

That knot of dread had swollen into a leaden ball by the time Allan reached Turgen's office door. *Just stand your ground. It's your decision, not his,* he mentally repeated like a mantra.

He paused before the dark wooden door. Luc's deep voice rumbled on the opposite side, the words muted. Damn it. He'd hoped he could have spoken to Turgen first. *It's your decision, not his.* Allan sucked a breath, holding that fleeting confidence, and knocked.

"Come in," Turgen called.

He opened the door on silent hinges. Master Turgen sat behind his desk, one hand on the polished top, the other at his chin. An eclectic assortment of antiques lined the walls and shelves, reminding Allan of his great uncle's museum. A trio of flintlock pistols hung on the wall behind the old man, each decorated in ascending degrees of ornament. In the corner, a blackened gorget and helmet stood on a carved stand, enameled with intricate symbols, though not as elaborately as Sir Eberlein's armor downstairs. Luc peered back at Allan over his shoulder.

"Mister Renault and I were just discussing you," Turgen said. "He said the hunt went flawlessly, until the end. Even then, you took control to save Samantha's life."

"Good to hear." Allan slipped inside and took the chair beside Luc. The chairs were designed with one arm so that anyone wearing a weapon on their left hip could sit without having to remove it.

Turgen withdrew his bony hands, resting them in his lap. It occurred to Allan how terribly old he looked. The skin of his neck hung loose above his immaculate tie. While never large, he didn't quite fill his suits the way he once had. Turgen's own holy sword and the student who had inherited it were both two years dead and he'd been withering ever since. The glass of brandy seemed to have restored color to his cheeks, but the excitement of the day had left his eyes tired. "With Taras ready to return to the field, I'll be assigning Chaya to Luc. You'll be assigned Taras and Sam. Providing how things transpire with Victoria, once she's ready, Luc will take Taras, while you take Chaya. That way each team has two knights and one student."

Allan and Luc shared a look.

"Makes sense," Allan said.

Luc nodded. "Any word on Master Schmidt?"

Turgen shook his head. "No luck so far. He'll be returning from London Thursday."

"Is he being assigned to a team?"

"I'll have him assigned as Base Knight. If he has any disagreement with that, it will be between myself and Max."

The knights nodded.

"As for our current problem," Turgen said. "Gerhard doesn't

yet understand what has happened to him. He doesn't believe."

Allan ran a finger along his upholstered armrest, touching the cold brass tacks like giant braille dots. "I got that impression myself."

Luc's chair creaked as he leaned back. "We need to show him."

"We do," Turgen said. "But Mister Entz strikes me as they type of man that must see it with his own eyes. No amount of video or personal accounts will get through. Though, he will get much of that. He's promised me one week."

"A week?" Allan blew a low breath, his mind flipping through any recent sighting and rumors they'd found. "That's not going to be easy."

"If we can't, and he leaves, we can't protect him. He's not trained. Umatri will exert his will to hunt."

"I know," Allan said.

"Good. You're the acting Librarian, Allan. It's up to you and Samantha to find a hunt."

Allan nodded. "We'll start right away."

The old man's gaze moved to Luc. "In the meantime, his training begins in the morning. If they can't locate a demon to show him, then he's going to leave here as well prepared as we can make him. Work the scheduling with Chaya."

"I will," Luc said. "We'll work him until he's too sore to leave."

"Just don't run him so hard he can't go on a hunt. He doesn't have to fight it, but he has to *see* it."

"Understood."

"Now." Turgen picked up the brandy snifter, almost idly. "I would like to speak to Allan alone."

Luc swallowed audibly. "Of course." He stood, giving Allan a moment's reassuring glance.

Allan traced the arm tacks, his finger running a figure eight between two of them.

The door closed with a *click*.

Turgen sipped his drink.

It's your decision, not his.

"Allan, I'm concerned as to why you accepted Miss Martin

as your student. And not just myself. Luc and Samantha have both expressed this with me already and Chaya simply hasn't had the opportunity yet."

"I didn't accept her," Allan said. "I offered."

"But why? We don't know her."

"She managed to track us down. She found us. We can use that skill."

Turgen nodded, as if considering the words. "She is quite attractive."

"I noticed."

"And are you sure that didn't influence your reason?"

"No," Allan said, the heavy dread suddenly compressing into a hot coal. He forced his voice calm. "It didn't."

"That's good to hear. It wouldn't be the first time a blonde has caught your eye."

"With all due respect," Allan said without moving his jaw, that coal igniting into full anger, "Anya tricked us all into believing she was one of us."

Turgen's hand came up, his eyes narrowing. "Please refrain from using her name."

"*She. She* was different. *She* didn't find us, she let us find her, make us think she was bonded. Victoria was attacked. I saw it. Her partner was killed. I saw that, too. She lost her job, went to therapy, and didn't give up. Victoria hunted us down and didn't come with any intention of joining. That's what makes her different. I have no doubt she hates demons as much as any of us."

"I understand that, but why your student? She's too close to your own age for her to inherit Ibenus."

"She can still bond to another weapon," Allan said.

"And if she doesn't?"

"Then I will keep her as my student. It is my right."

Turgen laid his hands on the desk top, one on top of the other. "Yes," he said, calmly. "It is your right. I cannot stop you. But I still fail to understand why you would choose her as your student. You may only have one and until she has bonded, or is dead, you cannot have another. Think of the future, Allan."

"Taras isn't that much older than Sam," he said more

defensively than he intended.

"Fourteen years, and their circumstances were different."

Not really, but Allan wasn't going to press the point. He sighed and touched Ibenus at his hip. "I can't ... explain it. It was just a feeling, and I still feel it. I *had* to offer it."

The old man studied Allan's face. "Are you saying Ibenus called you to act?"

"I think she did." Allan had spent the drive mulling the possibility but now, speaking it aloud for the first time, it suddenly became real. Why would Ibenus urge him to accept her?

"I see." Turgen patted his hand on top of the other, the green jeweled ring in his left little finger glinted with the movement. "You are her first protector that we've ever known, and her ... personal habits are still unknown. But you must admit that it is rather unusual."

"I'm not denying that."

Turgen picked up his glass and finished it. "However, while I cannot control who you take as your squire I will not allow her unobserved access to the Archives."

"I understand."

"She's your responsibility, Allan. I'm holding you accountable for her. I want her records. Find out who her therapist was. I have ways to get them."

Allan nodded.

"Well," Turgen said, the tension of the last few minutes seeming to wash away with the single word. "Is there anything else?"

"There is one thing," Allan said.

The old man rolled his palm upward, offering him the opportunity to continue.

"With the new assignments, have you given any more thought to our discussion?"

"Quite a lot, actually. In fact, my original plan was to begin grooming you once Gerhard's week has concluded. But ... you seem to have made other plans."

Allan forced through the urge to look away. "Then what will you do?"

"I considered Taras." He absently waved away Allan's coming protest. "But he's not right for it. Matt would be the perfect choice, but with Luiza and the baby ... transferring knights to replace them in Chile would be a problem."

"Who then?"

"Would I transfer?"

"No. Who will step in to fill your shoes with the museums?"

Turgen's lips pulsed tight, almost reflexively. "I'm not sure."

"We need to begin that soon. Train them. Get curators used to them."

"You believe I don't know that?" The old man's voice grew hard. "I had plans for you, Allan. But your responsibilities were already stretched enough. I'm not dead yet. I'll choose a replacement, but it can't be you."

Allan's eyes fell away as if watching the dream collapse and shatter onto the floor. "I meant no offense. I'm sorry."

"Not as sorry as I am."

EPISODE 138

CHUPACABRA

Bass thumps as a blurry image focuses into view, revealing a black and white picture of a creature standing in the woods, its eyes glowing in the camera flash. Another picture slides into the screen, covering it, this one depicting a clawed footprint in snow, followed by shaky video of a hairy beast running into an open sewer tunnel.

Red flashes filling the screen with a moment's crimson, and the footage now shows black and white security video, looking down on a woman being attacked by spidery insects the size of dachshunds. She falls and is dragged off camera through the white numbers rolling in the bottom right corner of frame. The music picks up, racing into a heavy metal riff as red flashes again, this time fading out onto thick, block letters: MONSTER SEEKERS.

"Hey, cryptozoologists," says a loud voice, reminiscent in accent and tone to a New England football coach. "TommyD here with a clip that will blow your minds."

The screen changes to an image of scraggly trees cast in ghostly blues.

"A pair of ranchers in Sonora, Mexico, uploaded this video," the voiceover continues. "After losing livestock to what they assumed to be coyotes, they set up in a blind and waited. What they found was much more sinister."

The image shakes and scans across scrub brush, the colors washed out, only the faintest hints of green and brown visible in the nighttime footage. Barbed wire glints along a trio of white lines stretched between posts. A shape dashes through the circle of light, the size of a wolfhound, a long rodent-like tail flickering into focus for only a moment.

"There! There!" yellow captioning reads, accompanying the whispered Spanish.

The camera shakes as the illuminated circle whips across gnarled trees and tufts of high grass. A hunkered creature looks up from the shadows. Batwing ears frame its long face. Vivid blue flashes in its eyes as it looks to the camera. Its lips curl, revealing a pair of curved frontal fangs.

"Jesus Christ!" the captioning reads.

A loud pop and the creature tumbles back. It staggers up, then another *pop* sends it rolling onto its side, large back legs kicking the air as if trying to run.

"You got it!" The camera swings onto a husky, unshaven man holding a rifle. His pupils glow pale in the night vision's light. The man looks off in the direction of the fallen creature.

"What was that?" the shooter asks. *"Did you see it?"*

"Yes. Let's look." The camera swings around, revealing chipboard walls, close up and washed out in the IR spotlight's glare. The camera looks down a trapdoor at a metal ladder, swings around, and the rungs move past in rapid succession.

"Come on!"

The shooter hurries down the ladder, rifle clutched in one hand. He leads the cameraman through the grass and past the twisted tree trunks, the camera shaking as they hurry. They slow and the shooter lifts his gun warily.

"What is that?"

The camera moves up onto a hairless animal, blood gleaming in the spotlight. Muscles throb beneath its dark hide. The creature's body seems to deflate, dimpling and creasing as it shrinks. Bones crackle and fur sprouts from the receding skin. The batwing ears shrivel and move higher onto the diminishing skull as the twin fangs, like bent nails, draw up inside it. Within a minute, only a coyote remains in frame.

"So there you have it," TommyD's voiceover continues. "Honest to God Chupacabra, completely corresponding with descriptions on the 1996 Jalisco photographs, the 2004 San Marcos videos, the 2011 El Paso pictures, and dozens more. Skeptics always claim that these reports are merely coyotes or foxes with mange and that no captured or killed specimen has ever proven to be otherwise. But now ... now we know why.

"Tell me what you think in the comments below, and if you have any videos or tips, please email me. As always, I keep my sources strictly anonymous. So keep your ears to the ground and cameras ready. The monsters are among us. Until next time, TommyD, signing out."

CHAPTER 9

Victoria stepped into the shower and closed her eyes. She leaned her head back, allowing the hot water to rinse away the sweat and lingering exhaustion. The unfamiliar bed in a house of strangers had made sleeping difficult. Without the Wi-Fi password and her phone still not returned to her, she'd simply lain there in the dark, replaying the weird turn her life had suddenly taken.

When sleep finally did come it was short-lived. Allan had roused her at six for a morning run. Bright-eyed, shaved, and wearing a dreadful neon lime green shirt, he practically pushed her out the door where they joined Gerhard, Luc, Chaya, and Sam.

The nagging suspicion that she was a prisoner was quashed when they'd left the estate's grounds and jogged in a haphazard line along the road outside. The bright lights that lined all of Belgium's streets replaced the feeling of being out in the country with one of being some of the last people on Earth. A tree-lined street, brighter than anything in Manchester, and no one on it but half a dozen runners and a few morning commuters. This whole affair wasn't at all what she'd imagined. Then again, she wasn't entirely sure what she had expected when Allan invited her to join them. Some run-down converted warehouse, or some mercenary training camp, perhaps? Whatever she'd envisioned, it certainly wasn't an antique-filled mansion with morning jogs and luxuriating in a marble bathroom. It reminded her more of some lavish spa or celebrity rehab center where millionaires atoned for their vices.

Missing her own shampoo, Victoria selected one of the bottles in the shower. Its fruity mint fragrance filled the tight stall as she stood there, letting it rinse, her mind wandering. She needed her phone back. Surely TommyD had heard of the fire. He'd be worried.

Just a quick message. That's all it'd take. That and the promise that his questions might soon be answered. Surely they'd let her have her phone back soon.

The shower done, she stepped out, nearly slipping on the tiles, ice-slick with condensation. Hazards of a marble floor. Toweling off, she wiped the foggy mirror and had opened her toiletry bag when a knock came from the door.

"Yes?"

"Can I use the shower?" Chaya asked from the other side.

Shit. Distracted with her thoughts, she'd forgotten the others would be waiting. She reached for her towel. "Yes, I'm done."

She barely had it on when Chaya squeezed in through the door, dressed in a smoky gray robe and her curly hair still tied up from their run.

"I'll be out in a second," Victoria said, quickly tucking her unused toothbrush back into the bag. She'd do that after breakfast.

Chaya only grunted as she turned on the water.

Victoria held her breath. *Get it over with now.* "I'd like to apologize … for … what happened." She turned to see Chaya disrobe, no modesty whatsoever. Victoria maintained eye contact, but not before noticing the gold Star of David hanging from her neck. Not exactly what she'd expected to see, given the obviously Muslim scimitar the woman carried.

Chaya looked at her, expression blank. "Have you apologized to Sam?"

"Not yet."

"Apologize to her." She stepped into the shower and moved behind the half-wall of frosted glass. "If you want respect, you have to earn it."

"I understand," Victoria said, fighting to keep her voice

calm. "I just wanted to say that I was sorry. I mean, we're under the same roof now and I don't want any bad blood from the other night."

"Then don't use my shampoo."

"Sorry." Victoria touched the zipper tab to closer her bag, but paused. *Can't earn her respect if you let her chase you out.* She pulled out her brush and toothpaste.

"There you are," Allan said as she made it back to her room. He'd changed to gray shirt and jeans, his sword casually hanging from his belt like it was nothing unusual. "Ready for breakfast?"

"Absolutely."

"Come on then. We have a long day."

She followed him through the mansion's halls, lined with their abundant mirrors and portraits of former members, each prominently displaying their weapons. They passed another of those gaudy bouquets, its smell not as eye-watering now that she was getting used to it. Either that or the growing aroma of food was distracting her senses. "I was wondering if we might go into town later. I have a few things I need to pick up."

"Of course." He led her into the kitchen where Orlovski was chasing sausage disks across a streaming skillet with a spatula. "Good morning."

"Morning." He motioned his head to a covered bowl. "Eggs?"

"Of course."

Following Allan's lead, Victoria filled a plate with scrambled eggs and sausage and carried through the door into the dining room.

"Orlovski always cooks the same thing when it's his turn at breakfast." Allan whispered. "The man loves his eggs."

"That's fine with me," she said, taking a seat at the long dining table.

Turgen sat at the far end, studying a tablet screen. He glanced up, giving them a silent nod before resuming his reading.

"I said that at first, too. You don't happen to be a gourmet chef or anything?"

She shook her head.

Allan shrugged. "Pity. We're in charge of supper Thursday."

A sudden nervous chill welled in Victoria's chest and flowed down her arms. "Oh."

Allan grinned as he forked his eggs. "Don't worry. None of us are what you'd call skilled cooks."

After they ate, Allan led Victoria down a flight of stairs hidden behind a steel, mirrored door. The posh rugs and ornate molding gave way to concrete walls and floors tiled in an elaborate and random mosaic of jade, obsidian, tigers eye, and a hundred other minerals and metals, most of which she couldn't even begin to identify.

"What is this place?" she asked, noting the very new and very expensive looking fire suppression system running along the ceiling.

"Previous owners built most of this in the Forties. The Order picked it up for a bargain after the war and added a little more during the restoration. It goes two levels down." He stopped before a metal keypad. "Don't worry. One of the first orders of business was ripping out all the swastikas." Allan typed in a five-digit code and opened the door. "After you."

Victoria stepped inside to an enormous library lined with a rainbow of books housed in thick glass shelves. Black singe marks marred many of the leather spines and she remembered Allan's story of the betrayer who had burned them. Several cases of photographs and antiques lined one wall beneath a collection of damaged paintings. A ring of tables occupied the center of the room. Samantha looked up from a computer monitor as Victoria stepped inside.

The dizzying mosaic continued across the floor. Victoria stopped as she passed a shelf, seeing a round steel vault door set into the wall beside where Sam sat. "This is incredible."

"Welcome to the library," Allan said. "Glad you like it."

"What's that?" she asked motioning to the vault. Above it hung a white and blue banner depicting an eight-pointed star within a circle, its spear blade points barely protruded from the enclosing ring.

"That is the real treasure. Come on." Allan crossed to the

room and began working the vault door's twin dials. He pulled the stainless handle and the door *thunked* and swung open, revealing not a room, but a recess. Medieval weapons hung from the inside wall and along the back of the door, brightly lit beneath hidden lighting.

Victoria stepped closer, eyes transfixed on the ancient arms. Some were ornate, decorated with swirling gold and gemstones, others, such as a black double-bladed axe prominently displayed in the middle, were strikingly simple by comparison. "Are these ... holy weapons?"

He nodded, stepping aside. "These are the orphans. Weapons waiting for a new protector."

Her eyes moved to a short spear hanging on the inside of the door. She recognized it, remembering the security video of a woman passing through a solid wall.

"Come on," he said. "Come closer. Give 'em a look."

Victoria stepped up to them, reading the polished brass labels affixed by each weapon. Several spots were vacant, and she spied Umatri's name above a pair of empty pegs. Ten weapons remained. "This isn't all of them, is it?"

"No. Some are on display at different museums. The rest of the orphans are split between the other headquarters."

She moved her hand toward a beautiful gold-hilted rapier, but paused and looked at Allan.

He nodded permission.

"Other headquarters?" she asked, touching the ivory grip, her fingers running along the smooth twists. The plaque read, "Feuertod."

"We have knights in India and South America, as well," Allan said "It's all right if you want to pick it up."

"Are you sure?"

"Of course." There was an excitement in his eyes. Restrained, but still evident.

Sam watched intently from her seat, her monitor seemingly forgotten.

Feeling a bit of a spectacle, Victoria carefully lifted the sword from its cradle, surprised how light it was. *Something so cherished should weigh more*, she thought. "Comfortable," she said, not entirely sure what qualities one desired in a sword. She lifted the blade before her, looking down its length at Allan.

"You like it?" he asked, his eager tone a like teenage boy sensing the possibility of snogging.

"I do."

"Can I see it?"

She offered the rapier over.

The eagerness vanished from his face and he accepted it. "It's a very impressive weapon." He returned it to its pegs, looking away as he did, but not before she saw the disappointment on his face.

What had she done wrong?

"Come on," he said, the sour expression washed away to cheerfulness. "Take a computer. I want you to show me something."

"What's that?"

He pulled a chair out for her. "I want to see how you find demons. We have six days to prove to Gerhard that they exist. So I want to see your magic."

She took the seat. Like most of the chairs in the mansion, it didn't have a left arm, which left her feeling a bit precarious like she'd somehow fall out of it without the rail.

Allan's cologne, spicy with vanilla, wafted as leaned over Victoria shoulder, thankfully on the left side, and entered a password.

Victoria clicked the browser and began to type. "A lot of the information is a bit haphazardly out there, but have you heard of Cryptozoo?"

"I know it." The wheels of Sam's chair clicked across the tiny tiles as she rolled closer.

The page opened, a plain white forum with a scrolling border of famous monster photographs. De Loy's Ape, Nessie, and two dozen others slowly glided along the outer edges. Across the top, emblazoned in dingy parchment-colored letters read, "Cryptozoo."

"Well it's by far the best resource I found." Victoria clicked the sign in and entered her information.

"You're VicMar?" Sam laughed. "I thought you were a man. I hate you."

"What?"

"On the forums," Sam said. "I'm FTrigg."

Victoria blinked. "You?" She chuckled. "You're an asshole." She smiled. "I know."

"You know each other?" Allan asked.

"We've had some disagreements," Victoria said, logging in. A bright red box glowed in the upper corner, telling her she had three unread messages. Heavy pinpricks of worry rolled along the back of her neck, and Allan's presence suddenly felt like a weight over her shoulder. Probably TommyD checking in on her. What if they asked her to look at them?

"Disagreements?" Sam said. "Epic fights. Nearly got banned because of you."

Victoria cocked a brow. "You deserved it. You and that ... Cheshire Grin."

"That's me, too."

"Really?"

"Yeah, I've got four names that I rotate through."

"Just trolling?"

Sam shrugged. "Disinformation. Try to glean any possible tips from there, but steer people away. I point them toward the ones we know aren't real and eyes off the dangerous ones."

"You're not that Emmi asshole, are you?" A nasty argument with them had nearly caused Victoria to leave the forum early on.

"No, that's just some other asshole. Total troll." Sam chuckled. "That's so funny it was you. You gave me some real hell about that mistcat vid."

"That's what you call them?"

"Mmhmm." She nodded to Allan. "He named 'em that. Real nasty bastards."

She looked up at Allan. "So it was real?"

"Quite," he said. "That was the Naples video?"

"Yes."

Allan's lips tightened. "Luc and I got it about two weeks after it hit the web. Nasty business."

Sam snorted. "Sick fuckers are what they are."

Allan turned to grab a chair. Seizing the moment, Victoria clicked her inbox, opening the screen, then clicking off it the moment it opened. "Cryptozoo is a good site," he said, taking the seat. "But I don't recall them having anything on the tengu. How did you find out about that?"

"The backroom." There was a moment's pang, like she's crossed some irrevocable line. "That's where they had it."

Allan brow creased. He shared a look with Sam. "What backroom?"

"Members only." She clicked the tab along the top, opening a new page "This is where the *real* discussions happen. It's where we organize our ..." She was about to say recon trips, but caught it. "Skills."

Sam leaned in closer. "I've never heard of this."

"You have to be invited in. We don't talk about it with the zoo. That's just where we ... chat with tourists."

"Can you invite Sam in?" Allan asked.

"I can nominate her, but the mod will have to decide."

Sam's nose curled like she'd just caught a whiff of something foul. "TommyD?"

"You know him?"

"Oh yeah," Allan said. "Nutcase. Used to post videos all the time. Claimed we were UN-sanctioned Men in Black or whatnot, covering up for aliens."

"Well he still uploads videos, but most of them he posts here now. At least the ones dealing with you."

"Us," Allan corrected.

"Us. But even if I nominated one of Sam's personas, he wouldn't approve it. She's not a believer."

Sam brushed her hair back over her ear and shrugged. "Then I'll make a new one. A real zealot."

"Good," Allan said. "Start two. Mask the IPs. Don't make them friends."

"Easy enough."

"Until then ..." Allan leaned in closer, bringing that spiced vanilla scent. "Victoria's got a door open. So let's see what we have to work with."

"Again."

Keeping his knees bent, Gerhard stepped, pulling back and thrusting the weapon into Luc's kidney-shaped mitt as his front foot come down on the floor.

"Again."

Gerhard stepped again, drawing and jabbing the blunted keris into the pad as Luc stepped backwards like a dance partner.

"Keep your elbow down. Again."

They moved this way from one end of the training room to the other, Gerhard catching glimpses of themselves in the mirrored wall beside them. The practice keris was a close approximation to Umatri, though blunted, its tip a rounded bulb. The handle was wrong somehow. Yes, it might match Umatri's in every microscopic dimension, it didn't feel right. It was a thing, a tool, a poor counterfeit that could never deceive Gerhard's hand. Once they reached the far end, they moved back, Gerhard retreating, and Luc advancing, each step proceeded by Luc's bark, "Again."

"Stop watching the mirror," Luc said once they finished the set. "Watch me. I'll watch you."

Gerhard nodded. His shirt clung to him as the sweat began to flow. The room had felt so cold when they'd first entered.

Luc dabbed his glistening bald head with the back of his hand. "You don't want to get tunnel vision by focusing too much. You should be able to see yourself without moving your eyes. Just be aware of the movement. It's tricky, but once you become accustomed it will be second nature. Now, switch hands, start again."

They continued, the sweat now streaming down Gerhard's back. It gathered along his forehead, threatening to run into his eyes but he continued to the big man's cadenced orders. Once finished, they changed, Gerhard now thrusting in and up from the side, back and forth with each step.

"You're getting weak," Luc said as they completed the final set. "We need to practice until your final attack is equally as strong as your first."

"It's my first day," Gerhard said.

"And if a demon attacked you tomorrow, is that what you'd tell it?"

He didn't answer.

Luc grinned, and pulled off the mitt. "You think we're crazy."

"No. I don't think that I—"

"Of course you do." He motioned to the wall of precisely organized practice weapons. "Unless you're crazy. Are you?"

"I don't believe so." Gerhard set the impersonating keris on its pegs, happy to be rid of it.

"We all think that at first. I did. Now we practice kicks."

Gerhard's legs were still tired from the morning's run, but he chose not to mention that. He'd already heard what Luc's response would be. His karate lessons he'd taken as a youth, a hobby that had lasted less than a year, came back to him as Luc walked him through front, side, and back kicks.

"These are the main ones you'll need," Luc explained once they were finished and Gerhard's legs felt like jelly. The final set had been particularly pathetic. "Should you decide to stay, we'll cover more, but these are the essential ones. You'll need to practice them often."

"You don't think I'll stay?" Gerhard asked, dabbing his face.

"I don't presume." He picked up his belt, the iron mace hanging from a black ring. "My job is to teach you."

Gerhard nodded, meeting the big man's eyes. He appeared sincere. "Why did you stay?"

Luc licked his lips and smiled. "Me?" He cinched the belt on over his damp-stained workout clothes.

"How did you come to be here? You said you didn't believe at first."

"That's a good question." Luc scratched his chin. "Most of us didn't at first. Master Turgen did. His mother was a knight. He grew up with it. But me, I played rugby for RCT. Had a girlfriend. She wanted to go to a museum together." He shook his head. "I wasn't a museum person, but I went. We were looking at a display of crusader artifacts. She was examining cases of helmets and armor, but I was looking at the weapons." Luc's eyes focused on something above Gerhard's head. Distant somewhere. "That's when I saw her. This beautiful mace and I just … stared at it. I'd start to look at something else, but then I would come back to it. My girlfriend asked what it was and I just told her I didn't know. I just … liked it.

"Next weekend she asked, 'What do you want to do?'"

Gerhard grinned at Luc's terrible impersonation of woman's voice.

"I said, 'Go to a museum.' She thought I meant another one but I wanted to go back to the same one, though I didn't say I wanted to see Velnepo again. I just said I wanted to have more time there. By the third time, she didn't want to go. She said, 'Luc, there's other museums.' So … I started going and not telling her. Every day. Then one day this old man strolled up." Luc shrugged. "You can guess what happened next."

Gerhard nodded.

"So I go to the chateau. Meet with Master Turgen. Everyone says, they could tell Velnepo would choose me. All of her protectors were big, even the women. All of them big and strong. They showed me the paintings, all these big people holding my mace. I thought, 'That's weird.' But demons …" He snorted. "I think they're crazy. Some cult. Probably going to kill themselves next time a comet comes by or something."

Gerhard smiled. The thought had occurred to him as well, though he wasn't going to mention it. Not to a believer.

"They showed me pictures. Told me stories." He shook his head. "My uncle tells me stories. All kinds of things. All bullshit. Can't fool me, I think."

"So what convinced you?"

"Velnepo."

Gerhard's brow creased. "How?"

Luc sniffed, the grin withering to cold sincerity. "Holy weapons are blessed with divine power. Once you understand that, believing in a demon is easy. Master Turgen is desperately hoping to show you a monster so that you believe us. The only proof you need is in the weapons. Umatri is trying to speak to you. Listen to him and believe."

"Flying lessons?" Victoria asked in a scared but excited voice.

Leading her down the western first floor hall, Allan casually ran his fingers through his hair, trying not to show how much he loved her growing smile. After six hours of scouring Cryptozoo and nearly a dozen other sites Victoria had known, and even a couple she hadn't, they'd gone to the city on a three-hour shopping spree for toiletries and other essentials. Having missed supper, no big loss he assured since Sam was cooking, they shared a simple meal before heading home. Now, it was time he started her real training, the part he was dreading. "Being my student means that I'm obligated to teach you everything I know. And I'm one of the Valducans' pilots."

"Airplanes?" she asked as if still into believing it.

"Well, one plane. It's an old Fokker Friendship. She's rough, tough, and old as hell, but she's good."

"So what's its name?"

"The plane?" Allan opened a door to a waft of old sweat, and vinyl masked below one of Master Turgen's bouquets.

"No, your cock. Of course the airplane."

Allan coughed a laugh and turned to meet a flat eye roll.

"Everything we've talked about and a dick joke is what surprises you? I was a copper." She stepped into the practice room, immediately cutting toward the mirrored wall, interrupted by a long ballet bar running its length. "Dance lessons?"

"Stretches."

She ran a fingertip delicately along the dark wood rail. "Brings back memories." She eyed him through the mirror as Allan hung his sword belt from one of the hooks near the door. "You still didn't answer my question."

"*Réflexion.*" He pulled off his shoes, tucking them beside the door and walked barefoot across the cool wood floor.

Victoria was inspecting a battered punching bag hanging in another corner, its surface scarred with duct tape.

"Since you've had experience with the basics," Allan said, stretching his arms above his head, "let's start with a warm-up, see what you know, then move on to weapons."

"Now we're talking." She slipped off her sneakers and joined him.

After some stretches, and practice moves, they pulled on padded mitts and boots.

"You're never going to win a hand to hand fight with a demon," Allan said, circling her.

Victoria's foot shot around toward him.

Allan stepped back, allowing it to pass before closing in with two solid hits to her ribs and stomach. "But familiars, followers, even the occasional policeman, you have to be ready." He jabbed and Victoria launched in like a cat, knocking his arm aside. Her glove made a hard *thop* as a back fist connected with Allan's chin. Her foot looped up behind his as she pushed and Allan went down, catching himself on one hand.

"I think I—"

Allan swept her legs before she could finish the sentence and Victoria came down hard. Grinning, he stood and offered her a hand. "What was that?"

Her hazel eyes narrowed on his extended hand. Allan could almost smell their desire for vengeance, but then she accepted it.

"I was saying that I think I got the idea."

"The idea, yes. But cops are trained to subdue. You need to incapacitate. Familiars don't fear. They don't have a sense of self. You can't interrogate them. They need be considered absolute threats at all times until their master is killed. Even then, be leery of them."

Her lips tightened as if about to say more but she simply gave a weak nod.

"I can't stress that enough," Allan said flatly. "They may look human. They may plead, cry, beg, but you can't for a single moment forget what they are. They'll come after you until they're dead, or rendered absolutely unable to. Many knights have been injured or killed because they forgot that."

"I understand."

Allan only hoped that she did, but chose not to beat it into the ground. "Good." He peeled the pads off his hands and feet, a trepidatious dread welling with each piece he removed. "So let's start what really matters." He handed her the pads. As she put them away, Allan retrieved Ibenus from her scabbard and returned to the practice floor, the sword at his side.

"We don't have any practice swords for her," he said, glancing to the racks of weapons mounted against the walls. "So we'll be using other ones to train. Still, you must become familiar with her."

"All right."

Allan tightened his jaw and offered her the sword. If he hesitated as Victoria accepted it she made no response.

She bounced it in her hand. "It's lighter than I would have thought."

"She's a hacker," he said, forcing a calm tone. He loathed anyone holding her. He felt naked without the blade but ... Victoria was his student. *Better get used to it.* "More like an axe than a sword. The first six inches there past the handle before the blade bows, it's not sharp at all. For a good swing you can grab the haft there," he mimed the movement, terribly conscious Ibenus wasn't in his hands, "and bring her down double-handed."

"I see," she said, squeezing the haft in her off hand.

"Most of the time, though, it's just one handed."

Victoria twirled the khopesh one side, then the other and hacked at some slow moving invisible enemy.

"So we'll have to train you with both swords and axes to get the full effect."

She spun, decapitating her imaginary foe, then took Ibenus in both hands, hacking down. "Am I making you uncomfortable?" She watched him in the mirror's reflection.

"N ... yeah." Allan sighed a breath. "I've never let anyone touch her before. It, uh, will take some getting used to."

"Never?"

He shook his head.

"Because she's your wife, sort of?"

"Sort of."

She nodded, the amused grin melting away. "So why me?"

"You're my student. To train you I have to trust you with her."

"Thank you. I didn't realize ... what that meant. I'll take care of her." She rolled it in her hand feeling the balance but without the playful air she'd had. "How do you make her blink?"

"I can't make her," he said, moving behind Victoria to adjust her grip. "That's her decision. I just have to trust that she will when I need her. But she won't do it for you."

"Why not?"

He guided her arm through a swing. "Holy weapons only work for their protector."

"So as long as you're around …"

"Don't be getting ideas, now."

She chuckled. "Never crossed my mind. Now that you mention it however …"

Allan smiled. "Then if you plan to bump me off and run off with Ibenus, let me show you how to use her."

"Good plan."

They practiced for over an hour, trading possession of the khopesh until Allan no longer counted how many times he had relinquished it. They moved through routines with wooden sabers, repeating the steps like dancers.

"I think this'll do for tonight," Allan said finally.

Victoria practiced the one-two step, wooden sword before her. "Are you sure?"

"Yeah. Got another run early in the morning."

"Oh. There's that."

"Always is."

They strolled back upstairs, chatting and walking a little slower than necessary. Allan rested a hand on Ibenus' handle as he went, enjoying the comfort of her back as his side. He'd need to clean off the fingerprints before bed, but that was nothing much. Truth was that he enjoyed cleaning her, polishing the bronze to a shine. She'd been in the hands of another. It was going to require some getting used to. He wondered if he ever would.

"Thank you for today," Victoria said as they reached her bedroom. "I, uh, was a little worried how my first full day was going to go."

"Not a problem." He smiled. "I said they'd get used to you. Definitely won some points with Sam. Wild that you knew each other … in a way."

"Not exactly on the best terms, though."

He shrugged. "You showed her the backroom boards. Trust me, that made a difference."

Victoria looked down at her feet. "One battle at a time, right?" She met his eyes. There, somewhere behind the gold and green something lurked. Sadness? Fear?

"That's right." Allan squeezed her hand, assuring her it was all right. "Just give—" When had he taken hold of her hand?

Victoria looked down the same moment as him as they both released their grips. Did she take his first or had he taken hers?

"I, ah, was saying, just take 'em one at a time. They'll get used to you."

"Yeah." She sniffed, her lips moving as if trying to wipe off any expression of discomfort. "Well, thanks again for today. I, uh, I suppose I need to send my mum a message. Let her know I'm okay. Thanks for letting me have my phone back."

"No problem at all. I'll fetch you in the morning."

"Bright and early." She opened her door and slipped inside without turning back.

Allan stood there for a moment, trying to figure out if he'd just fucked up. With a grunt, he squeezed Ibenus' grip and turned toward his own room. *Let's get you cleaned up, Love.*

EPISODE 159

AMIENS PT2—THEY STRIKE AGAIN

"Hey, cryptozoologists," TommyD says as the intro music fades down. He sits at a blonde wood table, one hand atop the other and a blank redbrick wall behind him. A trimmed sandy beard covers narrow cheeks. He wears a short-brimmed fedora the color of swamp water. Black Wayfarers rest atop a long nose, masking his eyes behind black glass. "Three weeks ago, I publicly posted a video about the Bird Man of Amiens."

A still image emerges from the corner of the screen, filling the frame: A dark cell phone picture of an enormous avian head emerging from water, a tied boat behind it giving it a sense of scale. Front-facing hawk-like eyes stare at the photographer like twin golden moons, a mixed expression of surprise and hate on its curiously human face.

"The Bird Man has been a local legend in the area for more than fifty years, garnering nearly a dozen photographs, half of which appear staged." Another frame expands from the other corner, pushing the still image away until they're side by side. A shaky video plays inside the left rectangle of a concrete bike trail whisking by, illuminated by a single light. "But this recent shot, alongside a cyclist's close encounter, is clearly the same creature." The camera wheels to the left to show a bird-headed man, a limp white terrier in its claws. The creature gives a silent scream and moves toward the camera and the frame turns back to the trail, jostling side to side as it races away. The camera looks back once to see the beast standing on the trail far behind, the dog forgotten.

"The locals have nicknamed their resident cryptid Henri. And until the cyclist video, no one has ever taken Henri seriously. Since my episode aired, it's been viewed twelve thousand times." The screen returns to TommyD, elbows on the table and fingers laced before him. "Several monster seekers have reached out to me through private channels, searching for Henri. Cameras were set up and we started trying to narrow down where Henri's lair might be. We were confident that we'd narrowed it down to a three kilometer stretch along the River Somme." He draws a breath, posture straightening. "Two nights ago there was a fire in one of the houses along that same stretch."

The screen cuts to footage of firefighters and police working around a black and smoldering ruin of a house in the early light of morning. "Authorities have confirmed the body of a man was found inside. While it's too early to tell if the fire was accidental, the contact that sent me this video also told me that a wildlife camera that they had mounted in the area has also gone missing. While this might seem like a simple coincidence to some, the events in Amiens only point to a pattern we've seen before."

The video footage changes to another burning house lit red and orange against a black sky. Blue and white lights flash against a backdrop of oily smoke as silhouette men race across the screen, hoses in hand. It switched again to a burned-out two-story warehouse, then to a farmhouse, each one with a date and location emblazoned across the bottom.

"It's no coincidence that house fires seem to always follow sightings, and then the sightings mysteriously end. So the question is, was the person, or people, responsible for those arsons the same that came to Amiens? Who wants to hide the truth from us?"

The image of a great gothic cathedral slides into view, its white stone facade encrusted with statues and heavy, elaborate reliefs. "Is it mere coincidence that Amiens is home to a bishop?

A bishop that could command men of faith? Secret men the Vatican claims don't exist?"

A black and white photo dissolves out from the church. Two men step from a round-nosed black sedan. They wear the dark suits and collars of priests. The older one peers somewhere off camera, his white hair only a wisp beneath a black hat. The younger one, a tall man built like a war hero with a broad chest and strong jaw looks directly at the distant camera, hard eyes displeased. His hair is slicked back and shiny like plastic. In his hand he holds a sheathed sword, its scabbard decorated with glinting metal. A label along the bottom reads, "Pisa – 1963" in capitalized red stencil font like some classified military document.

A color image slides down from the top. Again two men in somber suits and white collars. The first, a younger man with a ruddy tan and short-cropped curls walks through a bright green stucco doorway. The end of something long protrudes from his hand, mostly concealed by the door. Behind him, an older man with thin, slicked hair and a familiar strong jaw peers over his shoulder, cold eyes focused on the photographer across the street. He carries the same sheathed sword in his hand with the casual tension of a Spaghetti Western gunslinger. The blood-red stenciled date reads, "Buenos Aires – 1985."

"No, my friends, this is no coincidence. The pattern is all too familiar for us to ignore. The Vatican, it appears, has once again denied us the truth. Mark my words, we won't be seeing Henri again. Until next time, TommyD, signing out."

CHAPTER 10

"Have you seen this?" Victoria asked.

"What did you find?" Allan looked over from his own monitor, where a Lithuanian news report was playing a video of some creature that looked to him more like a sick bear than the monster it had claimed.

"Looks like one of those screamers in Manchester," she said.

"Where?" He pushed out his seat and leaned in beside her, momentarily forgetting his self-imposed two-foot rule. After last night's awkward hand-holding, he didn't want to make her uncomfortable or lend any validity to Master Turgen's accusation that Allan's attraction had clouded his judgment.

"Paris." She backed the clip to the beginning. A stylized white comet chased its tail as the video re-buffered.

Allan bit his lip and shared a moment's glance with Sam still seated at the next workstation. "Paris was one of the first places we encountered a mantismere."

Victoria looked up at him, the inner corners of her eyebrows raised, crinkling her forehead. "Mantismere?"

"Means mantis mother. It's what attacked you in Manchester."

"Mantismere," she repeated, seeming to ponder it. "Appropriate name."

Sam cocked a moment's smirk at Allan. He'd wanted to call it Spearbug but Luc, being the one that killed the first one they found, overruled him and decided the name.

The video started, its quality and framing obviously from a

cell phone at night. A pair of young men casually stood, cutting up, before a light-colored wall of large bricks. One wore a tight, open-neck T-shirt and jeans, his skinny arms decorated with tattooed swirls. He held a plastic soda bottle in one hand, its label torn away. The man beside him was laughing around a cigarette, his red-brown hair and blue buttoned shirt too perfectly disheveled to be accidental. Wind crackled through the microphone, drowning out men's voices as the tattooed man was imparting some evidently funny story, emphasized with exaggerated expressions. The video shook as the camera owner's laughter drowned out even the wind's noise.

The tattooed storyteller swigged his bottle and continued his monologue, his hand beside his face as if wrestling some invisible ball. The smoker beside him abruptly ceased his laughing and stiffened, eyes locked on something off to the side. The camera lingered long enough for him to slap his friend's arm before it whirled into the direction the man was looking. Something moved along the edge of an alley toward them, maybe half a foot high. Victoria inhaled sharply as a white doll's face emerged from the shadows, ghostlike with ink-black eyes.

"Oh yeah," Allan said, his voice a mixture of dread and excitement, as a faint baby's wail came through the computer speakers.

A pair of pincers unfolded from its oval mouth as the screamer scuttled into view. The mewling grew louder. The camera jerked upward to see a second one crawl from a broken second floor window, then back down to the baby-faced bug closing in. There was a scream and the plastic, labelless bottle sailed toward it. The screamer leapt up and landed against the wall, four feet up, as the bottle hit the ground, spraying its contents. The camera whirled around, everything shaking and spinning as the men fled, shouting and blubbering.

"That's it," Victoria said as the video went black.

Allan peered at the bottom on the frame. "Uploaded this morning. Over two hundred views in the last three hours."

"That's going to go up fast," Sam said.

Allan scanned the video description. "Where exactly was this?"

"Just says Paris," Victoria answered. "Five nights ago."

Allan's pulse quickened. "All right. Let's study the video. The building. What we see of the street. Search for other sightings, see if we can narrow it down."

Sam rolled back to her station. "On it, boss."

"How did you find this?"

"Link posted on Cryptozoo," Victoria said.

Of course it was. This was just getting better and better. "We'll need to run a few Doubting Thomases in the thread, see if we can steer interest away before someone wanders in there looking for a monster."

Victoria looked up at him, her face so close they could kiss. "Can't we use them?"

Allan stood, resetting the distance rule. "How?"

"The three of us searching Paris versus a hundred of them. We could find it faster if we let them help."

"No." He shook his head. "We can't afford someone going there with a camera in hopes of the next viral video or breakthrough discovery."

"We could warn them off it."

Allan cocked his brow. "And you think they'll listen? How many times is a volcano about to blow or a hurricane about to land and some git decides to go there to check it out?"

"If they knew what it was they'd stay back."

"No," Allan said. "They never do. Cryptid clubs are older than the internet. It's always the same. You can't tell me that that this TommyD guy and his flunkies won't go charging in there, and warning them to stay away will only drive them harder."

She opened her hands in surrender. "All right. Just an idea."

"That's fine." Allan slid back into his chair and clicked his mouse. "I want you to think of new approaches. I'm just saying why that one isn't feasible." He pulled up the video on his screen and watched it again. "Sam, see if you can grab some stills from this and edit them. Blow 'em up, point out errors. Maybe draw in a little line when that thing jumps, make it look like a wire."

"I can search for the location or I can photochop footage. Can't do both."

"I need you to." Allan checked the clock. He needed the

other Librarians. Master Sonu would be awake, afternoon his time. But Matt and Uwe were in Chile and probably wouldn't be up for a several hours. He began composing the emails to let them know what was going on.

Victoria's mouse wheel whirred in little clicks as she scrolled through the forum. "Speaking of TommyD, you have a chance to look at his latest video yet?"

Allan shook his head. "Not yet."

"I did," Sam said. "Blames the Vatican for taking out the tengu. Posted some pics of Father Gaze."

Allan paused mid-type. "He even around still?"

The corner of her lip curled in a shrugging motion. "Doubt it. Last image was from the Eighties."

"Who's Father Gaze?" Victoria asked.

"Priest," Allan said, finishing the message. "Last we saw of him was fifteen years ago."

"He always knew if you were taking his picture," Sam said. "Fucking creepy."

"So he's not with the Order?" Victoria asked.

"Oh no," Allan laughed. "He's one of the Vatican's boys. You ever hear how the Catholic Church has a group of exorcists they dispatch when one of the churches claims to have a serious possession? They'll show up, banish the demon and leave?"

She nodded.

"Well these guys are like that but more like the SAS. Demon hunters with the full power of the church at their back."

"And they have holy weapons?" Victoria motioned her head toward the orphan vault behind them, its door wide. Allan had opened it hoping that maybe one of the weapons might make a bond. Sam was unlikely, as she'd been Orlovski's student for years; Amballwa probably had her marked as his replacement by now. But Victoria was technically still fair game if one of the orphans decided her worthy. Keeping her in their view might help that along.

"Of course." Allan opened a link to the Creature Sighting Network, a smaller forum than Cryptozoo, but far more reliable. He started scrolling for posts about Paris. "The church has gathered thousands of artifacts over the centuries. Few legitimate holy weapons among them. Just a matter of time before one of them called to a priest or nun dusting off the relics."

"And ... we don't work with them?"

Allan's mouth tightened into a grin. He wondered if she even noticed she was calling the Order *we* instead of *you*. "No, we don't."

"Why not?"

He shrugged. "We've never been too keen on working together. No bad blood that I know of. At least there hasn't been in two hundred years. They mind their business, we mind ours. We're all fighting the same fight so no need to get in each other's way."

"So ... if the Valducans aren't the only hunters, how many are there?"

"Well, there's the Exorcists, us, the Takaira Clan operating in Japan, but they only have one weapon, two independent hunters that we know of, but we suspect there's a third one creeping around Liberia somewhere." Not finding anything on CSN, he moved on to another website. "If we can find them, we'll offer them a place, or at least help. Sometimes they join, sometimes not. We try to keep an eye on them, anyway."

"And do they watch us, the Church, I mean?"

"I'd be shocked if they didn't. I'd also guess that at least one person on the forums is in Rome and wearing a white collar."

"You'll love this one," Luc said.

Gerhard sat in a cushioned seat before a large screen. The private theater was more akin to a university lecture hall than a mansion. While the four rows of seating were certainly nicer than those he'd used at school, larger, more luxurious with leather and the ability to recline, the small folding desktops felt strangely academic. Maybe more like first class seating on an airline, though Gerhard had only seen such things as he'd shuffled past toward coach.

Luc sat beside him on the front row, scrolling through images on a small tablet. He'd offered a reprieve from the day's practice since Gerhard's muscles felt as though they'd been replaced with wood. The morning's run was humiliating, his legs functioning at a fraction of what they had they day before. So instead of kick training, Luc had been showing him videos of hunts. Green night-vision footage, between two and three screens at once, the audio composed of recorded radio chatter.

"This was my first hunt," Luc said. "You can hear me trying not to piss myself."

Gerhard smiled at the idea of such a man being afraid of anything. The screen flickered and went black. A map opened on one side, a cluster of red dots tracking up a blue road. "Vetrni?" he asked, reading the name of the closest town.

"Bohemia," Luc said. "Paper mill makes the whole town smell like shit after a night of drinking."

The GPS dots turned off the main road, eventually stopping near a cluster of buildings.

"Check. Testing. Check," said the first voice. The label "Nick" appeared as he spoke.

"Read ya loud'n clear," came a new voice, this one labeled "Tom," another name Gerhard didn't recognize. "Ya got me?"

"Read you," Nick said. "Luc? No, you turn it on like this."

"Testing?" Luc's voice rumbled.

The theater door opened, spilling light. An elderly man stepped inside, wearing a dark suit with no tie and a simple broadsword hanging from his waist.

"Master Schmidt." Luc fumbled with the remote, pausing the video and bringing up the lights. He stood. "You're back."

The old man nodded. "It's a pleasure to be home, Luc. Is everything well?"

"It is."

"Very good. I wanted to meet our guest." He smiled at Gerhard and extended a hand. He wore the same green-gemmed ring on his little finger as Alex Turgen. "I am Max Schmidt, protector of Lukrasus," he said in clear, though accented, German.

Gerhard rose to his feet and accepted it. "Gerhard Entz. It is a pleasure to meet you," he said, happy to be speaking the mother tongue. "Austrian?"

"I am. I apologize I was not here when you arrived. I trust

your stay has been comfortable?"

"Yes. It is a beautiful home you have. Luc was showing me some videos."

Max smiled. "Very good. Master Turgen explained you were not entirely certain about joining us here."

Gerhard swallowed, forcing a smile. "This is all … a little overwhelming so far."

"He tells me that you don't believe in monsters," Max said with a knowing amusement.

Gerhard smiled again, lips closed. He'd hoped to have made it a full day without this discussion.

"There's no shame in that." He absently gestured to the screen. "Have you seen them on there?"

"Luc showed me a werewolf." It hadn't looked unlike the movie monsters he'd seen his entire life, though with less green.

"Good." Max ran a thumb and forefinger along his narrow moustache and looked at Umatri resting in his scabbard beside Gerhard's seat. "Umatri hasn't moved for you yet, has he?"

"No." He wasn't at all convinced the blade could do as they'd claimed, dreams or not. The idea was just too ridiculous.

"He's shy. Ibenus is, too. Khirzoor can be explained as a party trick. But Lukrasus …" he patted his own sword, "she likes to show off. Would you like to see?"

"All right."

Max removed his shoes. Not exactly what Gerhard has expected. Schmidt stepped back and drew the sword with a dramatic flourish. "Each of us here has many duties." Max turned in slow spin, as if performing a waltz. "Do you know mine?"

Gerhard shook his head. "No."

The old man casually moved toward the wall. "I change the light bulbs." With that Max stepped onto the wood-paneled wall and twirled again, continuing his dance along it as if nothing had happened.

Gerhard's eyes widened. He took an unconscious step back, nearly colliding with Luc, who was grinning.

"When we moved here …" Max swayed side to side, working closer to the ceiling. "They said we don't need a ladder, we have

Max." He stepped onto the ceiling in one fluid motion. "So that is my job." He stopped, the sword flat before him and gave a small bow. "I can only do this in older buildings, mind you. One false step and I have to fix a hole." He walked across the ceiling effortlessly and stopped, his face nearly level with Gerhard's, though inverted.

Gerhard only looked at him, unsure what to say.

Max held his stare. He lifted the corner of his jacket and let it go. The fabric fell back in place, completely defying gravity.

"How?" Gerhard shook his head. "How are you doing that?"

"How do you think?" He looked down—up—at his feet. "No wires. Have you ever watched someone hang upside down? Their face turns purple. Is mine?"

"No."

"No. If you need your eyes to believe, then look. If you need to touch me, touch me. I am real. I am real and spitting in the face of physics. Isaac Newton spins in his grave as I stand here. What do you say to that?"

"I ... I don't know."

"Say you believe and I'll show you how I get down."

"The building is the key," Allan said, clicking through street view images of Paris. They'd scoured the forums for three hours as Sam constructed some impressive *proof* to debunk the footage's validity. Victoria had pieced together screenshots of the location they could use to figure out where the men had been when the screamers had shown up. It wasn't much. But it was at least a start.

"Broken windows, probably abandoned. Every one of them so far has nested in abandoned buildings. Can't tell the style, but looks to be an alley entrance so it might not face a larger street. Four floors. Bars on the bottom windows. Alley is paved in brick, not asphalt."

"You've just described half the city," Sam said.

"Then we just ruled out the other half. Check realtor sites, see if maybe it's on one for rent or sale."

The library's door locks clicked and the door pushed open.

"Master Schmidt."

"Allan." He nodded to Sam. "Samantha."

"How was London?" Allan rose and Victoria followed his lead.

"The competition was fine, but uneventful." He turned to Victoria, rising from her seat. "The same cannot be said about you, it appears." He offered her a slender hand. "I am Max Schmidt."

"Victoria Martin," she said, accepting it.

"It is a pleasure to meet you, Miss Martin." He turned to the side, offering full view of the sword at his hip. "This is Lukrasus, my charge."

She smiled a sort of hello at the broadsword.

"Victoria was a dancer, once," Allan said.

Schmidt's blue eyes lit. "Were you now?" Still offering the weapon toward her, his fingertips drew an inch of steel from the scabbard.

"Me?" She chuckled and shook her head. "That was a long time ago."

"It's never too late to pick it up again," he said, the faintest sadness to his voice. Schmidt lowered the sword, ceasing the display.

Allan tightened his teeth, pitifully attempting to mask his own disappointment. Lukrasus needed a new protector and Victoria fit the bill. *Give it time*, he reminded himself.

"I just returned from a dance competition," Schmidt said.

"Were you competing?"

He snorted. "No. No those days are far behind me. Now I just go to observe and scout the participants. Lukrasus," he said at the puzzled expression, "She only selects dancers, you see."

"Ah. I'm sorry it was uneventful."

He gave a rueful smile. "Lukrasus will choose when she's ready." At seventy-five, Master Schmidt was the oldest active knight in fifty years. Twelve years ago he'd retired, taking the mantle of Master, and passing the sword to his squire, Jean. Allan had been there when Jean caught a cultist's rifle round during an ambush. He'd died saving them. The bond to a weapon is forever, and with no other protector, Schmidt had no other choice but to carry her again.

"We think we found a mantismere in Paris," Allan said, changing the subject.

"Really?"

"Video hit the web this morning. We're just trying to narrow down where exactly."

"How long do you estimate?" Schmidt asked.

Allan frowned. "Soon, we hope."

"By soon, you mean now," Sam said with a self-satisfied grin.

"You found it?" Victoria and Allan both asked, Allan's voice echoing a syllable behind hers.

"Looks that way. While you were prattling it up, I was working."

"Where?" Allan peered over her shoulder at an image of a plain building nestled on a small street. The barred windows appeared the same, though it was shot in the daylight.

"Old flats in the Thirteenth District." Sam scrolled down the screen past several pictures of empty and decayed rooms, ceilings sagging and walls punched with holes and scrawled with graffiti. "Found it on an urban explorers page. People breakin' in for a little adventure. Couple shots of the interior. Look to be a year old, so should work fine."

"Good. Bloody good work."

Sam shrugged. "I know."

Allan turned back to Schmidt. The taut corners of the old man lips were turned up in that subtle proud grin that had taken him years to recognize. "I'll tell Master Turgen we found it."

Sam cleared her throat.

"That Sam found it," he corrected.

"The former arms masters," Chaya said, setting a shallow plastic tray in front of Gerhard, "thought that each knight should carry a sidearm they prefer. Good sentiment, but that led to everyone carrying different weapons that couldn't exchange magazines or ammunition." She set a tray in front of Victoria. "Assigning everyone the same weapon alleviates that problem."

Victoria glanced over at Gerhard's and Sam's matching HK

pistols, formidable with fat barrels and molded plastic grips. Then she looked down at the little Walther beside two small magazines, a tray of bullets, a plastic holster, and a black metal tube. "Don't I get one?"

"No," Chaya said. "Since Allan insists on pretending to be James Bond, you get the same weapon he does. That way you can swap mags if need be."

"Don't worry," Allan whispered. He stood beside her at the table, his own unholstered Walther resting before him. "You'll love it."

She looked back at the gun, hiding her frown. Allan was more clueless about women than she'd thought if he couldn't recognize an obvious power play.

"Since we run suppressed more often than not," Chaya continued, still pacing behind them, "you'll be practicing both with and without it. That little bit of weight on the end will really throw off your aim if you don't practice. Suppressed doesn't mean silenced. They're still loud. Not that wet fart noise movies tell you about."

Sam snorted a chuckle.

"But," Gerhard said, fingering the edge of the tray without reaching inside, "guns can't harm demons. Why should we devote this much to them?"

"Because demons might be the tip of the threat pyramid, but they're hardly the only thing," Chaya said. "Familiars are more common. Wounding a demon with a bullet of the correct materiel might help slow it down. Worst case, kill the body but live to hunt another day."

Gerhard nodded unsurely and reached a tentative finger inside the tray.

"First things first, load five rounds in each magazine, but don't touch your weapons."

Victoria loaded the tiny practice magazines, fighting the spring to get the last one in each. Chaya and Allan assured her that they'd break in soon enough. Once loaded, and coached on how to hold it, interrupted with a dozen safety reminders, Chaya let them shoot.

The range resembled more of a concrete ballroom beneath

the mansion. Round columns along the wall supported a vaulted ceiling, painted with a faded blue sky and dingy clouds stained with years of smoke and neglect. Five targets hung from a grid-work of metal tracks, suspended eight feet below the ceilings, running the full length of the room. Chaya set them for three meters.

"Not bad," Allan said after Victoria had emptied her second mag. Two of the shots had missed the man-shaped silhouette entirely.

Victoria glanced at the others' targets as she pulled off her huge earmuffs. Sam's grouping resulted in a single jagged hole in the paper man's chest, big enough for two fingers to slip through. Even Gerhard, who had never fired a gun until today, had all his shots in the space of a dinner plate. His lips drawn in a flat line, he studied it critically, obviously unhappy. There was something different about him. Colder, more serious than he'd been before. Allan's target was somewhere in between, as if he'd tried his hardest to make a three-inch ring around the center without actually touching it. "It's bloody awful."

"It's not bad for your first time." He put a hand on her shoulder, then quickly withdrew it. He'd been acting odd all day and once again Victoria regretted taking his hand the night before. At least, she thought she took it, though she didn't exactly recall doing it. But his reaction and sudden change since only confirmed her suspicion that she had made him uncomfortable.

"I've shot before. Remember?"

"Was that your first time?" He started reloading his empty magazines. "Shooting at the screamers?"

"Yeah. And I shot better than this."

"Then that's good. Fear makes you focused. For most people it's the other way around."

"Terrible," Chaya said from behind her. "You should stick with shotguns."

Sam's jaw noticeably tightened, two days of repaired rapport crumbling at the unfortunate reminder that Victoria had introduced herself with a 12 gauge to the side of her head.

"It's my second time to ever shoot," Victoria replied as civilly as possible.

"With that underpowered thing, I expect you to take out eyes at ten meters. I can't trust you with a sidearm until you can do that."

"Then give her one of the bigger guns," Allan said.

"No."

"No? Are you honestly refusing to equip my student?"

Chaya's mouth drew into a poisoned smile. "I'm equipping her with the exact weapon as her mentor. Masters Turgen and Schmidt both agreed that I should be Arms Master. You might outrank me, but not on this range. My decision is for unity among hunters. You chose not to adopt the sidearm that I selected."

A tense silence fell over the range.

"All right, then." Allan shrugged. "I'd like to upgrade to the new standard sidearm."

Chaya's mouth opened. "Yes. Of course." She took Victoria's gun and tray. "Just give me a few minutes."

"You don't need to do this," Victoria whispered once Chaya had hurried off to a pair of giant safes in the far corner.

"Of course I do. My job is to make sure you're outfitted with the best possible gear. If you prefer her gun, then that's what we'll use. I never shoot mine, anyway."

Chaya returned with a pair of larger pistols and accoutrements. The magazines were bigger, a lot bigger, and so were the bullets. The flat-sided suppressors were easily twice as long as the Walther's had been.

They loaded their magazines as Chaya continued working with Gerhard, moving the target back to five meters. Once they were ready, Chaya walked them both through the safety and handling lecture again, a distinct air of satisfaction to her voice this time.

Holding it tight, Victoria lifted the gun, and sighted it in on the orange dot in the paper man's chest. Bracing for the hard kick, she squeezed the trigger.

The kick didn't happen, at least not as much as she's expected. In fact, it hurt less than the smaller gun had. She's missed the damn dot, but the hole was right up against it like they were best friends posing for a picture.

"You like it?" Chaya asked with the same tone a waiter might use when offering the first taste of some fine and expensive wine.

"Definitely."

"Good. Allan, were you aiming for the head?"

The hole in Allan's target was perfectly centered where its nose should be.

"Not at all."

Chaya shook her head and they continued their practice. The steady cracks of shots filled the range as they all fired, riddling their targets with holes. Chaya moved up and down the line, offering pointers, correcting stances, and doling praise and criticism in measured amounts. Victoria's hits were at least all within the man's silhouette, even when the targets were rolled back to twenty meters. The groupings were still less than Gerhard's, who'd taken to shooting with a technical fervor that Victoria hadn't expected. He'd seemed so blasé about everything but his beloved keris since they'd arrived. There was definitely something different about him. His absolute focus on the perfect grip, stance, and follow up only reiterated it.

"So what do you think?" Allan asked as they reloaded their magazines. "You prefer it?"

"Very much so."

"Then it's settled." He sighed. "I'm going to miss my little gun. Always wanted to wear it with a tux."

She looked at him through the corner of her eye, brow arched. "You wear tuxes often?"

Allan shook his head. "No. Though I always thought it'd be kinda fun to go on a hunt in one."

The image of Allan, standing at the end of that filthy Manchester hallway, sword in hand and wearing a black tuxedo with shiny lapels and shoes, flashed in her mind. She gave a throaty laugh. "I'd like to see that. Seriously, though, if you prefer your gun, don't change it on account of me."

"Too late," he said with a smile. "This is best."

A guilty pang tightened in Victoria's chest. "Thank you."

They covered the targets' holes with black stickers and were about to send them out for silencer practice when the foam-padded range door opened and Luc stepped inside.

"Hold," Chaya called. "You come to practice?"

"The Masters called a meeting," Luc said.

Allan set his weapon on the table. "What's going on?"

"They've approved the hunt."

"Paris?"

"Paris."

Allan cocked his arm, hand clenched in a fist. He patted Victoria's shoulder. "You found it. Both of you," he added, looking to Sam who was giving him an *excuse me* stare. "All right, Gerhard, come with us. Chaya, can you...?"

"I'll take care of them," she said.

"Perfect. Thanks." He turned to Victoria. "You and Sam stay here. I'll catch you up once we're done."

"Oh." A prickly burr of resentment seemed to roll through Victoria's stomach. He was ditching her. "I'll see you then."

Allan and Gerhard gathered their things. The door thudded shut behind them, and the burr swelled like a puffer fish, the heat of its venom running through her veins. *So much for, "I trust you."*

Chaya cleared her throat. "Go ahead and attach your suppressors."

"So they're a bit of a boy's club, eh?" Victoria said, fighting the tight knurled knob affixed to the end of her barrel.

"How do you mean?" Chaya asked.

The knob gave and she unscrewed it. "All the men go off to plan but we don't. It was the same way in the department."

Chaya straightened. "It's not like that at all."

She removed the boxy silencer from the tray and began screwing it on. "Then why did they leave when—?"

"Let's get one thing straight that Allan obviously hasn't explained to you." Chaya strode over to where Victoria stood, chin up, and stopping just in front of her. She squeezed the handle of the scimitar at her belt. "The weapons see no difference in people. They choose the worthiest. So that means we don't have whatever hang-ups you're used to. When a weapon makes the decision, we agree to it. The Order was based on that."

She touched the scimitar at her hip. "My sword, Khirzoor,

did that. And as far as why I'm here, it's because I'm the Arms Master. You don't have a holy weapon, so the only one you get is from me. It's my job to make sure you know how to use it. You're about to deploy on a hunt. You haven't been trained. I have more firearm experience than anyone here so I'm the most capable at teaching you how to shoot. Allan can't shoot for shit, so I'm not at the meeting because if you're going to go hunting, I have to vouch that you can hold a pistol in the off chance that you'll need to. Is that understood?"

Victoria nodded, trying not to shy away from the Chaya's glare. The Israeli was a good two inches shorter but carried herself like she was ten feet tall. "I apologize. I was—"

"Is that understood?"

"Yes."

"Good. Now load your weapon and impress me."

CHAPTER 11

Gerhard stared out the van's window, not seeing the dark and shuttered shop fronts sliding past. Paris called itself the City of Lights and, while they were beautiful in some fairyland fashion, there were no lights here in this part of the city, and not at three in the morning when only the truly committed partiers were staggering home or already in bed. The city was sleeping, only minimal body functions of its legendary nightlife were keeping it alive. Absently, Gerhard rubbed his hands. Clammy. Numb. They didn't feel like his, like someone had stitched the hands of a dead man onto his wrists when he wasn't looking.

A dead man.

He might be dead soon. This might very well be his last car ride, sitting beside paramilitary cultists, whom he'd only just realized had reeled him into their insanity. He'd tried not to believe them. How could he? This was madness, hunting monsters. He'd laugh at his situation if it wasn't for the piece of him, that deep and elemental shard, that believed that tonight he'd see a monster and plunge Umatri into it.

It wasn't the videos that convinced him. Nor the fervor in which his new contemporaries believed. It wasn't even Schmidt strolling up walls and across ceilings, though that undeniably had helped. Umatri had convinced him. The dreams. His belief had begun crystallizing in his dreams, and when he'd first entered Paris two days ago and saw the streets and buildings, he knew the significance. They were different in that way in which all dreams altered familiar places, but it was undeniably Paris, and now he was here.

"Are you all right?"

Gerhard blinked and turned to see Orlovski beside him.

The Russian watched him over to tops of his glasses. "Nervous?"

"I'm … I'm fine," Gerhard said with the weakest lie in the world.

Orlovski patted his shoulder, the sensation muted through the Kevlar vest and holster strap. "You'll be good."

"Still look better than I did," Luc said from the front seat.

"How about you?" Gerhard asked Orlovski.

The Russian shook his head. "Just happy to be back in the fight."

"Ah," he said with what he hoped was tact. A year before Orlovski had suffered a mishap, explained only as *some asshole tried to amputate my leg with a shotgun*. The blast had shattered his femur. With this being his first hunt in thirteen months, and Gerhard and Victoria's first ever, it was decided that Luc, being Gerhard's handler, an appropriate if not irritating term, was to come as well.

"Well I'm glad you're back," Sam said from the driver's seat. "No more moping. Now you'll be happy, I'll be happy, and once Chaya gets her dog, I'll be even happier."

"Dog?" Orlovski turned to Allan in the back seat beside Victoria. "What dog?"

"No one told you?" Sam asked. "Chaya's getting a dog to commemorate her first kill."

"And I'm getting a cat," Luc said.

"No, no one told me this. Allan, you know I have a problem with those things."

"With cats?" Luc asked.

"With dogs," the Russian said, his voice rising several octaves.

"You have a problem with strange dogs," Sam said. "This one will be ours. You'll love it."

"I mentioned it to Master Turgen," Allan said, his voice calm. "He's in favor of it."

"So no one thought about asking me? I live there, too."

"And if it becomes a problem we'll deal with it," Allan said. "It's a big house."

"And if it bites me?"

"If it bites you, you deserved it," Sam said.

"It'll be dealt with," Allan assured. "I'm sure any dog Chaya gets will be the most behaved dog you've ever seen."

Orlovski's tightened lips writhed like something was trying to wriggle free. He turned back in his seat with a quick motion and he glowered at his knees as if something disgusting had slithered onto them.

"All right," Allan announced as they passed through a roundabout. "We're almost there. Stay on the lookout and get ready. We're exiting hot."

The mood in the vehicle instantly changed as if some switch had been flipped. Everyone's posture straightened. Fingers moved, checking equipment. A faint tang filled the vehicle. Fear? Adrenaline? Maybe both. Gerhard couldn't tell. His face felt hot and the body armor sweltering, like an oven. He needed air.

Still clutching Umatri in his lap, he moved his other hand, following their lead. The silenced pistol holstered beneath his armpit felt huge but partially calming. He traced the metal bead chain around his sweat-slicked neck to the plastic GPS unit shoved awkwardly beneath the vest.

The van turned onto a narrow street. The hunters peered out the windows, scanning the empty lanes. The principal lights came from the nearby high-rise apartments a block away. Orlovski and Luc had spent the night before gleefully shooting out the streetlamps with an air rifle in preparation.

"Here," Allan said, leaning forward behind Gerhard. He pulled the coil of plastic tubing from Gerhard's shoulder and let him loop it over his ear and push the bud in snugly. "Key up your radio."

Gerhard twisted the knob atop the little radio at his belt. The channels, they had told him, were specially encoded so no one might eavesdrop. Allan explained that the commanding view from apartment towers made cell-jamming useless, but it at least allowed for radios and the police scanners that would normally be rendered useless when running the jammer.

"You ready for this?" Allan asked Victoria, seated beside him.

She nodded. A long microphone extended from her headset, curling at the edge of her mouth. There was an uneasy hardness to her. Same as it had been that first day when they'd both arrived. Stiff and quiet. She'd livened up so much the last few days in Paris, especially with Allan and Sam. But that was gone.

They turned onto an even narrower street, the buildings' faces less than a meter from either side. A weight suddenly dropped in Gerhard's stomach as the building, the building he might die in, came into view.

"Looks clear," Sam said. She continued past it, giving Gerhard's stomach a surprise reprieve.

Were they not going in? Was this a practice drill? Maybe a joke.

"Okay," Allan said. "Circle back. Everyone, gloves on and masks ready."

The weight returned, heavier now with the moment's disappointment. Sam circled the block as everyone donned black latex gloves. The clammy hand-sweat made it even harder for Gerhard to pull them on. The hunters clutched their black, stretchy masks, rolled up like giant condoms. Gerhard twisted his around, trying to figure out where the eye slit was.

"Pull 'em on," Allan ordered as they turned again into the narrow street.

Gerhard pulled the mask over his head. The snug fabric trapped his breath, making it hot and humid against his face.

They rolled to a stop. Orlovski and Luc opened their doors in unison and hurried out. Adrenaline shot through Gerhard's veins, the weight instantly gone. Clutching Umatri, he scooted onto the brick street. Cool nighttime air blew across his bare arms and through the eye slit in the suffocating mask. He moved toward the green wooden door, scrawled with black spray-paint. A padlock hung from one side above a chipped scar where a previous one had been torn off.

"Be safe," Victoria said to Allan as she moved into the front seat.

"We will," Allan said. "Just listen to the scanner. Sam, circle around and plug the alley so no one else can come through."

"You got it, boss."

Allan shut the van door and hurried to where the hunters waited. The van rolled away, tires thumping over the uneven bricks. He drew his khopesh and a flashlight and gave a nod.

Luc slammed his mace into the door. The wood cracked loudly and came undone, bursting inside like confetti. Before the splinters had finished falling, Allan snapped on his light and was through the door, Orlovski on his heels.

"Go!" Luc whispered and Gerhard stepped through, fumbling for his light.

A narrow hall stretched before them, its stained floor made of white hexagonal tiles not much larger than a euro coin. Doors on either side stood open and dark. Brown smears ran down the stairway to the right, almost blending in to the layers of grime and graffiti. At the end of the hall, a paper-thin sliver of light peeked around the door to the rear courtyard, leaning in its frame as if it wasn't broken from the hinges. A wet, musty and fetid reek permuted through the stretchy mask.

They moved toward the first doorway, the plan to clear out the first floor before moving up.

Gerhard yelped as Umatri moved beneath his grip.

"Allan," Luc said, staring down at the keris. The blade slithered like a live and angry snake. Barbs bristled and smoothed along the waving steel and it bent toward the furthest doorway.

Terror and exhilaration stole Gerhard's breath as he watched the steel dance. Umatri was alive. He wasn't crazy. *An angel. I knew it.* But if Umatri was real …

As if on cue, a baby's coo sounded from the dark opening where Umatri pointed. Gerhard shivered, an icy terror coursing through his veins.

The hunters wheeled to face it.

A second coo came from up the stairs beside Gerhard, accompanied by a scuttling patter. Umatri's blade bent upwards. Gerhard lifted his gaze to see a white, chubby-cheeked doll face peek over the edge. Pincers unfolded out from its bristle-filled maw as a baby's laughter issued from that hard, unmoving mouth.

Gerhard screamed.

Infantile wails erupted from the neighboring room. Someone shouted but Gerhard didn't know who.

The doll-faced insect sprang. Its size rivaled a cat. Gerhard stumbled back into Luc. It landed against Gerhard's vest, the hooked feet grabbing hold. He shrieked and fell on his ass. The open pincers moved toward his face and it was still giggling that innocent laugh. Pulling his head away, he instinctively slapped at it, training forgotten and the blow ineffective. Umatri whipped down and struck like a scorpion's tail. The point skewered through the side of its head, bending somewhere inside its body and coming out its back. Its legs quivered, one still tangled in the fabric of his vest. Gerhard flung the insectile thing as hard as he could and it hit the wall with a solid *thump*, splattering inky blood before it tumbled to the floor.

He yelped as a hand grabbed him by the loop at the back of his vest.

Luc pulled him to his feet. "Get back!" He maneuvered Gerhard against the wall, one giant arm protectively across his chest. "You did good."

Umatri wriggled and danced, steam rising from the black ichor coating the blade. Gerhard's eyes followed the movement to where Allan and Orlovski hacked at more of the screaming bugs. Allan swung, vanished, reappeared over a meter from where he'd been and chopped one of the creatures in half. One flew from the darkness at him but Orlovski lunged forward, his kukri a silver blur. The doll-like head separated from the body with a spray of black goo.

"Is everyone all right?" Victoria's voice cried through the radio bud.

"Fine," Orlovski snapped.

"Bit busy here," Allan said. "No chatter."

Their lights cut white beams through the thickening steam that hissed from the withering dead things. Gerhard coughed at unholy stench of rotted meat filling the air, growing fouler with each breath. His arm still across Gerhard, and eyes up at the stairs, Luc scooted them toward the other hunters. Torn and filthy clothes littered the empty apartment, splattered with rusty brown stains. Four of the dead insects lay around them, their pale shells dissolving to slimy black meat.

More baby wails erupted from the walls and other rooms. Umatri flicked to the left as a large shape, the color of lacquered bone and striped in candy red, scrambled through the top of a bathroom doorway, plaster raining from the ceiling beneath its claws.

"Allan," Orlovski barked as he swung to face it.

The creature dropped to the ground and rose. Four arms extended from its segmented carapace. Two were slender and short, ending in three-pronged claws. Above them, the two longer and barbed arms tapered into scythe-like blades. Antennae twitched atop its wedge-shaped head, its mouth a boiling array of clicking mandibles.

Three more of the wailing insects scuttled through the door behind it and sprang. Orlovski spun, whipping his kukri knife and cleaving the right legs off one as it flew. At the same time, Allan leaped and swung Ibenus. He blinked, appearing to the side of the giant insect. The creature spun to face him, its bladed arms a blurred arc. Allan dropped, hacking the khopesh toward the floor. He vanished before the blade hit and reappeared mid-air before the monster, the down-swinging blade splitting its head with a sickly crunch. He landed, stumbling a little, as the monster collapsed.

Ghostly blue fire plumed from the bleeding wound, casting long shadows across the room. Dark steam erupted from the remaining baby-faced bugs as they dropped, legs drawing up and shells melting.

Gerhard gaped, wide-eyed as the blue fire spread over the beastly corpse and flickered along Allan's bronze blade. *Oh God, it's all true.* This was real. Demons. His head swam. They'd told him. Umatri had told him but he hadn't wanted to believe.

"The hell is this?" Orlovski shone his light into the dark bathroom.

The beam refracted off of a milky texture caking the rear wall, spreading out like thick webs to the tub. A cluster of irregular chambers, the largest approximately the same size as a one-liter thermos, honeycombed along the bottom. The structure crackled and sagged before Gerhard's eyes, dissolving like a wax sculpture in a kiln.

"We saw this in Manchester," Allan said. "Some kind of nest."

Disgusted, but unable to turn away, Gerhard watched a section peel from the tiled wall and plop to the floor, evaporating.

"There's more," Luc rumbled, his voice distant.

Gerhard blinked. Umatri was still slithering, this time pointing upward where more baby cries were sounding, drawing closer with the clicking of claws on tile.

"Back from the stairs," Allan ordered. Orlovski charged toward them but Allan was faster in getting out of the room.

They were still too late.

Four of the wailing bugs scuttled over the edges of the stairway, through the white iron railing. One moved across the ceiling. Gerhard thrust Umatri at one scrambling across the tiles, but the bug leaped back and to the side. Luc swung his mace down like a cricket bat. Ooze and bits of shell exploded in a mist. The creature sailed into the far wall with a hard *thock*, sticking in place as a pulpy mass of crab-like legs.

"Back," Luc barked, pushing Gerhard's chest with his huge hand.

Wrestling the dual urges to run for his life, or the growing, alien need to kill these horrors, Gerhard hesitated. Umatri danced and withed, his desire clear.

Luc bashed at another, punching a hole into the wall. It scurried around and hopped onto his leg and darted onto the back of Luc's vest.

Yelping, the big man twisted to reach it before it could bite. Gerhard moved toward it, Umatri raised, but suddenly Allan was there before him. The Englishman slapped the bug off with the flat of his sword and chopped off two of its legs as it tried to run.

"Gerhard," Orlovski shouted, "get back!" He swung his kukri at a closing bug, not close enough to hit it, but just keep it away.

"But—"

"Back!" Eyes still on the circling bug, he pulled Gerhard's shoulder. "Turgen will have our ass if you engage!"

A huge shape swung over the stair rail. The creature stood nearly two meters, stripes of greenish yellow ran across its bony armored plates. The mantismere hissed and spat. Its armored mandibles opened wide enough to fit both of Gerhard's fists. It raised its bladed arms and thrust them forward and down like a thresher. Luc lurched back, barely dodging the attack, but collided with Allan in the narrow hall as Allan finished off the bug he'd already maimed.

The mantismere lunged and raised its blades again in one quick motion. Unable to retreat, Luc closed the distance, his mace blurring in an arc. The deadly points vaporized as the mace smashed through them. Shrieking, the demon leapt backward, dark blood pouring from the broken ends.

Fresh crying sounded from behind. Gerhard wheeled as two more bugs came through an open door. He stabbed at one, the blade seriating as it moved. The screamer scuttled to the side but Umatri lashed out, bending toward it and taking a chunk from the creature's flank. The other bug raced up the nearby wall as Gerhard skewered the wounded bug with a second thrust. Wailing that horrible scream, the impaled creature's leg's flailed, its claws raking the filthy tiles. Then they curled inward and the shell blackened and melted outward from the death wound.

Blue light erupted behind him, filling the halls. Gerhard glanced back to see Luc standing above the flaming mantismere, its side completely caved in and greasy, flaming guts splattered on the neighboring wall. The screamer running across the ceiling fell at its master's demise, leaving a trail of reeking steam like a falling meteor.

The last infant wail ceased as Orlovski chopped the bug on the nearby wall, splattering he and Gerhard with some of its foul ichor.

"It didn't die with the master," Orlovski said, turning to the hunters.

"Then there's one demon left." Allan looked up the stairs,

then nodded to Gerhard. "What's through there? Basement?"

Braving a peek, Gerhard looked through the darkened door where the two bugs had come. Having first mistaken it for a closet, he now saw the narrow brick steps leading down into blackness. "Yes."

"Rest of this floor clear?"

Still panting, Luc nodded. Blue fire flickered along Velnepo's flanged head. "Yeah."

"Okay. You and Gerhard stay down here. Watch that basement and don't let anything escape. Orlovski and I will clear the upper floors." He glanced at the flaming monster at the big man's feet. "Move that body away from the door so no one can see it."

Allan and Orlovski headed up the step, leaving Gerhard painfully aware of the dark basement doorway beside him. Umatri's undulations had ceased, but that didn't calm him. What if there was a third monster? Maybe a fourth?

"Give me a hand," Luc said.

Not wanting to take his eyes from the doorway, Gerhard slowly made his way past the steaming mounds. His eyes watered at the stench that evoked memories from his thirteenth summer. A rat had died in the wall beside his bed, unreachable, and the stink of its decay accompanying him to sleep every night for a week, despite all the scented candles and room spray his mother had tried to mask it.

"Check your corner," Allan said through the radio.

"Clear," Orlovski replied. Footsteps creaked above as the knights moved along the second floor.

Gerhard stopped beside the burning monster. Blue flames flickered and danced over its entire length, brighter above the eyes, mouth, and gruesome wound. The steady flow of air coming through the smashed front door, and around the leaning back one, neither stoked or diminished the fire in any way. There was no smoke and no heat. While he'd been told about it, the non-fire disturbed him more than he'd anticipated.

Luc slipped Velnepo into his belt ring and bent before the creature's long-toed feet. "Grab it under the shoulders. We'll move it to the back room with the other."

Gerhard swallowed. Even with the gloves on he didn't want to touch it. Luc gave a sharp, commanding nod. Gerhard slid Umatri back into his sheath and, clenching his jaw, bent, reached through the dancing flames, and slipped his fingers beneath the dead thing's chitinous arms. He wondered if Umatri could even penetrate the hard shell.

Awkwardly they moved the corpse back up the hall, its hemorrhaged guts threatening to spill from the gruesome wound. A faint tingling worked along Gerhard's arms, making the hairs stand on end. He shivered, as if he could somehow shake the sensation off.

"I hate the way it feels, too," Luc mumbled, his voice so low Gerhard mostly heard it through the radio.

"It's in your head," Allan muttered through the radio. "Second floor clear. Heading up to three."

Together Gerhard and Luc moved the burning corpse into the rear room and dropped it to the floor. The sharp, insectile features on the first slain demon had softened since he'd last seen it. Its black eyes had shrunk and moved closer together, its nostrils rising up into a nose between them. The sides of its face had flattened, appearing more like cheeks. Burning blood and brains oozed out from its cloven skull. Luc drew his mace and led Gerhard back out into the hall to watch the exits and basement door. The radio buzzed as the other two hunters scoured the upstairs, searching every corner.

Three minutes later they came back down, having found nothing but trash and empty rooms.

Allan didn't speak as he returned, Ibenus ready before him. He gestured to Luc, who extended his thick arm and eased Gerhard farther from the basement door. Snapping a finger into the air and pointing, Allan directed Orlovski to one side. The Russian pressed his back to the wall, his kukri ready. Allan nodded, once, twice, and on the third he lifted his powerful light and darted in. Orlovski shot down behind him as if connected by an invisible tether.

Their footsteps thumped down the stairs. Lowering his protective arm, Luc stepped closer to the door and shined his light down after them.

Orlovski's voice came through the radio, "Clear."

"Check under the boiler," Allan said.

"Nothing."

"Fuck. You see this?" Allan asked.

Orlovski grunted.

"Gerhard, come down. We need you."

Gerhard tensed, excitement and fear. Needed him?

Luc motioned his head, urging him on, and Gerhard stepped through the door, Umatri before him, and headed down the narrow brick-lined stairway. It opened up to a hall with three doors and a giant spray-painted mural of a nude woman spread eagle on the floor. Light moved within the furthest room. Gerhard glanced in the others as he passed, a large closet with a tile shower and a laundry room with no machines. A cardboard sleeping pallet and a torn and spilled backpack rested against the laundry room's far wall.

The final room was wide, taking up almost half of the building's footprint. An ancient green and rust-streaked boiler dominated the far wall, so large Gerhard wondered if they'd simply constructed the building around it. Its thick door hung partially open, revealing more trash and refuse shoved inside. Beside it, hacksawed pipes led to a square where a presumably smaller, newer, and now absent model had once been.

Allan and Orlovski stood to the left of the giant boiler's door before a wide round hole in the floor. Remembering the urban explorer photos, he noted that a metal grate had once covered it, but it was nowhere to be found.

Allan didn't look up as Gerhard approached. "Is Umatri sensing anything?"

"No," Gerhard answered. The keris' blade hadn't moved since the last of the screamers had died.

Allan frowned and circled his light down the open hole.

Gerhard stepped over a broken wine bottle and joined them. The circular opening was about a meter across. Their bright flashlight beams revealed a long, brick-lined tunnel extending down so far their lights barely reached the bottom. Metal rungs protruded from the mortar down one side, their surface buried beneath dust and a rust patina. Something glinted in the hazy blackness. Metal? Glass? He thought of the empty spray-paint cans lying around. Maybe one fell down there. Easily twenty meters down.

"There's a tunnel leading off at the bottom," Orlovski said, angling his light as best he could.

Allan nodded. "Could be the sewers. Maybe the old mine catacombs."

"You believe it's down there?"

Allan nodded again. "We can't just send someone down one at a time. Not if it's waiting." He curled his lip, seeming to ponder it.

Gerhard looked at him, then to Orlovski, and returned his attention to the shaft, stretching down like a backdoor to hell. If there was another demon, and he believed there could be, he wanted it. He wanted its blue fire along Umatri's blade. "So what do we do?"

"I know it's in here," Luc grumbled from the open back of the van, digging through a rectangular tub. His deep voice came through Victoria's foam earpiece, echoing his words with only a moment's delay. They'd pulled the van outside the abandoned building's shattered door. Splinters hung from the hinges the same as they had in Manchester.

Victoria scanned the dark street, her gaze searching the high-rise apartments that loomed over the tops of the neighboring buildings, its rows and rows of balconies making it appear like a giant stack of wafers. Most of the windows were dark, but not all. She wondered if she'd even see a watcher up there if the lights were off. Could they see her looking for them? Maybe TommyD was up there. Though they'd never met, she owed the man her sanity, if not her life. Her mental descent after James' death hadn't led to the darkest of thoughts, but they could have if TommyD hadn't found her. Now he, or one of his agents, might be watching her through a high-power lens, likely one attached to a camera.

A feminine voice came through the scanner's speakers in assertive French, something about a traffic accident, Sam explained. So far, no one had called in the hunters.

"Here you are." Luc held up a roll of silver duct tape, the faint lights that gleamed off the sweat-slicked face visible through the mask's oval slit.

"You all right?" Allan asked.

Victoria turned back to where he stood, digging through a dull aluminum case. A trio of cameras and their necessary accoutrements filled the niches in the shiny black foam. "Fine. Just feel a bit out in the open here."

"I understand." Allan popped a little door on the back of one of the cameras and slid a rectangular battery in. "This shouldn't take too long." He winked. "We'll be back in a few."

"You want me to circle around again?" Sam asked.

He glanced down the empty street. "Stay here and watch the feed. Move if someone starts coming this way."

"Roger that."

"Good luck," Victoria said.

Allan gave a nod, his smile hidden beneath the black mask, but she could see it in his eyes. Camera in hand, he closed the van's door and darted back to the building, drawing Ibenus as he did.

Victoria slid back into the front passenger seat and rested the laptop across her knees so she and Sam could both watch. A black, gray-framed window dominated the screen with little icons running along either side. She couldn't help a glance to the short-barrel pump shotgun resting against the Australian girl's inner thigh.

Sam closed her hand over the microphone by her mouth and whispered. "You know everyone's going to assume you're screwing, right?"

A cold, defensive gush surged through Victoria's stomach, rising up her chest. She put a hand over her own mic, feeling the heat of in her cheeks. Was she blushing? "But ... we're not."

The young woman shrugged. "Doesn't mean they aren't assuming it. They've thought that about me and Taras for two years now."

"But you're not?" Victoria did confess that while Allan had said otherwise, she'd suspected there was more to Sam and Orlovski's weirdly close relationship. Their hands always touching each other's arms when they spoke, the way they seemed to carry entire conversations with only a look.

Sam snorted. "No. He's practically my brother. I'm just letting you know that people are going to talk. Especially with the way you two look at each other."

"How?"

She grimaced a little shrug. "There's just a flirty vibe."

"It's nothing."

Sam's brow arched knowingly. "But you still like him, though?"

Victoria nodded, the confession seeing to cement her unspoken crush.

"I knew it."

"You're not going to—?"

"No." Sam waved it off. "Don't worry. What's said in the van stays in the van."

"Thanks."

"Back when I first came on, Master Schmidt would come with me on these."

"Really?"

"He's too old to hunt any more, so he elected to show me how to run the surveillance. The things we talked about ..." She shook her head, exhaling a breath.

"Like what?"

She shook a finger. "What's said in the van ..."

"Ah," Victoria said. "Right."

After a moment's silence of listening to the hunters debate how to lower the camera, Sam said, "Honestly, it's pretty cool to have you here. Can get lonely, you know?"

"I can imagine." Victoria peered through the side mirror, making sure the street was still clear. Years of being a copper and never once did she fully realize the paranoia of seeing the blue lights. In that event, Standard Operating Procedure was to drive, radio the team to evac to a set rendezvous point. They'd drilled it in her. But now, now that she was here, Victoria couldn't guess what she'd do if she saw the police. Would she lose her senses, panic like so many suspects had, or would she freeze? It was so weird to be thinking this way. In the event they were apprehended, everyone had forged IDs, everyone but her and Gerhard, that was. Real IDs and phones, the ones linked to their real identities, were still in Brussels. Until the new identities were ready, it was even more imperative that she not get caught.

"You'll get a good idea as soon as Master Turgen splits us," Sam said, pulling Victoria back to the present.

"Well, until then, you have a lot to teach me." She removed her death-grip from the mic, but paused and squeezed it again. "I, um, wanted to apologize again for shoving a gun in your face. I'm … very happy we've gotten past that. I truly am."

"We'll get past it a lot faster when you stop bringing it up," Sam said. "I appreciate it, but it's really in your best interest to stop reminding me."

Victoria smiled. "Noted." She glanced back at the high-rise, hoping for the first time, that TommyD or his agents weren't actually up there. The idea of Allan or the other knights getting ID'd made her uncomfortable. They'd taken her in, shared openly, and offered their trust. Even Sam, who had every reason in the world to hate her, had moved past it. A barbed, regretful pang slid between Victoria's ribs at what she'd done. What she might have done. And what she'd promised to do.

They'll make you trust them, TommyD had written. *All cults and extremists do that first. That's how they work. They draw you in and make you feel important. But don't buy into it. Don't believe the lie.*

She ground her teeth, the needle sliding deeper. What the hell did he know?

"I think we have it," Allan announced.

Green light shone from the laptop's screen as the gray-framed window flashed to life. A blank wall appeared, washed out, only the barest features visible. The details sliding into focus. A brick wall, cut pipes hanging from the ceiling above spray-painted scrawl. The image whirled, losing focus, then coming in on Gerhard and Luc. Their eyes glowed through the slits in their ninja masks. The camera lowered, revealing a round manhole. A board lay across it, a notch chipped into the side above the very middle.

"I got you," Sam said.

"Lowering you down."

The camera moved lower, past their feet until stopping at an extreme close-up of a brick wall. It swayed little and the bricks began moving up at a slow, unsteady pace. The flashlight beams from above played off the tunnel's walls.

"Looks like there used to be a ladder," Victoria whispered, noting the bent and cut brackets jutting from the mortar.

Sam nodded. "Slow down, we're starting to sway."

The camera's descent stopped until the rocking ceased, and then it continued. The tunnel seemed to go forever, worn and irregular bricks rolling past as if on a video loop.

"Just a little over halfway down," Allan said as if reading Victoria's mind.

She braved another glance. The streets were still empty.

Blocks of digital static shifted across the screen.

"Reception is acting up," Sam said. "How much further?"

"Not much."

"If we lose it we'll need to move the computer in there."

"Just a little more," Allan said.

The brick wall ended, revealing a long, stone tunnel, its pale walls bright in the camera's infrared beam. The stones seemed to move.

Victoria's eyes widened as the image shifted into focus. "Shit! Allan, they're coming!"

Allan stood above the open pit, shining his light down as Gerhard fed the white nylon rope through the notched board and lowered the suspended camera. Luc had affixed little duct tape flags along the line, marking two-meter increments.

He breathed through his mouth, trying to avoid the sickly-sweet stench of the screamers they'd killed still clinging to his mask. He'd encountered enough rotted corpses over the years to know that all-too-familiar stench. It only took once and you'd never forget it. There was an article he'd read once where weapon manufacturers were studying various odors for non-lethal riot control stink bombs. They'd concluded that the most repulsive smell was that of rotted human flesh, a stink hardwired in people's brains as the foulest. He grinned, imagining the effect that tossing a couple dead screamers into a mob might elicit.

Sam's calm voice sounded in his ear bud. "Reception is acting up. How much further?"

The eighth duct tape flag slid past the notch. He shined his light along the passage's walls, guessing three more at most before the bottom. "Not much."

"If we lose it we'll need to move the computer in there."

He'd worried about the stone walls' interference but hadn't mentioned it, hoping it wouldn't be necessary. Another flag slid through the notch. "Just a little more."

The camera continued down, moving past the visible walls. Almost twenty meters. He held out a hand, signaling Gerhard to stop.

He was about to ask if it was enough but Victoria's panicked voice came through. "Shit! Allan, they're coming!"

A cacophony of screaming infants erupted up the shaft, distorted by echoes. Then they appeared, pouring around the sides and up the tube's walls like frenzied ants, mandibles clacking from their hard, emotionless mouths.

"I can see two mantismeres," Sam said, her voice unsettlingly calm.

Orlovski sheathed his kukri, drew his pistol, and started firing with metronome timing. *Pop ... Pop ... Pop.* Even suppressed the shots were loud enough to make Allan wince. The Russian didn't seem to notice. Bullets ripped through the ranks, shattering their child-like faces and sending bugs toppling back down the pit as more surged past them.

"Circle up!" Allan ordered. He drew his own pistol. The other hand braced it, holding the light as he shined it down. The closing wave was like a single boiling thing. Unable to focus on just one, he fired at the mob. His shots chipped up brick and wounded several, but nothing like Orlovski's methodical precision.

Gerhard dropped the line, sending one of the screamers crawling up it into the pit. Umatri's sheath rattled and shook, the writhing blade desperate for blood. He drew his pistol and began firing. His shots, like Allan's, were a wild hailstorm of bullets. Luc moved beside him, his own pistol out.

A hot shell, ejected by Luc's pistol, bounced off Allan's vest. His own shells were pelting Orlovski, but the Russian didn't react.

Orlovski's gun clicked empty. Keeping his aim on the monsters, he ejected the mag, letting it fall, and slapped a fresh one in. He resumed his firing, the screamers now just fifteen feet below them, when a mantismere swung out over the edge below. It charged upwards, its blade-like claws moving up either side of the tunnel. The dark steam from the dead screamers billowed up the shaft, making it difficult to see.

"There's a third one," Sam said.

Orlovski fired at the demon, taking it once in the head and once in the back. The holes closed as fast as they opened. "Silver with quartz tips." He ejected the nearly full mag and glanced at the next before loading it in. "Brass with blue spinel." He fired twice more but to the same result as Luc peppered it with his own ineffective shots.

"Camera's out," Sam said.

I think I shot it. Allan's eyes watered with the incredible and growing stink. It was like looking down a chimney. He prayed he didn't get sick inside the mask. His gun clicked empty. He jammed it into the holster and drew Ibenus. "There's too many!"

Luc grunted and shot a screamer just a foot below the edge before his own pistol's slide locked back. He drew Velnepo and glanced over at the giant boiler.

"Door," Allan said, guessing the big man's intent.

Gerhard and Orlovski's loud shots filled the brick room, blocking out the insects' wails as Luc turned to the boiler.

He slammed the mace down on the top of the square, cast-iron door. The boiler rang like a muted gong as the now bent door broke free of its topmost hinge. Taking hold of it in one hand, Luc swung the Velnepo into the bottom of the awkwardly-hanging door, knocking the other hinge free with another *clang*. Despite his hold, Luc stumbled, nearly dropping the door as the full weight came down.

The mantismere reached the top. Mouth wide and hissing, it lunged out the last foot toward Gerhard. The German fell backward dropping his gun as he clawed for his keris. Allan hacked with Ibenus, taking the monster in the shoulder and under the neck. The demon fell, barely missing the second one halfway up the tunnel. Blue fire ignited at the bottom, silhouetting the approaching horde in flickering light. A trio of screamers curled and fell at the demon's demise, their steam adding to the thickening cloud.

Dropping Velnepo in his belt ring, Luc seized the door in both hands, lifted it above his head, and hurled it down the pit. It tumbled as it went, chipping bricks and smashing or knocking bugs free. The mass of metal and carcasses slammed into the closing demon, sweeping it down in the wave.

Orlovski shot the last of the still-clinging screamers and a moment's silence fell. Allan's ears hummed from the shots. Then the wailing began again, but far less than it had been. Luc helped Gerhard to his feet. Both held their holy weapons ready.

"Boss," Sam said. "We could hear your shots up here. Police are going to get called."

Clenching his jaw, Allan peered down the smoky, blue-lit tunnel. One screamer was circling the bottom, but wasn't coming up. "We aren't equipped for this. Fall back to the van."

CHAPTER 12

Allan sipped his lukewarm tea. On the giant monitor, screamers surged toward the camera, their infant-like faces glowing green, appearing to float in the infrared, their eyes empty pits of blackness. Behind them, two mantismeres clambered into view, holding back as their minions led the assault. One walked upright along the floor. The other scuttled along the arched ceiling like the mewling soldiers. The camera jostled and began to spin slowly as they moved past, knocking into it. Then the broken limbs and steaming carcasses began raining down as Orlovski opened fire above.

He thumbed the button on the oval remote, pausing the video as the camera dropped. "The first two we caught completely off guard inside the building," he said, standing beside the wall screen like a professor. "However the nest was far larger than we'd imagined. Three more were downstairs and attempted an ambush in case we tried to follow them into the catacombs."

"Are you sure there were only three more?" Master Schmidt asked. He sat in the middle of the front row between Luc and Master Turgen. The rest of the knights filled the briefing room, eyes on Allan.

Allan nodded to Sam, seated to Victoria's right.

"That's all we saw before the camera went out," Sam replied. The dark circles beneath her eyes made her appear ten years older. She'd plowed through footage and archive records all night as Orlovski had driven them from Paris back to Brussels.

"Whether there's more or not, they likely won't return to the house." Allan clicked the remote and the screen changed to a map of Paris with an overlay of winding paths and blobs in glowing yellow. "We think the mantismeres have been using the old Roman limestone quarry beneath the city. The abandoned apartment was simply a convenient access to the surface, but there's hundreds more. Between the mines, the sewers, and the subways, the catacomb tunnels extend for over two hundred miles, with hundreds of potential accesses to the city."

Master Turgen squeezed his chin between thumb and forefinger, eyes intent on the screen, almost looking through it. "And there's been no other reports but the one that led us there?"

Allan hit the button again. Slideshow images of spray-painted tunnels, lit by flashlights and candles began scrolling past. "Not that we've found. I suspect the demons have been feeding on cataphiles, the people who live and explore down there. They could feed and possess them as much as they want and no one would even notice them gone. There's a small police unit that patrols the catacombs, terribly inadequate for its sheer size. If the demons avoid them, they could live down there indefinitely."

Turgen nodded, but more to himself than to Allan. "Do you suspect an eel?" There it was, the million-pound question. All eyes locked on Allan.

"I do."

A collective weight settled over the room, everyone's unspoken suspicions now voiced and now real with Allan's affirmation. Two years before, after Anya had orchestrated the deaths of over three dozen hunters, destroyed twenty-seven holy weapons, burned the Valducans' home, and nearly wiped the entire archive, she'd offered herself to become the body of Tiamat. In the brief time the Mother of Demons was flesh, she'd birthed a half-dozen flying eels. Each eel, ten feet long and wearing Anya's face, served as a nexus demon. Each victim they bit became possessed with a new demonic spirit unique to that eel. Mantismeres were one of those breeds, and if they didn't find and eliminate that eel soon it could unleash hundreds, maybe thousands, of mantismeres onto the world. Eels were considered top priority. So far they'd killed only two.

"The concentration of them is too high," Allan continued. "Mantismeres have only been found in Europe so it's likely still here."

Master Turgen's chair creaked as he leaned back into the leather, his posture straightening, seeming to regain that hardness Allan remembered. "Very well. Do any of our knights have experience in the catacombs?"

"Well," Allan said, "last expedition down there was in 2009. Out of that team Malcolm Romero is the only one still alive."

"Call him—No. I'll call him," Turgen said. "I'll tell him to come at once."

Sam perked up a little, a slight smile to the edge of her lips.

"Are you sure he'll come?" Luc asked.

The old man nodded. "I have no doubt."

"Who's Malcolm?" Victoria whispered to Sam but the whole room could hear.

"Mal?" Sam asked, still grinning. "Oh you'll love him."

"He went native," Orlovski said. "Got engaged, too."

Sam's eyes darted toward the Russian, skewering him with a sharp *shush*.

Allan couldn't help but smile himself. If they could get Malcolm, then they might even be able to pull this off. He was as stone-cold as they came, a natural leader and fiercely protective of his teammates. He'd stepped down as Team Leader a year before, went independent, a Valducan in little more than name.

Master Schmidt hadn't taken his eyes off the flipping slideshow. "Before Doctor Romero arrives, I want everyone to read the report from his mission into the catacombs. We'll find out what supplies he'll require and procure them at once."

Orlovski leaned over and whispered something in Luc's ear.

"We'll need to practice close quarter drills," Chaya muttered to Schmidt. "Attach tac lights to sidearms."

Master Turgen cleared his throat. "I'd like to announce that Gerhard Entz has chosen to join us."

Gerhard gave a small nod as the knights congratulated him, their moods a little less than enthusiastic at the moment.

"Welcome aboard," Allan said, clapping his hands. Gerhard hadn't spoken the entire ride back. Allan had mistakenly assumed the silence meant that the German was going to bolt the moment his week was up. Technically that was today.

"Tomorrow night we'll hold the ceremony to officially induct our newest knight into the Order. I will need to speak with some of you privately beforehand about your duties. Until then, many of you are understandably exhausted. Rest up. We have much to do in the next few days."

Ice clacked as Victoria sipped her drink, vodka and orange Fanta. Sam had named it funta, because it's fun. On the giant screen before them, an elf with impossible pigtails hacked her purple-glowing sword at a grunting orc, vaporizing it in a burst of sparks. The elf charged deeper into a cavernous tunnel, lit with wall-mounted torches. Caverns ... tunnels ... "There's no way we can scour two hundred miles of catacombs, not if they're trying to hide."

Sam let out a breathy growl. "I told you," she said, killing another orc, this time with some discus boomerang, "no talking about work. It's a night off. I didn't get one after the last job so I'm taking full advantage of this one."

"Sorry." Victoria sipped more of her Funta, trying to just let it go as Sam seemed to have. It wasn't working. "How do you do it?"

"What? The jump throw? It's all in the reflexes," she added in vaguely masculine voice, presumably an impersonation but Victoria didn't recognize it.

"No. How do you sit there so calm while the others are screaming and getting hurt and you can't do anything about it but listen?"

"Oh." Sam kept playing her game, jumping over a pit of spikes and snatching a floating crystal.

"Sorry," Victoria said, once it was clear she'd again spoiled her friend's down time.

"No." Sam paused the game and set the controller in her lap. "I get it." She picked her own drink off the desk of the empty chair beside hers and knocked it back. "It sucks. I once watched Taras get shot. Twice. They'd set up a camera in front of this house and they were coming around a corner chasing the target. I saw the shooter but ..." She shook her head. "His cry came through my radio as it hit him. All I could do was just sit and watch him bleeding out. Mal's yelling at me to keep listening to the scanner and watch the other cameras and Taras is just dying right there in front of me. I just wanted to start the car, drive up there, bring a med kit, anything but sit there."

"What did you do?"

"Stayed put. Followed orders."

Victoria imagined herself in that situation, Allan dying on the screen as she watched, unable to go to him, unable to help him. "How? How could you stay there?"

"It's what we do. If I hadn't, I'd have missed the scanner call. Police would have come, found us." She finished her drink. "I hated Mal at the time. But he made the right call. Our job is as critical as theirs. If we lose our cool it can spiral out of control. So we have to stay calm, calmer than them, so that they can stay calm. Got it? We have to be their rock."

That image of Allan dying still kept playing in Victoria's head, but she nodded.

"The worst is the silence, though." The leather seat creaked as Sam got up and carried he glass to the refreshment table. She scooped ice out of a polished copper ice bucket before pouring a healthy amount of Norwegian vodka. "When you're blind and can hear them fighting and yelling, then it all goes quiet and you're just ... waiting. Your brain starts running wild. Is anyone hurt? Is someone dead? That's when it fucks with you." The liter Fanta bottle hissed as Sam unscrewed it. She poured a dash in, not much more than to add color, then stirred the cocktail.

"I can imagine."

Sam picked the wireless controller back up and returned to her seat. "That answer your question?"

"Yeah."

"Good. Now, no more shop talk for the night." She held up her glass. "Agreed?"

Victoria clinked her empty glass against it. "Agreed." She rose and refreshed her drink as the redhead continued her game. Sam wrenched the controller up, as if the movement might transfer and help her character leap over a chasm.

After another round of drinks and mild increase in Sam's elf dying, Allan strolled in through the briefing room door. A slight flush brightened his cheeks and he carried an open champagne bottle in one hand.

"That's an interesting look," Victoria said, eyeing the strange ensemble—engraved breastplate, tall boots, and vibrant blue cape that matched the sash beneath his belt.

"You like it?" He gave a flourish, tossing the cape back over one shoulder, allowing full view of Ibenus on his hip. Instead of the usual black nylon scabbard, the sword rested within a dark leather one tooled with Egyptian hieroglyphs and accented in matching bronze.

"You look like you should be in this thing," Sam said, nodding to the screen.

"Don't be jealous. You'll have one soon enough."

"Yeah, but mine will have boobs."

He grinned. "But what will you put in them?"

Sam shot him a cold glare, eyebrow cocked. Then she glanced down at her T-shirt and shrugged. "Gotta get 'em somehow."

"Well, I think you look rather smart," Victoria said.

"Thank you." He held out the green fat-bottomed bottle, beads of condensation glinting across its surface. "Care for some?"

She motioned to her glass, still a quarter full of funta. "Need a new glass."

"Who needs a glass?" Sam extended her hand, wiggling her fingers.

"We are cultured people here." Allan tipped the bottle up, taking a draw before offering it over to Sam.

Victoria tapped her chin. "Is that a bacterial culture or fungal?"

"Why not both?" Allan said. "We make no prejudices."

Sam knocked it back, then came up sputtering. "Bubbles," she coughed, then offered it to Victoria. "So ceremony over, where's Taras?"

"He should be up soon."

"Good."

Victoria sipped the cold champagne, enjoying the fizz play across her tongue. She looked over as Allan lowered into the seat beside her. "Aren't you hot in that?"

"A bit." He tapped the breastplate. "But I so rarely get to wear it. Last time was ... Matt and Luiza's wedding. Chaya was knighted before she came over. So, two years." A tinge of sadness crept into his voice as his eyes momentarily dulled. "Too long."

She offered him the bottle.

Allan accepted it, lifted it in a mild toast, but didn't drink. "So what have you ladies been up to?"

"You're looking at it," Victoria said, motioning her head toward the video game and drink table. "So how did the knighting go?"

"Good. Very good. Gerhard has come around very well, all things considered. The both of you were instrumental in that. None of us will forget it."

"Great," Sam said. "Payback begins when you stop talking about work. Got it?"

Allan looked over at her, seeming a bit taken aback.

Victoria mouthed, *Night off,* and he opened his hand in surrender.

The door opened and Orlovski strode in. He'd already traded the armor and cape for a bright blue and white jersey emblazoned with a two-headed bird. Though he still wore the dark trousers and riding boots. He gave Victoria and Allan a simple nod, poured himself a funta and plopped down beside Sam. "You haven't made it out of the temple yet?"

"Stuck on the last part. I can't find the bloody key."

"It's easy. Just go back to the idol room."

After a quarter hour of watching Sam play as Orlovski backseat drove, Allan tapped Victoria's shoulder. She turned. He inquisitively raised an eyebrow and motioned his nose toward the door.

The corner of her lip tightened into a smile and she nodded. Bidding the two goodnight, they quietly made their retreat, leaving the two to their games.

"You read my mind," Victoria whispered once the door had closed behind them.

"It's a knight's job to read their student."

"I thought a student's job was to read their master."

"It goes both ways, I suppose. Whatever the case, if tonight's supposed to be a break, last thing I want to be doing is staring at a screen. I get that enough."

She chuckled. "Agreed."

"Any word yet on Paris?"

She shook her head. "Nothing. It'd be on the news if police came, but we sort of left the door in shambles so it's only time before someone finds the bodies."

"They should have found something by now." He glanced out the hall window as they passed. The lights in the trees outside cast scraggly shadows of branches across the green lawn. "You want to go for a walk?"

"Sure." She eyed the polished breastplate. "You want to maybe change out of that first, Lancelot?"

"Probably a good idea." They made their way across the mansion, seeing no one, only hearing Luc's laughter roared from the ceremony chamber as the passed the hall. "I'll just be a bit," Allan said, opening his bedroom door.

"I can help you with that," she offered.

He shook his head. "I have it, thanks." Allan stepped inside, but Victoria moved into the doorway before he could close it.

"Seriously, let me help you. I am your squire after all."

His lips tightened, embarrassed or uncertain. "Are you sure?"

"Beats standing out in the hall." She stepped inside.

The room was modest, a near duplicate of her own but with walls painted the color of dry oatmeal and burgundy curtains shot through with gold. A few trinkets and photographs hung from the walls, primarily of Allan and some of the other Valducans smiling before various monuments. One appeared to be at a wedding, presumably his best friend's. A polished wood sword stand rested atop the dresser beside a leafy potted plant. It was tidy, and clean, everything in its correct place. Even the bed was made, its sheets tight and perfect, like his mother might drop by any minute. Victoria thought of her own room and the pile of dirty laundry growing in the corner.

Allan was removing the cape from the rings, like miniature doorknockers, set in his shoulders.

"Here," she said, taking it from him. She looked around, unsure what to do with it, then draped it over the back of his chair. Ten seconds in and she was already making a mess.

"Really, this isn't necessary," he chuckled, removing his sword belt.

Meeting his eyes, she put her hand on his and smiled. "Isn't this a squire's duty?"

His already flushed cheeks reddened. "You're not that type of squire ... well, I suppose you are, but ... but students don't do that any more, removing armor and tending horses and—"

"Allan."

"Yes?"

"Hush. Let me do this. It's likely the only time I'll ever offer." She took the belt with Ibenus, noting his obvious discomfort at her holding it, and set it gently on the dresser before the stand. Really, the way he obsessed about that sword was weird. Surely he didn't actually think it was alive. That done, she unwrapped the blue silk sash from his waist and laid it over the cape.

Now confronted with the armor, she pursed her lips, trying to figure out how to begin. She started on his left shoulder buckle.

"There are tabs."

She lifted the end of the leather strap to find a pair of smooth knobs securing the side nearest the buckle, reminiscent to a handbag she used to carry. "That makes it easier." She popped the leather free, then easily undid the ones along his side. It came open like an oyster shell, hinging off the still-buckled right half.

Allan released a relived sigh as she slid it off. It weighed less than she'd expected. Though it probably wasn't the battle-ready armor from days of old, the twin plates mutedly clanged as she carefully set it in the desk chair.

"Thank you," he said, unfastening a button on his straight-collared jacket. "I have it from here."

Victoria pointed at the bed. "Sit down."

"Huh?" Panic tinged his voice.

"Boots."

"No, I've got it."

She gave him a look. "No, I've worn boots like those. Trust me, I'm doing you a favor."

He hesitated, seeming to search for a protest.

"Sit." She pressed her finger against his chest, gently pushing him down onto the edge of the bed.

"What's wrong?" Victoria asked as she slid her hand behind the heel of one boot and pulled.

"Nothing." He extended his leg out as she fought the stiff leather. "It's just a bit unexpected, you offering to help."

The stubborn boot came free. "Not that. I mean in general. You've been so edgy the last few days. Been worried I offended you."

"What?" he laughed. "No, not at all. Just been keyed up with this thing in Paris, that's all."

"Before that." The second boot came free with considerably less effort. She set it beside the other one and stood. "You've gotten all weird whenever I'm close. Like kid gloves."

His smile slackened. "Oh. I was … well, last week, after we sparred and I took your hand, you seemed offended. I didn't want you to think I was trying anything."

Victoria scrunched her nose. "You didn't take my hand. I took yours."

"You?"

"I'm pretty sure I would have noticed if you took mine."

"Oh. I thought I did that."

"Is that all it was? You didn't want to make me uncomfortable?"

He nodded.

She bent and took his hand in hers. "There. Does this make you nervous?"

Allan shook his head. Their faces were close now. A smoky aroma clung to his hair, sweet but with a bitter edge. "No." He rolled his palm over, squeezing her hand in return.

Tingles rolled up the back of her neck and prickled along her scalp. "Good."

He leaned closer, his warm breath playing across her lips. "Good."

They kissed.

A sudden rush of heat welled within her chest, flowing along her spine and surging to where he still held her hand. His fingers moved up to her cheek, sending electric ripples across her skin. Allan's other hand slid free of her grasp and glided up her arm, squeezing her shoulder and pulling her closer.

Pressing her hands against his firm chest, Victoria gently pushed him back. She tugged his lip in hers, holding for a few moments longer until she could force herself to finish the kiss.

Hunger glimmered in Allan's eyes. He reached for her again but she caught his hands and forced them to his sides.

"What?" he asked.

She grinned and touched the topmost silver button on his jacket. "I'm not finished with my squirely duties."

Allan laughed breathily and straightened, allowing her full access to remove the garment, which she did slowly. She savored his mounting impatience as she took her time. After the third button came free, revealing the white shirt beneath he reached out to pull her close again but she swatted the hand back, reminding him of her duties.

The jacket now open, she slid it off him, letting her hands caress down his arms. Victoria kissed his temple and down his jaw, then pulled away before the dizzying tingles made her forget her game. She stood and carefully laid the jacket on the bedside table.

Returning, she knelt between his legs and began on the shirt, kissing his chest as each undone button revealed more of him. Thin, hair-like scars traced along his collarbone. Twin purple scars ran along the side of ribs. She kissed each of the old wounds, then continued her task. The shirt open, she slid it free, folding it over and setting it atop the jacket.

The bed creaked as Victoria put a firm hand on his chest, pressing him onto his back. She looked at him with a devilish grin as she unfastened his belt then leaned in, kissing his shoulders and down the valley between his chest muscles. Blindly, her fingers fumbled with his trouser buttons. No zipper.

With an impatient growl, Allan twisted his leg, pulled her down onto the bed, and rolled, straddling her. "My turn," he said, pinning her hands by her sides

"But I'm the squire," she insisted, playfully struggling against him. "This is my job."

He pinned her arms back and pressed his weight down. His lips brushed against hers, tracing them with kisses. "And I said it goes both ways, remember?"

Victoria rolled her head to the side giving him access as Allan kissed along her neck. She let out a soft moan as his breath and lips caressed her skin with light nips. He moved down to her shoulders and chest, his advance halted by the collar of her cotton shirt. He followed the V-neck down, lips gliding across every bit of flesh the shirt allowed. His hand slid down her arms, along her sides. Lifting himself up, Allan pulled her shirt up and off, allowing her a moment's freedom before he tossed it somewhere behind him and pressed her back down on the bed, his lips seeking the newly exposed skin.

One by one he slid the lavender brassiere straps from her shoulder, kissing where they had been. The tingles rolled through her with each touch, somehow feeling deeper within her than mere sensation. But it wasn't just the ripples of energy that made her close her eyes as his hands and lips maneuvered lower, caressing her breasts while moving down between them. There was an electric, misty quality to it all, something new and only imagined in dreams. It felt as though her being was somehow floating an inch outside her flesh, extended beyond it, allowing her to feel more of him than where they simply touched.

Allan's lips were moving lower now, beneath her breasts. She bit her lip lightly as she felt the tip of his tongue play along the slope below her sternum and down along her stomach. He kissed along the edge of her jeans, the heat of his breath wafting deeper beneath them. Unfastening the button, he kissed lower. The zipper gave, sliding down as he pulled her jeans open. Victoria looked down to see his playful half-grin, then he pulled her jeans and underwear down over her hips. She shifted, allowing him to pull them lower, slowly peeling them down her thighs. Allan kissed her knees as the fabric slid away and his hands caressed her calves.

"Damn," he growled as he reached her sneakers, blocking the pants' descent.

Desperate to return to business, Victoria moved to help him, he pressed her back with a gentle hand.

"No. Let me do this."

She lay back and closed her eyes. His rough hand slid slowly down the length of her body, pausing to play across the hardened nipple still hidden beneath her brassiere. Allan made short work of the offending shoes, quickly removing them and setting them aside before he could continue his knightly task. The jeans hit the floor with a muted *plop*.

He gazed up at her, his eyes exploring her body, naked save the unstrapped bra. He nuzzled her knee, taking his time as he worked his way back up her legs, parting her thighs with kisses. Victoria let out a quivering sigh as Allan's breath caressed her sex. He moved in slower, the outside edge of his lips brushing against her as he explored the seam of her leg, still not touching her swollen lips, then kissing down the other side, breathing her in, teasing her.

She gasped as his tongue moved in, playing across her. Mouth open, she closed her eyes and savored the sensations, both physical and the rolling energy passing between them, working its way through every vein. She felt as though they were expanding, filling the room, a merging of energy and spirit. There was something more, something strange, yet beautiful. Victoria's eyes parted and there, the nucleus of that new and unfelt energy, was Ibenus, resting on the dresser. A corona of refracting ceiling lights gleamed off the polished bronze.

The thought of what that feeling was didn't have time to solidify as the waves and shocks of pleasure washed over her, drawing in and then exploding out. One hand grasped at the sheets as her other found the back of Allan's head. She clutched him there, desperate to hold him, feel some anchor before she might jolt away from him. A long trembling whimper escaped her lips, and she bit down before the entire house might hear.

Panting, she pulled herself away from him. She clutched his hand and groaned, "Kiss me."

He crawled up on top of her, their naked skin gliding across each other's with those rippling tingles. Pulling him close they kissed deeply, the passion mounting. She clumsily tried to maneuver off those cursed button trousers of his until she managed to slide them off. Chuckling at her eagerness, Allan pressed the full length of his body against hers, and she wrapped her legs around him.

They rocked together in unison. The energy mounted in waves and she met his brown eyes. "I love you." The word just slipped out but they were no less true. She been in love before, made love before, but nothing as this, pure and glowing.

He paused, seeming to weigh those words for an eternity that only lasted a heartbeat. "I love you, too."

"I love you," she repeated, then led him inside her, body and soul.

Victoria awoke with a start. She lay against him, her back pressed to Allan's chest and his arms around her. He shifted, awake as well. She turned her head, searching for the clock in the foreign room, wondering what time it was and what had woken them.

"Allan," Sam called from beyond the door, followed by pounding.

Shit! Victoria scrambled in a tangle of sheets to get behind Allan as the pounding came again.

"What?" Allan called back, sitting up.

There was no way she could hide in the bed if Sam opened the door. Maybe she could crawl behind it. Then she remembered the jeans and underwear strewn chaotically on the floor near the door.

"We have a problem." The handle rattled and began to open. Victoria rolled down onto the floor in a silent, ungraceful move she hadn't performed since the early days of college.

"Hey," Allan blurted, rolling on his side to create a human wall. "I'm naked, here. What is it?"

Victoria peered through the gap beneath the bed, waiting for the door to open. *Don't come in. Don't come in. Don't come in.*

"We're fucked," Sam said through the still-cracked door. "Master Turgen called an emergency meeting. We've been ID'd."

EPISODE 160

PARIS KILL SQUAD

"Welcome back, cryptozoologists," TommyD says as the Monster Seekers logo dissolves. A subtle crease at the edge of the frame reveals the clean white wall behind him to be a large suspended sheet. While the background has changed, the signature fedora and black sunglasses still mask his face. "I've been on a fishing trip and I'm happy to say that I've caught us a big one.

"Shortly after my last episode, where I discussed the Bird Man of Amiens, I was contacted by a gentleman in Paris, France, who videoed a close encounter of his own."

The image cuts to the familiar shaky cell phone footage as the smoking man slaps his friend's arm and the camera spins in time to catch the baby-faced screamer emerging from the shadows.

"My contact, who understandably wishes to remain anonymous, asked my opinion of it and I urged him to post it. It wasn't long before the footage went viral and our mysterious monster killers found it. It only took them three days to deduce where the video was shot. By that time, I was already there."

A daytime photograph of the same narrow street slides into view. "After the hidden cameras in Amiens were stolen, I decided on a different approach to either film these monsters or film those individuals that kill them."

The image changes to a shot of the alley, looking down from the side, this time at night. "At 0200 hours, a white van circled the block and two individuals systematically destroyed every streetlight within two blocks."

Several more pictures scroll past, each holding for a full second before changing, all taken from the same vantage point; then they zoom in on the van. One shows a blond man with close-cropped hair and slender glasses aiming down the barrel of a pellet gun. Another shows him turning his head toward an unseen driver. The next shows a bald black man peering down the air rifle's sight. Then it freezes and zooms closer on the last. The black man is smiling broadly, his elated expression so photogenic that it wouldn't look out of place in a magazine ad selling arms to would-be vandals.

"The following morning at 0300 hours the same van drove past." Pictures play as TommyD speaks, telling the story in hi-res images. "The vehicle stopped and four masked individuals exited, each armed with pistols and medieval weapons. They broke down the door and entered an abandoned apartment as the vehicle drove away. Eighteen minutes later the van returned and these two men removed articles from inside it before going back into the building. You can see by this close-up that the second one fits the size and race of the man pictured shooting out the lights. Neighbors reported shots fired and twelve minutes later all four perps ran back to the vehicle and fled the scene."

The image changes to video of two white police cars, blue lights strobing off the building fronts, the glare reflecting in windows. "Officers arrived half an hour later. Sources say that while no bodies were discovered, blood and shell casings were found at the scene. Whatever unfolded inside the apartment remains a mystery.

"But mysteries exist to be solved, my friends. We've identified this man," the close-up of the smiling black shooter fills one half of the screen, "as Luc Renault." A second picture slides into the other half of the screen. A large man, younger, but with the same broad toothy grin, poses for the camera. Muscles bulge from beneath a bright crimson jersey with a black collar.

"Renault played left prop for the Rugby Club Toulonnais until 2009 when he left at the height of his career. The retirement was sudden and without warning."

The images zoom in until only the smiling faces fill the screen. "Take a good look, cryptozoologists. This man is a piece in the puzzle. When we find him, we'll find our answers. Mister Renault, when you see this, and I have no doubt you will, this is your chance to do the right thing and share with the world what you know. This is TommyD, signing out."

CHAPTER 13

Gerhard closed his eyes, fleeing to the exquisite darkness behind his lids. It felt as though a steel ring pressed along the inner walls of his skull, ratcheting wider with every heartbeat, threatening to crack its way out. After the ceremony, he'd enjoyed several toasts with his new family. Never one to indulge in excess, he'd played it safe, sipping while they drank the expensive champagne and a Napoleon cognac that Master Turgen had opened for the occasion. He'd handled himself well. Then Master Schmidt had challenged him to a drinking contest over a bottle of schnapps.

Bastard.

The old man now sat at the front of the briefing room, freshly shaved and thin hair combed, sipping his coffee with no apparent signs of any hangover at all.

Gerhard winced as the door thumped. He squinted as Chaya came inside wearing a baggy shirt with no sleeves. Curly strands of hair poked awkwardly from her thick ponytail.

"What happened?" she asked.

"Have a seat," Master Turgen said. "Did you find everyone?"

"They're on their way," Sam said, following Chaya into the room. She took a seat at the computer by the front.

The others filed in shortly after, all asking what the emergency was.

"Now that we're all here," Turgen gestured toward Sam.

"Right." She tapped her mouse. "This hit the boards this morning."

Heavy metal blasted from the speakers along the wall, setting Gerhard's teeth on edge. He couldn't look at the video, having endured it once already. Instead, his gaze moved to the knights now seeing it for the first time.

The music faded down to be replaced by TommyD's angry voice, blaring out just that one decibel too high. "Welcome back, cryptozoologists. I've been on a fishing trip and I'm happy to say that I've caught us a big one."

Allan's and Orlovski's eyes widened as the video progressed, their faces falling with each second. Disbelief. Anger. Fear. Eyes locked onto the screen, Victoria's hand slid to Allan's knee, her open mouth a mixture of dread and pain, then closed into a scowl of the purest hatred. Luc watched the video for the second time, his expression cold and unreadable, as if he were listening to a doctor read a prognosis from a chart.

All eyes save Turgen's and Schmidt's turned to Luc as his name was spoken, but the big man remained impassive.

"What the hell do we do?" Chaya asked as the video wound to a close.

"We fucked up," Orlovski muttered.

"First things first," Master Turgen said after the screen went dark. "I want that van gone. Destroy it. I want no trace that it ever existed."

"Right away," Allan said. "It's not traceable to us."

"Good. Taras, secure a replacement vehicle. Make the necessary modifications."

Orlovski nodded.

"Luc, I'm sorry. We always knew this was a possibility. You're off the Paris team."

Luc's lips tightened to a flat line.

"How could they ID him?" Chaya blurted. "Just a photograph? How could he put that together so fast?"

"It only takes one person to recognize him," Allan said.

"Yeah, but that guy doesn't exactly look like a rugby fan."

"Maybe one of his contacts is."

Gerhard squeezed Umatri in his lap. "What do we do about this man?"

"Him?" Master Turgen asked, motioning to the screen. "Nothing. He's an irritation, but hardly the first to identify one of us." He turned to Schmidt. "Remember that British exposé in '92?"

Schmidt harrumphed humorlessly.

"This man is extremely dangerous," Allan said.

Turgen rested both hands on the cane between his knees. "I agree. He's just outed one of our knights. Luc will need to relocate. We'll get him out of Europe."

"But my family," Luc said, breaking the silence. "My nieces. I can't leave them."

"Nothing permanent, Luc." Turgen raised his palm. "But for the moment you need to go away. You can't visit them, either. This TommyD is surely watching them."

"He isn't charged with anything," Victoria said. "The video said no bodies. The most anyone could get him on is criminal damage for the lights, and they'd have to prove it was him. The picture proves nothing."

Schmidt shook his head. "It's not worth the risk. It could link him to the rest of us if he's spotted again."

"What happened to the bodies?" Gerhard asked. "Did he move them?"

Allan shook his head. "If TommyD knew what was in there he wouldn't have gone inside."

Chaya snorted. "He might have. He has no idea what he's playing with."

"Doubt it. He'd have shown that if he could. I'm sure the mantismeres reclaimed them once we'd left so no one would find them."

"The bugs hid them?" Gerhard asked.

"Don't let appearances fool you," Turgen said. "Demons might resemble animals, but they're not. They're extremely intelligent, retaining all the knowledge of everyone they've ever possessed. They'd know the bodies would lead people toward them. I imagine they've disposed of or eaten them by now."

"But why would they care?" Victoria asked. "The police can't hurt them."

"They can't harm the spirit, but destroying the body is quite possible. Fire. Explosion."

"Train," Orlovski added.

The old man bobbed an approving finger at him. "Destroying the body simply requires punishing it enough."

"So without Luc," Orlovski said, "what does that leave us?"

Schmidt blew a long sigh. "You'll have Allan, Chaya, Gerhard, Malcolm, and yourself with Samantha and Victoria running support. Five knights killed Tiamat and an army of demons."

"Naked," Allan added. "Don't forget that we were naked."

"I have full faith you can handle it." Schmidt said.

"That's rough," Matt said with a groan. His short sandy hair jutted out in every direction in a spectacular achievement of bed-head. "How's he taking it?"

Allan shook his head. The little window of him in the lower corner of the screen mimicked the movement, though opposite. Whether real or imagined, he could still smell Victoria's scent in the bedroom. Normally he'd have these chats with Matt in the Library, but Allan needed privacy for this one. He needed his best friend. "Not well. He hasn't said anything to me yet, but … Remember how he looked when the chateau was burned and we had to empty it out?"

"Ooh," Matt said with a wince. "So volcano pissed?"

"Yeah. He met with the Masters privately after the meeting. Not sure what they talked about, but I can promise he's still going to have to leave Europe."

Matt sipped from a giant gray coffee mug shaped like an Easter Island head. "Sucks that it happened, but we'll be more than happy to take him."

"Master Sonu has first dibs."

"Bullshit. Seriously, can you imagine Luc in Asia? He's like six seven. Just picture him trying to blend in."

Allan laughed. "I'm not saying he'll go there. They just have first call. Their territory is the largest."

Matt flapped his thumb and fingers together like a talking hand. "Dude, we've got four people in Chile. We don't even have a Master here. We're like the bastard children."

"That's not always a bad thing."

"No," he conceded with a slight shrug. "It's not. Once this Paris thing is over you should come down, give us a chance to meet this apprentice of yours."

"Love to," Allan said, grateful Matt had given him the opening he needed. "I, um, wanted to talk to you about something."

"What's up?"

"It's Victoria ... last night, after the knighting ... well—" A pang of terror shot through Allan's nerves as a baby's wail came through the speakers, invoking the memory of screamers surging up the hole.

Matt turned and looked at the camera. "Crap, hold that thought." He stood and left, leaving Allan the view of the Chilean Archives. They were smaller, only a few metal bookshelves and a glass case of visible artifacts.

Allan let out a long breath. *Just say it. He'll understand.*

A minute later, the crying slowed, then puttered out. Continuing to wait, Allan cemented his resolve.

"Here we go," Matt said, returning to frame, a fat-cheeked baby with olive skin and raven black hair in his arms. "Sorry about that, man." He waved the baby's hand at the camera. "I'm sorry, Uncle Allan."

"It's all right, Gabi," Allan said, his voice that high soothing tone he reserved only for children and animals.

Gabi seemed more interest in her toes.

"So," Matt said adjusting his hold on the infant. "Where were we?"

"I'm in love with Victoria."

Matt just stared at him. Then an amused smile curled at the corner of his lips. "What?"

"I'm in love with her," he repeated, enjoying the sound of it, enjoying telling someone. God, he needed that.

"You've known her a week."

"I know." He licked his lips. "I know how it sounds."

"It sounds flat fuck crazy." He gave an exaggerated grimace and looked down at the baby. "Sorry."

"I know. And if you had told me the same thing a week after you met Luiza I'd have said the same thing to you. Believe me, I know how this sounds."

"Good. Have you told her this?"

"She said it first. We, um, had sex last night."

"Hmm. Okay. I think there's an unwritten rule about doing your apprentice, but saying you're in love ... I'd call the screwing the least of the problems."

"I know," Allan said a bit more forcefully than intended. "But just hear me out." He drew a breath. "I've been in love before, at least I thought I was, but that was different. Teenage boy chock-full of hormones, all that. But with Victoria it's ... it's so ... different. This is more like how I feel with Ibenus than I ever have with a person. I mean, the fact I asked her to be my squire right off was weird, but I just had to. Like, I couldn't *not* do it. You know me. I'm not rash. Does that sound like something I'd do?"

Matt shook his head.

"At first I assumed it was a crush. I was thinking about her all the time. But then last night ... When you bonded with Dämoren, like fully bonded after Clay died and you inherited her, did you have this feeling like you were unraveled and then ..." he circled his hands, trying to formulate the words, "more entwined when you came back together?"

Matt leaned back, seeming to chew on it. He was probably the worst knight to ask that question to. Matt had bonded as a child when a bullet from the holy revolver lodged in his chest. To save him, Dämoren had done something no other holy weapon had ever done. It possessed him, bonding directly to him instead of simply through the weapon. The angel had once even manifested in Matt, transforming him into the living embodiment of itself. Finally, he said, "Sort of, I suppose. It was kind of like that."

"Have you ever done that with Luiza?"

"No. Well, it's different. I love her. We love each other very much, but the weapon bond is ... different."

"So never the unmaking?"

"No," he said, obviously a bit uncomfortable with the subject. "I can feel that she loves me. We do connect."

"I don't doubt that, Matt. But last night, with Victoria, it was that same feeling." He twined his fingers. "We merged. And Ibenus merged as well."

"Ibenus was in bed with you?"

"No! Oh God, nothing like that. She was in the room."

"Oh good. I was about to say ..." He had a grimace.

Allan laughed. "But, even then, I could feel her as well. I'm saying that Ibenus was *in* that merging. Spiritually," he clarified.

Matt frowned. "So Ibenus bonded with Victoria?"

"No. At least I don't think so. We haven't talked about it. This morning we got interrupted when that video hit the web."

"Have you told anyone else about this?"

"Just you, mate."

"And Gabi."

"Of course."

"Don't worry. She won't tell." He grinned and kissed his daughter's head. "Will you?"

Gabi peered up at him like she just realized Matt was there.

"Well you need to talk to Victoria," Matt said after a while. "But don't just outright ask about Ibenus. Watch her. Watch how she looks at it. Sidelong glances, maybe a need to touch the blade, anything like that. She might not know if she's bonded, so don't point her that direction. If she is, she'll naturally go there. Got it?"

Allan nodded. "Have you ever heard about anything like this?"

Matt shrugged. "No, but the weapons are all different. My whole life has been a first-case scenario, so who knows. But don't jump to conclusions just yet, man. Let it happen. And for Christ's sake don't let Turgen or Schmidt hear about this."

"Of course not."

"Good. This is dangerous territory, man. You be careful."

Victoria zoomed in on a photograph of an arched tunnel burrowed into a low hill, checking it in relation to a street view image in an adjoining browser window. "This one looks promising."

"Which one?" Allan rolled his chair beside hers. The back of his hand found her leg, his fingers giving a subtle caress.

She read the grid points they'd laid over the city map. "Location G 21." Victoria gave him a quick smile and wink. Despite the calamity starting their day, they'd found every opportunity for secret smiles and gestures. Touches, even a few quick, stolen kisses when they were alone and out of view of the mansion's cameras. It felt like primary school. Childish, true, but each moment of affection, given or received, filled her with an unbelievable joy. She'd never felt anything like this before. Though, she did wonder if she had thought that every time she'd felt love but knew it wasn't true. This was something more.

"Got it," Sam said at her own desk. "Oh, this definitely could work."

Allan reached over to Victoria's mouse and zoomed out on the image. "Not the best escape but I definitely like it. We'll put it on the options list."

"Best contender so far," Victoria said.

"As long as there's no high buildings looking down on it," Sam growled.

An angry pang of guilt killed the moment's joy at Allan's touch. Victoria hadn't known Luc was a former athlete. She'd only given his name, all their names, at least the ones she'd gleaned. TommyD's stunt put her at risk. What if they figured out she'd tipped him off? Would they kill her? Would Allan hate her? *Fuck TommyD.* The bastard had known she was still with them, yet he had to flaunt that he knew something about them. Now the world knew and Luc was suffering for it. Luc had been kind to her. He was Allan's friend, and now he was leaving. No seeing his family, just headed off to wherever they decided.

Now she was trapped. She couldn't tell Allan. Turgen already didn't trust her and hearing that she'd shared their information would be the end of her there. No doubt about it at all. Even if she expressed regret, it was still too late. The damage was irrevocable now. She wanted to tell TommyD exactly what he could do with that camera of his, but he had her cold. If she threatened to cut off his intel he could spill everything he already had and the Valducans would know she betrayed them. She glanced at Sam. Her friend. Sam who forgave her and made Victoria laugh with her stupid jokes and funta and whispered confidences. No telling how many pictures TommyD had of her in the van.

You really screwed this one up, didn't you? If she'd just waited to make her report, waited until she'd gotten to know them, to *know* Allan and Sam or Luc she'd have done it different. But it was too late now.

Allan gave her leg a quick squeeze before he rolled back to his monitor.

She smiled at him and he winked. Maybe he'd understand. If she couldn't stay, would he leave with her? They could go back to England together. Hell, they could go anywhere they wanted, just the two of them. They—

Ibenus' hilt glinted at Allan's belt. There'd never just be the two of them. *It* would always be the barrier. The other woman. Any fantasy of Allan running away with her withered to dust as she eyed the smooth golden metal sandwiched between black wood grips, seeming to call her hand. Last night she'd noticed how beautiful the bronze weapon truly was, but Allan's ... obsession with it. He'd never run away with her. He'd say that Ibenus wouldn't let him. A sword. She'd lose him to a bloody sword.

Ibenus wouldn't betray him, either. The bitter words rang through her head. *Fuck TommyD.*

Victoria licked her lips. She needed to focus. Dreaming of running off with Allan or pounding TommyD's head in wouldn't help. She needed to keep him from posting anything else. Get him to back off. There was no chance he'd stop altogether, but maybe for a little while, long enough for her to gather herself. She could tell him they suspected her.

But he might just tell her to leave. No, she needed time. Time and an excuse why the updates would stop.

She sipped her cold tea and leaned back, mind racing. Her gaze passed over the open weapon vault. The weapons. She'd tell him she was reaching the inner circle. Say that she would get a weapon. That'd shut him up. *"Don't blow my cover, I'm about to get access to the prize."* Yeah, that could do it. Slip him right into her pocket until she could figure out what to do about him. She'd keep the message short, rushed, say she might be off the radar and not to make waves until he heard from her again.

There. Victoria grinned, staring at the screen with the G 30 entrance but not seeing it. She just needed a few minutes alone to send the message.

The library door opened, breaking her train of thought. Victoria looked up as Master Schmidt stepped inside. A man carrying a metal briefcase followed closely behind. Tattoos traced up his dark tanned arms, disappearing beneath the rolled-up sleeves. A machete with white carved handle hung at the waist of his jeans.

"Mal!" Sam said, springing to her feet.

"Hey there." He gave her a one-armed hug lifting her off her feet as she wrapped her arms around him.

"If it isn't the prodigal son." Allan rose and gave him a strong hug. "It's good to see you."

"You too, brother." He patted Allan on the back. "How have you been?"

"Busy." Allan turned to Victoria who was rising from her chair. "I want you to meet my apprentice, Victoria Martin. Victoria, this is Doctor Malcolm Romero, protector of Hounacier."

Mal looked at Victoria, then back to Allan. He smirked as if about to say something but decided against it. He extended his hand. A bright orange and blue tattooed eye filled his palm. "Pleasure to meet you."

She shook his hand. "Likewise. I've heard a lot about you."

He grinned. "Hope it wasn't all bad."

"Not all of it."

"So what's this about?" Sam flicked at the short black ponytail high on the back of Malcolm's head.

"That? Tasha asked me to grow it out again, so I'm giving it a shot. Finally long enough to pull back. It's been driving me nuts, falling into my eyes."

Sam frowned, almost imperceptibly. "I like you better without it."

"If I could still grow one, I would." Schmidt ran a hand across his wispy gray hair. "Enjoy it while it lasts."

"So what's this I hear of you getting engaged?" Allan asked. "You plan on inviting us or is it some voodoo-only affair?"

"We're not exactly engaged yet," Malcolm said. "Just talking about it. She's ... working it out."

"Oh."

"You know how it is." Malcolm touched the machete's hilt. "Relationships are difficult for our kind."

A bitter knot pulsed in Victoria's stomach.

"Yeah," Allan said casually, seeming to laugh it off but the words still stung. He glanced uncomfortably to Victoria.

"So what's in the case, Mal?" Sam asked, changing the subject.

"This?" He lifted it up and set it on the table. "Little housewarming gift." He removed a key from his pocket and unfastened the twin locks. "Now you need to treat this thing like it's plutonium or a canister of mustard gas."

"Oh, you didn't?" Allan's eyes widened like a kid finding a Christmas pony under the tree.

Malcolm thumbed the latches and opened the case. Expecting a weapon or some form of bomb, Victoria scrunched her nose at seeing a white marble mask glaring hatefully back at her. It was a woman's face, her mouth open impossibly wide, revealing a pair of long slender fangs. Stainless steel bars enclosed it like a wicket-keeper's face mask with one rod coming up through the open mouth, making it impossible to remove without cutting it.

Allan's fingers moved toward it, then seemed to think better of it. "Lamia?"

Malcolm nodded. "She'd been lurking around New Orleans since the time of Lafitte. Found out about her last year during that ... incident. Managed to track her down." He pulled the tightly-packed foam from around the weird sculpture. The bars connected to a black enameled metal plaque.

"Niriffo?" Sam asked, reading the single word engraved along the bottom.

"That was her name," Malcolm said. "Real nasty bitch, too. Spitter. Had a pair of ghouls under her. It'd been a hell of a lot easier to just have killed her but trapping one, especially a breed that powerful, was a rare opportunity. Don't expect me to try that again."

Schmidt reached in and touched the bars. "This is phenomenal."

"Hold on," Victoria said. "Trapped?"

"The demon is inside it," Malcolm said. "It can't escape unless you put it on, hence the cage. Breaking it will release the spirit, but it won't have a body to go to. Dangerous as hell, so it'll require a dedicated security system."

"We will start on that at once," Schmidt said, his fingers still tracing along the bars.

"But why trap it?" Victoria asked.

"Because it's the best damned ward made," Malcolm said. "No demon can even get close to it. The obsidian ghoul masks had a range of about fifteen feet. But this thing, I'm guessing double that. Mount it before the entrance or the weapon vault and no one that's demon-corrupted will get through."

"But it's alive in there?"

"Yeah."

Victoria sneered, meeting the mask's loathsome stare. "I think it would have been better to have killed it."

Malcolm gave Allan a grin. "I like her." He looked back at Victoria. "These things are bad news. If Master Turgen hadn't specially requested it, I wouldn't have made it. But aside from holy weapons, these are the best weapons we have."

"Is this for Paris, then?"

"No," he laughed. "No, this needs to stay here. It's too fragile and far too dangerous to take in the field."

Good, she thought. The bloody thing was creepy as hell. It was as if those hateful white eyes were boring directly into her, cursing her. Then something clicked. *New Orleans.* She looked at the machete on Malcolm's belt, then the tattoos. "You're the Machete Man. From the video."

Malcolm gave a sour smile. "Yeah. Bad day and someone caught it on their phone." He blew out a sigh. "Not my finest moment."

"You heard about Luc?" Allan asked.

Malcolm grunted. "Already talked with him. He's not taking it too well."

"Can't blame him."

"Nope. Not in the least." Malcolm shook his head. "Of course I'll have to rethink my plans for Paris."

"What do you have in mind?"

"I got something." Malcolm licked his lips, then glanced at Schmidt so fast Victoria wondered if anyone but her noticed it. "Might sound crazy but I think it'll work."

"You want to share it?" Allan asked.

"Not yet. You find me a list of entrances?"

"Still working on it. We have a few possibilities so far."

"Good." Malcolm stuffed the foam back into the case and closed it. "Once I'm done with Master Turgen, I'll come back down and help."

Two nights later, they filed into the briefing room. Allan grunted as he lowered into a seat near the edge of the front row. Between scouring maps, photographs, practicing drills and climbing exercises, he ached from eyeballs to toes. Victoria slid in beside him, giving a subtle wink as her back was to the room. He smiled back.

Once this job was over he was going to take Matt up on that offer and take her to South America for a much-needed escape. Master Turgen wouldn't like it, of course, Allan skipping off to the other side of the world at the same time Luc was slated to go to Chile. But after a hunt this large they all deserved a little holiday. Of course he'd use the argument that he needed to train Victoria, tour the various archives. No one could argue with that logic. It was winter where Matt was. Maybe a little skiing was in order to relax. Then, after the slopes, he and Victoria could spend some time warming each other up with no Masters in the same hemisphere.

"This looks to be everyone," Malcolm said, standing from his seat. He thumbed the remote, bringing up a multi-colored map of the Paris underground onto the screen.

"In going over the reports of these mantismeres and encounters with the previous two eels, we have a lot of obstacles. The catacombs are enormous, up to seven levels connected by slopes and vertical well shafts. Large portions are either partially or completely flooded. Between that and cave-ins, most maps are only eighty percent accurate at best, at least for the hard to reach zones." He thumbed the remote and several areas of the map turned dark red. "We need to treat the catacombs as equal a threat as the demons. We can get trapped or, if one of us is injured, we might not be able to get them out. The water is damned cold and keeping dry is probably going to be impossible. Except for Orlovski."

Orlovski grinned and patted his kukri.

"Sound doesn't carry very far," Malcolm continued, "but firing a gun, even suppressed can cause hearing loss. Do not fire an unsuppressed weapon unless you have no choice. Ricochets are another concern. Chaya has made us all low-velocity ammunition with gem tips. Hopefully that'll cut it down but be aware of your field of fire if you do shoot. If we determine which elements hurt these mantismeres, she's going to bring enough gear for us to manufacture that type of ammo. We're all going to help her with that. Until then, if you shoot one, keep track of what gems and metals don't work. We'll narrow it down until we find it.

"Radios are another problem. Even on the highest levels, GPS won't work. Reception between hunters will be impossible over long distances, which means that once we go in, we're effectively cut off from the outside world, even each other. So to help with that, in addition to loading bullets, Chaya has something for us." He extended a hand to Chaya, who stood up.

She picked up a clunky gray box wrapped in tape and linked to one of the tubular night vision cameras with a coiled wire. "In order to boost our signal strength, we'll be setting radio repeaters wherever we need. By linking them to our cameras we can keep an eye on them or anything else moving around behind us. I coded them for our frequencies, so when they pick it up they'll retransmit it from that point. However, they're heavy so each hunter will need to carry one in. We also won't have near enough to cover the whole system so we'll have to move them regularly as we search."

"How many do we have?" Turgen asked.

"Nine. We'll need additional parts before we can make more."

"We've already put in an order," Allan added.

The old man nodded.

"The biggest hindrance is battery life," Chaya continued. "They pull a lot of juice to boost the signal so the cameras are now motion-activated instead of constant feed. When something trips them, they'll activate for two minutes after movement stops. If one of them goes dead, it'll break the entire chain, so we can't let them run dry, or leave them somewhere where they might get found."

The hunters nodded.

"On the subject of batteries," Malcolm said. "If your lights go out, you'll never make it out of there. We'll all keep extra batteries and lights. However, we're going to keep them dim red. That way bright lights don't kill our night vision."

"What about night vision goggles?" Gerhard asked.

"We'll have some nightscopes with us but we don't want to wear them. They're fine if you're shooting, but they distort your depth perception too much for using a holy weapon. Also, a big tube off your face is clunky and there's no way to keep the lens clean."

"Easy to say if you can see in the dark," Orlovski said, eliciting a few chuckles.

Malcolm grinned. "We all have our gifts."

Victoria leaned over to Allan's ear, "What does that mean?" she asked, her voice low.

"Tattoos," Allan whispered. "Each one gives him a power. One is seeing in the dark."

"In addition to all of this gear," Malcolm continued, "we're going to be carrying in plenty of food, water, and one med bag per team. We'll be down there for eight, maybe up to twelve hours at a time, so your kits are going to be heavy."

Allan raised his hand "How many teams?"

"Two." Malcolm flipped through some slides, stopping at an image of the tunnel at G 21. "We'll start here. Teams will go in." He flipped to another map of the tunnels, zoomed in on those around G 21. "Well set up a supply cache here, then continue down the southern branch to this intersection. Drop a camera there and Team 1 will continue on while Team 2 will circle around through this tunnel, meeting at this chamber. If there's any demons in there, we'll herd them. Otherwise they'll just lead us around indefinitely. Once we've made sure a region is clean, we'll pull out our cameras and move on to the next deep zone."

"Who are the teams?" Turgen asked.

"Ah." Malcolm cleared his throat. "Allan and I will serve as team leaders. The teams will be broken down on strengths and weaknesses. Allan's team will consist of him, Orlovski, and Gerhard. Orlovski can move across water, and while Gerhard is our newest knight, Umatri can warn of unseen threats."

"There's only five knights," Sam muttered, echoing Allan's thought.

What are you doing, Mal?

"My team will consist of myself, Chaya, and Master Schmidt."

A sudden burst of coughs and gasps filled the room.

"Excuse me," Turgen said. "You wish to take Max?"

Malcolm nodded. "I do."

"Absolutely not."

"Let me explain." Malcolm raised a finger. "Master Schmidt is an active knight. He will not be front-line but we need him. Specifically, we require Lukrasus."

"Malcolm, you just explained how physically difficult this will be. Max is seventy-five years old, do you—?"

Schmidt put a hand on Turgen's shoulder. "I can speak for myself, Alex."

Turgen let out a growling sigh and leaned back, that nearly forgotten fiery anger now in full force.

"Why do you require that I join?" Schmidt asked.

"Simple," Malcolm said. "You can move up walls. With Ibenus, Allan can move down any shafts providing he has room to swing, but no one can move up without serious risk. Lukrasus would allow you to move up and down. You can also attach ropes and act as short-range scout. You will not be asked to engage. That's for Chaya, myself, and the other team. Luc can serve as Base Knight in your absence."

Allan shook his head. No wonder Malcolm hadn't wanted to discuss the plan beforehand. It was mad.

Turgen leaned over, his voice calm and sympathetic, "If you're injured, they won't be able to get you out. You can't carry anyone if they're hurt."

Schmidt ran a finger across his moustache, seeming to mull it over. "I accept."

Allan blinked. *He can't be serious.*

"Max," Turgen pleaded. "Be reasonable. Please, I beg you."

"I am," Schmidt said. "I'm Lukrasus' protector. She is needed, and it's my duty to carry her when she is."

The remaining hunters exchanged looks but no one dared speak.

Malcolm gave a relieved smile. "Thank you, sir."

"When do we leave?"

"Tomorrow."

CHAPTER 14

They arrived shortly after sunrise, approaching in a pair of white, Mercedes-Benz cargo vans decorated with large magnetic signs emblazoned with an orange telecom logo. Allan slowed as he neared a battered chain link gate.

"Site's clear," Sam said from the neighboring seat, her voice echoing through his ear bud. She stared at the screen in her lap, watching the twin video feeds of G 21. The night before, shortly after their arrival in Paris, Malcolm had set the cameras in place.

Malcolm's voice came through the radio. "Let's do this."

Allan stopped just past the entrance and Orlovski pulled open the side door. Casually, the Russian strolled to the fence, tool belt slung at his side and his head low, face hidden beneath a yellow hardhat and mirrored sunglasses. He stopped at the gate and fidgeted with the padlock before pulling the chain loose and swinging it open.

Allan turned in his seat and backed the vehicle onto the gravel drive running alongside a pair of rusted railway tracks. Trees and shrubs lined the narrow canyon, shading the debris and discarded refuse littering the old rail line. After twenty meters, he stopped before a graffiti-coated stone block wall. Cars moved along the road above it.

Malcolm backed the second van in beside the first as Orlovski closed the gate and trotted to catch up. Pulling on his own hardhat, Allan killed the engine and stepped out.

The sky was clear, save for the white contrails marring

the perfect blue. Shards of colored glass glinted amongst the gravel as Allan circled around to the back and opened the rear door. He heaved out one of the locking plastic bins and carried it to the tunnel's entrance, setting it down before the gated door. Two of the iron bars were bent apart, rendering the barrier meaningless. The other knights, all dressed in matching uniforms of work boots, khaki cargo pants, and cornflower blue shirts, carried the other lockers over as Orlovski leaned over the gate and popped it open with a cylindrical electric lock pick.

Cyclists and pedestrians passed along the walkway above, none giving more than a moment's glance down at the apparent work crew. Hinges squealed as the gate door swung open.

Orlovski and Chaya began moving the supplies inside as Allan made his way back to the van. He found Gerhard there, wrestling one of the heavier boxes out.

"Let me give you a hand." Allan took one end and together they lugged it back toward the cavernous opening.

Gerhard studied the entrance as they neared, his mouth tight, lips colorless, eyes hidden behind the wraparound sunglasses.

"You all right?" Allan whispered so the throat mic wouldn't catch it.

Gerhard didn't answer right away. He nodded, licked his lips, "Yes."

"Scared?"

He nodded again. "Not like before. Now I know what's inside. That should frighten me more but ..." He shook his head. "It doesn't."

"The fear lessens but it never goes away." They carried the box through the open gate and set it down beside the rest. The tunnel was fifteen feet wide, its floor mulched with crumpled wrappers, cigarette butts, bottles, syringes, and countless other bits of trash. Every inch of the walls was covered in layers of spray-paint: symbols, names of forgotten lovers, elaborate and defaced murals, and more penises than he could possibly count. One ten-foot section was nothing but red skulls. Allan looked up, wondering how the artists had so completely covered the high, arched ceiling. He preferred to imagine them scaling the walls like lizards rather than by any rational means.

Schmitt stepped inside and removed his sunglasses. His face pulled into a deep half-smile as he looked around. He inhaled a long breath through his nose and his smile widened like a man sliding into a new car. "What Allan didn't tell you, Gerhard, is that while it doesn't go away, you also learn to love it." The old man didn't lower his voice enough and his words came in through the radios. He flexed his fingers. "You miss it when you haven't hunted in a while."

"Are you afraid, Master Schmidt?" Gerhard asked.

"Of course I am. Fear heightens our senses. That's what it's for. And please, during this hunt, call me Max. Same for all of you. No need for titles down here."

Allan glanced back, sharing a look with Malcolm and Orlovski, carrying the last of the gear. Schmidt had never asked to be called Max before. He was ... well, he was Master Schmidt.

Schmidt gave a little grin like he'd just told a dirty joke in front of a nun without her noticing. Then it was gone. He returned his gaze down the tunnel without a word.

Today looks to be an interesting day, Allan thought as he headed back toward the vans. Victoria was already setting up in the first row of the lead vehicle beside Sam. Both wore uniforms, their hair hidden beneath ball caps.

"Are you ladies ready?" he asked.

Sam gave a thumbs-up as Victoria nodded.

"Just remember, when you go to stretch your legs, keep yourselves hidden. Stay near the tunnel."

Sam looked up from her monitor. "That'll put a damper on the shopping adventure we have planned once you're out of sight."

He smiled. "Just be careful. If you see anything strange let us know and be ready to evac. Drive if you can, through the tunnel if you can't."

The playful gleam in Sam's eyes disappeared. "Don't worry about us. We know what to do."

"You be safe," Victoria said, the concern palpable in her tone.

"We will be."

Her lips tightened, seeming to hold back the obvious

statement, the words she'd whispered when they'd last shared a private moment. *I'm not worried about them. You be safe Allan. You.* Instead, she slid two fingers in her shirt pocket and extended her hand low. The squared edge of a folded slip of paper peeked from beneath her downturned fingers. "Happy hunting." Her voice came through the radio.

Allan glanced at Sam who was now very pointedly not paying attention. The sudden disinterest as obvious as a bad lie. *I figured she knew by now.* He accepted Victoria's hand, squeezing it, his thumb playing over her fingers as he accepted the paper. "Thanks."

Palming it, he hurried back to the tunnel where the others were already looting through the open boxes. He found his and pulled the lid open. Ibenus rested inside, atop pads, lights, ballistic vest, fresh clothes, and other gear. Bent over, Allan glanced back that no one was watching and opened Victoria's note. In crisp black handwriting it read:

I never knew love until I found you. Be safe.
-V

Allan kissed the note and slipped it into his trouser pocket before unbuttoning his telecom worker's shirt to reveal the black, elastic undershirt. Tucking it away, he pulled out the vest and strapped it on. The weight of the three-liter water bladder felt strange against his back. He'd never worn one outside of cycling. Hunts had never lasted so long that dehydration was even considered. Allan secured the rubber drinking straw at his shoulder and pulled on knee and elbow pads. That done, he fastened his sword belt and gave Ibenus a pat. *Ready, Love?*

Malcolm scanned a pocket-sized tablet. "Entrance should be a hundred and forty feet ahead."

Allan checked his pistol. Aluminum with rock salt tips. Hopefully one of those would work. He holstered it in the shoulder rig, then glanced to Chaya to make sure she wasn't watching before removing the little Walther from his gear. The tiny gun was pointless, he knew. He'd never hit anything with it, but it was also his good luck charm. He clipped the holster inside his waistband. *Just like James Bond.* That done, Allan clicked the LED lamp atop his helmet, releasing a dull red beam.

"Ready," Chaya said like she'd just completed a race.

The others quickly followed as Allan secured the last of his gear and heaved on the pack holding the radio. "Ready."

"All right, then." Malcolm nodded to Allan and both readied their watches, thumb and forefinger on either side of the digital readouts. "Mark."

Allan pressed the buttons.

"We'll check in every fifteen. No exceptions." Malcolm looked across the knights, critically scanning their gear, then nodded. "Let's go to work. Gerhard, keep Umatri out."

"Yes." Gerhard drew the keris and held it before him.

Motioning to Orlovski, Allan picked up one side of a locker while the Russian took the other. Malcolm and Chaya carried a second box as Schmidt, noticeably less encumbered with gear, followed.

The sounds of birds and traffic faded away as they moved deeper into the tunnel. Their crimson lights played off the painted walls but the details were hidden in shadows. Allan wondered if the lights would be enough, even after they eyes had finished adjusting.

"Here we are," Malcolm said as they reached a knee-high gap in the wall. The floor leading into the hole was worn smooth. Above it, dominating the chaotic tangle of spray-painted names and dates, read, *"Monde Souterrain"*—Underworld—in huge white-trimmed black letters.

"Are you sure this is it?" Chaya asked, eliciting a grin from Allan.

Malcolm shrugged. "Just for that you get to be the first to find out."

"Ladies first, eh?"

"Something like that."

They lowered their locker and Chaya knelt before the gap, seeming to consider it before crawling through.

A few seconds later her she radioed, "Careful with that first step."

Malcolm slid the box next to the entrance before he scooted

inside and pulled it in after.

Allan waited as the others followed in turn. His job was to take up the rear, keeping the less experienced warriors safely in the middle. Once Orlovski was down, Allan gave one final glance back to the distant daylight and the parked vehicles before he crawled into the catacombs.

Remaining somewhat parallel, the crevice's floor and ceiling both dropped three feet to a landing, then dropped again like demented funhouse stairs. The dizzying kaleidoscope of multi-colored paint only added to the effect. He banged his head on the second landing and was immediately grateful for the helmet. The air seemed to cool with each level, the summer heat now forgotten. Grunts came through the ear bud and echoed ahead as he lowered his way toward moving red lights.

Allan flinched in surprise as his wrist buzzed with vibration.

"First check in," Malcolm said through the radio.

"Everything fine here," Victoria answered.

After the third landing, the crevice continued into a low passage, eight feet wide, over twenty feet long, and just above three feet high. The other knights crawled through the low tunnel, pushing and pulling their lockers, while Max merely strolled upright along the right wall, his sword before him.

Now that his eyes were adjusting, Allan had to squint as his light reflected off the stone walls only inches from his face. Had it been brighter, the glare would have been blinding.

"It's probably good that Luc couldn't come," Orlovski grunted as they pushed the box out of the low hall and into a large chamber. "He'd have hated this."

"Just wait until it gets really cramped," Malcolm replied.

Allan stood, his helmet nearly brushing the ceiling. The room was wide at the south end, stretching over thirty feet to where it ended at a hall leading east and west side. A crude bench was cut along one side. Painted silhouettes gave the appearance of figures seated along its length. Spent tea-light cups filled niches randomly scattered along the walls.

Chaya inspected an arched tunnel on the wider side of the room. "Is this it?"

Malcolm nodded. "Yeah."

"Look." She crouched, her headlamp aimed at the floor. "Tracks."

Allan scanned the dust and eons of cigarette ash, seeing the layers of tiny V-shaped tracks running back forth across the room. "This looks promising."

"Where do these go?" Max asked looking down either side of the north-side entrance.

"They wander off to the rest of the catacombs," Malcolm said. "We'll set up our equipment here and leave a repeater cam to watch our backs."

"And if someone wanders in?"

"Not likely, but if someone does, Sam and Victoria will spot 'em."

"Damn right we will," Sam said through the radio.

Max gave an approving nod. "Very well."

As the others pulled out their gear and stacked the lockers, Allan cleared out one of the larger niches and positioned one of the cameras to get a good view of the other exits. That done, Malcolm led them through the arched southern passage.

The graffiti tapered off fairly quickly as they headed down a gentle slope. The air was still as a tomb. It didn't smell like anything, just the dust and occasional whiffs of Orlovski's aftershave.

Sporadic cracks traced along the pale limestone ceiling, some even fringed with tiny stalactites. They passed several more chambers; some like square rooms with doorways and windows into the hall, others no more than rough alcoves. They inspected each one, following the branching dead-end passages as far as they led before continuing down the main corridor. As Malcolm had warned, the map wasn't entirely accurate. Mortared walls sealed several passages, while others intersected at different points than expected.

Allan repeatedly glanced at Gerhard's blade, hoping for, yet dreading movement, but Umatri remained still. The tiny tracks along the floor still assured them that their quarry had frequented the area.

Every fifteen minutes, either Malcolm or Allan sent their scheduled check in. Once they realized that they didn't have a signal, they headed back until they reestablished contact and set up one of the repeaters.

Orlovski stopped and inspected a relief of a man carved into the wall. A candle stub, affixed with melted wax, rose from his cupped hands. The artist appeared to have lost interest about halfway through, leaving only the upper portion in high detail. Someone had painted it like a mime, red lips, black triangular eye makeup drawn in marker on the white face.

Chaya's lip curled as she passed it. "That's creepy."

"You don't like clowns?" Orlovski asked.

"No. It's creepy that someone would spend all that time down here carving it."

Eventually they reached a small round antechamber. The passage continued south, but a smaller passage, one yard square and set a good five feet off the ground, led east.

"Here we are," Malcolm said, unzipping his pack. "These will loop around on each other, running a kilometer before rejoining." He unzipped the back and removed a repeater camera.

Max drew Lukrasus and walked up the wall. Kneeling above the small opening, he peered down. "Looks to go in eight, maybe nine meters. Tracks along the floor."

Allan watched the old man, wondering what it felt like to choose your own direction of gravity.

Still peering down the passage, Max clicked his headlamp, unleashing a brilliant beam. "The passage turns once it opens back up." Rising to his feet, he stepped off the edge and plunged through the sideways hole. Fifteen seconds later his voice came through the radio. "Looks clear. Coming back." Max shot through the opening, then slowed before dropping feet-first onto the wall beside Allan's head with a grunt.

"Are you all right?" Malcolm said.

Max coughed and nodded. "Fine. Fine." He stepped back onto the floor with a slight limp. "Not as spry as I used to be."

"Be careful," Allan said.

Max waved him off and stepped back onto the floor.

"Seriously," Malcolm said. "If you hurt yourself we'll have to carry you out."

"I didn't live this long by being reckless. Stop worrying. I get enough of that from Alex. He's like my mother."

"All right," Malcolm conceded. "Allan, which one do you want?"

"The little one." The question was for Max's benefit. The night before, they'd privately discussed Allan taking the longer route here, allowing the old man to take the shorter, easier one. Max's pride wouldn't stand for it if he knew. So they didn't let him.

Malcolm set his bag on the floor. "We'll take a quick breather, little food, then split up. Herd any demons around and meet in the middle."

Crawling through the tunnel wasn't as bad as Gerhard had expected. Once removing his backpack, still holding the radio booster, he simply tied it onto Orlovski's rope, crawled down the narrow passage, dropped the two meters to the floor on the other end, and pulled it through. However, the crevice he was currently navigating was infinitely worse.

The horizontal gap was wide enough to fully extend his arms, but so narrow that his helmet had only a few centimeters clearance before contacting either the floor or ceiling. He lay face down, unable to lift his head enough to see ahead as he wormed his way with infinitesimal, jerky movements.

Bend the knees and elbows, push. Bend the knees and elbows, push.

"Almost done," Allan said ahead.

Dust rained down as Gerhard's helmet thumped the ceiling. He imagined the incredible weight pressing down on this unsupported and ancient roof. If it collapsed, would it kill him instantly or would he simply bleed out as Allan and Orlovski futilely dug for him from either end? At least he'd be buried with Umatri, but the idea did nothing to comfort him.

Bend the knees and elbows, push.

Sweat and the condensed humidity of his breath in the unmoving air ran down his face, gathering at the tip of his nose. He imagined hearing that horrible baby's cry as he was trapped here, unable to move or turn his head as chitinous feet scuttled toward him. The thought pushed him faster.

"Almost," Allan said, closer now.

Gerhard pushed and hands grabbed his shoulders and pulled. Allan got hold of the drag handle at the back of his vest, and together they slid Gerhard out and into a narrow room.

"Thank you," Gerhard panted, crawling to his feet.

"Just take a breather." Allan peered back down the gap. "All right, Taras, you're up."

Gerhard walked to the back of the chamber, savoring the freedom of movement. He'd never been claustrophobic, but he could now sympathize with those afflicted. He wiped the sweat off his face, smearing the grit and dust into mud. When he'd confessed that he was afraid, that was true, but not full truth. Gerhard's worry wasn't of the monsters. It was of something far less tangible.

He knew his place now, for the first time in his life. He was a knight. Husband of an angel. When they met these demons he wouldn't cower, he wouldn't freeze or let the others do the fighting. He needed to give Umatri that fiery blood. It was the only way to feel worthy of what he now was, and his fear was that of disappointment.

A muted buzz came from Allan's direction. The Englishman pressed his watch, silencing it. "This is Allan, checking in."

The scrapes and huffs of Orlovski slithering the gap sounded eerily loud in the catacomb's otherwise perfect silence.

"Can anyone hear me?"

Gerhard, tapped his ear bud. "My radio didn't hear you."

Allan checked his radio. "This is Allan. Checking in."

Gerhard shook his head.

"Mal, Victoria, Sam, does anyone copy?"

Again, no response.

"You try," Allan said.

"This is Gerhard. Does anyone copy?"

Silence.

"I don't hear anyone," Orlovski called from the gap.

"I haven't heard anyone on the radio in a while," Gerhard said, thinking back. There'd always been little comments or grunts picked up by the other knights' throat mics. An annoying amount. "Nothing since we started this." He gestured to the gap. "Maybe the signal can't get through."

Allan shook his head and look around. "But we should still hear each other."

"Should we go back?"

"I'm almost out," Orlovski shouted. "And I don't want to get thorough just to turn around and do this again."

"No." Allan looked up the passage. "We're almost to the junction. Check Umatri."

Gerhard drew the keris. The blade was still.

"We're over halfway," Allan called back to Orlovski. "Let's get to the rendezvous, see if Malcolm is there, then head back down the other passage. It'd take less time."

"Good enough for me."

Once Orlovski had made it another meter, Allan and Gerhard helped pull him the rest of the way.

"I don't care what's ahead," the Russian grumbled as he crawled to his feet. "I'll fight the devil himself before I'd do that again."

"I wouldn't go that far." Allan clicked his radio off, then on, and shook his head. "Come on, we're almost there."

The passage wound several times before gently sloping down. Occasional graffiti tag still marked the walls. The oldest Gerhard spied was a carving dated 1741, accompanied by a pair of names. Allan continued calling on the radio, but to no effect. Eventually the tunnel leveled out. After another turn, Gerhard's stomach sank when he saw their lights reflecting off the floor, casting the ceiling in red. Flooded.

"This is going to be fun," Allan said.

A narrow shelf, no more than ten centimeters wide, ran along one wall a hand's length above the water's surface. The tiny V-shaped footprints followed it like an earthen highway.

Gerhard clicked his light, strengthening the beam. The passage continued on fifteen meters until it sloped back up.

Orlovski drew his kukri. "Give me your packs."

Allan quickly pulled his off and handed it over.

The Russian pulled it over one shoulder, then accepted Gerhard's. "I'll be beside you in case you slip." He nonchalantly strolled across the mucky water as if walking over firm rubber.

"Just take it slow." Allan pressed his chest to the wall and started down the slender ledge

Running his tongue across the backs of his teeth, Gerhard sheathed Umatri, hugged the wall, and began sidestepping behind Allan. Ages of dirt and grit coated the path, making it slippery, worsened by the uneven slope to it that he hadn't noticed.

Orlovski walked between them, arms ready. Would he be able to stop them if they fell? Gerhard studied the brown water through the corner of his eye. How deep was it? A half meter? Ten? Would his gear drag him down to the bottom? His palms began sweating at the thought.

"... should be there," Max's voice crackled through the radio, giving Gerhard a start.

Orlovski's firm hand found his back before he could fall.

"Hello?" Allan shouted, his voice echoing through the hall and blaring in the ear bud. "This is Allan. Do you read?"

"Yes!" Malcolm replied. "There you are. Sam, Victoria, you there?"

"Here," Sam replied. "You had us worried."

"Is everyone all right?"

"We're fine," Sam said.

"What the hell happened?" Allan asked.

"One of the repeaters, we think."

"How?" Sam asked.

"Duplexer," Chaya said with an annoyed edge. "I think it was trying to transmit and receive on the same frequency. Jamming itself."

"Did you fix it?" Allan asked.

"No. We were heading back when it came back on," Malcolm said.

"Do we know which repeater it is?"

"No way to tell without checking them one at a time," Chaya answered. "They're cobbled together so it's likely a bad solder."

"So do we need to go back to check them?" Allan asked.

"We're almost to the junction where we set the last one," Malcolm said. "We're going to switch it out. What's your twenty?"

"Three-quarters of the way to the rendezvous."

"Good. Once we get it replaced we'll meet you there. Without having to check side passages it's a straight shot."

Allan brushed his foot along the path, sweeping bits of rock into the water. "Roger that. We'll see you then."

"So they have a straight path and we get this?" Orlovski muttered, his voice too low for the microphone to catch it.

"Doesn't seem fair, does it?" Allan whispered. "Them sitting around bored while we have all the excitement."

Orlovski snorted.

After several more tunnels, including yet another crawl, they were greeted with red lights ahead as they rounded a corner.

"What took you so long?" Chaya asked as they came into view. They were sitting on the floor of a low alcove. A teal and yellow braided rope was tied around a jutting stone. It ran across the floor and down a round, black hole dominating the center of the room.

"Seeing the sights," Allan said.

Stooping into the alcove, Gerhard peered down the open hole. A bright orange glow stick burned at the bottom ten meters below.

Allan peeled off his pack and sat. "We trust that?" He gestured to the rope.

Malcolm sipped at the drinking tube. "Feels solid. Only one way to know for certain. You all rest for a minute. We'll take it first."

Gerhard sat, his back against the wall, as Malcolm adorned a padded harness. Once cinched in, he looped the rope through a ring shaped like an 8 and clipped it onto the harness. Gerhard watched intently. They'd only given him an afternoon of rappelling practice. It was simple enough, but down here he felt as though he was watching it for the first time.

Malcolm tugged the line. "Ready."

Max drew his sword and crawled down the shaft like a spider. "Clear," he radioed once he was at the bottom.

Clutching the rope, Malcolm backed to the edge and slowly lowered over the side. Once down, Chaya pulled the line back up, the empty harness attached to the end, and she put it on. After her came Orlovski.

"You're up ... or down, I suppose," Allan said once Orlovski had made the bottom.

Gerhard's knees protested as he rolled to his feet, wishing he'd had more time to rest. He drew the rope up, the harness clips jangling at the end. Once he'd strapped and cinched the awkward harness around his thighs and waist, he clipped the ring onto the front of his belt and locked it in.

"On belay?"

Allan tapped his ear. "Say that again."

"On belay?" Gerhard repeated, a little louder this time.

Allan's lip curled into a frown.

Before he could say anything, Malcolm called up from below. "Radios down?"

"Down," Allan hollered back. "What do we do?"

"We need to check them. Make sure the girls are okay."

Allan shook his head. "If we wait for you all to climb back out, then go to the entrance, we won't have time to come back and get to what's down there. We'll lose a day."

"We can't leave Sam and Victoria cut off."

"I agree with that. Gerhard and I can check them. You four can keep going and we'll catch up."

"I can come up," Max called. "It's no problem for me."

"No," Allan said. "You stay with them if they need you. It's just a straight shot back."

"Are you sure?" Malcolm asked.

"It's fine. You set up a repeater down there. We still have one, so we'll go back, switch with whichever one is causing the issue, and catch up. Easy peasy, no time lost."

Gerhard waited, trying to make out the voices as everyone discussed below. He wanted to go down, blood a demon. Not run back and forth fixing bad equipment.

"Fine," Malcolm called. "Leave us the harness. Once you have it fixed we'll meet up."

Chewing his lip to hide his disappointment, Gerhard began unbuckling himself. It wasn't that he didn't understand why they needed to go back. He supported the idea. He just wished he'd volunteered to go down the hole before Orlovski.

"Let's go," Allan said once Gerhard had lowered the rope and harness back down. "No rest for the wicked, eh?"

Gerhard drew Umatri and they headed down the passage, keeping at a brisk pace. The tunnel that Malcolm's team had taken to the well was significantly shorter than the one Gerhard had, but the maze-work of side tunnels and branches required Allan to regularly stop and consult the map on his tablet. Even with those delays they made it back to where they'd split up in little time. The repeater Malcolm had already replaced rested on the floor.

Allan knelt before the gray box and flipped the switch. "Testing. Testing."

The radio was still silent.

"Figured that one wasn't it." Allan flipped the repeater back on and they headed further up the tunnels from where they'd come. They passed the creepy mime relief and the rooms they'd previously checked. Gerhard's eyes regularly moved to Umatri, but the blade was motionless.

The sloped tunnels felt steeper than they had when they'd travelled down them instead of up. Gerhard had to hurry to keep up with Allan's pace.

The next repeater sat atop a large flat stone resembling an ancient altar. The ring of spent candles around it only added to the look. Again, Allan clicked it on and off, fidgeted with the unrolled antenna coil and shook his head.

They continued on, finding the third repeater in a long hallway.

"Only one left," Allan said after completing the test.

Gerhard tightened his lips in frustration. At this pace the others might have the lower level cleared by the time they made it back. The tension in Allan's jaw told him that the Englishman felt the same way so he chose not to voice his anger. *A knight shouldn't complain.*

Without a word, they trudged up the long passageway until eventually reaching the wedge-shaped supply room with the painted shadow men sitting along one wall.

"This has to be it," Allan grumbled as he pulled the box out from its niche. He flipped the switch. "Testing. Testing."

Nothing.

"Oh you are kidding me." He flipped the switch on and off several times. "Piece of shit. Work, damn you."

As if it could hear him, the radio suddenly came to life in Gerhard's ear, catching the last word of Allan's frustration.

"Hello?" Allan asked. "Anyone hear me?"

Malcolm's voice came through in reply. "There you are."

"We're here," Sam exclaimed. "What the hell happened?"

"First repeater was out. We'll exchange it and head back. How's it going?"

"Nothing yet," Malcolm replied. "Let us know when you're getting close. Bring extra repeaters."

"Roger that." Allan turned off the buggy repeater, then took one of the spares from a locker and set it in place.

Gerhard packed the last of the extra devices into his bag and loaded the faulty one back into a trunk. Then, not having anything to do, he took a seat on the carved bench.

"About ready?" Allan asked once he was done.

Gerhard nodded. "Yes," a little more exhaustion to his voice than he'd intended.

Allan smirked. "I can tell. No." He waved Gerhard down as he started to rise. "You take a breather." He licked his dusty lips, eyes unfocused. "Sam," he said, his voice loud enough for the radio.

"Yes?" she replied.

"That camera out there that Malcolm set up, it's still there, right?"

"Yeah."

"We don't need that one out there right now, so I'm going to fetch it and bring it back down with us."

"Good idea," Malcolm said.

"Anything else?"

"Cold beer and a hot meal," Orlovski said.

Gerhard suppressed a laugh so it wouldn't clog the channel.

"I'll see what I can do," Allan said. "We'll let you know when we get closer to you."

"Roger that," Malcolm said.

Allan turned back to Gerhard. "You want to come out and get some air or are you good here?"

While stepping outside was definitely appealing, Gerhard was really enjoying this seat. Besides, re-acclimating his night vision afterwards didn't sound enticing at all. He shook his head.

"All right, you just stay there. I'll be back in a minute." He nodded to Umatri. "Keep an eye on him. Call the instant if he moves."

"I will."

Allan lowered and crawled through the wide gap exiting to the old rail tunnel. Removing his helmet, Gerhard ran his fingers through his hair, shaking out the bits of grit that had worked up inside. The ear bud itched. He considered pulling it out but decided against it.

He rested his head back against to cool stone, mind wandering as the grunts and murmurs of Malcolm's team played through his radio. He closed his eyes. How many days of this would they endure before they found this eel? A week? Two? Would he get that first kill or was he resigned to spend the entire time in the back, Umatri serving as their radar?

The radio went silent.

Gerhard opened his eyes, glaring at the repeater. "Not again." Groaning inwardly, he sheathed Umatri, pulled on his helmet, and started to stand.

A figure stepped into the entrance on the far, narrow side of the room.

Gerhard wheeled in surprise. The red beam from his headlamp fell on a man, his narrow face obscured by a set of black goggles, its eyes an array of jutting tubes, two facing front, with angles lenses at either side.

His blond beard, one side smudged with limestone dust, opened into a half smile. He wore a pair of sturdy headphones with knobs on one ear, similar to their electronic shooting muffs at the mansion. A red laser sprang from the pistol in the man's hand as he leveled it at Gerhard's chest. "You must be Gerhard Entz." His voice was calm. American, but familiar.

Gerhard didn't answer.

"You can't call your friends." He patted a bullet-shaped radio at his waist. "So keep your hands where I can see 'em."

Gerhard placed the voice. "TommyD?"

"Hands out," TommyD said, a stern edge to his tone.

Gerhard opened his hands at his sides.

"Now, with your left hand, only your left, take Umatri out and set it on the ground."

A new fear bristled and twisted in Gerhard's chest. Umatri? How did he know about Umatri?

"Do it. Slow." The laser bobbed toward the keris as he lifted the gun higher.

Careful, his eyes never leaving TommyD's, Gerhard reached across and gripped Umatri's handle. This man wasn't going to take him. No one was going to take him.

Umatri's grip flexed beneath his fingers, echoing the sentiment.

Umatri wanted blood.

"*Don't*," TommyD spat, "think about it. Slow. Nice and slow. That's right."

Gerhard relaxed the tension from his face. He nodded slow and purposeful. Then he sprung to the side, ripping Umatri from its sheath and charged.

The gun fired, its flash a brilliant yellow. The accompanying boom was so loud it vibrated Gerhard's bones.

Baring his teeth, Gerhard lunged, elbow bent, Umatri aimed before him.

TommyD hopped back, the writhing blade missing him by centimeters. He swung the pistol up at Gerhard's face, its muzzle a silver-ringed black eye.

It flashed again, filling the world with light.

Gerhard never heard the shot.

CHAPTER 15

Allan squeezed out from the gap and crawled to his feet beside the tracks. He squinted as he looked toward the vans, the distant gleam of sunlight so brilliant it burned into his eyes, the image remaining even after he closed them. Keeping his head down, he headed toward the exit.

The left van's door opened as he neared the gate and Victoria leaned out, smiling back at him. She was beautiful, her short blond hair poking out around the wire headset. He had to look like shit, caked in dust and dried mud.

She said something but he couldn't make it out.

He opened his mouth to respond when a *pop* sounded behind him. Allan turned. *What was that?* A second *pop* sent a spike of fear shooting up his spine. *Gunshot!*

"Gerhard?" he called, his voice chased by echoes.

Silence.

"Hello? Anyone?" Not waiting for a response, Allan ran back down the tunnel. He yanked Ibenus from her sheath, sprang, and swung, blinking a meter forward. He landed, nearly slipping on the gravel, and swung again. "Gerhard!"

Reaching the gap at the floor, Allan scrambled down, sword still in hand.

Hard stone banged his knees and shoulder as he clambered down the stepped crevice. He reached the low, wide passage at the bottom. Rolling to his side, Allan swung Ibenus, blinking forward. He swung and blinked again and again until he reached the edge.

"Stop right there!"

Still on the floor, Allan craned his neck. Gerhard lay on his back, his headlamp shining on the wall. Bits of bright plastic and bloody chunks splattered the floor, leading Allan's gaze to a jagged hole in the back of Gerhard's helmet. *No!*

A crimson laser beam cut through the haze of gun smoke, one end on Allan's chest, the other in shadow. "Don't move, Mister Havlock. Or is it, Sir? I've never met a knight before."

Mouth open in stunned confusion, Allan turned his head, his light finding the speaker. The man held a pistol, his eyes hidden behind night vision goggles.

"Now," the stranger said. Gerhard's killer. "You're going to set that sword on the ground and come out nice and slow."

Gerhard's shoulder holster was gone. Allan scanned for Umatri, finally seeing it tucked in the killer's black web belt. *Bastard.*

"*Now*, Allan," the man said. "Put the sword down."

"How do you know my name?"

The gun came up in reply, held in both hands. "Do it."

Fear vanished into rage. Allan swung Ibenus. A *whoosh* and he was standing upright. Allan lunged, swinging the sword again as the man, still aiming at the floor, fired.

The brilliant flash filled the room. Allan appeared a meter beside where he'd been but staggered as his foot landed. Searing pain shot up from his ankle and he fell against the wall.

The laser swiveled his direction. Allan tried to catch himself to move out of the way, but he only lurched to the side as another deafening *boom* roared. The round struck the wall, zinging. Chips of stone pelted Allan's neck. He fell backwards, yelping as he hit the floor.

Another shot. It hit Allan's vest like a hammer blow and he heard the *crack* of his own ribs. Ibenus fell from his stunned fingers. Ears ringing, and pain shooting from all over, Allan fought through the blackness swimming at the edge of his vision and rolled away as a fourth shot rang out.

He collided into one of the plastic lockers, stopping his roll, a jolt of pain from his injured ribs. Gasping for breath, he looked down to see the red laser dot playing across his body. "Stop," he croaked, unsure if he even made sound. "Stop." Further down, below the ruby dot, Allan now noticed that his ankle was unnaturally twisted to the side, blood pulsing from the bullet hole in his boot. A sudden heat rushed up his spine and coldness washed down. His focus zeroed in on the dark pool spreading below his foot.

"Don't fucking move!" the killer yelled, though it sounded faintly distant above the ringing in his ears.

Pulling his eyes from the crippling wound, Allan saw Ibenus resting on the dusty floor between himself and Gerhard's killer. His own killer.

"Hands where I can see them."

Allan opened his hands.

"Good boy. Now close your eyes."

"W ... why?"

"Close them. I don't want to kill you."

Allan closed his eyes.

"Good. Now with your left hand, palm toward me, I want you slowly remove your pistol and toss against that far wall." His voice was calm, like a man talking to a skittish horse.

Allan winced, his ribs protesting the awkward movement, but he managed to draw the silenced gun. There was a moment's thought he could swing it up, grip it and fire, but he knew he'd be dead before he even opened his eyes. The little Walther dug into his back where he pressed against the locker. Not all was lost. *Thank you, Commander Bond.* Keeping his palm out, Allan wrist-tossed the HK to the side and it clattered, maybe four feet away.

"Good."

The voice was familiar and Allan realized the only person it could be: *TommyD.*

Footsteps moved to where Ibenus lay. Braving a peek, Allan squinted one eye as the man knelt. The red laser dot jiggled along Allan's vest.

The quad night-vision tubes looked away as TommyD reached for Ibenus' handle. Seizing the opening, Allan threw himself to the side. He grabbed for the Walther as he rolled and came up, his thumb clicking off the safety.

The laser beam darted toward him and Allan fired.

Dropping Ibenus, TommyD backpedaled, his own gun blasting plumes of fire. Wild shots exploded around Allan, kicking up even more dust. Allan fired twice more, missing as he scrambled backwards like a crab and hid behind the lockers. Bullets pelted the plastic boxes. One shot through while two more slammed off something inside.

Allan came around the side, firing the tiny gun. Ducking, TommyD dove through the doorway behind him and hid in the perpendicular tunnel. A silence fell over the room, Allan's panting the only sounds. Each breath felt like a barbed carving fork digging in his side.

Gulping, Allan checked his gun. He wasn't out. That was good. How many shots had he fired? Five? Six? The gun only held seven and he didn't have any spare magazines for it. He could see the HK lying in the dust a solid five feet away. It held fifteen rounds and he had two spare mags.

TommyD swung out from the opening, gun raised. Allan ducked and hunkered as three rapid shots pelted around him. Blindly, he stuck his gun out from behind his cover and returned fire. The slide locked back. Empty.

Praying that TommyD had hidden from the ineffective shots, Allan lunged toward the HK, falling more than jumping. His broken ribs screamed from the impact. Gritting his teeth, he clawed until he found the polymer grip and brought it up just as TommyD was coming out for another shot. Allan fired, sending the killer back behind cover.

Allan clicked the light under the barrel, unleashing a brilliant white beam. He held it on the door, ready for the first hint of movement as he dragged himself back to the lockers. Mud squished between his fingers. Water pooled around the tubs from where one of TommyD's bullets had evidently struck the extra water bags. It swirled with Allan's blood that was now everywhere. If he didn't do something about that he might pass out before the fight was over.

Allan's thick belt was no good for a tourniquet. He needed something else. Lifting to his knees, Allan kept the gun trained on the door with one hand with his other blindly moved along the lid. The long suppressor and the tactical light made it feel infinitely heavier than his Walther had and he had to fight to keep the barrel still. He found the clasp on one side of the box and released it with an audible *thunk*.

Still no movement at the door. Allan reached across his body and popped the other latch free. TommyD leaned out, the gun already raised and the laser slicing through the dusty air toward him. Allan fired. The shot pelted the wall beside TommyD's muffed ear and TommyD fell back behind cover before getting a shot off.

Heart racing, Allan flipped off the locker's lid and reached inside. He touched the loosely coiled loop of antennae wire from one of the repeaters. He felt along it until he reached the end and unscrewed it from the unit.

Allan eyed the doorway. He was going to require both hands to tie the tourniquet but he didn't want to lower his guard. *Better make it fast.*

He drew a long breath, held it, then dropped behind the boxes and began tying the ten-foot cable at his knee.

A baby's laughter shattered the silence. Innocent. Terrifying. Close.

Fucking hell. Allan cinched the cable, his ribs burning at the strain, but the blood was still flowing from his boot. Frantically, he searched around for something to use as a winding lever.

An infant's coo, then shots erupted from the hallway.

Allan hunkered down, one hand on the half-tied tourniquet, the other grabbing his gun.

Sobs and wails poured from the passage ahead, punctuated by the rapid *pop, pop, pop,* and flashes of gunfire. Lying on his back, Allan aimed his pistol along the side of a locker.

TommyD launched past the doorway so fast Allan couldn't get a shot before the man was already down the left passage. The infant cries grew louder. Then four screamers scuttled into view, three along the wall and another on the floor, black ooze dribbling from a severed leg. They continued down the hall, not paying a moment's attention to the room where Allan hid.

A pale mantismere with burnt orange stripes came next. Allan froze as it stopped in the doorway. Its black eyes shied from the brilliant light of his gun and turned toward Gerhard's corpse. Ibenus lay just a few feet from it, far closer to the demon than to Allan. Its mandibles clacked like some old Morse message.

Shots came from somewhere down the passage. The beast swiveled its head, hissed, and hurried after its minions.

Allan released his breath. Keeping his eyes on the passage entrance, he drew the round, aluminum torch from his belt, worked it into the tourniquet wire, and began to wind it tighter. The all-too-familiar stink of rotted flesh prickled his nose. Evidently TommyD had killed a screamer.

His gaze moved to Gerhard's body, dead eyes staring upward. *This is my fault,* he scolded. *I shouldn't have left him alone.* That cocker might have pulled the trigger but Gerhard's blood was on Allan's hands. Now Umatri was gone.

The shots were growing more distant. Four more screamers ran past.

Allan scrunched his eyes to wipe away the stinging sweat. He was cold and he wondered how bad he was bleeding on the inside. He pictured the splintered bone chewing into his lungs with each movement.

No time for that. Just get Ibenus and get out. I need to warn the others. He looked down long enough to tie off the tourniquet. A new shot of terror hit, washing away the cold as he turned back to the doorway.

Two doll-faced screamers stood at the entrance. One cocked its head and giggled. Somewhere nearby another responded, followed by the clicking of tiny legs. Allan's grip tensed on the gun as the two bugs scuttled into the room. They stepped over Ibenus and headed toward him.

CHAPTER 16

"I suppose that answers that," Victoria grumbled as Allan raced back down the tunnel. The red light from atop his helmet seemed to strobe as he blinked his way back to the catacomb's entrance. She'd yelled that the radios were out, then he'd shouted Gerhard's name, and raced off.

"These repeaters are shit." Sam stared at the black screen that only seconds before had shown Gerhard sitting on a stone bench. "I say we disassemble them all and start over."

"Well, it'll give us something to do." Victoria shut the door before all the cold air could escape. Sitting here while Allan crawled around in a labyrinth looking for a fight was bad enough. But as Sam had warned, the silence was the worst. Rewiring electronics might help keep her mind off of it. She snorted. *Not likely.*

With the exception of those silent terrors while the radios were down, the day had been spectacularly dull. There had been a brief moment when a police car had slowed as it rolled past the drive's entrance, but then it continued on. *Nothing to see here. Just a repair crew. Carry on.* The police car, or another one, Victoria couldn't tell, had passed again two hours later, but didn't even slow.

The only other lingering itch was TommyD. She thought about him every time she or Sam stepped out to stretch their legs and every car or cyclist that slowed along the overpass sent tingles along the back of her scalp. He'd never responded to her scolding for that last video stunt and her promise to get him a weapon. Hopefully that meant he understood and was going to lay low and stop stirring the nest.

Of course that only delayed the inevitable. How could she ensure that he wouldn't post the other information she'd sent him? Once he figured out she wasn't going to come through, he'd simply just post all of it. Names, addresses, detailed demon and weapon dossiers. Enough information to ruin the Order. Even if they did somehow endure the exposure, she wouldn't. They'd leave her in the ashes, her name scrubbed from memory and only referred to as "The Betrayer" just like Anya. She wanted to tell Allan, but how? *I'm sorry, but before I got to know you and fell in love, and I really do love you, I sent every file I could find to the man who wants to expose you. Can you forgive me?* No, she needed to fix this before she confessed.

If she could only get TommyD to talk to them, maybe they could convince him why they needed to remain secret. Maybe he could help show why they needed to work together, release some of their information to save lives, use his network, and they could both benefit. They just needed to sit down and talk.

The headset crackled in her ear. At least the radio was working again. For now.

"Vid's coming back up," Sam said, almost bored. She gasped. "Oh shit."

"What?" Victoria turned to see the vibrant green picture and her stomach dropped. The image was foggy from the smoking carcasses of three screamers that she could see. Gerhard lay on his back, one of the bugs crawling over his face. Ibenus' blade glinted in the infrared's light, but where was Allan?

A pained cry came through the radio as if in answer. Allan dragged himself into the lower edge of the frame, his gun raised.

Victoria's hand went to her mouth. "Allan!"

Three *pops* sounded in the headset momentarily followed by Allan's firing those shots at another screamer charging through an open doorway.

"Help," he croaked. "Knight down."

The screamer leaped from Gerhard and onto Allan's back. Yelling, he rolled, batting at it with his gun. He jammed the barrel into its side and blasted it apart, splattering his face with black ichor.

"Mal!" Sam shouted. "Allan's in trouble. First camera. Screamer swarm."

Malcolm's voice crackled through. "Gerhard?"

"Dead." Allan wiped the steaming mess from his face and rolled.

Two more doll-faced bugs scuttled through the doorway.

"I'm on my way," Schmidt said.

"No, Max!" Malcolm yelled. "Come back!"

Victoria's hands balled into fists. *He won't get there in time.* Malcolm was yelling something at Schmidt in the radio but she couldn't hear it. Allan was hurt and was going to die right in front of her. *No.*

Without a word, Victoria drew her pistol from the open satchel beside her and pulled open the door.

"What are you doing?" Sam yelled, her voice shrill in the headset.

Victoria ran. "I have to save Allan." Her shoes crunched across the gravel. She sidestepped through the bent gap in the wrought-iron fence and ran down the train tunnel. *He's not going to die.*

Still running, the tunnel growing darker with each step, Victoria fumbled with the light under her gun. She jammed her thumbnail down into the rubber button and was rewarded with a brilliant beam.

"There's a mantismere," Sam called through the radio.

If the warning was intended to dissuade Victoria, it failed. *I have to save him.*

Muted gunshots popped ahead. Beneath the rapid staccato, babies screamed.

"Just passed the well," Schmidt said.

Victoria slid as she reached a wide gap in the wall framed in a bright corona of spray-paint and crowned with huge letters. The wails echoed out from the hole, but the shots had ceased. She scrambled through it. The floor dropped on the other side and she banged her knees as she hit the bottom. The screams were louder now, pushing her onward.

"It's got him!" Sam yelled in Victoria's earpiece. "Allan's down! Repeat, Allan's down!"

Navigating the stepped gap, Victoria came to a wide, low tunnel. The air was thick with gun smoke and that all-too-familiar stench of rotted meat. Inhuman shadows moved in the lights ahead. She ran toward them on all fours, one hand still clutching the pistol.

A spidery silhouette scuttled into view. A baby laughed.

Dropping to her elbow, Victoria lifted the pistol. The screamer's pale face shone in the spotlight, pincered jaws wide as it charged. The gun *thumped* loudly and the creature's chubby face folded in on itself as the bullet took it just below the left eye. The bug tumbled backwards, landing feet up.

She clambered past it as the screamer's shell began dissolving in dark steam. Another screamer charged toward her as she entered a room.

It leaped at her face, jaws open.

Recoiling, Victoria swung her pistol, smacking it with the big silencer. It hit the wall and she shot it as it struck the ground. Blood and brass shell casings speckled the floor as well as several black and gooey screamer corpses. A smeared trail led from a crimson pool to where two of the horrible bugs were dragging Gerhard's body toward an open doorway. Allan lay face up near the far corner, Ibenus only a foot away. Mouth open, he stared vacantly at the ceiling as a huge, six-legged mantismere hunkered above him, jaws clamped on his upper arm.

Damn, you. The demon had him. Had his soul.

"Passing the first repeater," Schmidt said in her ear.

Allan let out a rasping gasp as the demon released its grip, turning its black eyes toward her. Blood stained its chittering mandibles.

Victoria shot it twice in the head.

The demon reeled back, ooze dribbling from a ruptured eye. Then the holes closed, the eye re-inflated, and the monster hissed. The screamers released Gerhard's corpse and headed toward her.

Victoria swung the gun their direction, firing one ineffective shot, and the mantismere lunged. Stumbling, she ducked the demon's stabbing forelimbs. She scrambled to the side, peppering it with point-blank shots as the demon swung one of its blade-like arms in a blurring arc. Her foot came down on one of the dead screamers. It popped, spewing black guts, and she slipped on the greasy mess. Victoria threw her arm out the catch herself, skinning her palm as she hit the floor.

The mantismere loomed above her, its forelimbs raised like twin scorpion tails. A wailing screamer crawled onto her leg, ready to bite. Victoria threw herself to the side, knocking it off as she rolled. The mantismere's arms hit the floor behind her with a hard *thunk* that would have surely skewered her.

Firing back at it, she scrambled away as the demon swiped again. The gun's slide locked back as the last shot emptied. *Fuck.*

The demon hissed and two screamers started up the walls to either side. Allan's gun lay on the floor, its own light casting long shadows across the room. Its slide was back, too. Empty. There was still one magazine in the pouch below his right arm.

Victoria ran as the mantismere charged. As her hand moved toward it, a glint from Ibenus' blade drew her eye. With no time for both, she leaped over Allan's body and seized the sword.

The mantismere slammed into her, knocking Victoria on her ass. The beast loomed above and drove its piercing arms down.

Clutching the khopesh in both hands she brought it up, desperately trying to deflect the spear-like points.

Air *whooshed* in her ears with an instant's weightlessness and Victoria was now standing beside the creature as its points jabbed into the empty floor where she'd been.

"Passing the second repeater," Schmidt's voice said in the earpiece.

A sudden rush surged through Victoria's veins, singing through her body like taut piano strings. She hacked Ibenus into the demon's side. The shell split open with a solid *crack.* The beast shrieked, its armored plates bristling as it spun, nearly wrenching the imbedded sword from Victoria's hand.

She yanked it free, swinging it back for another strike as the demon came for her. The air *whooshed* again and she was now behind it. The euphoric tension in her muscles shot up her spine, blossoming behind her eyes with a sense of perfect clarity. In that pure calmness, she hated that monster and its screaming brood more than anything. With a primeval scream she brought Ibenus down into the back of the mantismere's plated skull.

The beast jerked forward, an oozing canyon in the back of its head. The screamers wailed as it stumbled, and then a flare of blue fire erupted from the wounds as it collapsed.

The screamers crumpled, their pale shells withering and blackening like a time-lapse of mold overtaking an apple. The demon's blood along Ibenus' blade ignited with the same icy blue flames now consuming the fallen mantismere.

Sam's voice came through the earpiece, sounding a million miles away. "Oh my god." Three breaths later. "Demon neutralized."

"What?" Malcolm said. "How?"

Only vaguely aware of the radio chatter, Victoria's gaze fixed on the gleaming bronze blade. A strange and beautiful weightlessness moved up her arms and fanned out down her body. She felt as if she were being unraveled, unmade. Then at the zenith of her disintegration, the fibers of her being rewove with new threads, beautiful, alien strands joining her. At their ends, she recognized Ibenus and Allan both being knitted into her, into each other. As they merged, a horrible pain swelled in each of her senses—smell, taste, the sound of it—and Victoria realized the source.

Allan! She pulled herself from her stupor and dropped by Allan's side. "Allan, talk to me."

His eyes rolled toward her, focusing for only a moment before fading off.

"You'll be all right." Blood ran from the Y-shaped, puckered gouge in his bicep. She clasped her hands across it as she looked around for anything to stanch the flow.

"There's a trauma kit in the supplies," Sam said.

Victoria spied the two stacked tubs across the room, riddled with bullet holes. She ran to them, finding the shattered remains of a repeater inside the top one. Pushing it aside, she popped the lid off the second locker. A red nylon bag rested along one side, a white cross emblazoned along the top. She yanked it free and ran back to Allan.

"Passing the third repeater," Schmidt said as Victoria drew the bandages from the bag.

She began wrapping Allan's arm, the blood instantly soaking through. "You'll be all right. Stay with me." His face was terribly pale. "We need to get him to hospital."

Victoria then noticed the loops of black wire tightly bound at Allan's knee. A slender metal flashlight was wound into the knot. Panic rising, she looked down to see the blood-caked hole through Allan's boot, wide enough to fit a finger but too narrow for one of the mantismere's bladed arms. A tourniquet implied he'd had time to wrap it.

She glanced over to Gerhard's body, his arms stretched above his head from when the screamers had dragged him. Blood and gore ringed the edges of his empty right eye socket. Brains spilled out the jagged hole in the back of his hardhat.

"They've been shot."

"Repeat that?" came Malcolm's voice.

A new fear rippled along the back of her neck. A jagged hole of shredded nylon marred the side of Allan's vest. She looked closer, seeing that it wasn't from a slash but a straight puncture. "They've been shot. Someone shot them."

"How? Have you seen—?"

A baby's laughter sounded behind her.

Victoria spun as pair of doll-face bugs peeked into the room, their inky eyes transfixed on her.

Grabbing Ibenus, she stood to face them as they scuttled around the rim of the door.

"Fresh contact," Sam called in her ear. "Screamers."

Keeping herself between the monsters and Allan, Victoria squeezed the sword's handle, feeling the power of it, the hunger. The screamers spread to either side, flanking her. Glancing to the left one, Victoria swung, blinked closer. She swung downward at empty floor. The air *whooshed* in her ears and she was now above the bug, Ibenus' descending blade cleaving it half. She wrenched the sword up, teleporting with the movement. Two blinks later she turned the blade into a low upswing and appeared beside the scuttling screamer in time for the khopesh to lop off its head.

More crying sounded from the doorway as another screamer, this one with a broken leg, shambled into the room. Behind it, a mantismere dropped from the ceiling and charged.

Victoria swung Ibenus as it neared, blinking out of its way. Before she could reorient herself, the beast whirled, flailing its arms outward. The flat of a blurring spear arm struck Victoria's side like a club. She hissed as the sharp, pointed bumps along it tore through her shirt, raking her skin. Stumbling, she managed to keep her grip on Ibenus and looked up just in time to deflect a strike aimed at her chest.

The hobbling screamer circled around behind her. She sidestepped another thrust, swung Ibenus, and appeared three feet away. The mantismere clacked its plated jaws, raised its arms out and up like a pair of angry cobras. It took a tentative step.

Victoria swallowed. There was no time for this. Allan was dying. She readied Ibenus before her, one hand on the grip, the other on the haft below the crescent blade. "Come on!"

The demon's mouth opened wide and hissed. It took a second step and paused. A red light grew across its pale surface. The beast swiveled its head toward the door behind Victoria. Air rushed past her ear. A dark shape blurred by and the demon flew back, its body splitting open beneath its raised arm. Black blood fanned out. The demon lurched around, left arms hanging limp beside it.

Max Schmidt crouched against the far wall like a spider, his head raised and red helmet lamp shining on the monster. Dark blood smeared the sword in his hand. Dust and scrapes completely covered Schmidt's body like he'd been dragged behind a car. The old man's eyes narrowed at the demon. He flew toward it, spinning his body around. The arc of his movement curved mid-air and he landed on the ceiling, his kneepads scraping with the momentum. The monster fell, blue fire spewing from its mouth and wounds, its minions fading at its death.

Panting, the old man gulped and dropped to the floor, slowing for an instant before he landed on his feet. "Demon ... neutralized." He slid Lukrasus into his scabbard and eyed

Victoria, gaze lingering on Ibenus still in her hands. "What happened?" he asked, turning toward Allan and Gerhard.

She lowered the weapon and ran to Allan's side. "Someone shot them."

Max limped over. He scowled as he saw Gerhard's body, then turned and knelt beside Allan. His skinned and bleeding hands moved down to the tourniquet then up over his body. "We need to get them out. Prep a saline bag. Samantha?"

"I'm here," she said.

"I need you to call Alex. Tell him what happened. He will make the necessary arrangements and call back."

Victoria rifled through the trauma kit and removed one of the plump saline pouches and a coil of clear tubing. "What next?"

Schmidt accepted them and began to work. "Give him Ibenus."

"What?" Victoria asked.

"The sword. Put it in his hand. It will help."

Puzzled, yet somehow understanding, Victoria placed Ibenus on Allan's chest and set his right hand on the handle. "Here you are." *Make him better, baby.*

"Good." Schmidt peeled the plastic wrapper from the tube and affixed it to the bag. He worked with the calm, purposeful demeanor of a man who had performed this many times before.

"What do you need?" Victoria asked.

"There is a folding stretcher in one of the lockers. Bring it here."

She hurried back to the plastic tubs and wrestled out a blue canvas bundle with rigid poles rolled inside. "What now?"

Schmidt inserted a hypodermic needle into Allan's arm. "Assemble it."

Heart thumping in her ears, Victoria unfolded the stretcher, making sure the poles were sturdy.

"Iben …" Allan mumbled.

"She's here." Schmidt patted Allan's hand. "Victoria, help me."

Carefully, they rolled Allan on his side then scooted him onto the stretcher. Victoria strapped Allan down, Ibenus against him, as Schmidt inspected Gerhard's body.

"Where is Umatri?" the old man asked.

"I haven't seen him."

Schmidt rolled Gerhard over, peering beneath him. "It's gone. As is his gun."

"They must have taken them." Victoria lifted one end of the stretcher.

"Who?"

"Whoever shot them. Are you going to help me?"

Schmidt cursed something under his breath. He warily looked back at the doorway behind him, then took one of the handles that Victoria was holding up. Together they dragged Allan's body to the gap leading to the tunnel.

"Malcolm," Schmidt said. "Site is compromised. Exit at one of the manholes we passed. Call when you reach the surface. Be on your guard."

"Roger."

They pulled Allan through the gap and up the steps. Schmidt did what he could, but Victoria performed most of the work. Allan's breaths remained shallow. He mumbled a few incoherent words as they pulled him up onto the second ledge but she couldn't make them out.

Almost there, baby.

Finally, they managed to get him up into the train tunnel and out of the stink of rotten meat. Sam had backed the van up to the wrought iron gate, the open rear door butted against the gap in the bars. She ran out to meet them as Victoria and Schmidt started down the tunnel.

"Did you get a hold of Alex?" Schmidt asked.

"I did. He'll call back when it's ready." Sam took the lower end of the stretcher from him and together she and Victoria began running toward the van.

Still holding the front poles, Victoria ducked through the gap and climbed up into the open back. "Carefully. Carefully." She guided Allan to the space Sam had already cleared open. The larger trauma case was out against the wall.

"I'll get the gate." Sam squeezed around the van and ran to the chain link fence sealing off the drive.

Victoria looked back at Schmidt hurriedly limping up behind them. "Let's go!"

"Not yet," he panted. Now, in the light, the old man's extensive scrapes and even a purpling bruise along one cheekbone appeared worse than she'd initially thought. Tiny bead of blood dotted a red cut along his jaw.

"We have to get him to hospital."

"And tell them what?" Schmidt growled, crawling up into the vehicle. "No, we wait for Alex's call."

"But—"

"No!" Schmidt's finger shot up. It was caked in blood and dust. "We wait for Alex. Now help me with him."

Max poured rubbing alcohol over his hands, washing away the grit, and pulled on a pair of gloves. He'd removed a pair of angled medical shears when Sam yanked open the driver's door and climbed into the seat, phone pressed to her ear.

"All right." She tapped something into the dash-mounted GPS. "I have it," and she rattled off an address. "I'll call when we arrive." She hung up the phone and started the engine. "Let's go!"

Victoria braced Allan as the van jolted to a start. Gravel crunched and pelted the underside as the van took off.

Schmidt hunkered over Allan's mangled boot and began cutting it off. Blood poured out of it as if it were some living thing he was dissecting. The van's carpet greedily sopped it into a growing red stain. Finally, he peeled the boot open and Victoria gasped.

Splinters of bone crowned outward from a devastating hole through his ankle. Allan's wire binding had ceased most, but not all, blood flow as red streamed from the pulped mess.

"Can you save it?"

"We'll need to move the tourniquet closer," Schmidt said.

"Can you save his leg?" she asked, her voice high.

Tires squealed as the van took a hard left. Victoria caught the IV bag before it tumbled away. She held it up, making sure no kinks were in the tube.

"I do not know." He shook his head. "The doctor may be able to save it. I'm more concerned with his life."

The van took another hard turn.

"Samantha," Schmidt said, pausing his work to hold on. "Maintain the speed limit. We don't want police."

"Sorry."

"Where are we going?" Victoria asked.

The old man slit Allan's trousers up past his calf. The skin was terribly pale. "Alex made arrangements with someone who can help."

"Who?"

"Someone interested in antiques and with access to doctors." Schmidt reached into the kit and removed a bright blue tourniquet with a knurled metal rod. He frowned at the wound and looked up at Victoria, his pale eyes mournfully sincere. "You killed that demon with Ibenus, didn't you?"

"I had to."

He nodded, his gaze distant as if she'd confessed an entirely different question. "Hold the sword to him. Talk to him. Let him know she still loves him."

"But—"

"Do it! If you want to save his life. Let him know that he isn't alone now."

Understanding, Victoria held Allan's hand against Ibenus' grip. She pressed her cheek against his forehead and closed her eyes. Instantly, that strange sensation came to the surface and she felt herself being re-knitted. It hadn't stopped since she'd last felt it, but had grown, crystallized into something far more intricate. Allan was still there, part of him now part of her. But that other entity was something greater than them both. Ancient. Powerful. Love.

"I'm here, Allan. I'm here with you."

Her essence seemed to flow and roll in an intoxicating weightlessness. She loved them both, Allan and Ibenus. And while she loved him more than she thought anyone could, her welling emotion toward the sword was beyond her comprehension. It was as a mother to her child, a child to her mother, and the special bond of lovers. This was no sword. It truly was an angel, an angel that loved her, loved them both.

"Ibenus is with us." She wasn't entirely sure if she spoke

the words aloud. "She's here."

She. It seemed a strange word for the sword, for the angel. The way Victoria felt its arms around her, through her, there was nothing feminine to that touch. Ibenus was a *he*.

Allan gave a shivering gasp.

Victoria opened her eyes to see him staring back but his eyes were focused somewhere far away.

"Ibenus," he breathed, not moving his lips. He met her gaze for the briefest instant, then his eyes closed.

"Allan?" She squeezed his hand. "Baby?"

No response.

His forehead glistened with moisture. Victoria felt her cheeks and realized she was crying.

"Keep holding him." Schmidt said. "You are doing fine."

Closing her eyes, she pressed herself again against Allan's wet face. "We're here with you."

The van made a sudden shift, a lane change, and a car horn blared outside. Ignoring Schmidt's orders for Sam to drive safely, Victoria lost herself again in the sensation that she, Allan, and Ibenus were one.

I'm here, baby.

A voice responded in her mind. *I hear you.*

She clutched him tighter. *Allan, I love you.* There was no response but she could feel him.

"We're here!" Sam called.

The van slowed and stopped. The electric whine of the driver's side window and a stranger asked something in French.

"*Monsieur Daigneau?*" Sam asked.

"You Max?"

"I am Max," Schmidt said.

Victoria looked up to see a narrow-faced man peering over Samantha's shoulder.

His gaze casually scanned the van, passing over her, pausing on Allan, then locked on Max. "Good." He withdrew from the window. "Back it up to the door."

Sam pulled the van forward, then turned and reversed the vehicle carefully back. It *creaked*, then popped gently up a curb before slowing to a stop.

Low, hurried voices sounded outside. Victoria licked her lips, about to ask what was going on, then the rear door clicked and swung open.

The lean-faced man stood beside a stocky guy with a neatly trimmed two-day beard that made the dimple in his chin look like a black dot. Behind them a dark-skinned man wrestled a long cardboard box that might have once carried a refrigerator out from the open door of a building.

Beardy's eyes moved to Schmidt's holster, sword, and then to Ibenus. He lifted the front of his shirt just enough to show the black of a pistol in his waistband. "No weapons."

Schmidt nodded. "Of course."

The man returned the nod, lowered his shirt, then motioned to the guy with the box. Taking one end, he climbed inside, pushing past Schmidt. One side of the box was open; the top and bottom ends were partially cut out and reinforced on the inside with black tape. He motioned Victoria to move and, once she'd leaned away, taking Ibenus with her, the man set the box over Allan, completely covering him.

"*Un. Deux. Trois,*" Beardy said, then he and the dark-skinned man, who looked to be Greek, lifted the stretcher and carried Allan out, across the short gap to the door and into the building.

Victoria started after them, but the lean-faced man stepped in her way. "No weapons."

Clenching her teeth, Victoria looked down at Ibenus.

"She'll be safe," Schmidt said, seeming to read her mind. "Sam will take care of the swords."

She didn't want to leave Ibenus ... but Allan.

"She'll be safe." Schmidt repeated as he pulled off the shoulder rig. "Go." Velcro *scritched* as he peeled open his bulletproof vest.

Drawing a breath, Victoria set Ibenus behind her, away from this stranger, and hurried out after Allan. She followed them up a flight of wooden stairs and down a short hall lined with frosted glass doors reminiscent of an old-style office building. The door at the end swung open to reveal a small room with plastic draped across the windows and covering the floor. At its center, a woman in a paper surgeon's mask stood beside a long table hidden beneath a sea green cloth. An array of gleaming tools filled a rolling tray behind her along with several electronic devices.

Snapping a gesture to the table, the woman barked something in French.

A young man in a rubber apron strode out from a bathroom, pulling on a pair of latex gloves.

The men set Allan on to the table and pulled away the box.

The woman shooed them back, then looked up at Victoria. *"Qui es-tu?"*

"I'm with him."

"Then shut the door and stay out of the way."

CHAPTER 17

Parisians prided themselves on their summer climate, considering air-conditioning a frivolous and pointless creation meant for those living elsewhere. On those rare days that temperatures soared above thirty degrees Celsius, the solution was to simply open a window. Unfortunately for Victoria, the windows of Daigneau's old office building were currently shut and hidden beneath drawn shades or draped plastic. Safe from prying eyes, yet sticky with the trapped heat.

She dabbed her neck as Malcolm and Chaya pored over a tunnel map. Sam sat at her computer, loading the footage from memory cards of the freshly retrieved repeater cameras and synching it with the audio. The smell of sweat, antibiotic cleaners, and coffee filled the empty four-room suite. The coffee pot had been working non-stop since their arrival.

Their single fan was humming away in Allan's room directly behind her. She desperately wanted to go back in there. What if he awoke to find himself alone in an unfamiliar room, a strange bed, tubes in his arms, and a plaster cast capping the stump where his left foot used to be? No. She had to be there when he awoke. She needed to console him, let him know that nothing had changed between them, and confess her sins. She was to blame for all of this.

She should have told him when she realized she was in love. But no, she led them straight into TommyD's trap at the apartments. Now Luc was in hiding, Gerhard dead, the man she loved was maimed, and to top it off, Ibenus had chosen her as his new protector.

What little sleep she'd managed had been sporadic, plagued by nightmares and paranoia that Allan had woken afraid and alone. The only calm she'd found was in cleaning Ibenus. It was almost meditative, carefully brushing the dust and dried blood. She felt like a curator restoring a masterpiece painting, each removed fleck revealing another facet of hidden beauty. Once finished, and she could see her golden brown reflection in the perfectly polished bronze, she did it again.

Allan had tried to verbalize what a weapon bond meant but she hadn't believed it. Naively, she'd thought of it the way some people might obsess over a treasured heirloom or automobile, valuable, but most certainly inanimate. But there was no possible way that Allan, or anyone, could articulate the sheer magnitude of what *it* truly was. She understood now and, in that, the gravity of Allan's loss was that much more tragic. He'd lost more than a limb. Losing Ibenus ... She had to be there when he awoke. She squeezed the sword resting across her lap. Ibenus had to be there when his eyes opened.

Master Schmidt and Orlovski had left immediately after Allan's surgery to take Gerhard's body back to Belgium. Malcolm's order was that no one could be near Allan without a holy weapon, and leaving Ibenus with him while he was unconscious was out of the question. A demon had bitten him and, even though Victoria had slain it, Allan was to be treated cautiously until they could prove he wasn't possessed.

Monsieur Daigneau, their unseen host that Master Turgen had bribed with a set of eighteenth century porcelain, had given them full run of the building until Allan was ready to leave. Doctor Laroux, the woman who had sawed off Allan's foot, was their only visitor. The woman's perpetual scowl could have been carved in stone. Whatever circumstances led her to being the personal physician to a Paris mobster had evidently left her wearing that eternal frown like a hideous scar. She came by every few hours to check on her patient and was never in the room without an escort armed with a holy weapon. The doctor never asked about the swords. Not asking questions probably came with the job.

"All right." Sam finger-massaged her forehead as she looked up with tired, dark-rimmed eyes. She rotated the laptop around so the screen faced the room. "It's ready."

Malcolm and Chaya quit their work and turned, neither of them sitting. Not willing to leave earshot of Allan's room, Victoria straightened for a better view.

Sam slid the cursor past footage of the knights setting up the first camera in the Ready Room. "Since we set up the cameras as motion controlled, it's real easy to mark when anything happened." The first camera went dark. Shortly after another window appeared, playing footage of the second camera being set up. Then the third, followed by the fourth, where Allan and Malcolm's teams split up. The screen was now divided into four quadrants.

"Okay," Sam said. "Just after fourteen hundred hours was the first radio silence. Ten minutes later, camera one flipped on." She clicked the slide bar and green appeared in the first quadrant. She clicked it again, expanding it until it filled the screen. A man in night vision goggles stood in the door. Despite his masked eyes, the familiar light-colored beard and narrow cheeks only verified what Victoria had already guessed.

"TommyD," she growled.

Malcolm nodded quietly, his jaw tight.

Chaya pointed at the screen. "There. Radio jammer at his belt."

They'd already guessed that, too. Once a jammer was in range of one repeater, the repeater merely boosted the jammed signal, creating a chain reaction for every radio on the network.

TommyD walked into the room, the eyestalk tubes of his goggles tracking around. He stepped off screen to where the lockers were, then returned, scanned the room again, and left through the north entrance he'd come from and down the east passage. A few minutes later, Victoria jumped as Schmidt's voice came through the speakers, breaking the silence.

"… should be there."

"So after Mal swaps camera one," Sam continued, fast forwarding, "we have some time before the next silence. Shortly after that, he comes back into the staging area."

As she said it, camera one came back on and TommyD wandered past. Two minutes after leaving the frame, the camera flipped off.

"Okay." Sam fiddled with the slide bar. "This is where it gets interesting. Camera two flips on as TommyD comes into view. Shortly after that, Gerhard and Allan set off four. They're headed toward each other. Allan and Gerhard made it to three first. TommyD sets off two again, a minute before Allan and Gerhard arrive."

"He was right in front of them," Malcolm said. "He must have seen their lights ahead and just stayed out of their range."

"Yeah," Sam said. "He was back in the staging area less than two minutes before them. I'm guessing he was hiding just behind that wall when they were in there and turned off his jammer while Allan was fiddling with the repeater. After Allan left, he just waited, then turned it back on."

On the screen, TommyD stepped back into the room. In the night vision, the laser appeared as an unbroken tether joining Gerhard to the pistol.

Anger mounted into disgusted rage as Victoria watched tragedy unfold, its conclusion already known. She looked away just as the back of Gerhard's helmet exploded in an arc of blood and brains.

"How the hell did he find us?" Chaya asked, as TommyD rifled through Gerhard's body. "There's no way he just *happened along.*"

Victoria's mind flashed to her phone, her computer. Was TommyD tracking her somehow? No. Her mobile they'd left at the chateau. Standard procedure to keep off GPS tracking since her name was linked to it. The computer maybe, but the Order had some serious scans in place for such things.

"He had to have seen the vans," Malcolm said.

Chaya shook her head. "We replaced the van he'd seen."

Victoria nodded. On the screen TommyD stood as Allan crawled into the room. "He might have been watching entrances. Noting which ones we'd likely use." Same trick she'd used in Amiens. Watch for the hunters and they'll lead you there. Bloody stupid to have left the vehicles there. She should have known better.

She shied away as TommyD opened fire on Allan. She saw the first shot strike Allan's ankle the instant before he blinked, then the stumble, the loss of Ibenus, and the final, silent shootout. Finally, the screamers appeared, chasing TommyD off down the west passage from where he'd originally come. Allan's terrible fight with the screamers played out on the screen. The audio came back on, capturing their shouts and Allan's shots, his pleas for help. Then the mantismere came. Ibenus only a yard from his grasp. Allan hadn't stood a chance.

A screamer exploded out from the low entrance and Victoria scrambled out. She watched the scene play out, though more in her mind than the captured footage. The demon fire filled the screen, washing it out, as she dispatched the monster not fully realizing the implication at the time. She squeezed Ibenus' grip. He had known Allan's life as a hunter was finished the moment he'd allowed Victoria to blink? That was the deciding moment, the passing of the torch.

Malcolm traced his finger along the map on the table. "There's a manhole a hundred yards down here. He must have escaped there."

"How do you know TommyD escaped?" Victoria asked.

"The mantismere wasn't bloodied when it returned. If he saw the vehicles at the tunnel, that'd been the closest place he could have accessed the mine."

"We should still check it," Chaya said. "Maybe he didn't make it out. If not, Umatri might still be down there."

"Agreed." Malcolm glanced at his watch. "Doctor Laroux will be back in forty-five minutes to check Allan. We can go once she leaves." He looked to Victoria. "You okay if we leave you for a while?"

"As long as I can stay with Allan. But go. If Umatri is there, bring him back." Victoria stood and started toward Allan's room. She stopped, seeing him there, hoses running in his arms, the elevated stump, short tubes protruding from the rounded end where his foot should have been. She squeezed Ibenus, calming the despair. "If you find TommyD, even if he's dead, shoot him for me."

Allan awoke to clouds, soft and pale floating overhead a hundred miles away. *Where am I?* An odd sensation tinged his side as he shifted. Grunting, he blinked and the world slid into focus.

It was a ceiling. Splotchy blobs of water damage stained the white paint. *What is this?*

"Allan?"

Then Victoria was there above him, her golden hair tussled and sticking out like she'd just woken up. Were they in bed together?

"Hey," he said, grinning. "You look like an angel." His words came out more slurred than he'd expected. They must have been drinking. He'd had the craziest dream about her and Ibenus.

Excited relief shone in her red-rimmed eyes. "He's awake!"

"Yeah, I'm awake." Allan turned his head to see the bags hanging above him, their clear tubes running down to his hand. Thick bandages bound his shoulder and bicep. Had there been an accident?

He scrunched his eyes trying to recall what had happened. He was in a room. Small. No decoration but a green plastic sheet draped along one wall.

Malcolm and Chaya came inside. He could see Sam back there behind them.

"Hey, brother," Malcolm said.

"Hey."

Malcolm extended his left hand, palm open. "Look at this."

Puzzled, Allan looked at the half-lidded eye tattooed on Malcolm's palm. "Why?"

"He's good." Malcolm lowered his hand.

"Did you just ..." Why would he give him the test? Allan turned to Victoria. "Where are we?"

Victoria set Ibenus on his chest and placed his right hand onto it. "You were hurt, baby."

Baby? She knew better than to say that if front of the others. The Masters would have his ass if they found out.

"Allan," she said, her hand squeezing over his. "You were attacked."

"Attacked?" He looked down at the bandages over his arm and around his chest. "When?" The words were no sooner out his mouth than he remembered dragging himself across the floor, screamers closing in and Gerhard's dead eye, the other a bloody hole, staring up at the ceiling. "Gerhard?"

"He was killed." Malcolm said. "Shot."

Allan's mouth felt dry. Images flashed through his mind, lacking context or order like some half-remembered dream. A man in black goggles, doll-faces bugs swarming, a red laser beam slicing the darkness toward him, a pale mantismere diving, its mouth wide. "TommyD."

Victoria nodded.

"He shot me. I remember shooting, then ..." He thought of his bandaged arm. How had he hurt that? "I was bitten?"

She squeezed his hand. "Yes. Yes, but you're okay now. The demon is dead. It's gone."

Allan nodded, recalling the fire now, its blue light flickering through half-closed eyelids. "You saved me."

Tears welled in her eyes. "Yes."

"You killed it." He remembered now. Blood pouring from his ankle, the tourniquet, the cold hopeless weight as the demon marked him. Victoria killed it with Ibenus. He felt the blood drain from his face. His head swam and a leaden weight settled in his stomach, threatening to drag him down.

"Yes," she said, the tears coming now. "I had to."

Allan tried to sit up, but Malcolm was there, his hand urging him back down. Allan pushed it away. If Victoria had killed the demon with Ibenus then that meant ...

He froze, eyes locked on the white, rounded cast extending down his leg, ending a hand's length above his ankle. Gone. His foot was gone.

Allan stared, his mouth open. He heard voices but they sounded like they were underwater. His gaze lowered to Ibenus. Victoria was still holding his hand against her, but Allan could sense the absence of that love he'd always known. Not gone, not entirely, but diminished somehow. Ibenus had chosen another. He was no longer worthy.

Hands guided him down, returning him to his back.

"Ibenus," he muttered.

"He still loves you," Victoria sobbed. "We both do."

He. Allan closed his eyes, his heart sinking. That single word sealed it.

"I'm sorry, Allan," Malcolm said. "This is my fault. I shouldn't have let you two go alone."

Allan nodded, not really listening. It was Mal's nature to assume responsibility. Allan squeezed Ibenus. His feeling toward it hadn't changed, but it wasn't the same. He felt as though he should cry but he couldn't.

Victoria's eyes were swollen, pleading for some affirmation. He needed to say something, something worthy of a knight.

"Ibenus is yours now. Take care of him."

Tears ran down the wet paths along her cheeks and she closed her eyes. "I will. I'll take care of you both."

A heavy silence fell, uncomfortable eyes averting.

"I know this is a lot to handle." Malcolm squeezed Allan's shoulder. "We'll head back home in the morning once the doctor checks you out. We have morphine if you need it."

Allan shook his head. He wasn't hurting. Then again, he was probably already on morphine. That'd explain why he was so itchy. "Where are we?"

"Paris. One of Master Turgen's clients set us up."

"I see. Did everyone else make it out?"

"Master Schmidt got banged up pretty bad coming after you. Controlled falls. Pretty much flew the entire way."

"Is he all right?"

"He says he is but ..." Malcolm shook his head. "You know Schmidt."

"Yeah."

Malcolm scooted aside, allowing Chaya and Sam access to hug him and tell him how happy there were he was alive. But he didn't feel alive. He didn't feel much of anything. His gaze kept returning to Victoria who was still beside him, holding Ibenus in his hand. Something lingered beneath the grief and relief in her eyes and the corner of her mouth.

"I suppose I can't get on to you for carrying that PPK of yours," Chaya was saying.

Allan exhaled a weak laugh. "First time I ever shot it on a job." *My last job*, he thought, the grin falling away.

If Chaya sensed it, she didn't react. "Well, I have it. I'll get it cleaned up for you. Maybe give it a trigger job while I'm at it."

Allan nodded. If only he'd shot that bastard when he had the chance. He mentally replayed the fight, wondering how it might have gone had Allan only hit him.

"Let's give him some space," Malcolm said, patting Chaya's shoulder. He looked at Victoria. "You two probably want to be alone."

"Yeah," she said, her words barely audible. "Thank you."

Allan was still remembering the confrontation as the others wished him well and made their way toward the door. His eyes widened as his memory came back. "Wait."

Malcolm was already outside the door. He turned back. "Yes?"

"My name. TommyD knew my name."

The others just stared at him.

"Are you sure?"

"He called me Allan. He said he'd never met a knight before." Even if TommyD had overheard Gerhard use his name, when would they have said they were knights? A horrible realization unfolded in his mind. It wasn't chance that TommyD had gleaned Luc's name, not if he knew they were knights. Allan sat up. "He knows who we are!"

"How the hell would he know that?" Sam asked.

Victoria sucked a breath, her face pained. "I'm sorry, Allan. I'm so sorry."

"What?"

"I wanted to tell you. I should have told you before but I was afraid."

"Of what?" Allan asked. "What happened?"

"TommyD," she said. "I told him. I told him everything."

Allan blinked.

"What are you talking about?" Sam asked, an edge to her voice. "What do you mean you told him everything?"

"I knew you were a spy." Chaya drew a pistol and leveled

at Victoria chest.

Victoria didn't even react to the gun. She squeezed Allan's hand. "I love you, Allan. I'm so sorry."

CHAPTER 18

The pain wormed its way around the medication around 2 a.m. Subtle at first, probing through the wall of opiates so slowly that Allan hadn't immediately recognized it. As with any surprise attack, the full assault began the moment Allan realized it was coming. Then at once he felt it all: the broken rib, the stitched bite in his arm where a cherry-sized chunk of muscle has been ripped out, and the leg.

The leg was the worst, a steady throb extending from the cast and up to his spine as if some winch were pulling on the nerve, winding it tighter, sending sharp flares along its length. He'd half-expected cold or itching or any of the phantom limb symptoms he'd heard of, but it was evidently too early for that. It felt like a vise was crushing his ghost foot, squeezing it impossibly hard past any point that flesh or bone could endure.

Doctor Laroux, who had visited Allan shortly after he'd first awakened, had explained the bulk of the pain wasn't real, that it was his brain panicking because the map of his body was wrong. She'd warned of the painkiller addiction that many amputees developed trying to win an impossible war.

Gritting his teeth, Allan had calmly explained that the arm, the rib, and the horror show of mutilation beneath that bloody cast were not imaginary, and while he'd keep her advice in mind for the future, he definitely needed something more than the aspirin she'd originally offered. The fat-cheeked woman only frowned, an expression made easier by the deep scowl lines that looked to have been cut into her face with a chainsaw, and gave him a bottle of painkillers. She then entrusted Malcolm with two more bottles, with orders that he was in charge of doling them out. The mere fact that she'd come armed with three bottles but didn't initially disclose that, told Allan all he needed to know about the gangland surgeon.

Laroux had made one passing comment about the blonde that hadn't left Allan's side, but didn't ask where she was. Allan wondered how the sadist doctor would react if she knew that Victoria was locked in another room, wrists bound, and Chaya beside her with a bad attitude and sword. She'd probably shrug and pretend she didn't see it.

That morning, after the doctor's final stamp of approval, they'd left and begun the four-hour trip back to the mansion. The arm and rib only made getting in and out of the wheelchair infinitely harder. Sam and Malcolm had to help him with that and push him. Two days ago he was a Lead Knight, an angel at his hip. Now he couldn't even move his own wheelchair. He still possessed Ibenus. Being a current prisoner it didn't make much sense to let Victoria carry it. Allan sat sideways in the van's bench seat, his leg extended before him, and the bronze sword in his hand. It wasn't right. It didn't feel the same. He was no longer Protector and he knew it. But Victoria ...

He turned his head to where she sat in the back, hands bound and Chaya beside her with a gun hidden beneath a bundled shirt in her lap. Victoria smiled weakly, the same smile a child might give a parent after accidently burning their house down, desperately fearful they've lost any chance for forgiveness. Not returning the smile, Allan swallowed and returned his attention to the window, absently watching the trees whisk past.

She had betrayed him. She had shared the secrets he had fought to give her. He had vouched for her and, in return, she had spat on his trust and lied to him. She'd revealed their names to a man intent to use that information against them. And while she claimed ignorance of TommyD's appearance, the betrayal was no less real. The messages telling him to back off while she procured him a holy weapon were the most damning. Chaya had wanted to put her down right then and there. Mal and Sam had reasoned that Victoria would be the most likely means of tracking TommyD down and rescuing Umatri. Allan agreed, though his true motivation for mercy was less tangible. He ran his fingers along the wood grip panels. Like it or not, Ibenus was Victoria's now. Ibenus had chosen her they day they'd met. Had it known this would happen? Was that why it had made him accept her? How could Ibenus have known?

Allan closed his eyes, shaking the new feeling of betrayal before it could take root. His vow to protect the khopesh was no less binding than it had been the day of their bonding. Protecting Ibenus' new guardian was part of that. That vow superseded everything.

The others wouldn't understand. He wouldn't have.

"Here we are," Malcolm said as Sam turned into the drive.

Allan drew a breath and held it. *Here we go.* His first true day of retirement. He hadn't considered what exactly his role would be now that hunting was off the table. Librarian for certain, though the library was downstairs. Surely they could work around that. But what else would he do? Tom became their chef after he'd lost his leg and a few fingers, but Tom could always cook. Maybe Allan would have to learn. Maybe he'd become the gardener, nurturing flowers and herbs to ward away monsters. Whatever it was, his new full-time job was to serve as a living example. A reminder for other knights as to what their own future might hold.

The gate opened and the van continued onto the drive. Allan released his breath. Now he had to deal with Master Turgen and look the old man in the eye. Turgen would never say, "I warned you," not in a million years. He'd be nothing but sympathetic, supportive, and kind. But Allan still had to face him with failure. Somehow that made it worse.

As they rounded the bend to the side of the manor, Allan noticed a small crowd gathering near the door. Turgen and Schmidt stood at the front. Directly behind them. *I don't believe it.*

The van stopped and Luiza Hollis was the first to open the door. Her black hair was pulled back into a thick ponytail. She wore a loose-fitting blouse of red silk tucked into tight jeans the color of walnut. Akumanokira, an olive green army katana with a polished copper handle, hung at her left hip. "Hey, stranger."

Allan's voice cracked with the surprise. "Hi."

"Hey, man." Matt said, stepping around beside her. Gabi was in his arms, intently staring into the vehicle.

"I can't believe you're here," Allan said. "Hi, Gabi."

Gabi's mouth opened into a wide grin, exposing her two teeth along the bottom front. Then she turned her head, following Sam's path out from her seat and toward the back of the van.

"We came right away when we heard," Matt said. "Flew in last night."

"You flew?" Allan smiled for the first time in days. "I'm honored."

"Yeah, so don't ever say I don't love you."

Sam squeezed past rolling an empty wheelchair. "Here we go."

Malcolm crawled from the front seat and squeezed up beside Allan. "Matt, can you give us a hand?"

"Of course." He handed Gabi over to Luiza and together he and Malcolm guided Allan out and into the chair. The cast restricted knee movement, which resulted in his leg sticking straight out before him like a battering ram.

"You good?" Malcolm asked, offering Ibenus once Allan was properly seated.

Allan pressed his tongue against to roof of his mouth until the dulled pain from his rib subsided. "Yeah."

"Hey, Mal," Luiza said.

"Hi." He kissed Luiza on the cheek. "You look beautiful." Malcolm gave Gabi an appraising look, his brow raised. "So this is our newest knight in training?"

"This is her. Say hello to your Uncle Malcolm."

"So you two figured out which weapon she'll grow up to use?"

She smiled to Matt, revealing white teeth. "We're still figuring that out. I think she'll take after her mother and use Akumanokira. Matt, of course, is rooting for Dämoren."

"My money is on Dämoren," Schmidt said. Short scratches

marred his left cheek, surrounded by a purple bruise.

Matt nodded. "Thank you." He patted the large revolver slung under one arm. Bronze wolf heads capped its ivory handle.

The old man tickled her belly. White tape bandaged most of his knuckles. "She's stubborn and a born troublemaker. Dämoren can't resist that."

"Hey," Matt said in feigned annoyance.

"Name one of her protectors that wasn't those things," Schmidt said.

"I'm not a troublemaker."

Malcolm snorted, eliciting a laugh from Luiza and Schmidt.

Matt gave Allan a look. "See what I put up with?"

"Sorry, mate," Allan said. "I'm with Schmidt on this one."

"Everyone's a critic."

Allan endured the condolences and well-wishes from the other knights. The tears at the corners of Luc's eyes when he said he wished he'd been there affected him the most. He'd never seen Luc cry, not even when their ranks were decimated. All of that was immediately forgotten as Chaya led Victoria out of the van.

All eyes followed her but Victoria only looked at Allan and Ibenus.

"Take Miss Martin to the first-floor guestroom." Master Turgen didn't try to conceal the venom in his voice. "It has its own lavatory and we know there's nothing hidden there."

"She came of her own free will," Allan said.

"No," Turgen said. "She might not have resisted but she didn't come freely until she was caught. We will discuss this later once you are settled."

Allan drew a breath to reply but a terse head shake from Victoria silenced him.

"Am I to be denied Ibenus?" she asked, meeting Turgen's glare.

The old man didn't look away. "Luc, please escort Miss Martin to her room."

Allan squeezed Ibenus in his lap as Luc and Chaya led her away. Their feet clomped up a wooden ramp that had been erected over the side entrance stairs. Sawdust clung in some of the corners along the walk from when someone had obviously used a leaf blower to clean up the fresh construction.

"Come on," Matt said, breaking the tense silence. "Let's get you inside before we add sunburn to your injuries." He pushed the chair up the ramp and stopped as Orlovski tapped out the keypad combination.

"We set new codes and passwords," Turgen explained somewhere behind Allan.

The door bolts thudded and Orlovski swung it open. There, in the giant mirror, Allan got the first true look at himself, his sunken eyes and three-day beard, an invalid pushed by his best friend as he held a sword he would never hunt with again. Allan looked away from the reflection, his gaze absently watching the inlaid symbols in the wooden floor tiles as Matt wheeled him down the hall.

His days away from the manor had dulled Allan's immunity to the pungent herb and flower bouquets. Soon he'd again be so used to them that he wouldn't even notice. He thought again to the prophetic vision, his likely future as gardener. He'd have to get a prosthetic, maybe a greenhouse where everything was up on tables so he could reach it from his chair.

"So this used to be some Nazi mansion?" Matt asked, breaking the line of thought.

"Yeah," Allan said. "Well, they didn't build it. Just took it and added the shelter beneath for barracks or balls or whatever it was they had in mind. Allies dropped a bomb on it and that was that."

"It's so weird."

"Why do you say that?"

"I don't know," Matt said. "Just not the kind of place you'd think about living. Bad vibes, you know?"

Allan snorted "Your American is showing again. Finding real estate on this side of the world without dark history is impossible."

"Eh, I guess. I suppose living in a Nazi mansion with a ballroom in the secret bunker is normal around here."

Allan laughed, setting off the fractured rib. Wincing, he

clenched his teeth until the pain passed. "It does sound a bit odd when you word it like that."

Matt guided Allan into a near perfect reproduction of his upstairs bedroom, though the door was on a different side and Allan normally didn't decorate with a million flowers. There was also a private bathroom. "Here we are."

Allan eyed the empty sword stand and grunted. Were they supposed to pretend Ibenus hadn't chosen a more capable protector?

"So." Matt sighed. "Here's the question of the day. I'm sure you need to take a leak and get yourself cleaned up. You need help?"

Allan craned his head up at him. "You offering to help me piss?"

"Whatever you need, man."

"I'm not a *complete* invalid."

"No problem. Just want to make sure you're okay."

Allan swallowed. Through the open door he could see the handles in and above the cast iron tub. He had one good arm and one good leg. He could do it. "Could you wait for me in here? You know, just in case?"

"Of course."

"Thanks, Matt. Thanks for coming. Both you and Luiza. It means a lot."

"You're family, Allan. No need to thank us."

The bath went about as well as expected. That is to say that it didn't. Between not wanting to soak the leg cast and the difficulties with his arm and rib, Allan settled on performing a glorified and rather messy sponge bath. Removing the film left from his bed in that abandoned building and the car ride had refreshed him. He still felt it coating his foot, and he desperately wanted to clean it and scrub between his toes where it felt particularly gross, but that foot wasn't there any more. Only its ghost desired to be cleaned and groomed as its widow had been. *Just ignore it.*

Shaving with his left hand had been more awkward than Allan had anticipated and he now had two nicks and a strip of missed stubble along his jaw line to show for it. Still, it felt good to be clean and to have done it himself.

As promised, Matt had dutifully waited outside. "Everything all right?"

"Splendid." Allan had figured out how to operate the chair with only one and a half hands, but he wasn't very fast and pulled to the left. In short, it was exhausting and not very good.

Matt sat beside the bed, watching him struggle through the door before Allan finally conceded.

"Can you give me a hand?"

"Of course," he said hopping to his feet and taking control. He parked Allan beside the desk and gathered the clothes from the bathroom.

Allan eyed Ibenus now resting in the stand and frowned.

"You want me to move it?" Matt asked, dumping the laundry into a basket. "I can move her closer to the bed if you like."

"Him," Allan corrected.

Matt's helpful smile vanished, his face an unreadable blank. "It doesn't ... feel right."

"I agree, but that's how Victoria sees him, so that's what he is."

"I don't care what she wants," Matt said. "She sold us out. Ibenus is yours."

"No he isn't. Not any more. He bonded to Victoria. She sees him as a he so therefore he's a he," Allan said rapidly, forcing the words before his voice could crack.

"But she doesn't deserve him."

"That's not your call. It's not mine, it's not Master Turgen's, or anyone else's but Ibenus'. He chose her and if he hadn't I'd be dead. Even if he hadn't," Allan gestured to his extended leg. "My life as a hunter is done. I can't carry him."

Matt tightened his lips and shook his head. "It's wrong."

"The weapons decide."

"I know. I mean calling Ibenus *he*."

"Akumanokira was a *she* until Luiza bonded to him. It's no different."

"That was different. Kazuo was dead. You're not."

"That doesn't matter," Allan said. "Ibenus has chosen.

Victoria sees him as male. It's that simple."

Matt glared at the khopesh. "I don't like it."

"Please," Allan said. "For me. Ibenus is a *he*. It helps me ... deal with it. Do you understand?"

"Yeah," Matt said with a noncommittal nod. "For you."

"Thank you." That tinge of betrayal rustled in the back of Allan's mind. He eyed the bronze sword. "I have a question."

"What's that?"

"Does Dämoren ever talk to you?"

Matt blew a breath. "I'm not the best one to ask this, but yeah. She has. Ibenus talking to you?"

Allan shook his head. "No. Never with words. But sometimes I get these feelings, you know? Like, I've had it where out of nowhere I just have to blink for no reason and I end up moving out of the way of something just in time. Taking Victoria was like that. I just had a feeling and I acted on it."

Matt grunted. "No Dämoren's never warned me like that before."

"So I keep wondering why Ibenus would have told me to take Victoria on. Did he know what would happen to me? If so, why didn't Ibenus warn me?"

"Ibenus couldn't have known this was going to happen, man."

"Why not?" Allan asked.

"Because Ibenus loves you, that's why. Do you really think she ... he wouldn't have warned you?"

"Maybe he knew he couldn't stop it so he chose Victoria to prepare."

Matt shook his head. "No. If Ibenus knew what was going to happen to you, he would have known about her."

"You're probably right." Allan scratched his arm. The painkillers were wearing off. *Time to beg Mal for another dose.*

Matt blew a sigh, washing away the distasteful expression. "So how about some food? You hungry?"

Allan's stomach gurgled at the mention. "Very. I'd even eat Orlovski's eggs right now."

Matt laughed. "I think we can do better than that." He opened the bedroom door and began wheeling Allan toward it, when Master Turgen stepped inside and rapped lightly on the frame. Schmidt stood behind him.

"All settled?" Turgen asked.

"Fine," Allan said. "About to get some food."

"Understandable. Do you have time for a word?"

"As long as there's food involved."

"Easy enough." He looked at Matt.

"Well, then," Matt said, taking the hint. "I'll go see if Luiza needs anything." He pushed Allan out into the hall. "I'll catch you later, okay?"

"All right," Allan said.

"Is the room satisfactory?" Turgen asked as Matt left.

"It's fine." He turned up to Schmidt. "I wanted to thank you for coming for me. That was ... that was incredible."

Max smiled. "No need to thank me. I would have done that for any of our knights."

"Well you did it for me, so thank you. I can't imagine how difficult that was."

"Extremely." He took the back of Allan's chair and began slowly pushing him toward the dining room. "My body is reminding me of that. There was a time I could have done that far faster and with less ... bumps along the way."

Turgen shook his head as he walked alongside them, his cane tapping the floor. "You're fortunate you didn't break anything or kill yourself attempting that."

"I wouldn't have attempted it if I didn't believe I could. As for risk, that is our business. It feels good to be earning scars again."

"Now you'll be here again, mending them."

Allan caught the image of the three of them in one of the floor to ceiling mirrors in the hall; a sad picture of lost glory.

"We'll provide you with the best doctors to help you adjust," Turgen said to Allan, his free hand gesturing as he spoke. "Physical therapy and recovery. Don't worry about any of that. I had been considering installing a lift for some time so we will go ahead with that modification if we decide to stay."

"We're leaving?" Allan asked.

"Very likely, depending on what TommyD knows and what

he's capable of. Some of our more ... precious items are being sent back to Chile. Luc will go with them."

"Are we sure Chile is safe?"

The old man opened his hand. "Victoria never knew where it is. So it's reasonably safe. Still, this madman has proven to be very resourceful."

Allan frowned. He liked this house. Loved it, actually. He'd designed the library and had spent countless hours hanging portraits and setting tiny tiles. His knees and back ached at the thought of doing that all again. Well, the tiling at least. Someone else would have to get portraits now.

Schmidt steered him into the dining room and set him before the table. The smell of cooking cheese and meat from the kitchen roused another grumble in Allan's stomach. Schmidt limped off through the door and Turgen filled water glasses.

He took a seat opposite Allan. "My deepest condolences, Allan. This is a terrible business."

"Thank you." He eyed the kitchen door. The old man could at least let him eat before the guilt-trip came down.

Master Turgen touched his glass, slowly rotating it like a jeweler inspecting a stone. "Wounds heal. But the loss of a weapon is more than physical." He met Allan's eyes. "I want you to know that if you need anything, anything at all, or just need to talk, Max and I are here for you. We understand."

"I will. Thank you."

Turgen sipped his water. "The bond will never go away. It merely changes, but only on the weapon's end. For us, relinquishing our control, our duty, is extremely difficult. I don't want you to feel alone."

"I won't."

The old knight leaned back into his seat. He idly twisted the ring on his little finger. "It is a misconception that hunters are immune to depression and that no hunter has ever taken their own life. However, there is a difference between suicide and giving up. Many former knights have wasted away, become dependent on alcohol or other vices. Tom and I used to spend many hours together after he had lost his leg. Eslarin was under Yev's protection at that time and Rowlind was under Gabriel's.

We were proud of our former students, but … seeing our blades in the hands of another, no matter how much we loved them, was never easy. When Gabriel was killed and Rowlind broken, I thought I was going to die."

Allan had been reaching for his own glass, but stopped at Master Turgen's mention of Rowlind. Master Turgen had never once discussed his sword after she was destroyed, her broken blade driven through his former apprentice.

"The only thing that kept my sanity," Turgen continued, "was the need to protect the Order. After Yev's murder and the destruction of Eslarin, Tom gave up. Of course he assured me that he was only grieving but I could see it in his eyes. When Anya betrayed us and set fire to the archives, Tom didn't hesitate. He saved the library, but I have no doubt he knew he would die to do it. I believe he wanted his final act to mean something."

Afraid speaking might shatter this strange openness, Allan sipped his water.

"You never knew Max before he'd passed Lukrasus to Jean. To you he's always been a Master, even after Jean's death. The man you hunted with in Paris was the old Max. Malcolm commented how unusual he was, joking and showing off, always insisting on being first to the danger. That was the Max I first met. Age didn't change him, not in that way. Passing his sword to another was what made him the … bulldog, I believe you've called him."

Allan smiled guiltily. He glanced to the kitchen door, making sure Schmidt wasn't there. "Among other things."

"I don't want your grief to make you a bulldog. I don't want you to give up and run towards death. I failed Tom, and to some extent I failed Max. I don't want to fail you, Allan."

The kitchen door opened and Schmidt came through carrying a plate.

"Promise me you'll talk to me if you need to," Turgen said as Schmidt set the plate down. Steam rose from the croque-monsieur, blanketed in melted cheese and folds of ham peeking from the edges. Allan's mouth watered at the aroma.

"I promise," Allan said, picking up his utensils. "Thank you, Master Schmidt."

Allan scarfed the sandwich down as fast as he dared without burning his mouth. The two men sat silently until he was finished.

"Better?" Turgen asked.

"Very much, thank you."

Schmidt smiled. "My pleasure. I would offer you a drink but … medication does not mix well."

Allan glanced at the crystal bottle of brandy against the far wall. "It's all right," he lied. A drink sounded marvelous.

"Allan, we wanted to discuss with you your new duties," Turgen said.

"I see." He really did want that drink now.

"We had previously discussed me taking you on as my replacement with antiques and my network. With recent events, I would like to move forward with that."

"I … I see," Allan said. He'd wanted this for so long, dreamed of it, and now that it looked to finally be happening he didn't feel anything. "I would enjoy that."

Turgen's somber face cracked with a moment's grin. "It's a slow transition. It will take years and, even then, not all of my contacts may follow along, so you'll need to make new ones, maybe even cultivate some that I could not."

"I understand."

"Your duties as Librarian won't change of course," Schmidt added. "This will simply be something additional."

Allan nodded, feeling a bit of relief, though the idea they'd revoke his job as Librarian hadn't even crossed his mind.

Turgen leaned forward, folding his hands atop the table. "The topic we wanted to discuss is that we have agreed that you would be a perfect choice for Master Knight."

Allan blinked. "Master?"

"Yes. You more than meet the required attributes."

Meaning I no longer have a weapon.

"You're a leader," Turgen continued. "Well respected, and we believe you can handle the higher operations and responsibilities."

"My leadership got Gerhard killed."

Turgen gave a resigned nod. "Knights have perished under

all of our commands. It's a difficult burden and it never becomes easier. Quite the opposite, truth be told. To achieve Master, a knight must be very intimate with loss."

"And all of you agree? Even Master Sonu?"

"Master Sonu especially," Schmidt answered. "He suggested you as a potential candidate two years ago."

"I see."

"You don't appear very," Turgen rolled his hand as if reeling out the words, "amenable to the idea."

"It's ... uh ... I'm just a bit overwhelmed," Allan said. "Forgive me, it's just with the past few days this all feels so sudden."

Turgen raised a hand. "There's nothing to forgive."

"Do you need an answer now? Can I have some time to process this?"

"Of course."

Allan sat in his new room staring at his laptop. He knew it would be days before Master Turgen requested a field report. The others, as well as the video footage, would detail most of it. But he needed to remember everything now, as crystal clear as possible. And not just the report from the catacombs, but everything that had transpired since meeting Victoria. Her life might very well hinge on something he recalled, and he was running out of time. They'd called for a meeting.

He glanced at Ibenus on the stand beside him, hoping the sword might somehow jog his memory. Instead, a sharp pain started in his missing toes, like long needles being slid into each one, joining near his heel. Clenching his teeth, Allan pressed his tongue against the roof of his mouth. *You're not real. You're not real.*

After a very long minute the pain receded, leaving an annoying tickle. Allan let out a breath and checked the clock in the corner of the screen.

Twenty more minutes.

Surely someone was coming for him. They couldn't possibly have this trial, or tribunal, or whatever it was without him. He shook the idea from his mind. *Just nerves.* He clenched his hands and continued to type.

A knock came from the door. "About ready?"

Allan turned as Matt stepped inside. "Yeah." He reviewed his notes and closed the laptop.

"So what did Turgen want?"

"They, um, offered to make me a Master."

"Wow." Matt's eyes widened. "Can't say I'm surprised. Well deserved."

Allan shrugged. "I don't know. It just doesn't feel ... earned."

Matt snorted. "Really?"

"It's like they're just giving it to me as some consolation prize. Oh, you lost your foot and sword? Here's a promotion."

"That's not it at all." Matt shut the door. "Allan, they're offering it to you because you deserve it. Tom never became Master when he was hurt."

"Yeah, but—"

"No." Matt folded his arms. "Seriously, if Schmidt, Turgen, or Sonu were to die today, who would replace them? You killed a god, man!"

"Naked," Allan said. "No one ever mentions that part."

Matt nodded. "Yeah, that does add to the story, doesn't it? But seriously, who would you choose? Malcolm? No. He's all barbecues and Mardi Gras floats now. Luc? Sure. He'd be good."

"Luiza?"

"She'd be great, too. Me? No, they won't even give me a team. You heard Schmidt earlier. They were joking but it's still true. Taras? Maybe one day. He's too ... intense. Uwe?"

They both laughed.

"What about Daiyu?" Allan asked.

"Never met her in person."

"She'll make an excellent one."

"Good for her," Matt said. "But they're asking *you*, man. Do you honestly think they'd offer the Order to you just to make you feel better?"

Allan thought about that. "You're right."

"Doesn't happen often. Hell, you should ask to be stationed back home. You'll love ordering me around. You like fishing?"

Allan shook his head. "Not really. But I think I'd be staying here. Master Turgen wants to groom me on the museum circuit and his connections. Said it'll take a long time."

"Really?" Matt grunted. "You know I'm the antique expert, and you don't see him asking me. And you still think they're not serious about wanting you to become a Master?"

"I said you were right. Now you're just pushing it."

"Just want to be sure it's through that thick head of yours."

"Consider me scolded. And thanks. It's what I needed to hear."

"It's time," Luc said.

The knot of apprehension tightened in Victoria's stomach. She'd known it was coming, watched the clock counting down the minutes. But now she felt herself at the precipice, like those criminals she'd once arrested must have. Though their penalty was only prison. Hers could be far worse.

Chaya, leaning against a chest of drawers, motioned her pistol, ordering her to stand.

Forcing at least a mask of confidence, Victoria stood. "Let's go."

Luc opened the door and led her out into the hall, Chaya behind her. The mansion was silent, the only sounds being crickets outside the windows and their own footsteps on tile. Her stomach rolling somersaults, Victoria rubbed her wrist absently. Chaya had at least offered the courtesy of removing the sturdy zip ties when Victoria had needed to use the toilet, though she insisted on her keeping the door open. Luc had been kind enough to look away but Chaya, never one for modesty, watched the entire show with cautious eyes. Once done, they'd left the restraints off.

They passed the staircase and continued along the corridor. She'd imagined this drama playing out in the second-floor briefing room, the entire Order stadium-seated before her. Now that she thought about it, it was obvious that Allan's injury would have made that problematic. She hadn't been given a chance alone with him since he'd awoken, the opportunity to tell him how she felt, that nothing had changed with them. Now, she feared, she never would. She'd never kiss him or hold Ibenus again.

No. *That isn't going to happen.*

She'd come too far, earned an angel's love, and they sure as hell weren't going to deny her Ibenus. He had chosen her, found her worthy, and by God so would the Valducans.

They entered the dining room and they were all there, seated along three sides with one empty like a Last Supper painting. No, not all. Sam wasn't in the tribunal. She was likely watching over the baby Victoria saw when they arrived. Babysitting would definitely put a damper on funtas. Victoria wondered if she'd ever see Sam again.

Master Turgen and Schmidt sat in the middle. Ignoring the stern faces, she met Allan's eyes. He sat between Turgen and his friend Matt. Allan gave an almost imperceptible nod, assuring, and at once Victoria's fear abated.

She could do this.

Master Turgen gestured to the single empty chair opposite him and she walked to it, chin high. She was Ibenus' champion and she wasn't going to quail before these people.

"Miss Martin," Turgen said once she'd taken the hard, high-backed seat. "We have questions we want to ask you about your activities with TommyD."

"I know why I'm here," she said, confidence mounting with each word. "I've shown you everything I sent and discussed with him. Luc," she said, turning to him. "I am terribly sorry that my actions brought this down on you. One day I hope you will forgive me, but I don't expect it of you now. That was my fault and I hurt you."

Luc's cold expression remained unchanged.

"And what of Gerhard?" Turgen asked. "He can't simply forgive you. And now Umatri is in the hands of his killer, the same man you betrayed him to."

"I have freely admitted to everything I've done, but ... TommyD's appearance in the mines and the terrible things that he did, was nothing I was privy to. I told him to stay away. I had hoped to buy time to correct the mistakes I had made."

"But you still didn't tell us," Schmidt said. "That was the final mistake."

Victoria folded her hands across her lap, fingers intertwined.

"And what would have happened to me had I told you? Would I still be here?"

"No," he said. "But Gerhard might still be alive. Allan might not have been injured."

"The only definite is what would have happened to me. Having no knowledge of TommyD's intention would have gained you no insight into his ambush."

"Then how did he find us?" Chaya asked.

"I don't know. But I suspect he was looking for the getaway car. Would my confession have led you to not using Samantha as eyes on the cameras?"

Chaya narrowed her eyes but didn't answer.

"We were all already paranoid he might find us," Victoria continued. "In fact, your not knowing how he found you the first time led to everyone being even more cautious than you would have been otherwise."

"Now you're speaking hypotheticals," Turgen said, steepling his slender fingers before him.

"What I want to know is why." Malcolm's eyes didn't hold the loathing contempt as Chaya's or Turgen's. More like a physician determining an ailment. "Why did you betray us?"

"I already told you that," Victoria said.

"Indulge me," still studying her.

She swallowed. "James, my partner, was killed by a demon. I was written off as mad because no one believed me. And then I discover that your Order has kept these things secret out of some fear of what people might think, but with no consideration for how many would suffer for not knowing. I was angry. I wanted the world to know what was out there and how to protect themselves, and I wanted them to know damn well who was letting them die by not telling them."

"Do you not remember why?" Luc rumbled. "I told you."

"Yes." She nodded. "You told me that people would kill you for the holy weapons and you were right. I ..." Victoria fought the welling tears. *Not now.* "I didn't understand at the time."

"And what was that?" Turgen asked.

"I didn't know the extent that TommyD would go. As I said, I was angry. I lashed out before I grew to know what kind of people you really were. Most importantly, I didn't understand about the weapons."

"I told you about the weapons," Luc said. "Allan, I know, explained it."

Allan nodded but still hadn't said anything. He looked as terrified as her, his lips pursed and colorless like he was afraid moving them might break something, but Victoria couldn't tell what was behind those eyes. Was he scared for her, of her, what?

"I was told," she said. "And it was explained as clearly as I believe you could have. But I didn't understand. *How* could I understand what the weapons were? Before any of you were bonded, could you have understood what they were?"

"But you had seen the monsters," Luc said. "And you didn't believe us?"

Anger flashed, heating her cheeks. Victoria opened her mouth, closed it. "There's an enormous difference between belief and understanding," she said carefully. "Gerhard came *believing* in the weapons, but everyone was scrambling about trying to show him a demon because he didn't *understand*. Why then is it hard to believe that I didn't understand what all of you take for granted? The weapons, the bond, what that *means*."

"She's right," Allan said. "I didn't help her understand. That is my fault."

"Don't blame yourself," Matt said. "She knew what she was doing."

"Matt's right," Turgen agreed. "She has already admitted she came intent on betraying us."

"And it was my job to *make* her understand," Allan said.

"Don't excuse her," Schmidt said. "No one blames you."

"But it's still my fault. She was my student and it was my job to make her understand."

"She came intent on destroying us," Chaya said. "You're only mistake was accepting her as your student."

Turgen raised a silencing finger. "Sir Allan's errors in judgments are not what we are discussing."

"So what are we discussing?" Victoria asked. "I've told you everything. I don't know where TommyD is. There is nothing more I can tell you. So what possible outcomes does *this*," she swept her arm across the row of seated knights, "have? Or are you just pretending to be a court?"

Turgen glowered at her. "Miss Martin—"

"Is it death by firing squad, or the sword?" she asked. "Is that the debate?"

"No one is going to kill you," Malcolm said, earning every eye in the room.

Chaya snorted. "That hasn't been decided."

"We don't have a choice." Malcolm leaned forward, his seat creaking. "Ibenus has chosen her as protector. We know that."

"So you just want to let her go?" Matt asked. "After what she did? One knight is dead, a weapon is gone, and Allan's in a fucking wheelchair, man."

"You think I don't know that?" Malcolm snapped. "Taras and I recovered Gerhard's body. I scooped his brains up myself. But that still doesn't change the fact that Victoria isn't responsible for what happened to them."

"She admitted she sold us out," Luc said.

"She has. But the fact remains that she is bonded to a holy weapon." Malcolm turned to Matt who was still glaring at him. "You once told me that no holy weapon has ever bonded with their protector's killer."

Matt nodded, seeming unsure where this was going.

"So," Malcolm continued, "if we believe that a weapon can see into our soul when it makes the bond, then Ibenus would have known of Victoria's betrayal. Therefore, if she was in any way responsible for what happened to Allan, Ibenus wouldn't have bonded. And if she's not responsible for Allan, then she can't be responsible for Gerhard." He looked over the room, letting that sink in. "Ibenus has chosen Victoria. As knights, we must honor that decision. Killing her would defy our vows."

"Where was this when I was brought on board?" Matt asked. "You threatened to kill me. Now you want to protect someone that has openly betrayed us?"

"That was different," Malcolm said. "You were possessed. We'd never encountered that before. Allan told me that I should trust you because you were bonded. He was right. I was wrong. And I'm not making that mistake again." He returned his attention to Victoria. "So to answer your question, the outcome is that you either stay or you go. Either way, Ibenus is yours."

"Sir Malcolm," Turgen snapped. "While I respect your opinion, you can't speak for us all."

Schmidt shook his head. "He's right, Alex. Victoria is not to blame for Allan."

"We'll she's not staying here," Chaya insisted.

"Agreed," Orlovski said with a nod.

"I have no problem with that," Malcolm said.

"Glad we agree on something," Matt said. "But she can't leave until we have Umatri back."

"So are we just supposed to keep her in chains?" Malcolm asked.

"You want her just walking around here?" Matt asked with a wide gesture.

"If Victoria goes, I go," Allan announced.

Victoria met his eyes as stunned exclamations erupted around him.

Turgen placed his hand on Allan's arm. "Allan, there's no—"

"No," Allan said, holding Victoria's gaze. "I'm still sworn to Ibenus. I go where he goes." He turned to the old man. "I accept your offer, Master Turgen. I'm honored to do it. But if Victoria leaves, I'm going with her."

"Allan," Turgen said. "You're putting us in a very difficult situation. We can't trust her."

"Then let's give her the chance to earn it back. Let her hunt. The eel is still the highest priority. After that ..." A hardness grew in his voice as he met Victoria's eyes. "She can earn her way in by killing TommyD, and retrieving Umatri, and whatever information TommyD might still have on us. Would you be willing to do that?"

Victoria nodded. "Gladly."

"So there." Allan awkwardly pulled Ibenus out, setting him on the table, handle facing Victoria. "That is my proposal. Either we agree and she stays and earns lost trust or we both leave tonight."

"Allan," Matt said, "You're in no condition to leave right now."

"Then don't force me to."

Schmidt drew a long breath. "I'll agree. But as long as she is in this house she cannot be outside her room without an escort or have any access to the archives."

"Agreed," Malcolm said.

Orlovski tongued his cheek, sizing her up. He looked at Allan, back to her, and gave a slow nod. "Agreed."

A silence fell as the knights were deadlocked, four to four, one Master each way. But Victoria no longer cared. Whatever they decided, she'd have Ibenus and she'd have Allan. The rest of them could go to hell after that. Then she'd go to Paris and kill that bastard for what he did and return Umatri if for no other reason than to atone.

"Agreed," Luiza said, sealing the majority.

Brow crinkled, Matt turned to his wife. "You can't be serious?"

She smiled humorlessly. "Why not?"

"After what she did. You're willing to hunt beside her."

Luiza shrugged. "Mal's right. Besides, the last time I took a risk on a hunter I married him."

Matt shook his head, lips tight, but didn't speak.

Victoria held her smile, she met Luiza's stare and gave a silent thanks. Allan was beaming, the same satisfied glow he'd had when they'd found the Paris building from the video. The bitter taste of that betrayal returned, spoiling Victoria's elation. She didn't deserve his trust. Not until she atoned. Then her gaze returned to Ibenus. They needed to get back to Paris.

Schmidt rapped the table, silencing the whispered conversations. "Now that we have a strategy for Victoria, we still need to plan our next move. With Allan's condition, and my own ..." he gave Turgen a defeated frown, "physical limitations, I will be unable to accompany you to Paris. That still leaves six hunters."

"Excuse me," Victoria said, raising her hand.

"Yes?" Schmidt asked.

"I would like Ibenus now."

There was a hesitation. This was the commitment. Schmidt smiled, a sliver of teeth beneath the gray moustache. He opened his palm, gesturing to the sword. "He is yours."

EPISODE 161

SUBTERRANEAN WARZONE

"We have a special episode for you, cryptozoologists." TommyD sits before a wall of pockmarked beige stone. A slate gray helmet with a square LED lamp has replaced his trademark fedora, though he still wears his black Ray-Bans. "I'm here with a special report that only Monster Seekers will tell you about."

Familiar photographs of black-clad figures exiting a parked van and storming an abandoned building play across the screen. "After our last episode where we brought you absolute proof that a secret team of covert monster hunters exists, including the identity of one Luc Renault, I continued my investigation."

Video footage fills the screen—descending stairs, brick walls moving past in the harsh camera light. "Once the police finished their investigation of the Paris apartment where the kill squad was sighted, I took a peek inside." The camera turns down a hallway, briefly scanning two empty rooms before entering a third. A giant furnace dominates the rear of the chamber, hinges bent and torn from the missing door. The camera pans across a dark stain on the floor, then slowly approaches a yawning round hole. "A shaft beneath the apartment led straight down into the Paris Underground, a labyrinth of abandoned mine tunnels and sewers." The camera peers down the round tunnel, seeming to lower as it zooms. Far below, the light plays across a pile of debris, dead rats, and glinting metal at the bottom.

"The Underground has been a popular site for explorers, the homeless, illegal activities, and parties for centuries. There's hundreds of miles of tunnels and it could take a lifetime to see it all. This also makes it the perfect lair for cryptids. So I decided to go down there and see what I might find."

A shaky video fills the screen and black bars crop either side, indicating it as from a mobile phone. Over a dozen youths hop around, shoulder to shoulder, their necks and wrists encircled with slender glow sticks. Electronic music thumps, its sounds distorted by echoes and the inadequate microphone. Spinning lights seethe and strobe across the graffiti-coated stone walls around them as they dance and drink. A girl in her early twenties laughs in front of the camera. A smudged smiley face in blue glowing paint decorates her left cheek. Her glassy eyes are all pupil.

TommyD's harsh voice comes in, crisp above the poor audio. "This footage was found on a cell phone not thirty feet from one of the many ladders leading to the surface."

Screams erupt, drowned out beneath the music. Partiers drop their plastic cups and surge past the camera, pressing the owner against a wall. Behind them, doll-faced insects the size of small dogs pour from a darkened hall, skittering along the walls. Shrieking victims flail and fall as the pale monsters spring and latch on to them. The wails of crying infants ululate beneath the still-thumping bass. Two giant insects emerge from the darkness and the camera whirls away. It jostles madly as the owner flees with the shrinking mob. The tunnel is black, lit only by a few wildly waving lights, luminous body paint, and multi-colored glow sticks. The music fades as they run but the wailing cries grow louder. Finally, the phone tumbles to the ground, landing face-up, the stone ceiling visible in the phone's LED light. A pale carapace scuttles past and the screams continue, silencing one by one.

"There was no trace of anyone nearby," TommyD continues. Baby coos and giggles sound from the still-playing footage. "Though there was blood. The trail led a hundred yards to this …"

The video changes to a dimly lit scene of an arched chamber littered with bottles, dead glow bracelets, clear plastic cups, and crumpled clothing. A white folding table stands against one wall, an open Styrofoam cooler atop it. The camera's sweeping light elicits ghostly afterglows from the phosphorescent spray-paint scrawled across the walls and ceiling. A pair of barrel-shaped speakers occupy two corners. One lies on its side beneath a smeared red-brown handprint.

"Who these poor victims were is still unknown. Many partying tourists pass through the City of Lights and, unless someone escaped, no one might know of this illegal rave or what happened to their loved ones. I myself encountered these monsters during my exploration."

The video cuts to the image of a doll-faced insect emerging from the gloom of colorless night vision. The camera jostles and a crisp laser beam swings into frame. Two more creatures scuttle along the walls behind the first. The laser cuts through the hall, the end flaring on the lead insect as pincers unfold from the black slit of its mouth. It cocks its head slightly, then coos like an amused infant. A loud *pop* and a brilliant flash fills the screen, washing out the night vision in white. High shrill screams, like a dozen terrified babies, wail through the speakers. The image contrast restores. The insect's corpse lies on its back, smoking and smoldering black. The other monsters charge, mouth wide as they weave side to side.

The laser beam slices toward one but the screaming bug jumps to the left as another shot rings out, blinding the camera. More shots, and then the cameraman is running down empty passages, his breath hard and panting. The camera swivels around again. Three more bugs scuttle behind him. The laser moves wildly, trying to lead one before more shots blind the night vision.

"Oh shit, oh shit, oh shit," repeats like a desperate mantra as the cameraman continues to run, racing past dark chambers and blurred graffiti. He turns again. The insects are closer now. A giant six-legged creature with a wedge-shaped head runs along the floor behind them like a fox hunter behind his dogs.

The chant continues, the words blurring together. "Oh, shit, oh, shit, shit, shit, shit ..." Beneath that and the clomps of racing feet, the child-like screams grow louder.

The camera spins violently to the side, the owner slamming into a wall as he takes a hard right. He continues running, his words now just an unintelligible noise. He turns again, pausing before a wall set with rusty bars. Looking up, the rungs lead up a narrow shaft to a pinhole of light above. Without looking back, the cameraman hurries up, the bars now racing past the screen in rapid succession.

The wails distort in the echoes and the camera peers back. One of the nightmarish dolls has started up. The camera jostles, then a pistol swings into view. It has no laser, but instead a long square silencer. The gun barks a metallic *chunk* and the wall above the closing beast puffs, blasting dust and shards of masonry. The gun fires twice more, hitting the monster and sending it down to the floor. Two more of its kind scuttle into view along the bottom.

The camera pans up. Brilliant daylight flares through a rectangular hole in the center of a manhole high above. The camera surges towards it. A gloved hand reaches up, pressing the lid. Metal grates and light eclipses around the disk, washing out the image.

"I barely escaped," TommyD says, the video returning to him before the wall. "Had I not found an escape, I can promise you that I wouldn't have made it out, and the secret of what lies beneath Paris and what happened at a recent rave would go unknown. But not by all. There are some who do know. There are those mysterious killers of monsters who we have witnessed, but have yet to come forward with the truth. And while I, as many of you, have always hoped that one day they might share the truth, I now know they will kill to keep it from you. You see, my friends, I met them, too."

Footage of a dark passage fills the screen, an arched tunnel, seeming to go on forever. Bits of debris and broken rock line the corners, leaving a dusty path between them. Lights move in the distance. The camera pauses, watching a pair of figures make their way closer. One wears a sword at his belt. The other carries a long wavy-bladed knife, its edges occasionally gleaming in the glow of their headlamps.

"I found these two coming toward me shortly after my discovery of the party kill-site. Despite my apprehensions, I braved speaking with them, to tell them of what I'd discovered."

The black and white footage cuts to a slender man in a filthy bulletproof vest and a helmet with a light. A pistol butt peeks out below one armpit. A black, irregular shape, like something on the lens blocks the lower portion of the frame. Only the most scrutinous viewers might notice that the distortion along the edge remains curiously consistent as the autofocus adjusts.

"Excuse me." the voice, while slightly different, is still clearly TommyD's, despite the microphone's poor placement or quality. "Please, I don't mean to startle you."

The man wheels, eyes wide. He takes a step back and his dark brow furrows.

"I found something. There's—"

"TommyD?" the man asks, his accent German.

"Yes, but listen."

The German stands rigidly still. Then one hand slowly reaches across his body, vanishing beneath the lens' black obstruction.

"Please," TommyD shouts.

The camera jostles and a second man leans out from behind a pair of stacked plastic bins, a small pistol clutched in his hand. The gun fires, the flash blinding the swinging camera as it tries to adjust.

"No!"

The camera flash fades as the German wrenches the kris blade from his belt and dives to the side. More gunshots erupt and the camera swings wildly, unable to focus. From the blur, the German's face lunges forward, his mouth open in a scream, his serpentine blade raised. The brilliant laser springs into frame, gleaming off the man's bared teeth and up toward his eyes. A gun fires, the flash filling the screen and it fades back to TommyD seated before the stone wall.

"Again," he says, shaking his head. "I barely escaped. Had I not been armed, I have no doubt they would have murdered me. Many of us had hoped that these mysterious hunters were silent guardians, protecting us from what lurks in the shadow. That is not true. What these men and women are hiding is something they'd kill for. Monsters, humans, it doesn't matter. There's a secret war, my friends, being waged right now, below the streets of Paris. The monsters are on both sides. And *we* are trapped in the middle.

"From Paris, France, this is TommyD, signing out."

CHAPTER 19

"How do we look?" Malcolm asked, turning the van onto a dark street, his voice echoing in Victoria's ear bud.

Hunkered in her seat, the backpack pressing awkwardly against her, Victoria scanned the windows along the empty avenue. Nothing. Above the rooftops, a white beam from the Eifel Tower blocks away, sliced across the clouds. "Clear."

"Clear," Chaya said, followed by Luiza, Matt, and finally Orlovski seated beside her.

"Okay," Malcolm said easing the vehicle along the curb. "You know the drill. Ready in three ..."

Despite this being their fourth night, Victoria's heart pounded like it was still the first. Sweat ran down the back of her neck.

"Two ... "

Mouth tight, she crouched behind Orlovski, her hand squeezing the nylon handle of the second backpack.

"Go!"

The van doors swung open. Orlovski charged out first. She was right behind him, the sticky night air hitting her already hot cheeks. Ibenus bounced against her thigh as she ran. Crouching beside a wide manhole, she surveyed their surroundings as Orlovski slipped a metal hook into the cover's slot. With a grunt and the grating of steel on concrete, he heaved it to the side. Matt and Chaya came next, each taking a separate point to look out. Luiza shut the doors and ran to them, katana in hand as the van rolled silently away.

Without a word, Matt reached down the opening, cracked a bright green glow stick, and let it fall before he climbed down. Chaya followed, her movement concise and graceful, zero hesitation. Once she was a few feet down, Luiza gave a sharp nod and Victoria pulled the extra pack onto one shoulder and swung her legs into the hole. Her boots found the thick rungs set along the side and she started down, pausing long enough to click the red light atop her helmet once her head was below the surface.

Maddening swirls of graffiti coated the ancient masonry, most of it completely illegible. Four feet down, a grimy ledge filled one half of the shaft, creating a platform wide enough to stand on. She set Malcolm's gear onto the landing, happy to be rid of its awkward weight, and then pulled the hanging sword closer so it wouldn't catch on the platform's lip before continuing down. The sounds of the already quiet city faded, replaced only by the metallic pings of boots on the ladder below her. Eons of dust and grit coated the round rungs, making them slippery. More rained down as Luiza began her descent.

Lowering her head to shield her eyes, cascading dirt tinkled off Victoria's helmet and ran onto her sweat-moistened neck. Ignoring it, she continued, the air growing chillier with each rung.

"Watch out for the last step," Matt said.

A few seconds later, Malcolm's voice came through the radio. "Parked, locked, and heading back."

A green light grew brighter beneath her feet. The claustrophobic walls opened up as she lowered into an arched room. More graffiti decorated the three walls, and Matt and Chaya stood off to the side.

"Careful," Matt said.

The ladder ended two feet from the floor, above a pile of cigarette butts and crumpled wrappers, their shadows long in the glow stick's jade light. Carefully, Victoria eased herself to the bottom and stepped out from beneath the gritty rain. A carved stone block in the wall read, "1853." The spray-paint vandals had left it completely untouched, as if some reverence had stayed their hands.

Matt gave her an emotionless glance, then returned his attention to the small plastic bottle clutched in one hand. The faint pinkish hue of the water inside seemed heightened under his headlamp's red glow. Minutes before they'd made their final approach, Matt had stuck his finger with a diabetic's lancet and squeezed several drops into the water. Blood compass, he called it. Evidently the blood would gather in the direction of any nearby demons.

What a weird power, she thought.

She eyed the snarling bronze wolf heads jutting from the holster beneath his arm. The holy revolver, while impressive, wasn't silenced. Victoria only hoped she wasn't beside him when he fired it down here. By contrast, the blocky machinegun he carried slung from his other shoulder sported a comically huge suppressor.

"Careful at the bottom," Matt warned as Luiza emerged from the ceiling.

"Thank you," she replied, a musical tone to her voice. She hopped down and walked over to them, brushing her hands together. She wore her katana along her back, beneath the black pack, its metal handle nearly flush with her head.

Metal grated above, followed by a muted *clang.* "We're all in," Malcolm said.

Victoria ran her fingers along Ibenus' smooth handle as she waited for the knights to come down. How she wished Allan could have been here, given her a kiss for luck. Not that he would have. They video-chatted nightly, but there was still that distance, and more than just the miles between them. He didn't fully trust her. She didn't blame him. But he believed in her, and that's what she needed.

Now she was down here, with five knights who didn't trust her, two who hated her, one murdering bastard lurking around and, of course, the monsters. In the nine days since Allan's maiming she'd had the dreams he'd spoken of. Her in some Arabian landscape, creatures emerging from the sands. She wanted to kill them, sure. But more than that, more than anything, she wanted TommyD.

Standing orders were to take him alive if they found him.

Squeeze him until they recovered Umatri and the footage he'd taken. She ground her teeth at the thought of that awful video he'd posted that morning. The image of Gerhard's death, the blatant fucking lies. *Fucking bastard.* He still hadn't communicated with her. But the fact he hadn't named the Order and everything else meant that he was still honoring her request. Didn't it?

Malcolm and Matt might posture, making their threats and claims of what they'd do to him, but TommyD was hers. He was going to see her face, know what he did. Ibenus would taste his blood. There would be more. Oh, she had plans. But first ...

"All right," Malcolm said as he followed Orlovski down into the passage. "Let's get to it."

First I need the Order to trust me.

They followed the hall single file, Malcolm in front, Luiza, the second Team Leader, on the rear. Victoria was in the middle, between Orlovski and Chaya. The passage was almost coffin-shaped—narrow at the floor, subtly widening until eye-level, then it quickly came together with three tapered steps, forming a kind of arch. Victoria could easily have pressed her palm flat against the ceiling. After thirty or so feet, it turned. A rusty wrought iron gate, its top crowned with spikes, stood open. A pair of chipped holes marred the wall where its latch or lock had once been. They continued on, giving the ancient relic no more than a passing glance.

There was no smell, no sounds but their boot steps and shifting gear. The passage opened into a long, vaulted chamber. Faint lines across the stone floor showed it had been swept. And a colorful array of empty glass candle holders and various trinkets formed a semicircle before a skillfully painted mural depicting a Virgin Mary with a bearded dwarf suckling at her disproportionately large breasts. Several cataphile maps referred to this as *La Cathédrale de la Vierge Profane.*

Chaya gave the shrine a non-committal grunt as she passed it.

"At least it's not a mime," Orlovski quipped.

Taking the eastern exit from the cathedral, they followed the next tunnel twenty yards past a pair of rounded chambers to where it ended at a long stairway, hewn from the solid stone.

Matt checked the compass, shook his head, and they headed down.

The cool air became heavier as they descended. Victoria could smell the stale moisture before the first of their lights reflected off the smooth surface of the flooded passage. The water was the creamy tan of parchment, so cloudy that their lights only penetrated it by millimeters. Crimson light played off wall and ceiling, extending further and further into the darkness. Narrow ledges ran either side, about a foot above the water.

"How far does it go?" Chaya asked.

"Fifty meters," Victoria said, recalling the map.

"Taras, you're on point," Malcolm said.

Drawing his kukri, Orlovski squeezed his way to the front and stepped onto the water. The surface bent beneath his feet, sending distorted reflections down the tunnel.

Once he had made it a few feet, the rest of them moved forward, straddling the flooded passage. The low ceiling required even Victoria to stoop, head down, legs wide as she shuffled along, her incremental progress measureable in inches. Her pack scraped along the ceiling. The position left her feeling vulnerable, exposed above the unseen depths. She imagined the pale, black-eyed doll's face rising out from the murk beneath her. What would she do it if one did? *Kill it,* she decided.

Movement caught her eye. Adrenaline shot up her spine and down to her fingers. Her headlamp zeroed in on an unfurled condom lazily bobbing in the milky water like a dead jellyfish. Victoria released a breath. Her surging pulse slowed and she continued onward. Her hips ached from the awkward movement but she pushed through it. No way was she going to complain or, God forbid, fall.

Steps led up and out of the water. They took a moment to recover and stretch back out before continuing on.

After a half hour of walking, crawling, and searching several side passages and empty chambers, Malcolm held up a hand, halting the procession. He lifted his head and sniffed. "You smell that?"

Victoria sniffed and shook her head.

Luiza was the only one that nodded. "Yeah." She drew a deep inhale and curled her nose.

"Compass doesn't see anything," Matt said.

Malcolm drew Hounacier. "Keep your eye on it."

Weapons ready, they moved forward, searching the crags and shadows. They passed one room that was simply a round pit. A swirling pattern of rocks and broken glass covered the floor ten feet below. Malcolm stopped at an intersection and sniffed again, then gestured to the left.

Victoria licked her dusty lips, her hand squeezing Ibenus' wood grip. A faint stink tickled her nostrils, growing stronger with each step.

"Jesus Christ," Orlovski muttered, the back of his hand across his nose.

They rounded a corner. Dim light issued from a hole in the wall a dozen yards ahead, a lone window shining in the blackness.

Victoria breathed through her mouth, trying to avoid the pungent reek of shit.

Malcolm killed his headlamp. "Stay here," he whispered. Hounacier out, he crept into the shadows. He stopped just below the opening and removed something from his vest.

Malcolm lifted a square mirror atop a telescoping metal rod. He peered through the crude periscope, moving it around, then motioned. "Clear."

The hunters hurried forward, the stench growing palpable as they neared.

Matt was the first to reach him. "What do we have?"

"Kill site."

Pushing her way beside Chaya, Victoria peered through the narrow window into a room. The air that touched her face was warmer than the rest of the catacombs and carried a metallic tang. A column of stacked rocks, held together with globs of mortar stood in the middle, shadows spoking outward from it, cast from a trio of discarded flashlights. Glistening blood splattered the walls, running down the pale stone in long trails where it joined the puddles in the floor. A red-soaked backpack lay strewn open, contents spilling from a slashed hole in one side. A wet mound of purple and pink organs was piled on one side. A crinkly length of intestine ran away from it, along the floor, over one of the lights, and out the door like a discarded water hose.

Bile rose in Victoria's throat and she turned away, allowing Luiza a peek into the cave of horror.

"Nothing on the compass," Matt said, checking the bottle. "With all the rock, range is for shit."

"They couldn't have gotten far." Malcolm removed a tablet from his pack and flipped it on, flooding the passage with pale light.

"It's messier than we've seen," Orlovski said. "Previous sites were clean of remains. They'll probably come back for the rest."

"Maybe. Maybe not." Malcolm's fingers moved across the screen, expanding the map. "If they took live victims the eel might corrupt them before the cleanup crew arrives."

"I don't see another way through," Victoria said, peering over Malcolm's shoulder. "This cut through window isn't even showing."

Malcolm scrolled through the maze-work of tunnels beyond the room. The passages' colors ranged from white to orange, depending on depth. Blue signified flooded or regularly flooded regions. Red markers indicated exits to the surface. Behind their position, a noodle-work of green passages, the least prevalent color on the map, depicted where all they had cleared. "This looks to be the only way." He flipped off the screen. "Let's go."

Matt was the first to peel off his pack and slither through the waist-high window. Dämoren out, and trained on the doorway, he stepped over the red pools, making room for the next hunter.

One by one they crawled inside. Over the course of the last few days, they had the system down. Something squished beneath Victoria's boot as she came through and she resisted any urge to look. Twin rows of prong-shaped dots, like curved V's, speckled the walls and floor. Bloody footprints. Eyes watering from the stench of blood and disembowelment, she re-shouldered her bag and followed the knights into the adjoining hall.

The prints continued for several feet, appearing black under the red caving lights, the occasional smear where something dragged the floor elicited memories of Gerhard's limp body being hauled away.

Blood compass and revolver in front, Matt led them down a low tunnel thirty yards before it split. The blood spots were fewer, difficult to find, but Chaya spotted one that led them to follow the south tunnel. They walked in silence, headlamps searching the walls. Victoria ran her thumb nervously along Ibenus' grip, straining her ears for the sounds of scuttling feet or a baby's laughter.

The passage shrank lower and lower, forcing them to hunker and eventually crawl. Any traces of blood were gone, but the occasional claw print in the dirt assured them their quarry had passed this way. After twenty cramped minutes on their knees and elbows, the tunnel intersected a wide arched passage. A single rust-colored smudge marked the exit's lip.

Careful not to touch the blood, Victoria crawled free and dropped to the floor. Stretching her tight muscles, she surveyed her surroundings. The prevalence of spray-painted graffiti told that this tunnel served as an arterial route for cataphiles, a subterranean highway.

"Which way?" Luiza said, arching her back.

Eyes squinting at the screen, Malcolm checked his map.

Matt crouched, inspecting the floor. "Tracks lead this way."

"Here, too," Chaya said from the other direction. "Looks to be a lot of traffic."

"This is a huge section." Malcolm flipped the map around for everyone to see. "Too much for us to clear in one day." His dusty fingers hovered above the screen, tracing the paths on their descent from pale yellow to the bright hazard orange of the deepest depths.

"Running out of time if they took prisoners," Matt said. "You said so, yourself."

"I still think we're going to find the eel somewhere deep. One of the flooded chambers."

"So which way?" Matt asked.

"It's not that simple," Mal said, turning the map toward him. "We have several possibilities."

"Then we'll split up," Luiza said.

Victoria bit her lip. They'd split several times before, but never when they had proof that demons were nearby. Not wanting to be the naysayer, she eyed the others, hoping someone else might mention it.

"Agreed," Malcolm said.

Hand on Amballwa, Orlovski let out a low breath. "Are we sure about this?"

Thank you, Taras.

"We know they're around here." The Russian looked both ways up the hall as if expecting screamers to emerge.

Chaya coughed something under her breath. Orlovski shot her a flat look. "That what you're in to?"

The Israeli gave a teasing shrug.

"Three should be sufficient," Luiza said.

Malcolm tapped his screen. "Be careful. We know they're close. We'll meet back here in two hours."

In a life of chasing monsters and hiding from people out to kill him, Matt had hunted in twelve countries and three continents. He'd stalked forests, mountains, desert, snow, swamps, cities, and roadside towns that could measure their population in single digits. And in that impressive buffet of miserable and shitty places to kill or be killed, Matt hated mines most of all. It wasn't the sense of being buried alive or a fear of toxic gas. He could handle that. It was just that nothing ever went as planned when a mine was involved. Things always went sideways.

Now they were traipsing through the weirdest damn mine in the world. His body ached from days of crouching and crawling. Every night, he had to blow a pound of gray-brown crud out of his nose. He was banged, scraped, bruised and there was no end in sight. Exploring the Catacombs could take years, and that was providing that what you were looking for wasn't actively hiding from you. Matt just wanted to get back to Belgium. He missed Gabi like crazy. At first he thought a little vacation from the crying and diapers might be pretty nice, but now they were nearing a full week and he wanted to hold her. He didn't complain to Luiza about it. She was taking it harder than he was.

He also wanted to see Allan, make sure he was doing okay. The daily video conferences weren't enough. Allan was like a brother and, aside from Luiza and Gabi, was the only family he had. Well, maybe Schmidt to some extent. Schmidt and Matt's adopted father Clay had been tight, sort of like him and Allan, so he kinda muscled his way into Matt and Luiza's family, like some crazy part-time uncle that shoots machine guns and challenges you to drinking contests. There was also Ester, Luiza's mom, though she wasn't a Valducan. Luiza's dad had been a knight, as had his father before him, so Ester at least understood the life.

"Hold up," Luiza said as they reached an intersection.

Matt halted, keeping his attention to the passages ahead and to the right. Chaya maintained rear guard. He checked his blood compass. Nothing.

Pale light blinked on behind him, flooding the area in colors other than shades of red and black. "Right tunnel," Luiza said, and then the light went out.

She put the tablet away. Luiza motioned her head and they followed. The tunnel turned a series of right angles, eventually widening into a large chamber easily forty feet across. At its center, between a pair of questionable support columns, their lights gleamed off a miniature castle built of clay with bottle glass windows and tiny, dusty banners along its towers.

Luiza led them past it without a second glance.

Matt checked the compass. Still nothing. They'd been going for forty-three minutes. Another twenty, twenty-five and they'd need to head back. They'd lost radio contact with Mal's team after the first half hour. He didn't like being cut off. What if they needed help? Maybe they found a demon, or one of them got hurt. What if that murdering son of a bitch TommyD showed up? Matt couldn't help but wonder what Victoria might do if that happened. Would she stay true to her word, a word that meant jack shit to him, and plug the bastard? Or would she pop Mal and Taras in the back of the head, steal their weapons, and take off?

Why Luiza trusted her, Matt didn't know. Luiza just said that she did, and that was that. Matt knew better than to push the point once her mind was made up. Still, it felt like she was siding against him. For Allan' sake, Matt hoped she was right.

Alcoves lined the passage beyond the room, each haphazardly packed with yellowed and crumbling bones. In Paris' long and bloody history, burial space became a premium. After centuries of bodies buried atop bodies, graveyards formed pregnant hills. Sometimes they burst, spilling rotted corpses into neighboring basements. Eventually, Parisians made the bold decision to exhume the millions of dead and transfer them to the old quarries. Several hundred thousand were stored in the official ossuary, a special section that was sealed off from the rest of the mines. It was now a tourist site, the bones cleverly arranged in artistic patterns, walls of skulls and pillars of femurs. But the bulk of those bones were unceremoniously deposited down here. While bones and the dead didn't bother Matt, not after the life he'd led, the sheer volume of it was staggering.

"Did we take a wrong turn?" Matt asked as they reached a mortared wall sealing the passage.

"Shouldn't have," Luiza said, a hint of uncertainty in her voice. She unzipped the pouch with her tablet.

Not one to pass the opportunity, Matt removed his pack as well and set it on the floor, happy to be rid of the weight. Chaya followed suit. She stretched, her vest *creaking* with the movement.

The glow from Luiza's screen flipped on. "The map says it goes through."

"Map is wrong." Matt wandered the fifteen feet back to a brick wall along one side of the hall that sealed two-thirds of a side passage, leaving a crawlspace along the top. He peered down the narrow tunnel. The floor was solid bones, ribs, broken craniums, vertebrae—thousands of bodies worth, four feet deep and stretching beyond the end of his light like a river of death. "Christ."

"That tunnel should cut through," Luiza said. "Maybe that's what they were referring to."

"Is there another way?" Matt clicked his headlamp, increasing the beam. The trough extended at least sixty feet before opening up at the far side. It reminded him of one of those ball pits he played in as child, but nowhere near as inviting.

"I'd rather not go through that," Chaya said, craning her neck.

"I bet there's a prize down there if you dig."

"You first."

Luiza fidgeted with her map. "If we go back a kilometer, it appears to loop around. Passage might be flooded though."

Matt dimmed his light. "Don't think we have time."

"Me neither." Luiza frowned, her chocolate eyes studying the passage of bones. "By the time we made it through that, we'd have to turn back around and hustle."

"Well," Matt said, taking the cue. "I say we mark this as a spot to return to and head back. Maybe Mal's team found something."

"I'm down with this," Chaya said.

"All right." Luiza clicked off her tablet and slid it back into its waterproof bag. "Let's see what the others found."

Matt heaved his pack back on. He gave an unconscious glance to the bottle in his hand and froze. The blood-pinked water was clear. Along the side, the one facing the bone trough, a sphere of blood pressed against the inner wall. A surge of excitement shot up his spine, banishing the exhaustion. "Contact."

The two knights spun, hands moving to their swords.

Matt motioned his head in the direction the compass pointed. The red bead was sliding along the bottle's wall. The demon was moving.

Luiza looked at it, drew her katana, and moved toward the half-wall in a crouch.

"We going for it?" Chaya asked, sliding Khirzoor from its scabbard.

"That a problem?" Luiza's tone was ice cold, serious.

"Just making sure." Chaya's humor seemed to have risen by the same degree Luiza's had vanished.

"I go in first," Luiza said. "Chaya, then Matt. Stay close so Khirzoor hides our sound." They nodded and she was up and over the wall. Bones clicked and crunched as she slithered through the gap. As her feet slid inside, Chaya grabbed the lip and pulled herself up before Matt could even offer to help. Once she was through, he scrambled up, scraping his helmet on the low ceiling.

Bottle still his hand, he wriggled across the dead. The ancient bones crackled beneath him like dry rotted sticks. His padded knees and elbows sank into them with each movement. Chaya's boots pistoned inches from his face as she crawled, and he had to keep his head down to prevent one from taking him in the face.

Above the pops, rattling, and scrapes as they hurried, a baby's soft coo echoed from up ahead. *Shit.*

They scrambled faster. A giggle. Gabi's chubby face flashed in Matt's mind, a sound that once brought joy now perverted.

"Visual!" Luiza called.

Children's screams erupted in the tunnel, echoing all around them. How many? Four? Five? Matt's pack slammed into the ceiling as he tried to hurry and his foot became buried in bones. They were almost halfway through now. They needed to get out before they were trapped. He glanced at the compass. The blood sphere had split.

"Two demons!" he called. The minions wouldn't show on the compass, only the mantismeres themselves. Six screamers per monster.

The sharp *clack, clack* of a suppressed pistol made him wince but they kept crawling.

One of the red beads slid away from the other, moving around. More shots came from ahead. Wisps of gun smoke danced in the beam of Matt's headlamp.

A giggle came from behind, sending a cold shiver down Matt's neck. He rolled and looked back down the passage past his own boots. A pale, doll-faced insect stood in the opening, its eyes liquid black.

Its mandibles opened and it cooed.

Shit!

Spidery legs reached around the edge and a second screamer crawled up into the trough.

"They're behind us!" Firing Dämoren in here would deafen them all, but the holy revolver wasn't needed for these fuckers. Dropping the compass onto his stomach, Matt clawed for the

Ingram slung tight across his chest.

The first bug cocked its head and scuttled inside as a third one climbed into view.

Matt pulled the machine pistol up, not bothering to remove the protective sock he'd put over the barrel. Spreading his knees and feet as wide as possible, he squeezed the trigger. The burst came as a metallic roar.

Old bones exploded in plumes of dust and the monster blew apart. Steam poured from the mulched corpse, bringing a gut-wrenching stench. The other two bugs wailed. Matt swung the gun toward them, shearing the legs off one with another burst, but the other one leaped to the side and burrowed beneath the bones.

Fuck!

Putrid steam and smoke filled the tight tunnel. Eyes watering, Matt searched the bones. He caught a glimpse of movement as another screamer hurried inside, but it was gone before he had the gun up.

A bowl-shaped cranium wiggled, the bones shifting beneath it. Screaming, Matt pulled the trigger, unleashing an explosion of grit and shattered bone. Hot brass bounced off the walls, tinkling around him. One shell landed in the crook of his neck, scalding him, but he kept firing until steam wafted out from beneath the powdered bones and the Ingram's bolt clicked.

"Go! Go! Go!" he yelled, scrambling along his back, one hand fumbling at a magazine pouch. The compass rolled off him, but he snatched it up, holding it beneath his chin. Matt slapped the fresh magazine in and fired at something moving at the exit. He had no idea if he even hit it.

They were almost out. Luiza's gun was still firing. Splinters of bone dug into the backs of Matt's arms but he kept going. His ears rang but he could still hear the shrill wails.

The bones between his legs shifted, forming a mound. The tips of mandibles poked through and Matt rammed the Ingram's barrel directly against them and fired. Shards of bone pelted his face as he drilled out the area, moving the gun in a circle. Black ooze splattered his thighs and hands.

Dark steam belched from the rubble, the cloud so thick

he couldn't even see his own feet. He choked on the stench, struggling not to vomit.

"I'm out!" Luiza shouted.

Matt kept crawling backwards, tears running down his face. He slid over the greasy remains of one of the screamers Luiza had killed, smearing it down his back.

"Look out!" Chaya yelled.

Matt kept kicking his way backwards. Clattering came from behind him, but he couldn't turn his head to see. Luiza was yelling something, and then blue flickering light filled the tunnel.

Matt pushed himself further and the ground seemed to vanish beneath his shoulders. He was out! The compass fell from beneath his chin as he twisted around and pulled himself from the hole, nearly falling to the floor.

Panting, he looked up. Luiza was standing above a six-foot insect encased in icy blue fire. Flames dripped from Akumanokira's blade as she looked around.

"Here," Chaya said helping Matt to his feet. She clutched her scimitar in one hand, the other on her pistol. Four more black and rubbery screamer corpses littered the floor, each spewing their vile stench.

"Where's the other one?" Luiza asked, her head swiveling around.

Matt fetched his bottle from the floor. The bead pointed beside them, but there was nothing there, nothing but a wall. "I don't know."

"How did they get behind us?" Chaya panted, shining her pistol's light down the trough tunnel.

"I don't know," Matt said. "The demon moved around and they were there." He looked at the compass again. The red bead was moving. The range was shit through solid rock, so it had to be close.

"There should be a tunnel here." Luiza motioned her sword at sealed passage like the one before. The other end of the hallway stopped at a bone-filled pit.

"Where did this one come from?" Chaya searched her light across the ceiling.

In the blue fire of the burning demon, Matt noticed the tiny footprints from screamers across the dusty floor. They ended at the sealed wall. Tiny trenches, like scuff marks extended at the very edge. "What the hell?"

He stepped closer. The wall appeared no different than the dozens of other sealed passages. Matt touched the ancient mortar. It gave slightly. He scraped a fingernail and a sliver flaked off like dried snot. *Son of a bitch.*

Matt brought his boot up and kicked the wall. It gave a hollow thud and crack like the sound of breaking Styrofoam. He kicked it again, and one of the stones fell inward.

"Here!" he shouted, breaking more rocks free. The wall was thin, no more than a hand-width thick. He pulled one of the loosened stones and the whole wall shifted under the strain, hinging off the top before the rock came free.

"What is this?" Luiza shined her light through the hole Matt had torn.

He gripped the edge of the hole and pulled. The entire wall moved with a crackling groan, pivoting upward like a dog door. There must have been a counterweight of some kind, allowing it to swing so easily. Matt was able to lift it three feet before it wouldn't go any further. "Like a trapdoor spider."

Chaya and Luiza shone their lights down the hidden passage beyond.

Matt caught the faintest hint of vinegar beneath the stink of the steaming bugs behind him. He peered up at the gooey mortar along underside of the door, some kind of hardened mucus. He wondered if a black light would have helped in spotting it. *Too late now.*

"We need to tell the others about this," Luiza said.

The blood bead was still moving in the bottle, away from them. "We need to kill that demon. If it warns the others, they might bolt. We'll never find them."

Luiza sucked her bottom lip. She looked at the door, then back down the passage. "Then let's go get it."

CHAPTER 20

The day that Thomas Doershuk's life had changed was the day he first tried amphetamines. Twenty years old, believing he was invincible and ready to conquer the world, Tommy's life took the surreal twist from promising musician to resistance leader in the secret war by way of addiction. How it was, Tommy was in a band with his best friend Aaron Lemming. Together, they embarked on a cross-country adventure from Danbury, Connecticut, to LA, playing gigs along the way. Aaron introduced him to meth and, by the time they made it to California, Tommy was masterfully versed in the ways of addiction.

Addicts develop a hyper-evolved set of skills that only those helplessly obsessed with illegal drugs can possess. Skills that allowed you to look at a room of strangers, instantly gauge who might be in the know, and to have the courage that only real addiction grants, to approach this complete stranger and try to score. An addict's life is also about networking. Once you have established those connections, you must maintain them, grow on them, diversify in case one link gets pinched or runs dry. This skill, prized by businessmen, is second nature for a truly proficient addict. Finally, the addict knows when those rare and unexplainable strokes of luck come by, that you must seize them without hesitation.

Tommy and Aaron had believed that was the case when a hot brunette had invited them back to her friend's, who was a cook. The friend was supposedly away and she knew where the stash was hidden. But when they arrived, they got the drugs and the little hottie got in the mood. She'd taken Aaron to the back, leaving Tommy to snort rails, and promised to take care of him next. They'd been gone all of two minutes when tweeker-bladder kicked in. Tommy went looking for a place to take a piss and came across Aaron. That little brunette with her short hair and shorter skirt, was now tall, seven feet, hairless and gray, her baby blue crop-top hanging from her emaciated frame. Aaron's throat was torn out, blood everywhere. His pants were around his ankles and the monster was eating his leg like a turkey dinner. Seizing the junkie's power to act on luck, Tommy got the fuck out of there.

The monster chased him, running on all fours behind Tommy's old Honda, its pale eyes reflecting the red of his taillights. It nearly caught him, but the little four-cylinder finally got enough speed to send him racing away on the desert highway, his heart hammering louder than the engine. Tommy never touched meth again. And while the chemical addiction was long gone, Tommy never forgot the skills it had given him. He had a new addiction: hunting monsters.

"Light's going off," Gregorie said around his cigarette.

Tommy looked up from his laptop to the pillar of black plastic boxes stacked on an olive metal shelf. A green LED quietly blinked from the one labeled "9." Something was moving. Was it them? None of the other sensors had gone off. He glanced to the other stack, the six labeled with letters instead of numbers. The lights were dark. Nine was near trap C. Would it take the bait?

The motion sensors were crude but had good range down here. He wasn't able to get radio cameras, nothing as nice as the Valducans had. But cameras required more battery, more bandwidth, and were much harder to hide. All he had were game cameras, which required physically going to them and downloading any videos they'd made. Crude, but they worked.

Gregorie sucked a hard drag off his cigarette. "You want to check it?"

"Let's give it five minutes," Tommy said.

The Frenchman nodded and blew a long stream of smoke.

The blue-gray haze floated lazily up, then was sucked into a rusted pipe extending down from the ceiling. The pipe had served as a chimney for resistance fighters during the Second World War. They'd hidden down here in their bunker, far below the streets, plotting their bombings and assassinations while navigating the subterranean highways below the Nazis' feet.

Tommy had installed a fan at this end to cycle the air. Its hum echoed in the steel tube, creating a steady, ghostly tone. It was Gregorie who had run the power down in the form of a heavy-gauge extension cord, the bright yellow of its bulbous head masked beneath a patina of grime. But Tommy didn't complain. He'd slept in far shittier and far less exotic places than this twelve-by-nine stone room.

Finding Gregorie had been a godsend. Tommy knew his addict's intuition had led him to the notorious and near mythic cataphile. Gregorie didn't do interviews. He didn't lead vacationing college kids on illegal tours. He prowled the catacombs like a ghost, his tag marking every corner of this hidden world. It graced the wall beside him, a stenciled stick figure, its head a curving G with a little googly eye. Above that, a meticulously carved Croix de Lorraine, the double cross of the French Resistance.

Knowing to never pass up a stroke of luck, Tommy offered him five hundred Euros a week to be his guide and to help him procure ... difficult supplies. Items like a gun.

That gun had saved Tommy's ass and brought him even more treasures. He patted the wood grip of the kris dagger at his belt. More of a short sword, really. Victoria had told him that the weapon was centuries old, though in its perfect condition he wouldn't have believed it. But Tommy had seen the blade move with his own eyes. He knew it was magic, but it still hadn't moved for him. Victoria had said that the monster hunters, these self-proclaimed knights, bonded with their weapons for them to work. So Tommy had spent every day wearing it, waiting for his energies or whatever they were to align and unlock this amazing power.

It had been sheer chance that he'd even encountered the demon hunters. Using the profile he'd built, many of the gaps filled in by his little spy, he'd noted likely places the Valducans might access the tunnels. There were far too many to watch them all. So Tommy just made a habit of swinging by any while he was running errands topside. Pure luck he'd happened on the two vans. He'd seen two figures through the window tinting and knew, just *knew*, it was them. Not one to pass up a stroke of luck, he checked it out. Now he had a second gun, a silencer, some weird ammunition with gemstone tips, and an honest-to-God holy weapon.

Shooting the German and Allen wasn't planned, but they deserved it. Their silence had killed hundreds, maybe thousands of people. But more than that, they'd tried to quash him, make him look the fool, just another raving madman. One on one he'd taken them both. If they could kill monsters and he could kill them, then he was the real apex predator down here. And he was going to tell that to the world.

Tommy smiled. This was going to be bigger than anything. Bigger than the moon landing. The supernatural was real. Magic was real. Once the world knew, everything would change, and his name would forever be linked to that. How many lives would he save? How many lost souls, unable to believe in anything any more, would find faith? His chest tightened at the joy of what he was going to do.

"The other light is on," Gregorie said.

Tommy swung his head. Trap C's receiver blinked green. *Got one.*

None of the other motion detectors had activated. No telling how long it might be before another came. Tommy closed his laptop and stood. Gregorie hadn't believed in monsters, though he did claim the tunnels were haunted. Finding the rave site and phone footage had made convincing him easy enough. It was time his newest convert saw a monster with his own eyes. "Let's go."

Gregorie pulled his greasy tangle of hair back and slid the Russian infrared goggles on. The cataphile had protested wearing them at first, but five hundred a week had changed his mind.

Tommy loaded his laptop into his pack. It'd probably be

safe here, but the old junkie in him knew better than to leave anything valuable unguarded. They couldn't lock the door from the outside. He strapped the jammer onto his belt, but didn't turn it on. No need to jam his own sensor network. He pulled on his own high-end goggles and electronic shooting muffs and flipped them on.

Gregorie twisted the wheel set in the rusty iron door. It resembled an old-fashioned vault or submarine hatch. Dark shiny grease caked every moving portion. It opened with a heavy groan.

Crackled plaster coated the outside of the door. Whether it had originally been painted to match the limestone walls or if decades of dust had colored it, Tommy couldn't tell. It was far from a perfect camouflage, but still effective against a passing glance in poor light. Stepping through, he navigated the short, crooked passage leading toward trap C.

They walked in silence. Gregorie wasn't much one for talking, and that was fine by Tommy. After several more turns, they came to a passage wide enough to drive a car through. A cluster of crusty pipes ran along one edge. Tommy's gaze moved along it, noting sensor four hidden up there. Even with night vision it was difficult to spot.

"This way," Gregorie said, turning at a side tunnel Tommy had passed.

Tommy hid his embarrassment behind a cough. Mistakes showed incompetence, made others doubt his judgment. He hated being doubted. He'd endured it far too long.

The passage wound through a web-work of tight turns around empty chambers. They passed sensor eight, its plastic dome peeking from a pile of rocks.

A shrill whine echoed somewhere in the distance.

Tommy threw up his hand. "Shh."

Gregorie stopped and looked at him, his expression unreadable beneath the goggles.

"I heard something." Tommy rolled the dial on the hard plastic muffs. In addition to dampening loud noises, they amplified fainter sounds.

There it was again. Crying. A hot surge of exhilaration

welled in his chest. He turned his head slowly, allowing the microphones to catch it. The sounds were definitely ahead. "Okay." He touched the kris' handle. "There's one ahead."

Gregorie frowned, the first real hint of actual fear. Tommy had insisted Gregorie carry a gun and the cataphile drew it from his waistband.

They moved cautiously forward, the child-like wails growing louder.

"I hear it," Gregorie whispered, his lips tight.

"Shh."

Eventually they reached a narrow side hall from which the sounds emanated.

Tommy drew the blade and peeked around the corner.

The side tunnel extended only eight feet. On the floor in the back, a pale bug thrashed and screamed from inside a clear box. Its spidery legs pounded against the walls as it hopped about. Holding the blade out front, Tommy moved in and locked the box trap's twin door latches.

The monster screamed again, attempting to turn, but couldn't in the confined space.

Carefully, Tommy lifted it up by the handle and pulled it out from the alcove. "Look."

Gregorie took a sudden step back as Tommy swung the box into view. The screaming bug lunged at the walls, banging so hard it nearly came loose of Tommy's grip.

"It's safe." Tommy's dad had taught him how to make the traps when he was ten, assembling his first out of scrap wood. These were bulletproof glass with steel hardware. Setting it down, Tommy flipped up his goggles and clicked on his headlamp. "It can't get out."

Blood and fur smeared the back wall and the insect's porcelain-doll's face, remnants of the rat they'd used as bait. Pincers quivering, it unleashed a furious scream.

"Hey there, little guy." Tommy tapped the glass and the bug rammed into the side to get at him. "You're going to be famous."

"I don't believe it," Gregorie breathed. He'd taken off his own goggles and stared, but still refused to approach.

"Believe it." Tommy held the kris before the angry insect,

running the point along the inside of one of the air holes.

The creature backed away, black eyes locked on the magic blade. The twin pincers folded and withdrew into its bristled mouth slit.

"Yeah, you know what this is." He rattled the tip and the bug flinched. "So be quiet."

"That fucking thing understands you?" Gregorie hissed, his voice rising.

"It's not stupid." Grinning, Tommy slid the blade back into its wooden scabbard. "You want to help me carry it?"

"Fuck that." The cataphile cocked his head to look at him without shining his headlamp in Tommy's eyes. "You want to bring that thing in the bunker with us?"

"I told you. It can't get out."

"How you know?"

"Because it can't."

As if in response, the bug rammed into the side with a solid *thump.* The creature staggered back, then giggled.

"I don't want it in there with us," Gregorie said. "Fucking evil."

The creature's giggles grew louder, welling into a weird, shrill cackle. It began bouncing, its claws clacking against the acrylic bottom.

"Shut that thing up!" Gregorie hissed.

Tommy slapped the top of the box, but the bug kept jumping. The laugher growing into a scream. Tommy drew the knife and poked its tip into one of the holes, but the thing just kept screaming.

"Shut it up!"

Continuing its cries, the creature looked directly at the cataphile in dead, expressionless defiance.

"Quiet." Tommy pounded the top again. He wanted to shake the box but couldn't risk injuring his prize. Gritting his teeth, he stood and flipped his goggles back down. "It'll tire. Let's get back."

"I don't want—"

"I'm paying you."

Gregorie's lip curled back from nicotine-stained teeth. He

resignedly shook his head, pulled on his goggles, and killed the headlamp.

Tommy lifted the heavy cage like some industrial cat carrier. "Come on."

Somewhere behind them, a baby screamed. Faint, but distinct in the muffs' amplified audio.

Shit. Tommy's balls tightened. He turned back, but the passage was empty. "We need to go. Now."

Gregorie in the lead, they started back. The bug continued hopping, jarring the box, but Tommy held tight. Behind him, a second infant's wail joined the first.

"Hurry." Tommy slid the dagger away and took the trap in both hands. The bug poked its legs through the tiny holes, jabbing his palm. "Shit!"

The box fell and tumbled to the ground, landing on its side. The bug clattered and kicked, pausing its screaming.

Gregorie turned as if to help, but froze. "You hear that?"

The other wails were louder now. Closer.

"We need to go." Tommy took the handle and gripped the bottom where there weren't any holes.

"Jesus!" Gregorie ripped the revolver from his pants.

Tommy turned. A doll-faced monster scuttled quietly along the wall toward them.

The blast from Gregorie's gun nearly made Tommy drop the box again. Had he not been wearing the muffs the sound would have surely deafened him. Limestone chipped a full foot beside the closing insect. Two more shots and the beast fell, legs curling and steam pouring from a hole in its cherub face.

All at once, a cacophony of cries erupted from the hall. Something moved at the edge of the infrared's light,

"Go!" Tommy yelled, but Gregorie was already running. *Fucking pussy.*

Heaving the box trap in front of him, Tommy ran as fast as he could. Unable to see his feet, he stumbled over the uneven floor, nearly tripping. The cries grew louder.

Turning, he saw two more of the bugs twenty feet away. Tommy dropped the trap and drew his forty-five. The laser sight came on as he squeezed the handle, its dot a brilliant flare in the night vision. Holding the gun both hands, he zeroed it in on the first creature and fired. The bug exploded in a spray of goo and legs. The other one scrambled to the side, but a second shot sent it tumbling back. It tried to right itself, but the laser found it and the third shot blew it in half.

The bug in the box was trying to get at his foot through the holes. The tumble had broken one of its legs, now hanging limp, but it didn't seem concerned. Still clutching the gun, Tommy seized the box by the handle and ran.

Around a corner he saw Gregorie ahead at an intersection. Something flashed in his hands, a brilliant glow, then spewing sparks.

"Come on!" Gregorie called.

The heavy box swung with each step, threatening to pull Tommy over.

"Drop it!"

Tommy kept running. A thick fog spewed from Gregorie's hand. He hurled a clay smoke bomb down the passage, past Tommy's shoulder, leaving a trail of sulfur-reeking smoke.

Without a word, Gregorie turned and ran down the right passage. Huffing, Tommy tried to keep up. He tripped. Fingers reflexively tightening, the pistol went off, blasting the wall. He fell over the box, smacking his shin and landing with a painful grunt. The gun skittered away, its laser winking off as it left his hands.

More cries were coming. His skinned palm stinging, he clambered to his feet. The bug was still banging inside the box. *Fuck it. I'll trap another.* Not wasting time to find his gun, Tommy ran, limping in the direction Gregorie had fled.

Sweat ran down his face and neck. It gathered along the goggles' rubber seal beneath his eyes. A terrible *clicking* was gaining on him but he didn't dare look back.

Panting, he reached the main tunnel. He turned to see another of the damn bugs just a few feet behind him, beyond that, one of the bladed-armed big ones scuttled along the wall. Ripping the silenced gun from its holster, Tommy shot. Dust and stone chips blasted as he tried to hit the scurrying insect. Finally, on the seventh or eighth shot, he hit it, unleashing a stench like a sun-baking corpse.

The big monster hissed, its mandibles clacking. More screams came from the distance. Tommy shot it once and ran.

Faint light moved along the passage ahead beyond a curve. He couldn't get to the bunker without passing whoever was there. The clicking claws were gaining, the screams growing louder. There was no turning back but there was an exit ahead. He just needed to get to it.

Rounding the curve, silhouettes moved in the glow ahead. One held something long in its hand. A sword?

He was almost at the turn off. Just a few more yards. The lights came up his direction, but Tommy ducked beneath the rusty pipes, his shoulder slamming the wall as he took the side passage. His side cramped from the running. His aching legs couldn't keep this up for much longer. *Almost there.*

The tunnel turned and he splashed through ankle-deep water. Iron rungs protruded from the wall ahead. Salvation.

Something hit him from behind. Screaming, Tommy fell forward into the cold muddy water. Sharp legs scuttled up his shoulder. Giggling in his left ear. Tommy rolled, sunken rocks digging into his side. The mud had smeared the goggles' lenses. He was blind and the bug clambered across him.

Arms flailing, he struck the hard carapace. He still had his gun. Tommy grabbed the thing and tore it free, but the spindly legs latched onto his arm.

Twin needles stabbed his hand with a crunch he felt more than heard. Icy cold shot up his left arm. His fingers twisted as the muscles seized. Roaring in animal fury, Tommy rammed the gun's muzzle into the bug's side and fired, and fired, and fired.

Bits of leg and shell spattered his face and open mouth. Gun smoke and that god-awful reek filled his lungs. He couldn't feel his arm below the elbow.

Dropping the gun, Tommy yanked the useless night scope off and clicked his light.

The creature's severed head was still attached to him, pincers locked onto the side below his little finger. The shell blackened and steamed and Tommy tore it free, ripping his skin, but he couldn't feel anything in his arm.

Water splashed. Rapid clicking sounded from the blackness. Turning toward it, the white beam from Tommy's headlamp fell on one of the giant bugs. Pale green traced the edges of each of its body plates. It raised its bladed forelimb like a praying mantis and moved in.

"Fuck you." Tommy drew the magic kris from his belt and lunged, throwing himself beneath the descending forelimbs. The wavy blade slid up under one of the ventral plates and the monster squealed. Its jaws slammed down on the helmet like a hammer blow, but they didn't break through.

Tommy yanked the blade half out, unleashing a spray of hot blood, and rammed it in again. Staggering, the beast tried to pull away but Tommy pushed forward, pounding the blade like a jackhammer. "Fuck you! Fuck you! Die!"

The monster fell backward into the water, but Tommy didn't stop. Straddling it, he drove the blade in as hard as he could, sawing its insides until the creature fell still.

Tommy pulled the long blade free and stood, panting. It didn't burn like he'd been told, but he'd done it. The thing was dead.

He spat. "Apex predator, asshole." Tommy sheathed the monster-killing blade back into its scabbard. His hand, his arm, all of him was coated in the creature's sticky blood. He needed to get out of here. Surely the Valducans had heard him.

The numbness in his left arm extended up to his shoulder blade but the spreading had stopped. He sloshed up to the ladder and looked up. *Fifty feet, one-handed.* It was the only way out. Tommy gave one final glance back to the monster he'd killed, drew a breath, and began to climb.

CHAPTER 21

"Shh." Malcolm raised a hand, and cocked his head. "You hear that?"

Victoria stopped, listening. Silence. The soft *ping* of dripping water. She held her breath. Earlier, the faint, hollow rumble of a subway car had passed overhead. But now, the tunnels were dead silent, save the drips and their breathing. She shared a look with Orlovski and they both shook their heads.

"What—?" Orlovski started but Malcolm silenced him with a karate-chop motion of his raised hand.

Victoria continued listening. Slowly, she shifted her weight between her aching feet.

There! Three faint *pops*, each no louder than a breaking matchstick, sounded ahead. *Shots? Who's shooting? What are they shooting at?* The distance was impossible to judge. The mines ate sounds but it couldn't be far.

Orlovski nodded that he'd heard them, too.

"All right," Malcolm whispered, clicking off his helmet light. "Hold back forty feet but keep me in view." He transferred the blood compass Matt had given him to his other hand and drew his horn-handled machete. He crept forward. Brick arches ran the length of the tunnel like stone ribs. Malcolm kept to their shadows, the pale dust covering his body added to the camouflage.

Sliding Ibenus from his scabbard, Victoria waited until Mal neared the edge of their red lights' range, and began to follow,

Orlovski beside her. They kept their beams just off Malcolm so as to not silhouette him so much.

Another shot echoed ahead. Closer.

Malcolm crouched at an intersection and waited for them to catch up. Once they were on him, he ducked beneath a bundle of rusty pipes and started up a square tunnel as wide as a street.

Shouts came from ahead. A figure came around the corner, sprinting toward them. A pair of blocky night goggles with a single jutting tube in the middle covered his lean face.

"*Secours! Secours!*" the man shouted, waving an arm, the other shielding his eyes from their lights. The blued metal of a revolver glinted in his hand, though he wasn't pointing it at them.

Malcolm stepped out before him, machete raised and left palm out front. "Arrête!"

The stranger yelped and jumped back in surprise, nearly falling. Malcolm thrust his palm out harder. "Look!"

Panting, the man looked at the hand, then at Victoria and Orlovski closing in.

"He's clean." Malcolm lowered his palm. "Ah! Ah!" he said as the man moved the hand clutching the pistol.

The man froze. Malcolm pointed to the floor and the man carefully set the pistol down. He peeled off the night scope. Dusty curls of hair framed his face.

"We need to run," the man said in heavily accented English. He looked back over his shoulder. "They're coming."

"What is?" Malcolm asked.

"Monsters. Bugs."

"Where did you get that?" Victoria motioned to the pistol.

Faint baby cries echoed in the distance.

The man looked back. "We must go."

"The gun, the goggles, where did you get them?" Victoria asked. "Tommy."

"Tommy?"

A half-dozen pops sounded up the hall, sounding like pneumatic hammer.

"That's a silenced pistol," Orlovski said, taking a step forward. "Tommy? Where is he?" Victoria demanded.

The cries were growing louder.

"Back there," the man said. "He's crazy."

"There!" Malcolm pointed down the hall.

Victoria looked, but saw nothing. More wails sounded.

Shoes scraped on rock. She spun back to see the cataphile running away. "Stop!"

She started after him, but Mal touched her arm. "No."

"But he knows where TommyD is."

"And he said he was this way." He picked up the revolver.

Tightening her lips, Victoria glanced back, but the cataphile was gone. "Bollocks."

Weapons out, they hurried down the passage. Malcolm motioned toward a hallway on the right side.

"I saw something through there."

Clicking sounded further ahead, followed by a child's laugher. Victoria raised Ibenus as a mantismere and three screamers rounded the tunnel only a few yards ahead.

"Close up," Malcolm ordered, taking a step back. They formed a triangle with Orlovski at the right and Victoria at the left.

One of the screamers skittered up the wall and jumped, jaws wide. Malcolm threw up his hand and the creature slammed backwards as if it had struck an invisible wall. The other two scuttled around, one moving behind the dusty pipes while another charged toward Victoria's feet.

She swung Ibenus down to meet it. Air whooshed in her ears with an instant's weightlessness and she was beside it, the descending bronze blade cleaving it in two. Inky blood squirted across the ground. Screaming, the half-bug tried to crawl with its remaining forelegs. It rolled its head up, jaws open, then fell still and began spewing steam.

Three loud pops echoed from the tunnel beside them.

Victoria turned as the mantismere lunged toward her, its twin blades stretched before it.

Malcolm dove between her and the beast, his palm raised. The demon hissed, recoiling from the palm tattoo and Malcolm sprang toward it, Hounacier arcing down at the monster's head.

The beast dodged to the side, one of its saber arms deflecting the machete's blade. Malcolm ducked as the second arm swung at him. The beast corrected its miss and brought the blade back up, but Orlovski charged in, slashing his kukri up beneath the arm with a hard crack. Hissing, the beast stumbled to the side, blood spurting from beneath its limp, useless arm.

Victoria was about to go in for a killing stroke but something moved at the corner of her eye. A screamer hurried along the pipe behind Orlovski, its shadow long in her head-lamps beam. "Behind you." She sprang toward it, swinging Ibenus. A whoosh and she was there, her blade coming down in front of the springing insect. While she didn't cut it, Orlovski managed to get out of the way before it could hit him. It landed on the floor, long legs scrambling away as both their blades came down just a moment too late.

The mantismere let out a rattling hiss and swiped at Malcolm again. Blocking it with his machete, he brought his boot up and kicked the beast square in the abdomen. It stumbled back and Orlovski slammed Amballwa into its side, tearing an enormous gash. He was out and away before it could turn on him.

Malcolm edged in for another attack.

"Look out," Victoria called, swiping Ibenus down on another screamer moving up behind Malcolm.

Mal threw his hand out and the little beast shrank back, stopping long enough for Ibenus to chop it down. More putrid stream filled the hall. Eyes watering, she turned to see Orlovski lunge, ramming his kukri into the mantismere's back. One of its smaller, clawed arms scratched blindly back, slapping him.

Malcolm brought Hounacier down onto the demon's neck with a bone-like crunch. Blue fire erupted from its wounds and the beast fell. The last of the screamers, circling around behind Orlovski withered. Coughing and panting, Orlovski yanked Amballwa free. "Everyone okay?"

"Yeah," Victoria said, trying not to breathe through her nose. In the light of the blue fire, she noticed a notch in Ibenus' blade where he had hit a rock cleaving the last screamer. "Shit."

"Battle wound," Malcolm said. "We all get them. Kill a demon and it'll mend." He ducked beneath the pipes and started down the side passage. "Come on."

Victoria touched the rounded portion where the blade curled back. *I'm sorry.* Clenching her jaw, she ducked and followed.

Icy fire danced along Hounacier's bloodied blade. Holding it up like a torch, Malcolm led them down a narrow corridor. If a demon was ahead they'd have to fight it one at a time. Victoria kept special attention to their rear. The all-too-familiar stench of rot they'd just escaped grew stronger as they moved deeper. Malcolm stopped at an intersection, sniffed, and headed down the side hall.

The stink was worse here. It felt oily in the catacombs' unmoving air, a greasy film that soaked into her hair, clothes, and skin. Mal's foot splashed ahead and soon Victoria was sloshing through cold, ankle-deep water as Orlovski strolled atop it like Tactical Jesus.

"Hello there," Malcolm said.

Coming around a corner, she spied a corpse. A dead mantismere lay on its back, a wide cut in its pale stomach. The sharp edges of its form had softened; its head widening at the jaws, the saber limbs shorter, with ridges resembling fused, elongated fingers as the blades. Its plated chest bulged slightly, a pair of faint nipples beginning to peek through. The transformation was fast compared to what she'd witnessed before, her first time in a filthy Manchester building as her partner bled out. Black steam boiled out from the bloody water. Bits of rotting meat and screamer legs splattered the walls.

"Why isn't it burning?" she asked.

"Killed the body but not the demon." Malcolm looked up a series of bent rungs. High above, a half-crescent of night sky shone through an open manhole.

"What could do that?"

"Umatri," Orlovski said. "Bastard managed to stab it."

"But I thought he couldn't kill it. Did he bond?"

"No." The Russian picked something out from the corner. "If he had bonded, the soul would burn." He lifted up a black pistol. Muddy water ran from the handle and familiar square suppressor. "In case we doubted it was him." He cleared the filthy gun and shoved it into his pack. "Fucked but salvageable."

Malcolm sheathed Hounacier and started up the rungs. "He

couldn't have gotten far."

An infant's wail sounded in the distance behind them.

"There's more of them." Victoria lifted Ibenus and faced the passage.

"Mal," Orlovski said.

"He's getting away," Malcolm hissed, fifteen feet up the ladder.

"You want to run through the streets dressed like this, searching for him?" Victoria asked. "The demons are *here*."

"He has Umatri."

"And we'll get him back."

More sobs joined the first, growing louder.

"She's right," Orlovski said. "If those demons see their burning friends they'll bolt. This is the closest we've been to finding the eel."

Malcolm stopped. "And this is the closest we've been to TommyD."

"Don't worry. TommyD's mine," Victoria said. "Just not now."

Malcolm was silent for a moment, then gave a frustrated growl and started back down. Eyes blazing with anger, he drew Hounacier and moved to the front. "Then let's get to it."

They moved down the hall, back toward the main passage, the distorted cries becoming clearer with each step.

Orlovski drew his pistol and cocked the hammer. "I want to take the minions out fast so they can't swarm us."

Pale firelight flickered along the walls ahead. Long, spidery shadows skittered past. Malcolm rounded the final turn and the crying erupted into a wave of screams. Mal threw out his palm and charged, Victoria on his heels. A pair of cowering screamers backed away, one not fast enough as Mal slashed Hounacier, chopping off one of its pincers. Oily blood dribbled from the stump. It shrieked, loud and terrible, but was cut off as Mal's boot stomped down, spewing guts across the stone.

The hunters scooted under the pipes into the wide passage, the air still thick with dark, rank steam. Four screamers circled, hopping along the walls and floor. Victoria stepped toward the closest, but Orlovski took it out with a pair of rapid shots.

"There!" Mal shouted, pointing his blade. Further up the hall, a mantismere retreated around a bend.

Orlovski's pistol fired twice more, one shot pinging off a pipe. A screamer scrambled to get behind them but a third shot sent it to the floor, legs curled and blackening.

Not wishing to damage Ibenus by chopping at the screamers along the stone walls, Victoria drew her pistol. Sword in one hand, and gun in the other, she swung, blinked, and shot one that charged Orlovski from behind.

Malcolm chopped the last bug off the ceiling. "Come on," he shouted, running down the hall.

They ran, their red lights bouncing across the walls. Coming around the curve, the passage was empty, seeming to stretch forever.

"There." Malcolm motioned to the rubbery, steaming screamer corpse inside a side passage entrance. Brass shells gleamed on the floor around it. A red bead in his blood compass pointed in the tunnel's direction. "It's getting away."

They followed the winding tunnel, pausing long enough to scan the empty chambers they passed to be sure no monsters were lying in wait. Malcolm paused at a Y intersection and checked the bottle again. The blood sphere pointed vaguely to the left, not enough to be sure in this maze-work if that was the way to go. Malcolm ventured a few feet into the right passage, lifted his nose and inhaled deeply. He turned and repeated down the left side. "This way."

Around a corner they found a clear rectangular box laying in the hall. Long metal bolts ran through the thick acrylic, holding it firmly in place. Inside was cloudy, foul steam leaking from the rows of holes along the side.

"What the hell is this?" Orlovski asked.

"Live trap," Malcolm said. "Idiot was trying to catch one."

A glint of metal behind a rock caught Victoria's eye. "Look at this." She holstered her gun picked up a chunky two-tone pistol, stainless and black. A red laser sprang from the right grip panel as her fingers encircled it. A shiver ran her arm. This gun killed Gerhard. It took Allan's foot. Her grip loosened and the laser went out.

"Store it away," Malcolm said. "It's not suppressed so don't shoot it."

Remembering Chaya's training, she cleared the huge bullet from the gun, clicked the safety, and jammed the pistol into a side pocket of her pack, happy to be rid of its touch, then hurried after Malcolm and Orlovski.

The smell of sulfur itched her nose as they continued on. Yellow smoke swirled at the edges of their light beams, growing thicker.

"Smoke bomb," Malcolm coughed. "Cataphiles toss them to escape pursuit."

The lack of air movement made the cloud dense and impossible to see through. Victoria held her breath as they trudged deeper through it. She watched her feet as to not trip on the uneven floor. Eyes, watering, they pushed past the wall of smoke and continued on.

"Damn it," Malcolm growled. The red bead was gone from the compass. "Hurry up. We can catch it."

Still coughing, they hurried down the tunnel, passing a pair of dead screamers, then another.

"Found it," Malcolm said, holding up the bottle. They turned down a tall, narrow corridor, eyes scanning the holes and alcoves along the walls.

A *coo* sounded from the darkness ahead. Victoria drew her pistol.

The passage continued, sloping gently downward. Malcolm's compass pointed to the right wall but the tunnel was straight, no exits on either side. The blood bead rolled along the bottle's wall as they continued. The demon was now to the right and behind them.

"There has to be a switchback up here," Malcolm said.

The tunnel leveled out, ending at a small, muddy chamber littered with puddles and rocks.

"The hell?" Malcolm peered around, his light searching the walls and ceiling.

"Wrong turn?" Orlovski asked.

Victoria looked back up the passage. "We didn't pass— Bloody hell."

A pair of chubby-cheeked screamers skulked along the ceiling toward them. Their pincers opened as her red light fell across them. Squealing with laughter, they charged. Victoria raised her pistol, firing at the closest one. The bug wove back and forth, dust and rock blasting around it. Orlovski swung in beside her, crouching. He dropped the other screamer with two rapid shots. The remaining bug leaped toward the wall and Victoria nailed it mid-air, sending it tumbling to the floor. Legs twisted, it tried to rise, but a final shot blew it apart.

"Where did those come from?" Orlovski flipped on his pistol's light, unleashing a brilliant white beam down the entire passage. Three more screamers emerged from shadows, racing toward them.

"There!" Victoria pointed her smoking pistol at a red-striped mantismere scuttled out from beneath a section of raised wall forty feet up the tunnel. The wall shut behind it like a door flap, only to open again as another screamer hurried out.

"Form up!" Malcolm ordered, stepping behind them. "Victoria take the right. Taras, left."

The hunters moved forward up the tight passage. The bugs swarmed forward, the demon shepherding behind them. Victoria tracked the closest screamer. Once it closed within ten yards, she fired. The bug leaped to other side of the passage where a shot from Orlovski blasted it into pieces. Gritting her teeth, Victoria aimed at the next one and began to shoot. It was moving fast, laughing as it reached a dozen feet away before she managed to hit it on the fifth shot.

"Pace your shots," Malcolm said.

Orlovski swung his pistol and shot another with a quick double-tap. The Russian's face was calm, unhurried, like he was just practicing at the range.

Holding her breath, Victoria steadied her hand, bracing it with the one holding Ibenus. She waited until the glowing night sights fell between the last screamer's black eyes before pulling the trigger. Dark, reeking steam filled the passage, making it even harder to see.

Antennae twitching, the mantismere rushed along the ceiling above its splattered brood.

"Get ready. Victoria, you have range." Malcolm threw up his palm as the demon closed in. It froze, saber arms coming up to shield its eyes.

"Now," Malcolm ordered.

The hunters closed in. Victoria hopped as she swung Ibenus, the blade passing between the demon's raised forelimbs and cleaving onto its head. The monster fell, ghostly fire spewing from its split face as it crashed face down at her feet.

Releasing a sigh, Victoria checked Ibenus' blade. The notch was gone.

"Reload," Malcolm ordered.

Victoria ejected her magazine. Two rounds left. One more screamer and she'd have been out. She loaded a fresh mag and slid the near empty one in her pouch, praying she wouldn't need it.

"Bastard tried to lead us to a trap," Malcolm said, pushing his way to the front. "Corner and overwhelm us." They stepped over the burning and steaming corpses to where the wall had opened, finding a four-foot-high sealed passage. It appeared no different than any of the other hundred closed doorways they had seen, but under Orlovski's bright and direct light, the gloppy mortar between the stacked stones held a faint, silvery sheen.

"Cover me." Hounacier in hand, Malcolm knelt before the wall, feeling along the edge. He hooked his fingers beneath one of the stacked stones and pulled. The wall swung open like a dog flap. Malcolm peered beneath it. "Tunnel opens up a few feet in."

"What do we do?" Victoria asked. "We need to be heading back to meet Luiza's team."

Malcolm frowned. "We could be back here in two hours."

"If they know we found this they're going to be ready for us." Orlovski said.

"I'd rather we go in with six instead of three," Victoria said.

"Agreed," Malcolm said, still peering under the door.

"They could run," Orlovski said. "We'll never find them again."

"Yeah, and if the three of us go in there without reporting

what we found no one might find us ever again."

Orlovski shrugged. "Then close that before they notice we—"

Mal's hand shot up, silencing him.

Tensing, Victoria squeezed Ibenus' grip, ready for anything.

"Hello?" Malcolm said. "Hello? You two not hear that?"

"Hear what?" Victoria whispered.

"Luiza, do you read?" Malcolm slid part way beneath the hatch. "Chaya, Matt, anyone there?" He set the blood compass on the floor, unhooked the radio from his belt, and pulled it inside. "Is anyone there?"

Victoria lowered to the floor and peered under the door. Gauzy strands, like pearlescent caulk, held the rear side of the door together, forming a twisted hinge at the top. A faint vinegar odor emanated from it, sour and unpleasantly sweet. The crawlspace extended fifteen feet before opening up. Malcolm lay on his stomach, his radio before him like a torch.

Static crackled in her ear bud. A woman's voice came through. "... are you ... read ..."

"Luiza?" Malcolm crawled further inside. "Do you read, over?"

"Mal ... ound ... ver."

Malcolm crawled entirely into the passage. "Repeat that."

"We ... ound nest, over."

"They found the nest," Victoria whispered to Orlovski kneeling beside her with a puzzled expression.

"Copy that," Malcolm said. "We found a trapdoor."

"The ... down."

"Repeat that."

"Mal," Orlovski hissed. "Compass!"

Victoria glanced back at the bottle lying beside her. Twin red spheres moved along the curved inner wall ahead.

Gunshots echoed in her ear bud.

Malcolm looked back, the light of his headlamp momentarily blinding Victoria. "Luiza's team found the nest. Signal is stronger in here." He drew a glow stick from his vest, cracked it, and hurled it down the crawlway. "Grab the compass and follow me."

CHAPTER 22

"Here," Orlovski said, offering a hand as Victoria emerged from the crawlway into an arched tunnel. She crinkled her nose, fighting the urge to sneeze at the vinegary reek.

Curved channels spiraled along the walls like the inside of a giant gun barrel, freshly cut and white, lacking that ancient dinginess she'd grown accustomed to. The floors were absent of loose rocks, the stones being arranged in swirling patterns along the floor and irregular, rib-like arches. The orange light from Mal's thick glow stick on the floor only added to the surreal surroundings. "This is unexpected," she muttered, running her toes across the small, pearl-colored gloops bulging between the paving stones. She pressed hard, feeling one crunch beneath her boot.

Orlovski shined his light down the passage. "Quite the little artists, aren't they?"

The two red beads in the bottle slowly rolled along inside ahead of them, beyond the curved wall. The demons were moving but she could see no exits leading that way.

Malcolm's dark eyes scanned the floor, his lip curled in a mistrusting sneer. "Watch your steps. This is their court." He reached out for the compass, which Victoria offered over.

Weapons drawn, they headed east, leaving the orange glow behind. Following Orlovski's lead, Victoria activated her pistol's under-barrel light, shining the brilliant beam along the dark recesses. The patterns in the walls and floor changed as they moved deeper, ranging from intricate designs to nothing at all, save for an absence of loose rocks, and white-chipped telltales that the tunnels had been recently worked.

"Luiza," Malcolm said. "Can you hear me?"

"Lou ... clear," she replied in the radio. Gunshots popped in the background, an indecipherable yell, maybe Chaya, then two more shots.

"What's going on?"

"We chased ... inside. Few skirmishes. Most ... rying bastards."

"Everyone all right?"

"We're good. Used a lot of ammo," she said.

"Any idea where you are?" Malcolm asked.

"Not really. They've changed it."

"Well, we're getting close. Signal is getting better." Malcolm paused, shining his down a crawlway, then continued on. Victoria glanced through it as she passed, seeing the back of another trap door.

A faint *coo* trailed up from the passage behind them. Victoria swung her light around, searching the hall but seeing nothing. She held her breath, listening. She flinched as something touched her shoulder.

"Come on," Orlovski whispered, his eyes scanning the tunnel. "They have to know we're here. Let's find the others before they come for us." He cracked a bright green glow stick and dropped it on the floor. "Maybe we'll see shadows if one moves past it."

They continued on, Victoria regularly checking behind them. The green light faded as they rounded a turn. The hall split several times, opening into various chambers, traces of old graffiti still clinging to the freshly furrowed walls. An elaborate gossamer construction dominated one chamber, completely covering three walls. Geometric tubes, like some over-sized wasp nest, studded the far side. Most of the cells were empty, but a few were sealed with rounded caps.

"Christ," she breathed.

Orlovski's light played across the sealed chambers, revealing pale doll faces, as if preserved beneath cloudy cling wrap like packaged toys. "Fuck this."

One of the eggs shuddered, the screamer inside writhing. The surface stretched. Twin pincers emerged, slicing through the membrane, unleashing a gurgled cry. Malcolm rushed inside, his palm up. The creature froze and Hounacier slashed across, killing the monster in its womb. Black froth sizzled out. More of the cells began to twitch. Malcolm hacked and chopped, shredding the nest and everything inside it.

Screams erupted behind them, coming both ways up the hall.

Victoria spun, her chest tightening. She moved the light up the hall, searching for the first sign of movement. *Here we go.*

"Let's move," Malcolm snapped, steam wisping from his bloodstained machete.

They hurried down the passage. The cries grew closer, rising and falling in waves. The tunnel opened into a domed chamber. Patterns of white stones crusted the upper curve like a cathedral mosaic. Screamers seethed out from the far doorway, spreading out across the etched walls. Victoria fired into the mass of legs and faces pouring in but hit nothing.

The light on Orlovski's gun zeroed in on a single bug among the throng. He fired, splattering black, and moved to the next. "One at a time. Pace your shots." He killed another, then another, the shots in rhythmic time.

Circling back to back, Victoria focused on one moving along the ceiling. She fired, blasting stone. *Damn it.* Clenching her teeth, she sighted it again and blew it in half with a perfect shot. *Don't get cocky,* she joked in her mind. She moved to the next one, firing as it lined up.

More wailing bugs poured in from the doorway they'd entered. Victoria shot two of them before they joined the ranks swirling around them.

Pausing his firing, Malcolm threw out his palm to a wave surging across the floor. The front line reeled back, the ones behind them spilling over only to recoil at the eye tattoo's power. Malcolm and Orlovski peppered the ranks with bullets before they could recover.

Dust trickled down through the beam of Victoria's light. She looked up. Several of the screamers dug at the ceiling stones, pincers gnawing between them. The sheet of stones sagged as it peeled free. It rippled and bulged, more loose rocks shifting beneath it. A fist-sized stone fell, thudding between her and Orlovski. The Russian didn't appear to notice as he emptied his magazine in a closing wave.

"Roof," she yelled. "They're bringing it down!" She shoved Orlovski out of the way as dust and rocks began to fall.

"Move," Malcolm shouted. Palm out front, he ran for the exit, shooting and stomping bugs as he cut a path. A crackling rip thundered above and stones rained down as they fled. Dust billowed past, enveloping her and dimming their lights. A flat wedge beamed off Orlovski's helmet, eliciting a grunt. Victoria lurched to the side as a head-sized rock smashed down right in front of her.

A screamer scuttled toward her, jaws open. She lifted her gun just as a falling rock smashed the screamer to pulp.

Eyes stinging with dust, Victoria charged toward the glow of light moving ahead and dove through the exit.

"This way!" Malcolm shouted.

Someone was firing a few feet away but she couldn't see through the dust. The screams were lesser now, most of the brood killed serving as distraction. Spidery legs clawed at her calf, the pronged tips digging into her skin. It scrambled around to the outside of her leg. Yelping, Victoria swatted the flat of Ibenus down, knocking the creature free before its jaws found her.

The lights ahead cut to the side. Choking on dust, Victoria rounded a corner to find Malcolm and Orlovski.

"Are you okay?" Malcolm coughed. The white powder completely covered him.

Victoria rubbed at her teary eyes. "Yeah."

"Thank you," Orlovski panted. Crimson spread across the dust on the back his hand from a ragged cut.

"No problem."

New cries called from the darkness behind them. Victoria raked her gritty tongue along her teeth and spat. "They're still coming."

Malcolm checked the bottle. Five red spheres moved inside the plastic walls, three behind them. Two were ahead. "They're just sending the minions. They could do this all day. We need to find them. Put 'em down." He peered up the corridor ahead. "Come on."

They hurried down the tunnel, their lights bouncing along the walls. Fresh cries joined the ones behind them. The hall split and Malcolm chose the left passage. It led to another egg chamber, though the cells were all empty. Victoria wondered if their former inhabitants had been the ones they'd faced in the cathedral. The tight hall continued on, winding through several turns before it ended at a blank wall.

"Shit." Malcolm shone his light around, searching for an exit. "Wrong tunnel."

Victoria glanced down the passage behind them, the incessant wails growing louder. *I fucking hate that noise.*

"Back," Malcolm ordered. "Before they trap us."

Weapons ready, Victoria led the retreat, charging toward the advancing cries. The narrow walls scraped her shoulders as she ran, pausing long enough at each turn to make sure it was clear before continuing on. The egg chamber was just ahead. They only needed to get there first, spread out side by side, and kill the bugs at the entrance.

Victoria checked the next corner and froze. Spindly legs curled around the far corners. Too late.

"Contact." She brought the gun up as the doll face emerged into view and she fired. Another screamer launched itself into the hall before the first blackening corpse hit the floor. Victoria fired, missing it by a hair, but the next shot splattered it.

She moved forward, pistol trained on the corner. A screamer lunged out as she drew near, its jaws open. Victoria fired, knocking it back, but still alive. She squeezed the trigger but nothing happened.

Damn it. She'd forgotten to reload. "I'm out!"

The screamer staggered to its feet, inky blood running from a gash in it side.

"Down!" Orlovski shouted behind her.

Victoria dropped to a crouch and Orlovski's gun fired above

her. The screamer tumbled backward in a mist of black slime and Victoria was up, Ibenus before her as she charged the last few feet before turning into the egg chamber.

Screamers raced from the shadows, closing in. Victoria swiped, blinked, and lopped one off the wall. Spinning, she blinked again and appeared behind another. The bug halted, looking around for its now missing prey. It started to turn but Victoria's boot crunched down on top of it, squirting an arc of foul guts across the floor.

Orlovski rushed in beside her, his pistol *popping*. Within three seconds of entering the room, the cursed screams had silenced.

Victoria stole a moment to load her last magazine as Malcolm checked the door. She'd have given anything for those shots she'd wasted earlier.

Luiza's team was chattering in Victoria's ear as they fought their own wave of monsters.

"Come on." Malcolm surged into the lead. They hurried back to the last intersection and started down the path.

A loud *boom* came through the radio, followed by an echo up the hall.

"That Dämoren I hear?" Malcolm asked.

"You know it," Matt replied, a second shot punctuating the sentence.

"We have to be close," Malcolm said. "Everyone keep an eye out for lights so we don't shoot each other."

They hurried down the tunnel, crouching as the ceiling shrank lower and lower. Infant wails and the muted *pops* of suppressed gunfire sounded ahead. They passed the back of another trapdoor and emerged in a tall, narrow tunnel. Human bones, dry and yellow with age, accented the stones along the walls and floor, arranged in wavy lines like some impressionist seascape. Red and blue lights moved in the darkness ahead.

"Luiza, that you?" Malcolm called.

"We see you," Luiza replied in the radio.

The corridor widened to over ten feet. A side passage broke off to the left before the hall ended at a narrow, floor to ceiling fissure in the far wall. Lined with tiny finger and toe bones, the crack opened to no more than nine inches at its widest, tapering at the top but continuing down, as if forever. Pale blue light flickered on the far side, showing the wall to be over six feet thick. A figure stepped into view, silhouetted by the ghostly demon fire, a red light atop its head shone through the fissure cutting a crimson path across the passage.

"Mal?" Luiza called.

"Yeah," Malcolm replied. "Everyone all right?"

"We're fine. We can't find any way through."

Mal glanced back at the side passage. "They have to meet somewhere."

"Listen, we found a hidden door that goes deeper into the nest. Do they have it all tiled on that side?"

"Yeah."

"They're hiding doors behind it. The demons have been holding back there and sending all their drones out. We were just lucky enough to see them using one, otherwise we wouldn't have found it."

Victoria scanned the paved patterns in the walls and floor, suddenly hyper-aware of how easily a door might be hidden. How many had they passed? How many demons and screamers waited on the other side, readying to swarm out once their backs were turned?

"We almost caught TommyD," Mal said.

"Where?" Chaya asked.

"Just before we found the nest. Dumb bastard was trying to catch one in a trap."

"Did they get him?" a hopeful edge to her voice.

"Got away. Dropped his gun and Gerhard's pistol."

A distant giggle pulled Victoria away from the conversation. Orlovski must have heard it as well, his pistol light coming up, scanning the floors and entrances.

"No Umatri?" Chaya was asking.

"No. But he stuck a demon with it so we know he still has it."

Another giggle. Listening, Victoria stepped away from the crack. *What is that? Scratching?* She pulled the bud from right ear and cocked her head. A faint scurrying, like a hundred tiny rat claws within the walls. But she knew they weren't rats. "Mal." Fear tinged her voice more than she'd intended.

Malcolm turned. A *coo* drifted from some indeterminate direction.

"They're coming," Matt said. Wails sounded in the distance on their side of the wall.

"Mal." Urgency sharpened Luiza's words. "Listen, intel was wrong. They can make more than six screamers. A lot more."

"We found nurseries," Malcolm said. "Like bullets in a gun. Kill one, another hatches."

"Three beads," Matt yelled. A tidal wave of baby screams surged up through the crevice.

"Don't waste your time on the drones," Luiza shouted. "Follow the compass to the demons. Kill the masters."

Chaya tossed a glow stick down the crag. It tumbled between the narrow walls, briefly lighting a mass of black-eyed doll faces before being swallowed up beneath the spidery mass.

"Contact!" Chaya shouted.

More wails sounded from the halls. Malcolm glanced at the compass and stabbed Hounacier toward the side passage. "Two that way."

Ibenus in hand, Victoria hurried after Malcolm as screaming bugs boiled out from the gap and far tunnel. Shots sounded behind her, and voices squawked through the rubber bud dangling beside her ear.

The passage curved around. More infant wails came from ahead. The tunnel split Screamers poured up from the right-side passage. The left appeared clear.

"Down here," Malcolm shouted bringing his palm up at the closing bugs. "They're trying to herd us the other way."

The screamers recoiled from the warding tattoo and Victoria lunged forward, cleaving through the ranks.

"Keep moving." Orlovski's gun popped, blasting one as it peeked out from a crevice in the wall. "They're right behind us."

Victoria chopped a screamer and front-kicked another scurrying across the wall, crushing it into a row of vertebrae. Hot steam filled the passage like a sauna. Tears welling at the stink of rotten meat, she moved onward, deeper into the tunnel as they fought their way through the swirling horde.

Orlovski's shots continued behind them, but Victoria didn't look. They rounded the hall, entering a circular chamber, its walls tiled with the faces of human skulls. Jagged clusters of teeth jutted from the eye sockets, glistening like ivory crystals.

Victoria scanned her light across the room. "No exit." She eyed the ceiling but the morbid tile-work didn't cover the entire dome.

"Son of a bitch," Malcolm yelled. The twin beads of his blood compass pointed straight down. "They're under us."

Following the compass' direction, Victoria searched the floor for a seam, but only for an instant before Orlovski charged in, running backwards, his gun trained on the flood of screaming bugs.

"I'd give anything for your old sawed-off," Orlovski panted. Black blood speckled his cheek and glasses.

"Close up." Malcolm stepped toward the doorway, dropping the bottle and drawing Hounacier. "Don't let them get inside."

Nearly two dozen screamers closed in, a dizzying mass of legs and cherub faces. Victoria's chest tightened. *Too many.* Her arms and legs ached. She couldn't keep this up. *No! I'm not dying here.*

Victoria looked again at the blood compass, following the line from the beads to the bone-tiled floor, and fired. The round shattered a domed skull cap by Orlovski's foot, opening a black hole.

"What the hell are you doing" he shouted, flinching away.

Rapid clicking sounded from the floor. A jagged-edged trapdoor flew open as a gold-striped mantismere lunged out toward the Russian. Orlovski stumbled back, yanking his boot away before a bony scythe arm speared the floor.

Victoria lunged for the demon, but Malcolm beat her to it. He spun, cleaving his machete blade through the top of the mantismere's emerging head and brought his palm up to halt the closing horde.

The scalped demon spasmed, arms flailing. A plume of blue fire erupted from its open skull, cascading down its body as it slid back down into the open hole. Several of the closing screamers withered and fell from the tunnel walls and ceiling, plopping to the floor.

A second demon clambered over its fallen brethren. Black eyes locked on Malcolm, still fighting the surviving screamers. It raised its forelimbs to strike.

Victoria swung, appearing beside it. She chopped Ibenus into its back, splitting the chitinous plates with a meaty crack. Squealing, the monster fell to the side as Victoria wrenched the bronze blade free.

The demon raised its four arms to shield it from the next blow but Ibenus cleaved through two of them, sending the severed ends flying and burying the blade into the demon's chest. The mantismere arched, legs kicking, and then ghostly fire burst from its mouth and wounds.

Dead screamers thudded to the floor, steam spewing from their blackened shells. Malcolm chopped the last survivor as it tried to scuttle away. He spun on his heel, his eyes blazing with rage. He scanned the room, the red beam of his headlamp panning across the ceiling and walls, before his gaze fell on the dead demon. He looked at Victoria, her sword sheathed in bloody demon fire. "Good work."

"Thank you." She panted, not really sure what else to say.

Orlovski stood above the half-open trap door. Pale demon fire flickered up from the pit, lighting his face. Victoria cautiously peered down into it. The demon copse lay sprawled eight feet below beside a pair of melting screamers. Crouching for a better view, she saw a sloped passage leading deeper, its curved and carved walls reminiscent of an intestine.

A clatter sounded behind her. Victoria wheeled to see a sagging section of tiled wall, peel from the rock face. Streamers of milky goo trailed from the falling bones like melted glue.

"Nest is dissolving." Keeping one eye on the pit, Orlovski checked his pistol and slid it into his holster. "More we kill the more it'll crumble."

"Luiza," Malcolm said, "We found an entrance."

Remembering she'd removed her ear bud, Victoria pushed it back in to place to hear Luiza say, "… to the party."

"All right. You heard her." Malcolm picked the blood compass off the floor. He nodded to Victoria. "You found it. You want to go first?"

"Damn right." Ibenus in hand, Victoria carefully lowered herself into the tunnel. The freshly cut channels in the wall offered plenty of purchase. She dropped the last two feet and landed beside the dead mantismere. Burning brains oozed out from the demon's open skull. Matt was shouting something in her ear bud, his words lost beneath a machinegun's roar.

The oval passage coursed gradually down like a lava tube or subterranean river, though Victoria knew there were no natural caves here. The chaotic uniformity of the spiral-cut grooves and diamond-patterned tiling made it difficult to gauge the tunnel's length. Keeping her gaze down the tunnel, Victoria drew a glow stick from her vest, cracked it one handed, and hurled it as far as she could. The spinning orange light bounced off the ceiling and followed the wall, skating along the curve like a funhouse slide. In the final moment before slipping out of view, it silhouetted a screamer hugged along a far wall.

"Got one bug," she called up, spotlighting it in her pistol's white beam. The screamer hopped to its feet, cooed, and scuttled away.

Malcolm climbed down and stepped over the demon corpse. He held the blood compass out. A cluster of red beads formed at the bottom like caviar. "Looks to be the place."

"About damn time." Orlovski swung down, boot clomping on the floor. His lip curled as he eyed a tiled section of floor. "Watch out for trap doors. Just warn me before you start shooting them."

Malcolm drew Hounacier and started down. "No promises."

They'd made it only a few yards when the mewling cries started ahead. A mantismere scuttled around the far wall and dropped to the floor. A second moved in the shadows behind it. Screamers surged past them, their quivering jaws wide.

"I'll make a hole," Malcolm shouted, running toward them.

Victoria ran after him, her foot nearly slipping on the smooth, uneven stone.

The screamers were almost on them. Malcolm threw out a

hand, palm wide. The closing bugs recoiled. One lost its grip and fell from the ceiling. Victoria charged past, Orlovski at her heels. She leaped and swung Ibenus, blinking forward. The sloped tunnel matched the arc of her jump.

The mantismere raised its twin spears, ready to impale her. Victoria swung just before they met. A *whoosh* and she was now behind the demon, her sword cleaving into the side of the second mantismere behind it.

The wounded demon hissed and lurched to the left. It swung its arm, clubbing Victoria's hip as it tried to pulled away. Fighting to keep hold of the sword, Victoria wrenched Ibenus free with a wet *crunch*.

The demon behind her turned, mandibles clicking like a rattle. Victoria swung Ibenus, blinking away as the saber arms came down. Hissing, the demon took a step toward her, but then Orlovski slammed into it from behind, his kukri chopping into the back of its head as it fell.

Blue firelight filled the tunnel, little comets slinging from the Russian's still hacking blade. The demon Victoria had wounded tried to rise, feebly pushing itself up by the forelimbs, blood pouring from the open chest wound. It crumpled and began to burn, the last of the screamers withering at its death.

Malcolm didn't even slow as he jogged past. "Come on." The passage continued down. Pieces of silk-mortared rock and bone slid free, their builders now dead. "This way," Malcolm said as he reached a split in the hall. Cries echoed ahead but there was no sign of more screamers as they moved deeper, the passage so steep they had to make small steps to keep from falling.

The tunnel leveled out below. Victoria jumped, falling ten feet, and swung Ibenus. She blinked and landed with no more impact than from a slight hop.

A wide, round chamber opened up before her, its walls completely covered in honeycombed nest. Victoria coughed. The vinegary reek burned her throat. Most of the chambers were empty, a few still dripping slime from recent hatchings. Sealed cells twitched and stirred as Victoria's light passed over them.

Not waiting for the others, Victoria sprang into the room.

She chopped and hacked at the birthing monsters, slinging goo and bits of shattered nest as she worked.

Feeble cries came from around her as more screamers struggled to free themselves. Blinking around the chamber, Victoria killed as many as she could.

"Christ," Malcolm growled as he dropped the last few feet into the room. He immediately started on the neighboring wall, cutting his way the opposite direction as Victoria. "Taras, get your ass down here."

Orlovski slid down, cursing as he landed. He drew his pistol and began clearing the bugs racing across the ceiling. The gun's slide locked back. "I'm out."

Victoria chopped the last of the hatching bugs and drew her pistol. "Here," she said, ejecting the magazine. "Full mag."

Orlovski winced as he stepped toward her, favoring his right leg. "You need that."

"You're a better shot." She patted her mag pouch. "I have a half one left," she lied. It only had two. Of course there was also TommyD's two-tone pistol in her pack, the gun that had crippled Allan and killed Gerhard, but she knew she'd never fire it, not even if the devil himself came for her.

The Russian's brows knitted as if about to protest but he simply nodded. He reached out, accepting the mag. Red clumps of caking blood ran from the back of his hand and soaked his shirt sleeve to his elbow pad.

"You're hurt."

He nodded. "It's nothing." Orlovski popped the magazine in and thumbed the slide shut. "Thanks."

They followed a curving tunnel down toward the sounds of wails. Gunshots echoed in the distance. They were getting close.

A few screamers emerged from an intersecting passage, but the hunters quickly overtook them with now practiced efficiency. The tunnel opened into a great vaulted chamber, far larger than anything they'd encountered; easily a hundred feet across and just as wide. Their lights played off the murky water that hid the floor, casting rippled reflections along the forest of support pillars.

"Fucking hell." A terrible mixture of awe and hopelessness swirled in Victoria's guts as she halted at the edge. A narrow, stone ledge ran along the right wall, leading to a broad landing, a dark passage beyond.

A slender bridge extended before her, its surface pitted and glinting like a crystal sponge. It arched gracefully above the water's surface where it joined other bridges at a low island near the far side. A thick pearly column dominated the little mound, twisting upward like a giant unicorn's horn riddled with wormholes.

Several mantismeres scuttled along its surface, weaving in and out of the large burrows. Demons and screamers swarmed across a single bridge linking the island to a balcony on the upper left corner, twenty feet above the water. Red lights and the *pops* of silenced pistols came from the tunnel just visible beyond the ledge's rim.

A hulking mantismere with a brilliant red and purple shell clambered over the balcony's edge. A gunshot boomed and the demon pitched backwards, body igniting before it splashed into the water. The burning corpse bobbled up to the surface, its blue light filling one half of the great flooded hall.

"Luiza," Malcolm shouted into his radio. "We're ahead of you."

"Thank Christ," she grunted. "Chaya's hurt and they're overrunning us."

Malcolm raised his pistol, the white beam spotlighting the monsters from behind. "Can you see that?"

"Yes. Hold it steady."

Bracing his arm, Malcolm held the light in place. Several of the beasts turned, noticing the trio for the first time. A few broke ranks and started toward them, moving along the walls and slender bridges.

Amballwa in hand, Orlovski stepped out onto the brown water and fired his pistol at the closing screamers. Victoria eased up beside Malcolm, Ibenus ready.

Blood sprayed across the upper landing. Demons split in half as if some invisible scythe had just ripped through the mob. Burning corpses and severed limbs tumbled from the circle of

Malcolm's light. Across the room withering screamers fell from bridges and walls, splashing into the water like hailstones.

A four-foot span of bridge before Victoria began sagging under its own weight. Another, spanned between two columns crashed down, one end melted from its anchor.

Orlovski was still firing at closing screamers, their ranks noticeably shrinking. "They're breaking for it." He motioned to a trio of mantismeres fleeing across the bridge that connected the tower island to the tunnel at the far right.

"Head them off," Malcolm ordered. "I got this." The monsters in his light now dead, he panned it to the side, catching two more demons in the beam. Just beyond them, Luiza stood in the hall legs apart and katana in both hands. Stepping to the side, she slashed the blade across the long shadows cast by Malcolm's light. An arc of blood and demon fire and the two monsters fell as if the blade had struck them.

Setting her teeth, Victoria sidestepped along the narrow lip of stone as fast as she could. More shots echoed through the room, punctuating the mewling cries.

"They're getting away." Orlovski said, hurrying beside her his feet silent on the water.

The demons reached the landing and ran, escaping into the darkness of the far passage. The great tower sagged like a cone of ice cream under a summer sun. More demons fled out from the compressing burrows. Some retreated along walls and intact bridges while others scuttled to meet the hunters.

Matt stepped up to the balcony edge above, Dämoren out. Gouts of flame flashed from the holy revolver's tip and demons fell. Mantismeres scattered, rushing for cover behind columns and crags. A trio charged across the bridge as Victoria and Orlovski reached the landing. Dämoren boomed and one of the demons crumpled forward, chest exploding in fire.

Victoria and Orlovski met the remaining two as they closed in, blades swinging. Side by side they fought, parrying blows from the monsters' twin blades. Victoria blinked, appearing behind one and hamstringing it. The demon fell and Orlovski was on it before Victoria blinked back. The second beast thrust its spears at the Russian, but Victoria hooked them with Ibenus and kicked the monster. It stumbled back, trying to catch itself, but she rammed the blade up through its thorax, driving six inches of polished bronze out the demon's back.

"Mal!" Luiza shouted through the radio.

Boot on the demon's chest, Victoria wrenched Ibenus free. She turned to see Malcolm fighting a pair of mantismeres that had dropped from the wall above.

"I'm coming!" Orlovski sprinted across the water with a limping gait.

Tingles of being alone danced up the back of Victoria's neck. Gripping Ibenus, she glanced nervously around. Burning corpses lit the chamber in hues of icy blue, hazy in the steamy air thick with the stink of vinegar and rot. Chaya stood slumped against the wall of the upper tunnel, arm wrapped in a red bandage and face pale. Matt loaded the giant revolver as Luiza stood near the edge, katana ready.

Malcolm seemed to dance between the flanking demons, Hounacier a blur, *clacking* off bony sabers. He threw his palm into one demon's face, stunning it long enough for him to skewer the other monster. It fell burning into the water as a third mantismere leaped between the pillars like some jungle animal and landed on the wall above him.

She started to cry a warning when something slammed into her from behind. Sharp pain shot through Victoria's back. She hit the floor hard, her helmet the only thing saving her from a split skull. Ibenus fell from her stunned fingers and skittered across the floor.

The stabbing pain below her shoulder twisted and ripped free, eliciting a howl. Someone was shouting in her radio but she couldn't make it out over the terrible *clicking* just above.

Legs pinned, Victoria twisted to see the mantismere raise its forelimbs. Blood tipped its right point and Victoria was at once acutely aware of the wetness spreading down her back. The beast's black eyes locked on hers. The sabers came down. Victoria rolled, dodging one, while the other raked across her vest. The demon gave a guttural hiss and chittered its mandibles angrily.

Craning her head, she saw Ibenus on the floor. She reached

out but it was too far. The demon's weight shifted, readying for another strike.

Beyond the sword, Victoria spied Orlovski running toward her across the water. "Down!" The Russian leaped, springing upward as if propelled on a trampoline. Cresting his ascent, he hurled Amballwa. The spinning kukri flew toward her like a silver disk. Victoria pressed herself into the floor, bracing for the blow. The holy blade slammed into the mantismere above her just as Orlovski came down with an enormous splash, vanishing beneath the water.

"Taras," Chaya cried, voice echoing across the chamber and blasting through the radio.

The flailing demon rolled off Victoria's back. Scrambling, she grabbed Ibenus. She swung, appearing upright and facing it. The monster rolled, clawing at the jeweled kukri buried in its upper chest. Victoria lopped the mantismere's head off, unleashing the blue fire.

Hesitantly, she touched the wetness pouring down her spine and the back of her legs. Expecting blood on her glove, she released a sigh at seeing only water. The beast had punctured the drinking bladder in her pack. Her shoulder still hurt but it was a small price for what she'd expected.

"Taras hasn't come up," Chaya yelled, her voice ragged with panic.

Fear stealing her relief, Victoria wheeled to see the water still sloshing and bubbling where the Russian had gone under. Malcolm was racing along the ledge toward her, machete coated in burning blood and the bodies of three demons behind him. Blood trickled from a fresh cut along his right wrist.

Victoria ran to the edge and dropped to her knees, scanning the surface. There was no sign of him. *Shit. Oh, shit.* If Orlovski drowned trying to save her— *No, he has to be here.* She thrust her arm down into the frigid water. *Please. Please.*

"Eeeel!" Malcolm roared, pointing his Machete at the tower.

Dämoren's shots rang like a chain of thunder claps.

Spouts of water from missed bullets geysered around a long rubbery form sliding from the base of the tower. One round punched through its flat tail as it kicked up a splash before vanishing beneath the surface. How long it was she couldn't have said, but it was definitely bigger than the ten feet Allan had told her, a lot bigger. And now it was in the same water as her arm, the same water where Orlovski was drowning.

Sliding further over the ledge Victoria swept her arm, blindly feeling. *Come on. Come on.*

A cold current moved across her arm. Brown silt stirred, and then a gloved hand burst from the surface only a few feet beside her, the droplets splattering her cheek. The hand sank then came up again, clawing at the edge.

"Taras." She clambered toward it as the hand sank again and drove her arm after it. Blindly, her fingers found his muscled forearm. He clamped onto her wrist and she heaved him upward, her wounded shoulder screaming at the strain.

Orlovski erupted from the water, coughing and sputtering. His glasses, pack, and vest were gone. The Russian pulled himself to the edge gagging up muddy water.

Victoria pulled his arm. "Come on. It's in the water!"

Panting, Orlovski blinked as if trying to understand. A serpentine swish broke the surface behind him.

"Out! Now!" Malcolm ordered, his boots pounding the ground toward them.

As if on automatic, Orlovski pulled himself up, swinging his legs over the lip.

A pale, noseless face burst from the water behind him, its open mouth a multi-rowed symphony of fangs.

Victoria fell backward in surprise, landing painfully on her ass. Orlovski screamed. The monster shot out to strike when Dämoren boomed. Blood exploded from the eel's flank. The beast jerked, slamming against Orlovski as it fled from the water, swimming through the air.

Victoria swung Ibenus, appearing upright. She lunged at the eel as it slithered past. The glistening tail whipped to the side, Ibenus missing it by inches.

Two more shots rang. One kicked up stone and the other tore a ragged gash down its side. The beast rolled in the air, slinging blood and dirty water. Shrieking with a woman's voice, it flew away, undulating through the air, and vanished down the passage.

Malcolm charged after it. "It's getting away."

Victoria turned to Orlovski.

Coughing, the Russian waved her on. "I'll catch up."

She turned to follow Malcolm but paused. Orlovski had no light.

She offered her pistol. "Here. Two in the mag, one in the pipe."

He accepted it, still hacking. "Go!"

Gripping Ibenus tight, she raced down the tunnel after Malcolm's bobbing light. Chips of rock and bone sagged and dripped from the walls, trailing strands of melting silk. It caught in her clothes and along Ibenus' blade. A single hole burrowed through the vinegar-stinking web, plowed open by both the eel and Malcolm's passing.

She spared only glances at the passing rooms of crumbling nests and mosaics. Her boots crunched over the loose gravel and she had to blink to keep from losing her footing. The passage curved, revealing Malcolm's light close ahead.

He crouched beside an open pit, pulling a coil of nylon rope from his bag. The climbing harness lay crumpled at his feet, hardware glinting. "It went down there."

Cautiously, she peered over the edge. The round shaft was easily five feet across, smooth walls straight down. Fresh blood streaked the white stone. An orange glow stick blazed forty feet below. "Bloody hell."

Malcolm swiveled his head around the room. "Need to tie off somewhere. Luiza, how fast can you get down here?"

"We're getting Chaya in the harness now," Luiza replied. "She lost mobility in her right side when one of those little bastards bit her."

Orlovski's light jogged down the passage toward them.

Victoria peered back down the well again. If the eel got away this would start all over. Another city, another horde. Gerhard's death would be for nothing. Allan's suffering would be for nothing.

Malcolm shouted something behind her, but Victoria wasn't listening.

She raised Ibenus before her. "I'm going down."

Malcolm's frantic jingling stopped. "What?"

"Taras can help you down. Catch up." Without waiting a reply, Victoria stepped off the lip and plunged into the pit. Wind flapped her clothes as she accelerated. Her stomach lurched and rose. Holding her breath, she watched the orange light flying up toward her.

Closer.

Closer.

She swung.

Whoosh.

Victoria landed with a light jolt, knees bending. Ibenus before her, she whirled, ready for an attack. The passage was empty. Sagging tile-work covered three walls. To her left, a single tunnel led away, a hole in the curtain of hanging threads. She clicked her headlamp to full brightness and drew her final glow stick, unleashing a green light with a crunch.

She pulled the chattering plug from her ear and listened. Silence.

Holding the glow stick high so as not to blind herself, she started down the passage. Occasional drops of wet blood sprinkled the floor. Her old partner James would have said it was bleeding like a stuck pig, though he admitted to having never seen a butchering. Now he was dead and the mother of his killer was wounded. Desperate.

The tunnel opened into a broad chamber, just a few feet taller than herself. Boulders littered the far side. Two passages opened to her left. Torn webs framed the closer one.

Victoria started for it, but noticed a spattering of blood leading to the right. She spun, to see the giant human-faced eel woven into the rocks, easing out toward her.

The monster paused. It blinked its black eyes. "I don't know you."

"No," she breathed, taken aback that it had spoken.

"You carry Zhygan. Ibenus." It cocked its head curiously. "Is Allan dead?"

"He's alive."

"I see. I knew him. Very well. He used to hover around me,

peeking down my blouse. He didn't know that I knew."

"Anya?" Victoria took step back, eyes locked on the human-faced monster.

"So he told you about me. Allan was always trying to fuck me." The creature smiled, revealing a hint of those wicked fangs. "But I wouldn't."

Malcolm's shouts echoed up the passage beside her. He was coming. *Just keep it talking.*

The demon's head remained motionless, but the rest of its body slid out, slowly coiling, the muscles tense. Blood dribbled from its bullet wounds, spattering the dust. "Appears he finally found a slut that would."

"Fuck you."

The eel tittered. "You're not my type."

A sudden warning flashed in the back of Victoria's mind.

Not taking time to think, she swung and blinked away as a mantismere that had been sneaking up behind her skewered the now empty air. She slashed, hooking the blade around and into the back of the monster's skull. Blue fire filled the room, chasing away the shadows.

Shrieking in rage, the eel sprang, jaws wide.

Victoria ducked, coming up as the eel stuck at her again. Leaping to the side, she hacked Ibenus into the monster's belly as it passed, splitting through the rubbery skin. The eel crashed into the floor, coiling and writhing. Blood and organs spilled from the terrible gash. The demon screamed, lashing out toward her.

Feinting an attack to meet it, Victoria swung, blinked, and appeared beside the monster. The eel looked in time to see the arcing sword but not in time to avoid it. Ibenus chopped into its neck, severing bone in a spray of blood.

Brilliant amber fire burst from the gory wound. The demon eel balled and rolled, its head flopping by only a sliver of connected skin. Shielding her eyes, Victoria stepped away, afraid of being struck in its death throes. Golden orange flames dripped from the khopesh's bronze blade, beautiful like liquid sunrise.

Footsteps clomped up from behind her. She looked back to

see Malcolm racing up the tunnel.

He stopped and stared at the burning eel. Blowing out a long sigh, he turned toward her. "Are you all right?"

She nodded, releasing a shuddering breath. "I'm fine."

Malcolm snorted, then laughed. "Damn right you are." He pulled her into a hug.

Victoria winced, her wounded shoulder screaming.

"You fucking did it." He broke the embrace and pumped his fist. "Luiza, Victoria killed the eel. Repeat, the eel is dead."

Vaguely aware of the chatter in the bud dangling beside her ear. Victoria watched the burning monster. It was gone. The last of the mantismeres had been born. They were an endangered species now. She'd done it. More than anything she wanted to tell Allan, tell him Ibenus, *their* sword had killed it.

But she couldn't go back. *Not yet.*

"Come on." Malcolm patted her shoulder. "We need to see to Chaya. Get her to a doctor. The rest of the demons have made a break for it. Maybe we can catch the stragglers before they escape."

Victoria nodded. She gestured to the cut in Malcolm's wrist. It was straight, like a knife wound. Nothing like what the mantismeres did. "Are you all right?"

"This?" Grinning he wiped at the blood, eyeing it appraisingly. A faint scar was visible there in the bright amber light. A ghostly shape like a beetle. "Don't worry about it. Little reward for a triple-kill."

"Then let's get out of here."

CHAPTER 23

"Smile for the camera, bitch." Tommy tapped his computer's touchpad. The black and white footage restarted, showing an arched catacomb tunnel extending into darkness.

Two figures emerged from an intersecting passage thirty feet ahead. The first, was rail-thin, tall, his charcoal black skin nearly the same shade as his clothes. Despite his lankiness, there was an elegance to him, as if each movement had been carefully choreographed. A short axe with a long, slender head, hung from the man's belt. He glanced either way up the tunnel. The light of his headlamp flared as it passed the hidden night vision camera, and he continued on. A petite woman followed behind him. What he first mistook for long hair, Tommy now recognized as a shawl draped along the back of her neck. She carried a thick broadsword, almost too large for such a small woman. Her gaze zeroed instantly on the camera, blinding it under her headlamp's glow. She held the stare a full five seconds, her head appearing like a miniature sun, before turning away and continuing on.

Tommy clicked the pad again, stopping the video. Smiling, he saved the clip under the title, "Scarecrow and Mrs. Sword – Paris," and moved it to his "Hunter Footage" folder. Pins and needles tickled his numbed fingers as he typed. The swelling in his arm had gone down, though it was still puffy. A numb streak still ran the length of his arm, spreading down his little finger and half of his ring finger. The ulnar nerve, he'd learned.

But he had full mobility so he wasn't worried.

Tommy sipped his Corsica Cola, a French Coke knockoff that he strangely preferred. The footage he'd gathered before fleeing the catacombs was hands-down the best he'd ever taken. High-resolution videos of those crying spiders and even of the larger clawed monsters.

He wondered how much more his little cameras might have gathered over the last week. Probably a lot, he guessed. But he sure as shit wasn't going down there for them. Gregorie hadn't returned his messages. The cataphile was probably dead. Tommy felt a slight twinge of guilt about that but he mourned the cameras more. Gregorie was only a man. The right footage would change the world. He needed to find someone to retrieve them. Maybe Victoria, once she finished her little blackout from him.

She'd come a long way in the months since they'd first met online. Shy at first, reluctant to participate on the boards, but was always on, scouring hundreds of old topic threads. Eventually she'd opened up and shared her story. Some had called her crazy, but not him. He'd heard of the Manchester police killing and had already figured out who she was by her IP address and comments she'd made. Instantly, he'd recognized the fire in her, the anger. Like himself, Victoria had lost someone, and that was the foundation for their bond. Once the world knew the truth, she'd have her vindication. She'd be famous like him. She'd earned that.

Tommy cocked his head. A police siren wailed in the distance, faint, but growing louder—that silly *wee-ooo-wee-ooo* noise heard in every movie set in Paris. Knots of paranoia latticed up his spine. Touching the kris knife in his lap, he glanced to the second monitor beside him. Three parallel feeds played across the flat screen. The first was a fisheye view outside his apartment door, the camera mounted behind the peephole with silver duct tape. The other two looked out over the street from behind his curtained windows, the cameras tucked in the corners so no one might see them. A little police car raced through one feed, its blue lights pulsing. Then it passed through the other, and continued on down the street, sirens dopplering as it hurried away.

Scolding his paranoia, Tommy shook his head and returned his attention to his computer. He opened Cryptozoo.

The message icon blazed red. There, he found six messages from Victoria, all sent in the last two hours. *Speak of the devil.* They all read, "Emergency. Call Me."

Fear mingled with excitement. He opened the first one, seeing a phone number. The line beneath it read, "It's done."

Navigating between pedestrians, Victoria followed the sidewalk, her primed senses overloaded with all the movement around her. Her eyes darted to each new stimulus, instantly gauging if it posed a threat. Retuning topside was going to take some getting used to. The wheels on her long rolling bag clicked across the square paving stones behind her. A jackhammer clattered in the distance, drowning out the steady drone of traffic.

Resisting the urge to glance over her shoulder, she stepped into a shallow alcove and stopped before a blue-painted door. She pressed the button for "302" on the tarnished brass pad and waited.

The phone buzzed in her pocket. She fished it out and read the text.

"You here?"

"I'm here," she replied. *Who else would it be?*

Ten seconds passed before a high-pitched beep sounded. She opened the door and stepped inside. Passing a pair of apartments, Victoria stopped at the base of a narrow staircase. No lift. She eyed the steep wooden steps and drew a breath. *Don't bother offering to help.* She heaved the bag onto her shoulder, the weight threatening to pull her over, and started up. Its contents rattled mutedly with each step.

She blew a hard sigh once she reached the fourth floor, finally able to set the bag down to use the wheels. 302's door opened as she reached it. TommyD's head emerged, shy and turtle-like as he looked around. His short blond hair was parted neatly. She'd always assumed him bald with his penchant for hats.

His shit-brown eyes paused on the black bag, then moved up her body appraisingly, before meeting hers. "Come in."

He stepped back, opening the door wider and Victoria rolled

the bag inside. The narrow flat ran the depth of the building—a single room, partitioned off with a book case. Ancient, beige masonry made up the outer wall, the rest were eggshell white. It was so clean it might have been a showroom, except for the mounds of electronics, dirty dishes, and empty cans piled across the desk, an island of chaos amidst the order. Pedestrians and street traffic moved across one of the two desk monitors, as well as the hallway behind her. Victoria noticed the camera on the back of the door. The second monitor appeared to be Cryptozoo. *Perfect.*

Reporters silently blathered on a muted television, the report cutting to earlier footage of a van engulfed in flames. The grisly details scrolled along the bottom and while she couldn't read them, she knew what they said: five victims burned beyond recognition and an arsenal of guns inside.

"I'm very happy to finally meet you," TommyD said, offering a hand.

Hiding her disdain behind a smile, Victoria accepted it. His hands were softer than his macho-persona had led her to imagine. Bandages crisscrossed TommyD's other hand, the jutting fingers pink and puffy. "What happened?"

"Oh." He slid his good hand above the injured one, shielding it from her view. "One of those little baby things got me. It's mostly healed now."

She nodded. "Good to hear." Chaya's leg and arm had swollen, too. But after Doctor Laroux pumped her full of steroids, Benadryl, and God knows what else, she'd made full recovery in three days.

"Can I get you anything?" TommyD asked, his voice higher, obviously eager to change the subject.

"Where can I put this?"

Tommy looked around and motioned in the direction of the bookcase. "The bed."

She rolled the clunking bag past the television and case to find a large bed, rumpled, but made, like a child's feeble and rushed attempt to appease a scolding mother.

"Is anyone else here?" Victoria asked, eyeing the mound of dirty laundry piled in the corner.

"Just me."

"We'll need to get out of the city as soon as possible." She heaved the bag onto the bed. "They'll be looking for me."

"That's not a problem." He chewed his lip, gaze moving hungrily across the bag. "Did you get everything?"

"I gathered everything I could fit." She pulled the zipper and opened it to reveal a thick roll of gray sheets. A pair of sword handles protruded from one end.

Tommy helped withdraw the heavy bundle and laid it out on the bed. Ignoring the modest collection of guns still in the bag, he flipped the fabric aside and let a long, low breath. Four swords, a curved knife, and a black mace rested inside, all clean and of perfect quality. "Very nice."

"These and the keris you got makes seven. We could arm two squads with that."

He ran his fingers along a sword hilt, following the engraved lines. "This is outstanding. What about the axe?"

"What axe?"

"The one the black man was carrying."

She shook her head. "Luc carried a mace. There wasn't any axe."

He lifted his gaze to meet her, eyes narrow with suspicion. "I saw an axe." His voice carried a dangerous edge. "I have footage of it."

Victoria held out her hands. "I honestly don't know what you're talking about."

"So there was no other black hunter with you?"

"None."

"Then why did I see him? I saw them!"

"I … I don't know. Maybe it was someone else. Maybe the Valducans sent a second team. They didn't trust me, not after … what happened." Her heart pounded. What the hell was going on?

The accusatory suspicion seemed to cool, but lingered.

"So I'd love to see that footage," Victoria continued. "If there are more knights in Paris we need to know. After I killed them, burned them up, they're going to come after me. We need to get out of here."

"It's all right," he said, the anger seemingly gone. "I'll take care of you. Don't worry."

"All right." She rubbed the back of her neck, scratching a paranoid itch. Christ, this man's madness was infectious. What the hell was he raving about? She needed to keep control of this before it got bad. "Whatever you say."

His attention was already back to the weapons. "I recognize you." He lifted Ibenus off the bed. "How does it work? That Allan guy was teleporting or something with it."

"It's tricky." She fought to keep her voice even. How dare this bastard touch Ibenus. Victoria held her breath. *Stay focused.* She cleared her throat. "Do you have Umatri here?"

"Yeah." He moved the khopesh around slow, parrying invisible blows. "I can't get it to work."

"Bring it out and I'll show you." This was it.

Tommy bounced Ibenus a few times, then looked up as if he'd just heard her. "Sure." He set Ibenus back down, handle toward him, beside a beautiful museum-grade reproduction of an Italian broad sword. Reaching behind his back, he drew Umatri from beneath his shirt.

"All right," Victoria stretched across the bed for Ibenus. "Let me show you." A comforting calm flowed up her arm as her fingers encircled the wooden grip.

There must have been something in her expression as she smiled at him, something that tipped him off. Instantly his mood flipped. Eyes wide, he lunged, stabbing the keris at her.

She rolled across the weapons as the wavy blade buried through the sheets. The flanged mace head jabbed painfully into her ribs. Growling, Tommy ripped Umatri free and slashed at her still extended arm.

Victoria swung and blinked away before it could hit. She appeared upright, lunged, hacked downward, and blinked behind him. He whirled around just as Ibenus buried into his skull. Umatri clattered to the floor as TommyD crumpled, legs twitching.

Victoria pulled Ibenus from his head, unleashing a stream of blood across the wooden floor. His shit eyes stared in frozen disbelief. She glared at him. "That's for Allan and Gerhard, you son of a bitch."

A dark stain spread across his crotch. Stepping over the

piss and blood, Victoria picked the fallen keris off the floor. "I'm sorry, Umatri." She set it down on the bed and rolled the dead man over, removing his wallet and Umatri's wooden sheath tucked in his belt. The blood was spreading faster than she expected. There was a lot to do and not much time. She unzipped a side pocket and removed a pair of gloves from a plastic bag and pulled them on.

Grabbing shirts from the mound of laundry Victoria wiped up most of the blood, making a little pillow for him to catch the rest and elevate his head. She hurried over to the filthy desk and opened Cryptozoo. He was still logged in. *Thank God.* She searched the member list for Samantha's newest alias, MoonHuntress, and clicked the box, granting full admin rights.

Cryptozoo was theirs.

She removed a memory stick from her pocket and plugged it into the computer. She searched, grabbing files and dropping them in as fast as she could. As they loaded, Victoria removed her phone and called a number.

As it rang, Victoria watched the surveillance monitor.

On the street below, a black-haired woman with a stroller answered her phone. "Yes?"

"It's done. I have Umatri and the files."

"Any problems?" Luiza asked.

Victoria glanced over at the body, noticing a splatter of blood on one of the white walls. *Shit.* "Nothing serious. Come up. I'll buzz you in."

Victoria pulled TommyD's legs over the edge of the tub with a grunt. A slow trickle of blood ran from his head toward the drain. She'd managed to drag the body across the flat with minimal mess, though there would need to be some serious scrubbing. Not long ago, the thought of moving corpses and cleaning blood would have horrified her, but she was becoming strangely used to it. Helping haul five bodies of former mantismeres up and out of the catacombs to incinerate in a van had broken her of any squeamishness. But the ruse had worked, and now she had one more corpse to show for it.

A knock came from the door.

Victoria hurried from the bathroom, stepping over a red smear. The surveillance screen showed Luiza and Matt standing outside. Since Tommy had never seen them before, the two hunters had been selected to serve as backup and keep an eye on her. Luiza had told Matt to go on home to their daughter and Allan, but Matt refused, saying he had no intention of leaving his wife alone with Victoria and that was that.

"Come in," Victoria said, cracking the door.

Luiza squeezed in first, empty stroller before her. "Looks to have been exciting." she said, noting the blood.

Matt came in next, eyes wary. "Where is he?"

"Bathroom." Victoria locked the door and offered him Umatri. "I figure we can move him out of here after dark and get rid of him. Clean this up, make it look like he left."

"Move him?" Matt's brow rose. "Why not leave him here?"

She motioned to the computer. "Because we own him now. His entire network, videos, contacts, files, everything."

"Okay? So let's pack 'em up and get out."

Victoria shook her head. "You don't understand. We can't let anyone find him."

He nodded, realization dawning. "You want to impersonate him?"

"Exactly."

Luiza approached the mess of computers and food wrappers. "Why didn't you say this before?"

"Master Turgen wouldn't agree to it. He doesn't want to use the public. He'd prefer to hide like we always have. If we own Cryptozoo we have access to nearly every tip that comes out. We have a thousand believers that we can use, not tell them everything, mind you, but just enough to save lives. We can direct and misdirect as we see fit. I wanted it to be a done thing before I offered it."

"You're right." Matt shook his head. "He won't agree to it."

"He's not the only Master," Victoria said. "Allan thinks it's a brilliant idea."

Matt shared a look with his wife.

Luiza shrugged. "She has a point."

"I've already made Sam an admin," Victoria said. "We'll

start slow. Remove everything we don't want out there, Luc's name, for one. Then gradually start making changes as we like."

"What about his videos?" Matt asked. "No new videos and they'll notice he's gone."

"We'll figure it out. Some might suspect, but as long as there's no body no one can prove otherwise. We'll make our own videos under the Monster Seekers channel and people will get used to it."

"I like it," Luiza said. "I really like it. A direct tip line."

Matt nodded. "I do, too." He looked at the keris. "You did well. I'm … I was wrong about you." He offered his hand. "I'm sorry."

"I am, too," she said, accepting it. A weight seemed to lift from her shoulders, so old and familiar she hadn't realized how heavy the burden had become. She drew a breath, fighting tears. "Thank you."

"Just keep one thing in mind," Matt added. "If you break Allan's heart …"

The tears welled, threatening to run down her cheek. Allan, she couldn't wait to see him again. Victoria wiped her eyes. She hugged him. "You have nothing to worry about."

Matt squeezed her close, patting her back. "Then welcome to the family."

CHAPTER 24

Victoria let out a grunt as she pulled the hard riding boot past her heel. They were definitely a lot more fun to take off than to put on. She stood and turned before the giant mirrored door in her bedroom, adjusting the band collar of the navy blue Nehru jacket.

"Ready?" Luiza asked.

Victoria eyed the gleaming breastplate in the knight's hands. Engraved parallel lines ran from either side, meeting at a V-point at the middle. Luiza's own armor was the same, although the metalwork along the collar was accented with copper and brass, signifying her higher rank. A small pendant hung prominently at the Brazilian's chest, a polished shard of jagged metal framed in twisting gold.

"Ready," Victoria said.

Luiza carefully lowered the clamshell plates over Victoria's head, then began adjusting the straps along the shoulders.

"I still say you should have gotten one with boobs," Sam said from beside the bed.

"It's meant to be practical." Luiza tightened the straps and the armor pressed Victoria's breasts toward the middle. While the higher hips were definitely femininely formed, there was nothing sexual about the armor's shape.

Sam snorted. "What's practical about steel armor? It's meant to look good so give it some tits, maybe even strapless."

Refusing to rise to the bait, Luiza rolled her eyes. She

cinched the buckles along one side, forcing Victoria's posture even straighter. "How's that?"

"It's good," Victoria said, twisting a little.

"You get used to it quickly but you want to have it snug. Otherwise it starts rubbing."

"No it's fine." She turned to Sam. "What do you think?"

Sam looked down at Gabi, sitting in the plastic walker Schmidt had bought her. "Uh-huh. I concur." She nodded. "You look like a badass."

"Perfect."

Luiza glanced back at the bedside clock. "Go ahead and put Ibenus on. It's almost time."

Removing a sapphire blue sash from the back of a chair, Victoria wrapped it around her armored waist and strapped it down with a belt in the fashion Allan had shown her. Once it was secure, she removed Ibenus from his stand and slid him into the tooled leather scabbard.

That done, Luiza draped a matching blue cape over Victoria's back, affixing it to the door knocker rings at the shoulders. Victoria checked the mirror again and gave an approving nod. Badass was an appropriate term. She turned, smiling as the cape whirled with the motion.

"You look great." Luiza affixed her own cape and knelt before Gabi. "Mommy will be back in a bit." She kissed the toddler on the head. "Be good."

"Oh we'll have fun," Sam said. "Maybe play with Tsel while Chaya's busy." The Malinois pup had caused quite a stir since Chaya had bought it. It had only taken two days to win Orlovski over.

Sam gave Victoria a hug. "You look great."

"Thanks."

"I expect you upstairs once this is done. Just because you're a knight doesn't mean we don't hang out any more."

Victoria grinned. "I'll be there."

"I'll have funtas ready."

"I can't wait."

Luiza opened the bedroom door. "Ready?"

"Ready."

They left the room and headed down the empty halls, side by side, capes billowing. The only eyes watching the display were those of the painted dead, staring down from their portraits. Despite the regal appearance, a familiar and almost forgotten fear seemed to roll over inside Victoria's mind. Was she sure about what she was doing?

Yes, she assured herself, banishing the silly thought. *Ibenus chose me for this.*

They turned down another hall. A pair of tall candle holders framed an arched door. Orlovski stood outside it, wearing his own armor and cape with Amballwa at his waist. Victoria couldn't tell exactly what it was, but the perfect crispness to his uniform was unbelievable, like he was born for it. Seeing their approach, the Russian nodded, stepped inside, and closed the door behind him.

They stopped before the door, Luiza to her left. Like all the others in the mansion, the handle was encrusted with various gems and metal studs. But unlike those, the door itself wasn't modern. The dark iron-shod wood looked to have come from some ancient church or fortress, something meant to stop invaders. Rounded scars and impact dents alluded that it might have once served that very function.

Victoria swallowed. Despite her resolve, a nervous tingle played along the inside of her ribs. Before any doubts could surface the door opened, swinging wide.

Candlelight filled the room, casting everything in a yellow glow like in an old photograph. Orlovski stood at the edge of the door, chin high and eyes staring straight before him. Chaya stood to his right in the same statuesque pose, the hilt of her sheathed scimitar jutting out a little. Matt, to her right, then Luc and Malcolm completed the line. Beyond them, Masters Turgen, Schmidt, and Allan stood at the rear of the room before a white and gold banner, facing the door. Their heavily engraved breastplates glinted in the flickering light and their own cloaks were the same vibrant green as the emerald rings they wore. Schmidt wore his sword, but Turgen and Allan had none. Allan winked as their eyes met.

Luiza stepped forward and Victoria quickly followed,

keeping pace. It smelled of frankincense and a strangely bittersweet aroma she couldn't place. The heavy incense smoke cast ghostly coronas around the dozens of candle flames. Passing the line of knights, Victoria couldn't help a sidelong glance, noticing the orphaned weapons from the vault proudly displayed along the wall across azure velvet.

The door groaned and thudded closed behind them and Luiza and Victoria halted before the green-clad Masters. The gilded and embossed image of a sword with a wide, tapered blade decorated Turgen's breastplate. A longer, cruciform sword decorated Schmidt's, its shape and octagonal pommel an exact replica of Lukrasus. Ibenus' bowed shape gleamed from Allan's chest. The banner behind them depicted the familiar eight-pointed star, its bladed points barely protruding out from the enclosing ring.

Turgen narrowed his eyes accusingly, all grandfatherly friendliness gone. "Victoria Martin," he rasped, his voice loud as if he were speaking before a parliamentary hearing, "you stand before us, seeking entrance into our Order. Do you choose this of your own free will?"

"I do."

"Who among our family speaks for this woman?"

"I speak for her," Allan said.

"Master Havlock," Schmidt said, eyes still locked on Victoria, "is this woman truly wed to a divine instrument?"

"She is."

"Have you taught her what sacrifices this vow demands?"

"I have."

"Do you find her intentions pure?"

A moment's grin pulled at Allan's lips, breaking the somber expression. "I do."

Victoria pursed her lips, fighting her own smile. There were some impure intentions for later on, she knew.

"Do you find her worthy of our Order?" Schmidt asked.

"I do."

"Swear it on Ibenus."

Allan placed his hands on the gold khopesh on his chest. "On Ibenus, I find her worthy of our Order and worthy of my own divine instrument."

Schmidt gave an approving nod and Luiza stepped back, leaving Victoria alone before the Masters.

Turgen, who hadn't removed his cold gaze from Victoria during the exchange, addressed her again. "Draw your charge and kneel, Victoria."

She slid Ibenus from his scabbard and carefully lowered to the floor, a move made difficult by the rigid armor and hard boots. Knees on the unforgiving tile, she met the master knight's eyes.

"Victoria Martin, do you vow to protect your charge with your very life, to hold his well-being before your own?"

"On Ibenus, I swear it."

"Do you vow to protect the other divine weapons, holding their safety above your own?"

"On Ibenus, I swear it."

"Do you vow to protect the Order, and its secrets?"

"On Ibenus, I swear it."

"Do you vow to protect your brothers and sisters even at the cost of your own life?"

"On Ibenus, I swear it."

Turgen lifted his gaze to the room. "My brothers and sisters, you have heard this woman's professions. If you accept them, seal her vow with your own."

Master Schmidt drew his sword. The faint rasp of another sounded at Victoria's back. Lifting the sword, the old man stepped forward and lowered it, resting the blade on Victoria's shoulder. Other blades came down as well, *tinking* as metal met metal. Luc's heavy mace head came down last, one of its iron flanges gently prodding Victoria's neck.

Hand on Schmidt's shoulder Allan took a step. The first step she'd seen him take since his injury. He'd refused to wear the temporary prosthesis around her until now. Releasing his hold, he lowered his hand and placed it on Victoria's head.

Master Turgen came last, resting his hand beside Allan's. "The Order of Valducan accepts you into our fold. Rise, Lady Victoria Martin, Protector of Ibenus, and embrace your new family."

The weapons still upon her, Victoria slowly rose to her feet.

She nearly stumbled but a hand from behind caught her and helped her up. The weapons withdrew and Turgen stood before her.

The old man smiled proudly. "Welcome, Sister."

"Thank you, Brother."

Tears framed Allan's eyes. He swallowed and wrapped his arms around her, their breastplates softly thudding. "I love you, Victoria."

Victoria held him tight, her cheek against his. She closed her eyes, savoring the energy knitting between them, unhindered by the steel armor. "I love you, too."

EPILOGUE

"Do you know where Kerri went?" Abby asked, her already high-pitched voice rising above the chaos. Girls giggled and chatted all around them. A pack of scowling parents circled an instructor, speaking in raised, accusing whispers. Hip hop blasted through the ballroom door as someone stepped inside.

Dodging a line of Junior dancers in matching tuxedo leotards and top hats, Mei shrugged. "I think Missus Connolly asked her to help with the Jazz team."

"You want to get some food?"

A pack of young women filed out of the dressing room ahead. Their matching turquoise T-shirts read, "D-Lite Studio – Chicago." Tara Isom, her blonde hair wound in a tight bun, led the tittering herd, the others orbiting around her.

Damn it. Mei looked away. She wasn't in the mood for shit-talking right now. It was their last year to make it to Nationals and Tara was dead-set to dole out a lifetime's supply for their final competition.

"Aw crap," Abby muttered. "She's coming this way."

Mei spied the open door to the right, a familiar three-color logo of an elongated blowing leaf beside it. Head low, she made a beeline for the safe haven. She slipped inside, escaping the noise and gym-sock stink that permeated every other corner of the convention center.

Rows of glass cases lined the meeting room's wall, each displaying a collection of antique armor and weaponry. The miniature museum was weird. Normally all the outer rooms were reserved for dressing and green rooms, but not this one. El Sable Energy Corporation, the event's largest sponsor, had brought the exhibit. Whatever medieval weaponry had to do with dancing or South American wind farms Mei had no idea. But it had instantly become her favorite place in the entire event—an island of calm and mystery among the chaos.

A few parents, mostly dads, strolled the aisles, their eyes moving across the artifacts without really seeing them. If they had, they'd be at the back corner. As if on auto-pilot, she wandered deeper, knowing where she was headed, even though she hadn't planned it.

Abby blew a sigh. "I think she's gone. You want to get food now?"

"That's okay." Mei waived dismissive hand. "You go on. I'll catch up."

"What? No come on. I'm hungry. Aren't you?"

Passing a long case containing a gold-encrusted conquistador helmet, Mei stopped before a standing suit of polished, but dented armor. A card along the side explained that it was relic from the Second Crusade. "I am. Just give me a few minutes, all right?"

Abby huffed. "What is it with you? This is our last year and you're obsessing over this shit. Come on. We're eighteen and in Vegas."

Ignoring the armor, Mei gazed at the simple broadsword before it. "I'll find you in a bit. See if you can find Kerri and we'll go out."

Abby gave one of her trademark growls.

"I'll meet you at the front in twenty minutes," Mei said, eyes still on the sword, but could see Abby's reflection behind her in the glass. "Promise."

"Fine." Abby tucked a blonde strand behind her ear. It fell out almost immediately. "Twenty minutes." She spun with a dramatic flourish and strode away, leaving Mei alone with the beautiful sword.

She couldn't say what it was that drew her to it. Most of the others were far more decorative, with etched gold and silver accents. But something about the simple elegance of this one enchanted her. The straight tapered blade, the rounded crossbars—it was pure function. The only adornment was the octagonal knob capping the cord-wrapped handle.

Mei knelt, leaning closer until her breath fogged the glass. What type of sword was this? There was no card saying where it was made or anything about it, only the armor. She closed her hand, remembering the feel of it in her dream last night after she'd first seen it.

"Something catch your interest?"

Flinching, Mei looked up to see the reflection of a tall, slender man standing behind her. He was old, too old to be one of the dads. Grandfather, most likely. "Oh." She smiled, hiding her embarrassment as she rose. "Sorry. I didn't mean to get in the way."

"It is quite all right." His accent sounded European, though she couldn't tell which flavor. "Do you like armor?"

"Me? No, no. I ... was checking out the sword."

"Ah." He smiled. "Beautiful, isn't it?" There was something in has manner, an excited neediness.

Mei glanced behind him. A pair of dads stood off to one side, staring at their phones. A trio of younger boys were ogling a nearby case. It was safe in case this guy got all creepy or something. "Yeah. It just looks ... comfortable."

"It is." The old man offered a slender hand. "My name is Max Schmidt."

"Mei Tseng," she said, accepting it. The old man's grip was firmer than she'd expected.

He nodded as if to himself. "Chinese?"

"Yeah, but I'm from Sacramento."

"And you're competing here?"

"I am. Our final round is tonight."

Max's blue eyes glistened. Was he crying? "I'm sure you will do well."

"Thank you. Are you all right?"

"Yes, yes." Max dabbed his eyes. "You remind me of someone, that's all." He motioned to the sword. "It has a name, you know? Lukrasus."

"Really?" Mei scanned the case again. "I don't see it anywhere."

"Oh it's not on there. Lukrasus is *my* sword."

"Yours?" she turned back to the old man.

"It is. I represent El Sable Energy."

"Oh," she said. This guy didn't look the least bit South American. It was bad to talk with the judges. What about the sponsors?

He nodded. "I was a dancer when I was younger. My late son, Jean, was as well."

"I'm ... sorry." She needed to get out of here. If someone saw them talking ... *Missus Connolly's going to kill me.* "I don't think we're supposed to be talking. You know, with the competition and all."

"There is nothing wrong with it. I am not a judge, simply a fan."

"Oh, good." Smiling, Mei began eking her way around him. "Well, I need to meet my friends. We're going for lunch. But it was nice meeting you."

"Would you like to hold Lukrasus?" Max asked, the words stopping her cold.

"Really?"

"Of course." He chuckled. "As I said, it's mine. Maybe she will give you luck."

She? The sword was obviously a *he.* Nothing feminine about it, but Mei wasn't going to argue with him. "I'd love to. When can we do it?"

"Right now."

Mei blinked. "Really?" Her hands trembled, just like they did before a big performance.

Max laughed. "Really."

"But ... my friends are expecting me."

"And they'll be fine without you." He winked conspiratorially. "Won't they?"

Mei nodded, biting her lip.

"It'll only be a minute," Max said. "I'll fetch the key."

Mei turned back to the sword as the old man hurried away. Her heart thudded in nervous anticipation. "Lukrasus," she whispered, savoring the name. Somewhere deep in the back of her mind, Mei thought she heard the sword answer. It was beautiful.

About the Author

Raised in the swamps and pine forests of East Texas, Seth Skorkowsky gravitated to the darker sides of fantasy, preferring horror and pulp heroes over knights in shining armor.

His debut novel, *Dämoren*, was published in 2014 as book #1 in the Valducan series; it was followed by *Hounacier* in 2015, and Ibenus in 2016. Seth has also released two sword-and-sorcery rogue collections with his Tales of the Black Raven series.

When not writing, Seth enjoys cheesy movies, tabletop role-playing games, and traveling the world with his wife .

Visit Seth's website: http://skorkowsky.com/

Curious about other Crossroad Press books?
Stop by our site:
http://store.crossroadpress.com
We offer quality writing
in digital, audio, and print formats.

Enter the code FIRSTBOOK
to get 20% off your first order from our store!
Stop by today!